Imperfect Delight

IMPERFECT DELIGHT

A Novel

ANDREA DE CARLO

Translated by Brett Auerbach-Lynn

37INK

ATRIA

New York London Toronto Sydney New Delhi

37INK

ATRIA

An Imprint of Simon & Schuster, Inc.
1230 Avenue of the Americas
New York, NY 10020

This book is a work of fiction. Any references to historical events, real people, or real places are used fictitiously. Other names, characters, places, and events are products of the author's imagination, and any resemblance to actual events or places or persons, living or dead, is entirely coincidental.

First 37 INK/Atria Paperback edition June 2018

37INK/**ATRIA** PAPERBACK and colophon are trademarks of Simon & Schuster, Inc.

For information about special discounts for bulk purchases, please contact Simon & Schuster Special Sales at 1-866-506-1949 or business@simonandschuster.com.

The Simon & Schuster Speakers Bureau can bring authors to your live event. For more information or to book an event, contact the Simon & Schuster Speakers Bureau at 1-866-248-3049 or visit our website at www.simonspeakers.com.

Interior design by Rhea Braunstein

Manufactured in the United States of America

10 9 8 7 6 5 4 3 2 1

Library of Congress Cataloging-in-Publication Data is available.

ISBN 978-1-5011-7977-8
ISBN 978-1-5011-7978-5 (ebook)

Imperfect Delight

WEDNESDAY

ONE

Late on the morning of November 18, 2015, there was a blackout throughout the Canton of Fayence, department of Var, region of Provence-Alpes-Côte d'Azur, with repercussions affecting the entire public transit system, telecommunications, radio and television broadcasting, food preservation, security systems, computer networks, and various types of businesses, including La Merveille Imparfaite, the gelateria at the top of the stepped cobblestone lane that slopes down from Rue Saint-Clair toward the market square in front of the church.

Just a few minutes earlier Milena Migliari, the gelato maker, was looking out the doorway of her shop and thinking that you didn't need a calendar to see that tourist season was long over. You only needed to feel the stillness of the air, in which the echoes of the laughter, the revelry of voices, the exchange of looks, the rustling of fabric, the shuffling of footsteps, and the clicking of cell phones of late summer still seemed to hang suspended. You only needed to look around the corner at the main road to see how few cars passed beneath the town hall with the words Hôtel de Ville painted in flowing script, the pale blue shutters, the French and

EU flags, the vases of drooping geraniums long past their prime; how few continued past the storefronts of the restaurants, bakeries, and real estate agencies and then on, toward Mons or Tourrettes or Callian or who knows where. The cold was uncertain, confounded by an undercurrent of enduring warmth; the sky was a faded blue that couldn't seem to make up its mind to yield to gray. Standing out amid the general silence was the staccato hammering of a construction worker in one of the lanes below, and the music from the radio in the laboratory.

When the lights in the gelateria dim completely and the radio goes quiet, the only sound left is that of the distant hammering. Milena Migliari looked around, went back inside, exchanged a puzzled look with her assistant, Guadalupe, behind the counter, before going into the lab: even the hypnotic and reassuring hums of the refrigerators had stopped. She went back outside, turned the corner onto the main road, needed only a few steps to realize that the power was out in the entire town.

Gelato's equilibrium is unstable by definition, though it takes some time before it becomes unsalvageable. And Milena Migliari has always felt a mix of anxiety and fascination for unstable equilibriums: it might depend on her own personal history, as Viviane claims, on her never having had a solid familial framework, never having put down roots anywhere. And now the fruits of her labor are in jeopardy: the ingredients sought out with infinite care, the procedures honed over time, expensive equipment to pay off, a budget to respect.

She makes a conscious effort not to get upset, to wait patiently for the power to be restored. She looks at the wall clock, which luckily runs on batteries, makes a few calculations: in the counter's refrigerated pans the gelato can resist for two hours for sure, even three with this outside temperature. She chats with Guadalupe, goes back to the lab every so often to look at the batch freezer, the maturation vats, the blast chiller, the positive-temperature refrigerator for fresh ingredients: off, off, off, off. Not a pilot light on, not a fan humming. Her anxiety grows, pushes her to pick up the phone, call the electric company and the city to get some information; but the only responses are from voice-mail systems or incredibly uninformed, vague, and uncaring human beings. They don't reassure her one bit, quite the opposite.

Milena Migliari goes back out to the main road, talks to the bakery owner who knows as much as she does and is just as worried, shakes her head. Then she goes into the real estate agency next door: two of the employees are staring fixedly at their cell-phone screens, a third is vainly calling for information. She returns to the gelateria and tries to calm down, listens to Guadalupe's account of her cousin's birthday party in Quetzaltenango that she joined via Skype. Every few minutes she looks at the wall clock, goes to check the lab. She tries calling the electric company again, the city: nothing. She paces back and forth, from the counter to the lab, the lab to the counter, her cell phone pressed to her ear, her heart beating faster at the thought of the power returning who-knows-when and the temperature in the pans rising to the point of no return. Still nothing happens, so before the situation gets any worse she makes a decision: she tells Guadalupe to help her fill up cones and cups, to distribute them to anyone passing by outside.

But tourist season is indeed long over: on the streets of the old town are only a few elderly ladies with grocery bags, a few slightly furtive North African laborers, a few northern European tourist couples looking lost, a few worried storeowners trying to figure out how the situation is going to pan out. If the blackout had occurred in July or August, or even September, she and Guadalupe would have been able to give away all their gelato in half an hour, and it would have been great publicity for the store. As things stand, they practically have to beg the rare passersby to accept a free cone or cup. Baffled faces, distracted expressions, raised chins, hurried steps: it's incredible how offering anything for free arouses suspicion. To convince people. they smile profusely, make reassuring gestures with their head and arms, explain that they're not asking them to give blood or join a religious sect. But progress is so slow that after a while Milena goes back inside and starts filling up the one-pound containers, starts taking them to the real estate agencies and faux-Provençal handicraft stores, to the restaurants. It's ironic, because in summer she is inundated with requests she's unable to satisfy, having to explain time and again that her production is limited, her preparation slow and complex, that she can only satisfy a limited number of people at a time. But now, between the blackout and the lack of tourists, no one seems excited about the enchanting yellow-red of Maquis arbutus berry, the golden brown of Montauroux jujube, the vibrant green of Mons gooseberry. Sure, a couple of people thank her, but mostly it seems like they're doing her a favor by accepting for free a container that a couple of months earlier they would have fought to pay for. And when she explains with a hint of urgency in her voice that the gelato needs to be eaten soon, to avoid it losing its ideal consistency, they look at her like she's an obsessive freak, whose concerns are totally inappropriate given the situation in which they all find themselves.

Milena Migliari goes back inside, makes more useless phone calls, gets more useless answers. She checks the temperature in the counter pans with the infrared thermometer, which also luckily runs on batteries: 14°F. Still okay, but it keeps rising, naturally. She already pictures herself poking around dejectedly with the spatula in little puddles of various colors. She and Guadalupe look at each other in despair. It's not just the imminent loss of the gelato; it's a much vaster feeling of decay, extending to the very confines of her life.

When the telephone rings, she jumps up to get it, surprised that one of the unfeeling bureaucrats she reached out to has taken the initiative to update her on the situation. She presses the receiver to her ear, her hand trembling slightly with agitation. "Hello?"

"Is this La Merveille Imparfaite in Fayence? The gelateria?" The woman's voice on the other end of the line sounds slightly harsh, over the background noise of a moving car.

"Yes, what can I do for you?" Milena Migliari tries to sound professional, but given the circumstances, she isn't very successful.

"I've just read some amazing things about your gelato." The voice has a slight foreign inflection, but her command of French is absolute.

"Well, thank you." Milena Migliari doesn't know whether to feel more reassured that her work is appreciated or pained that soon it's going to melt right in front of her.

"*Milena Migliari, an Italian living on French soil, captures with miraculous sensitivity and perspicacity the quintessence of ingredients that are rigorously natural, rigorously local, and rigorously in-season, and offers it to the palate of the refined connoisseur in incomparable cups and cones of the most delicate and vivid colors. . . .*" The woman is clearly referring to the write-up by Liam Bradford, the fine-foods blogger who happened to pass through in July and was blown away by her Saint-Paul red apricot, her Tourrettes midnight-blue plum, as well as by her Montauroux fior di latte.

"Well, I do my best." Milena Migliari says so because she thinks she has to say something, but immediately feels stupid. She recalls reading the review on her home computer, seeing the photo of herself and Guadalupe behind the counter, looking like a couple of fugitives from justice; how she felt gratified but also destabilized at seeing the fruits of her long research, born of instinct and experimentation, translated into these slightly alien words.

"*We said tomorrow, that was the bloody agreement! No, no, no, Friday is too late, for God's sake!*" The voice on the phone is speaking English to someone else in the car, in a tone so suddenly aggressive that it almost seems like a different person.

Milena Migliari makes a face at Guadalupe, as if to say that she has no idea who's on the other end of the line.

"I'm terribly sorry." The voice turns back to her, once more in French, once more in an amiable tone, though not quite as much as before. "Do you deliver?"

"That depends." Milena Migliari is taken aback, and a bit distracted by Guadalupe, who continues to stare at her questioningly.

"Depends on what?" The voice seems on the verge of losing patience with her, too.

"On how much you want, where, and when." Milena Migliari thinks that in all honesty, right now, she would be willing to drive dozens of miles just to deliver a single one-pound container: it would give her the sense of having saved at least something from the general disintegration.

"I want twenty pounds. In Callian. Immediately." Yes, there's a substantial dose of hardness just beneath the surface.

"Sorry, how many pounds did you say?" Milena Migliari is sure that the woman has gotten her French numbers mixed up: in the three years since she opened her gelateria the largest orders have been for two two-pound containers; and those in the middle of August.

"Twenty. Two-zero. Half of forty. Every flavor you have." Zero doubts, zero hesitation; now she *is* growing impatient. "Is it possible?"

"Of course it's possible." Milena Migliari struggles to shake off her disbelief.

"Wonderful, I'm so happy!" The enthusiasm in the voice is disconcerting, as much as the recent shift from amiability to impatience.

"So am I!" Milena Migliari can't help but be excited, though the doubt does surface that this could be some sort of prank. "Would you give me the address?"

"Chemin de la Forêt, Les Vieux Oliviers." The voice enunciates each word, to make them stand out with the greatest possible clarity over the background noise. "The name is engraved into the tree stump, to the right of the front gate. You can't miss it."

"All right." Milena Migliari would like to ask something else, but doesn't know exactly what. "Then I'll see you soon."

"See you soon!" The person at the other end of the line seems content to have reached a satisfactory conclusion and hangs up.

Milena Migliari puts the receiver back in the cradle, stares at Guadalupe for a second or two, and then recovers, her movements regaining their normal speed. "Help me fill up ten two-pound containers. Every flavor."

"*Ten?*" Guadalupe looks stunned.

"Yes, ten! Ten!" Milena Migliari takes the Styrofoam containers off the shelf, lines them up on the counter.

Guadalupe recovers as well; in no time they're both scooping frantically.

TWO

NICK CRUICKSHANK DRIVES his white Piaggio Ape Calessino, with its soft-top roof and white fabric seats, along the sienna-colored asphalt path that cuts between the rows of olive trees. The sky is a pale blue and it wouldn't be a bad morning given the season, but he has a headache and a touch of nausea from all the whiskey he drank last night with that idiot Wally, despite the Bloody Mary antidote he had Madame Jeanne prepare for him when he got up. This motorized tricycle looks ridiculous, but it's pretty fun to use; the manufacturer sent it to him as a gift from Italy, probably hoping it would appear sooner or later in some photo shoot or music video of his. Come to think of it, for a long time now people have been giving him things as gifts that he would be more than happy to buy, while he has to keep paying for those he'd gladly do without. For example, it's been decades since he was able to spend a cent on a guitar or an amplifier, or a leather jacket (when he was still allowed to wear them), or even a silk scarf, and meanwhile he has to continue coughing up money for his two ex-wives and their five children, and all their endless requests. Yes, it's a paradox, but then his life is *made* of paradoxes, really. Like drinking a

Bloody Mary to remedy the consequences of a hangover. But years ago his personal doctor, James Knowles, confirmed that there is something to it, the properties of the tomato combining with the ethanol of the new drink to drive out the toxic methanol in the blood, or something like that. Anyway it's not much of a problem anymore; for a few years now his life has been all too healthy, with a few rare exceptions when someone shows up to tempt him, like last night.

His discomfort is, at any rate, far more generalized, and now this electrical blackout is piling on a feeling of imminent catastrophe. Aldino discovered that the power is out in the whole area: How do you manage not to think, at least in passing, that someone has blown up the power plant to carry out a well-planned massacre? It's not a question of being paranoid; the world is simply becoming a pretty nerve-racking little place, where it's better to keep your guard up if you want to give yourself a slightly better chance of avoiding a bad end. Consider the precautions they now have to take at the Bebonkers' concerts: metal detectors at the entrances, security guys outside the dressing rooms, armed guards beneath the stage, bulletproof vehicles. And just the same you know that it might not be of any use, that two or three imbeciles brainwashed in a madrasa financed by those Saudi bastards could still slip through the cracks without anyone knowing the first thing about it.

It's reflections like these that make him want to accelerate, even if this contraption can only get up to around thirty miles an hour at most. Nick Cruickshank gives it full throttle, tries to milk the 200cc motor for all it's worth. The result is that the Ape follows an uncertain trajectory, rocking violently at the path's slightest undulation. Now and then one of the back tires scrapes on a lump of dirt in the grove, sending bits of reddish earth shooting up in the air; he has to jerk the wheel forcefully to get back on course.

Amid the olive trees are three workers intent on sorting out the orange and yellow and green nets that have become tangled up, thanks to the alpacas that for some reason decide to chase each other here of all places, despite all the open areas they have on the lawns and in the woods. Nick Cruickshank takes one hand off the handlebars to wave hello, though the workers are far away and their expressions seem more diffident than cordial. But as a foreign proprietor who got rich from what to them might not even seem like work, and with this large villa and dozens of hectares of land right in their own backyard, he feels obliged to be gracious. Assuming this really is their own backyard, because when he gets a better look at them, despite the vehicle's bouncing around, their faces seem more Middle Eastern than French. Come to think of it, they could easily be Islamic terrorists hiding their AK-47s among the olive nets and waiting for the right moment to riddle with bullets a symbol of the pagan and corrupting West. Aldino told him that he verified the identity of all those working on the property with the local police, but these guys could easily have arranged false documents, or killed three real workers and taken their place.

Nick Cruickshank feels a preconcert tension rising inside him, sufficient to drive the methanol from his blood more effectively than Madame Jeanne's Bloody Mary. It occurs to him that his morning pick-me-up could become one of those ridiculous and tragic details that the media dig up when they go rummaging through the life or, even better, the death of people like him. He can already envision the headlines in the *Sun* or the *Mirror*: THE LAST BLOODY MARY OF NICK CRUICKSHANK. The more he thinks about it, the more his arm and stomach muscles contract, the less he's able to look away from the worker-terrorists entangled in the orange and yellow and green nets. Then the back right wheel scrapes again on the dirt, and the single front wheel skids; the Ape swerves irresistibly toward the olive grove. He tries to yank on the handlebars to regain control, but he can't: the motorized tricycle will have to go it alone. It bumps across a patch of dirt, drags the olive nets in its wheels, banging and rattling, miraculously avoiding tree after tree, but it's clear that it's going to crash somewhere, sooner or later. In fact, it heads straight for a gnarled and wrinkled trunk, thick as an elephant's leg: the front wheel slams into it, the entire ridiculous metal structure reverberates.

The impact is much less violent than he expected, probably because of the nets caught in the wheels, and because the tricycle certainly wasn't going very fast. But nonetheless it is an episode of stupid mechanical violence: it flings him against the handlebars, and though he tries to soften the blow with his arms, it knocks the wind out of him.

It's worse when he gets out, doubled over and breathless, and sees the three Middle Eastern guys in the distance immediately shed their workers' disguises and transform into terrorists. They come running toward him, a ferocious light in their eyes, a brutal eagerness to complete their mission. They certainly weren't expecting to see their task facilitated this way, to find their target within their grasp, immobilized and stunned, instead of having to hit him on the move and from a distance. They'll see it as confirmation that their mission is holy and just, guided directly by the hand of Allah.

Nick Cruickshank thinks for a moment that he could try to escape; despite the shock of impact and the lingering hangover he's in far better shape than many of his colleagues, ruined by a life of excess. He left that life behind a good ten years ago; he does at least an hour of exercise a day, a five-mile run, a long swim, a horseback ride, eats well, has totally eliminated meat from his diet. Furthermore, the three terrorists are still about forty yards away, impeded by the nets they were pretending to rearrange; if he started zigzagging between the olive trees he might have a chance. But the fact is that the idea of being mowed down while running away like a coward after crashing an Ape Calessino just seems so undignified, so uncool. It's not a question of keeping up appearances to the very end. But there is undeniably an image to uphold, and it's an issue that doesn't regard him alone, but also all his fans, and even those nonfans who consider him a behavioral benchmark. Looking back at his life since the Bebonkers became famous, you won't find a single occasion on which he has started running to get somewhere, or away from something. He once blew off a concert in Birmingham (and infuriated the other band members) just to avoid rushing to catch a train, even though it was still on the platform and he was only a few dozen yards away, with a determined sprint he'd certainly have made it. Another time he skipped out on a ceremony with the queen at Buckingham Palace simply because he couldn't be bothered to set his alarm at an unpleasant hour (back when he was still waking up late). But there too it was a question of style: on his résumé there isn't a trace of nervousness, hastiness, anxiety, insistence, breathlessness, struggling against the current. Excess, yes; anger, even of the destructive variety, yes, he certainly won't deny it, but always in the service of asserting a principle, or of artistic and existential exploration. This is why for years now he has come to be known (among his fans, in the media, even in certain jokes) as the incarnation of cool: for the combination of elegance and natural nonchalance with which he does or doesn't do things. On the other hand, it isn't an act; it's how he *is*. Always has been, ever since he was an unhappy and restless child in Manchester and didn't seem to have the slightest thing in common with what he saw and heard and felt around him. It's not coldness, it's not emotional neutrality: you only need to listen to one of his songs to know that he's the *opposite* of emotionally neutral. The fifty percent of Irish blood in his veins should suffice. If an explanation were absolutely necessary, you could say it's a tendency to see things in a far-off perspective, which inevitably reduces their relevance significantly. It would also be tough to find cowardice among the character flaws he's been attributed over time (by journalists, ex-wives, other members of the band). If anything, they've all rebuked him constantly for being too willing to take risks, with drugs (in the past), with women (in the past), with aggressive fans, with powerful cars, with spirited horses, with ocean waves, and so on. At least there's some truth to this: ever since as a scrawny third-grader with stick legs he floored that fifth-grade bully with a totally unexpected uppercut and then kicked him senseless, he's known how to look fear in the face and tell it to fuck off.

So instead of slaloming desperately through the olive trees, Nick Cruickshank turns toward his future killers with an expression of extreme casualness; he raises a hand in a tired and ironic replica of the greeting he made from the Ape, when he still thought they were actual workers, maybe even fans. He's slightly crooked and a little shaky on his legs, but in general he doesn't think he's giving off a shabby image of himself; he straightens up, adjusts the foulard rolled up over his forehead, even manages to don a provocative smile, before they start shooting. It occurs to him that an end like this might even make sense; that it might even be a sort of crowning achievement. It's certainly no less than he deserves: no one ever forced him to become a global catalyst of love and hate, aspirations and frustrations, admiration and jealousy. Over the course of his career he could easily have died in dozens of more stupid ways: from an overdose like several of his colleagues, suffocating in his own vomit like Jimi, drowning in the swimming pool like Brian or in the bathtub like Jim, crashing in a helicopter right after a concert like Stevie Ray. All in all, this might be a noble end, which could turn him into even more of a symbol, like what happened to John, who in life might not have been a great guy but in death turned into a beautiful martyr. Of course it will be necessary to wait and see just what he becomes a symbol of: unfiltered and uncompromising creativity transferred from art to life? The freedom of Western culture attacked by Islamic fanaticism? The fans and media will have to find the answer; personally, he couldn't care less at this point.

His three soon-to-be killers are now only a few yards away, but though they're clearly out of breath and look at him with extreme intensity, strangely they hold neither Kalashnikovs nor pistols nor knives, nor do they seem intent on attacking him physically in any way. In fact, one of them points to the Ape that crashed into the tree, then points at his legs. "Okay?"

Nick Cruickshank needs a couple of seconds to transition from being about to die in an extremely cool way to feeling extremely stupid. He nods. "Okay, okay."

The three look at him with inquisitive faces, look at one another; they might not be terrorists, but they're certainly not fans, either. In truth they don't seem to have the slightest idea who he is, what to think of him, or what's just happened.

Nick Cruickshank gives another decidedly self-deprecating smile, though he's none too sure that's how they'll interpret it. Relieved? No. Embarrassed? That neither. More than anything he's fed up: a damn fine morning this is turning out to be. He nods good-bye to the three workers, crosses the olive grove with all the nonchalance he can muster, reaches the driveway, sets off in the direction of the house. Now that he knows he's being followed by a collective stare, albeit limited in number and not particularly invested emotionally, he emerges from his dazed state of shock and his movements gradually regain their elasticity: he sets his toes down before his heel, in that undulating gait that years ago some moron, later imitated by many other morons, called the "Nick-walk," and which at any rate makes him feel more in possession of his faculties with every step.

"*Monsieur!*" There's a voice coming from behind him, over a mix of rustling and squeaking.

Nick Cruickshank turns around calmly, thinking that maybe the three men *are* terrorists after all, though quite tentative, or maybe just waiting for the best moment to do him in.

But they've just finished pushing the Ape out of the olive grove, and with great difficulty: they present it to him, panting, with the same perplexed expressions as before.

Nick Cruickshank shakes his head, at himself and at them, smiles again, opens his arms out wide; he goes back to reclaim his stupid motorized tricycle, only slightly the worse for wear.

THREE

Milena Migliari gets Guadalupe to help her attach the rolled-up little messages to the containers, already filled and taped shut. The idea came to her when she was still making gelato at home and selling it to local restaurants. She has always enjoyed finding the short phrases inside Chinese fortune cookies, or on the little tabs of the herbal tea she and Viviane drink in the evening: discovering tiny revelations, possible connections to her current state of mind or activity. So she began looking for phrases in the books she loves, and transcribing them with a fountain pen on little pieces of straw-colored paper, which she then tightly rolls up and binds with a little red string. Whoever buys a container receives one. It is a little time-consuming, especially in the summer, when the gelateria is working at full capacity, but she likes to dedicate an hour each night to finding the phrases and copying them down; likes to imagine people's faces at home when they unroll her tiny messages, before tasting the gelato or after tasting it, or best of all, *while* they're tasting it.

Guadalupe helps her put the first five containers in a cooler and properly seal the cover, then helps her fill up the other five, working determinedly with the spatula. Fortunately the consistency is still good, and should stay that way until delivery. It would certainly benefit from a few minutes in the blast chiller, but oh well. Every so often Milena Migliari looks at Guadalupe, they both laugh: this monster order at such a desperate moment is a sort of miracle, difficult to believe. But the truth is that to her it seems like a miracle every time someone comes into the store; she still hasn't completely gotten used to the idea that there are people who like her gelato to the point of coming here even from far away, and returning several times in the course of a week or month to taste new flavors or enjoy the ones they've already tried, knowing full well they'll never be quite the same. She even wrote as much in light-blue marker on a sign hanging on the wall: *Every flavor changes, from one time to the next; don't be upset when you don't find the exact replica of what you liked, but try to appreciate the differences.* One of the things she figured out right from the start is that she gets no satisfaction from repeating the same identical recipe over and over again, even when it's particularly good: the true joy is in the experimentation, the implicit risk, the possible surprises. Naturally this leads her to make mistakes, to follow a hunch that seemed promising and instead leads to disappointing results; but she allows for it, it's part of the game.

The choice to use only local and seasonal raw materials also means that they can run out, sometimes in a few days, and that it takes a whole year to get them again. This is probably the aspect of her work that's most difficult for others to understand: even the customers who know her best sometimes get upset when they discover, for example, that the Châteaudouble elderberry of the previous week is no longer available, or that they'll have to wait until the following November to savor Bargemon pomegranate again. Viviane often tells her that this is just purist fanaticism, that there'd be nothing wrong with freezing local ingredients to be able to use them for a longer period of time, or even buying outside the local area, as long as the products are of the necessary quality. But to her it would seem like cheating, and anyway she's convinced that the magic of her gelato lies in the variability of her flavors according to the season, place, outside temperature, the mood of the person tasting them. Considerations like these are what led her to the name of her gelateria. ("Philosophically intriguing, but wouldn't simply 'La Merveille' be better? Or 'Gelato Italiano'? Or, I don't know, 'Le Bon Goût'? Or maybe 'Soleil de Provence'? Since it is supposed to be a *business*, aiming for the most part at *tourists*?" as Viviane commented three years ago, when it was time to decide. And of course she was saying it for her own good, and for their common good, with the practicality that Milena usually finds so reassuring.)

But the fact is that she simply isn't interested in making good gelato for tourists; she wants to explore the mysterious nuances of each flavor, discover the connections between sensations and images and memories, traverse complexity to reach a maximum of simplicity. She spends hours each week talking with small farmers and sellers at the local markets, taking note, reflecting, experimenting; and more time on the Internet and at the library, reading up on everything she's been able to find about the science and mechanics of taste, from the writings of Theophrastus to illustrated children's books to new and old cookbooks to treatises on biochemistry and nutritional science. The research is thrilling, though it's painstaking and not very profitable, except in the middle of the summer. She invests all the physical and mental energy she has, but if she didn't enjoy herself immensely as well and wasn't at least able to make someone happy, she'd rather quit right away, find herself another job.

Now the other five two-pound containers are ready, their little messages all attached. Guadalupe helps her place them in the second cooler, take both into the shop. Milena Migliari takes off the gloves, hairnet, and overshoes she always wears in the lab, puts on her coat and cap, grabs the two coolers by the handles, reassures Guadalupe that she can manage fine on her own, turns the corner, and walks quickly up the main road, toward the public parking lot where she left her van.

FOUR

IN THE KITCHEN Madame Jeanne looks at him with a worried expression. "*Ça va, Nick?*"

"*Ça va, ça va.*" Nick Cruickshank takes a bottle of unfiltered organic apple juice out of the refrigerator, pours some into a thick glass cup, drains it in a few swallows. His body has an intense need for restorative liquids: he immediately pours himself a second glass, empties that one too, pours himself a third. If one thing has stayed with him from his drug period, it's the tendency to indulge his body's needs as quickly as possible, never to leave them wanting.

Madame Jeanne continues observing him: rotund and soft in her striped apron, a wide face, skin like milk, small, alert blue eyes, the manner of a good country mother always slightly apprehensive for her child, indulgent but also severe when it comes to protecting him or bringing him to his senses for his own good.

Nick Cruickshank goes toward one of the windows, with the tickle of pleasure and annoyance he feels every time he's observed with insistence. If he thinks about it, ever since he's had the means he's managed to find a series of women to take care of his domestic existence, and thus, at least in part, of his emotional balance. There have been at least four or five of them, of different origins, languages, and skin colors, with the common trait of being credible, substitute, albeit paid mothers. But Jeanne is by far the best of all of them: the one who has invested the most naturalness and authoritativeness in her role, the most sincere feelings. The paradox (here's another) is that his *real* mother didn't have any of the characteristics he has sought out in these surrogates; she was a thin and nervous woman, intelligent and restless, much more interested in painting and writing poems than in taking care of him or his brother. When it came to urging them to read a book or listen to classical music or visit a museum she was all too insistent, but he can't remember ever having seen her bake a cake, or produce one of those displays of feminine generosity and sweetness that even back then he so desperately needed. Try as he might, he can't recall a single enveloping and comforting hug, a single kiss of comprehension or encouragement. Sure, a few caresses on the forehead when he got sick, but so rare as to be almost baffling. And yes, she did get him a little gray cat that time he came down with the measles and became delirious with fever and was nearly on his deathbed; but as soon as he recovered she gave it away to his cousin Rae in Yorkshire, because she had neither the time nor the patience for cats. What he remembers most about his mother are her ironic expressions, her sarcastic comments, her biting observations, her critiques dictated by an aesthetic sense so evolved that practically nothing was up to her expectations, her lack of indulgence for the mediocre or trite. It was probably (in fact, certainly) a privilege for him to have to measure himself against such a demanding mind during his formative years, and much of what he's been able to accomplish in later years likely derives from it, but his childhood was certainly no barrel of laughs. Even after, with him now grown up and famous, it's not as if he ever received much gratification from his mother; unless you consider gratifying a comment such as "Well done, with this rock business you've found yourself a job that not only doesn't force you to leave adolescence behind but requires you to stay there indefinitely."

But as a child he also discovered the existence of a brand of femininity completely different from his mother's high-strung and elusive variety, thanks to the rare, precious visits of his father's sister, Aunt Maeve. Every now and then she would bring him chocolates, or a picture book that she'd read to him while holding him on her knee, caressing his hair, smothering his head in kisses. When he grew older she would take him to the movies, to see the Westerns or war films he liked so much; after the film they'd go to a tearoom, to drink Darjeeling black and eat scones with whipped cream. Aunt Maeve didn't give any credence to his mother's implacable division between highbrow and lowbrow discussion topics, noble and ignoble subjects: she liked telling him even about frivolous episodes concerning relatives or acquaintances, movie or music stars, members of the royal family. She was always ready to laugh, in a marvelously earthy and luminous way; even now he remembers her perfume, the whiteness of her skin, the softness of her hugs. He wrote "My Wondrous Enveloper" thinking of her, though everyone's convinced he was inspired by some amorous girl with whom he had had a fling. It certainly wasn't by chance that his mother treated Aunt Maeve with the impatient condescendence of refined culture for raw instinct, mixed with a dose of English haughtiness for the Irish; she was almost certainly jealous of her, for everything she meant to him. Anyhow, after his father ran off to Ireland, Aunt Maeve's visits became rarer still, ceasing completely when she left for Australia with a man from Sydney she had met at a dance hall. From there she sent him cheerful and humorous postcards, with pictures of emus and kangaroos, people in bathing suits on endless beaches; then she died. It was a terrible loss for him, but the seed of desire for a warm, caring femininity had long since sprouted inside him, become a part of who he was.

"*Tu es pâle.*" Madame Jeanne comes closer to get a better look at his face, turned as he is toward the window. She has this visual, audio, olfactory, tactile way of monitoring his physical and mental well-being: she might make him stick out his tongue to see what color it is, use two fingers to stretch his eyelids open to check that his eyes are nice and clear, stick a hand under one of his armpits to be sure he doesn't have a fever.

"*Je vais bien, merci.*" Nick Cruickshank now tries to wriggle free from this excess of maternal attention because he still hasn't completely recovered from what happened out there in the olive grove. Come to think of it, the other paradox (once more) is that he's been able to find that warm and caring femininity more in the women who take care of him *as a job* than in the women with whom he's had serious relationships. Really: almost all of the latter have been from his mother's category, rather than Aunt Maeve's. Intellectually acute, maybe artistically gifted, but emotionally unstable and limited in their affections, if not frigid. And to think that, from the age of twenty on, he certainly hasn't lacked for choice: he must have met thousands of them on tour alone, on three or four different continents. But he's never been drawn to idolizing fans, or the poor, damaged mannequins always hanging around the postconcert parties or record industry events, or the models or actresses his colleagues like so much, drugged out of their minds by the transient gleam of fame and its connected material advantages. Okay, maybe he *has* been attracted a few times, but the attraction has lasted a few hours or days at most, and inevitably left him in a state of desperate solitude, staring down into the abyss. Sure, he's met a couple of women capable of bringing a little serenity into his life, but by some perverse mechanism he's always ended up ruining things with them: just look at how it went with his first wife. It's like he's condemned to rediscovering in his life partners the same characteristics that made him miserable with his mother: it's crazy, really. Several years ago he read a book by an American psychologist that talked about this very thing, the unconscious return to the causes of primary distress; but being conscious of the problem obviously hasn't been of much use, judging by his sentimental choices before Aileen. With her it's as if for the first time he's discovered the existence of an intelligent, energetic, and creative woman who also wants and is able to take care of him, and it's seemed like a sort of miracle. Not that she has ever baked a cake for him either (with the diet he's been on for years, he wouldn't eat it anyway), but she's dedicated herself with the utmost intensity to every aspect of his life, from his stage attire to his song lyrics, to his houses; she's even established good relationships with his kids, even with his ex-wives. Intuitive, reactive, ready to offer advice and suggestions anytime they're needed, helping him and when necessary urging him on, convincing him, for example, to rid himself of the objects and people keeping him chained to his previous lives with the shackles of nostalgia and guilt.

Fortunately, the substitution of Madame Jeanne has not been among the many changes that Aileen has demanded here at Les Vieux Oliviers. Not that she hasn't broached the subject, truth be told, but she eventually realized how important she is to him, and decided to put up with her at least temporarily, despite the territorial tensions and questions of form that arise between them at regular intervals.

"*Est-ce que tu veux deux oeufs battus*?" Madame Jeanne is firmly convinced that a well-fed man is a happy man: her first reaction when she sees him a little out of sorts is to offer him a couple of scrambled eggs, maybe with a little drop of rum.

"*Non, merci.*" With one long swallow he drains the third glass of apple juice, goes to set it in the sink. He's always liked thick glass; this too must be something he gets from his childhood, from the memory of the bottles the milkman used to leave on the doorstep in Manchester. Is it possible that he's repeatedly gotten himself into situations of emotional unhappiness for fear that serenity and stability would make him lose his inspiration? Has it been the emotional equivalent of limiting himself to a diet of rice cakes and water for days on end to try to revive the desperate creative energy of the early days?

"*Un peu de guacamole, peut-être?*" Madame Jeanne continues scrutinizing him protectively. When he hired her ten years ago she had a marked mistrust of avocados, almost didn't consider them edible; it's wonderful how in order to make him happy she's been able to overcome her own preconceptions, expand her repertoire.

"Can I have a fucking pint of coffee, now?" Wally Thompson has entered the kitchen: thinning grizzled-blond hair scattered across his head, eyelids swollen from last night's drinking and smoking, tattoos on his arms and legs revealed by gray gym shorts and a black cutoff T-shirt with the Guinness logo, white terrycloth slippers with the golden initials of the Paris Ritz.

Madame Jeanne glares at him: with the sole exception of the master of the house she doesn't like having the sacred space of the kitchen violated, particularly by someone such as Wally, who represents the very type of rude and debauched friend she'd prefer to see him avoid.

"Madame Jeanne will make it for you now." Nick Cruickshank heads him off, pushing him back out of the kitchen. He turns around to motion at Madame Jeanne. "*Du café pour ce baudet, s'il vous plaît.*"

She nods, the faintest hint of a smile: she understood perfectly, but her expression remains disapproving.

Wally reluctantly allows himself to be pushed out into the hallway, dragging the rubber soles of his slippers over the ceramic tiles; he stinks of alcohol, smoke, sweat, the expensive cologne that on him still smells out of place, even after decades. Wally looks at him, with those annoying eyes of his. "Already up and about from the break of day, eh?"

"It's almost half past noon, Mr. Thompson," Nick Cruickshank responds drily, because it's how things have always been between them, and because he considers him largely responsible for the earlier accident among the olive trees: if he hadn't made him drink so much last night and hadn't given him that supercharged weed it's almost certain he would have been able to see the three workers for what they were.

"Oh, my apologies, Mr. Clean." Wally gives him a couple of jabs in the ribs, tries to rile him up. He has always been the jackass of the band, ever since the beginning, and certainly hasn't improved with age: he's merely become less funny, greedier for money, more bitter that in all these years the Bebonkers have only recorded three of his songs, thus depriving him of the constant flow of royalties that Nick Cruickshank and Rodney Ainsworth enjoy. But between records and concerts he has still earned infinitely more than if he had ended up in any other band or done any other type of work within his capabilities. And it isn't true that they've all ganged up on him, as he claims: he simply doesn't have any real talent as a composer. He's a good bassist and that's it. An *amazing* bassist, they might as well admit it, who never misses a beat, never lets their rhythm slacken. If he were capable of writing good songs, they would have taken them on the fly, at least in leaner years. But all he's been able to come up with are some good bass lines (even some memorable ones, sure): that's his comfort zone, his natural limit. When he tried to put together a band of his own in the nineties, that embarrassing calamity known as the Blues Angels, it was plain to see just what type of masterpieces he was capable of. But try telling him that: they've nearly come to blows several times, because of the veiled hostility he carries inside him. How many times has he wanted to get rid of Wally, substitute him with a session man to call in for recording and tours, as the Stones did, eliminate once and for all the torture of having to deal with someone convinced that their amazing talent is being thwarted.

But Wally Thompson is also one of the people whom Nick Cruickshank has known the longest, with whom he's spent the most time. Adding together rehearsals, recording sessions, concerts, car, bus, and plane rides, days in hotels, lunches, dinners, smoking, drinking, waiting in dressing rooms, they've spent *decades* together, and this creates the same type of inevitable familiarity you have with a relative. But a relative whom you've gone to battle with, with whom you've been through the best and worst adventures imaginable, from being completely down in the dumps to being over the moon to plummeting back down to earth again, and so on. This is why it was simply unthinkable not to invite him here; just like it would make no sense to expect him to behave any differently than usual.

"So?" Wally scratches his rear end, looks blearily around the living room: slovenly, the protruding belly of a beer drinker (and any other alcoholic substance he can get his hands on). "What's the program for this afternoon?"

"The program is that everyone does whatever the hell they

want." Nick Cruickshank thinks that inevitable familiarity at least has the advantage of not needing to be overly concerned with politeness. If he'd had the choice he would have much preferred to take it easy for an extra day, maybe read a book or watch a few episodes of one of his favorite television series, but oh well. The fact is that after decades of chaos and continuous noise, in the studio, at home, onstage, offstage, he's developed an immense appreciation for silence and solitude, for not having anyone around to disturb his thoughts and bombard his eardrums.

"Ah." Wally looks at him with the expression of someone who, for lack of his own resources, is always hunting for invitations, suggestions, instructions, which he's likely to bitch about later.

"Where's Kimberly?" Nick Cruickshank gestures toward the room he and Aileen assigned to the Thompsons.

Wally's expression conveys a generalized neglect; he scratches himself between the legs. "Fuck do I know. In the can, or on the phone, or rubbing some shit on her face."

Nick Cruickshank would like to tell him to try to make an effort to better himself, even a small one, even for five minutes, just to surprise other people, if not himself; but it would be like asking a donkey to run the Kentucky Derby, so terribly useless. And then you might as well be up front about it: it's not like the world of rock music is populated by people of extraordinary intelligence, let alone culture. The most widespread characteristic is a lack of precise thinking due to the lifestyle, the continuous interaction with a fundamentally infantile public, the use of immature attitudes and language as authentic tools of the trade. Wally Thompson doesn't particularly stand out among their colleagues for stupidity or ignorance; in fact, he falls more or less in the norm. Indeed, it's those who have aspirations of betterment that are looked on with suspicion, if not open hostility; getting caught reading a novel that isn't pure trash can be sufficient to be branded a pretentious know-it-all. He still remembers Rodney's reaction on seeing him reading *Madame Bovary* on an airplane, or Joyce's *Ulysses* in a hotel suite ("Oh, pardon me, Mr. Professor!"). He has to admit that in this regard, his mother was right: the world of rock is *founded* on permanent regression. Better to conceal any attempt at personal growth, if there is one, or at least compensate for it with the occasional relapse into vulgarity and mental haziness.

Suddenly the stereo, the floor lamps, the signal on the modem all turn on simultaneously. They hear Aldino's voice coming from the hallway. "The power's back on!"

"So no plans?" Wally doesn't register the information: it's absolutely possible that in his state of morning opacity he wasn't even aware of the blackout. He stares at him with those watery irises, his lips in that ugly half smile. "You make people come here from halfway around the world and you can't be bothered to organize fucking anything?"

Nick Cruickshank feels the urge to tell him that he should be grateful he was invited to stay in this house with that slutty wife of his, but he restrains himself, for hospitality's sake. He gestures toward the windows, quite brusquely. "If you want, maybe tomorrow we can take a little horseback ride."

Wally looks at him as though he's extremely disappointed by the proposal, but emits a grunt, nods.

Nick Cruickshank rotates his index finger in the air to say *catch you later*, heads for the door. He thinks that maybe he should call Aileen to see how her photographic expedition with the local derelicts in Lorgues is going, or alert René to prepare the horses for tomorrow morning, or find any occupation that keeps him away from useless attempts at nontrivial conversation with Wally "The Wall" Thompson.

FIVE

Milena Migliari drives her orange Renault Kangoo on the road that runs through the plain beneath the foothills where the villages are perched, past construction material depots and swimming pool retailers and parking lots for diggers and so-called Neo-Provençal-style houses built on every available lot. Every so often she has doubts about having coming here of all places to live and work; but then she thinks that all she has done is to follow an inescapable current, beginning when she met Viviane at the yoga center in the hills of Le Marche, and continuing with her decision to come join her in France, their increasingly structured living arrangement, the purchase at rock-bottom price of the house with the glass-covered patio from the eccentric notary/amateur painter, the leasing of the ex-bar for the gelateria when it no longer seemed possible to find a suitable space. She has never been one to make long-term plans; not even medium-term ones; not even short-term. She has always lived in the here and now, with the idea of leaving room for things to happen when they have to happen, adapting in consequence. She's always had a pretty fatalistic attitude toward events, and a tendency not to give either too little or too much weight to them based on preconceived scales of importance. For example, this story of the phone call from the super-nice and super-agitated English lady who wants twenty pounds of gelato today, of all days: it doesn't radically change her economic situation, but it is a message from the universe telling her to keep her chin up, that pleasant surprises are always possible. Unless of course it's a terrible joke by someone who enjoys toying with other people's lives. It will be clear soon enough; she's already rounding the curves that lead up to Callian, and the plateau just above the village where Chemin de la Forêt is located.

The roads in this area are mostly narrow, and you have to be careful because the locals drive as if they're absolutely convinced no one will ever be coming in the other direction. She frequently has to slam on the brakes at the last second or veer off to one side, to avoid a frontal collision with some recklessly speeding idiot. And with each passing curve her anxiety grows, as it does before every appointment. It doesn't matter if it's with the dentist, a friend, or a client, as in this case: the idea of having to meet a specific person in a specific place for a specific reason makes her nervous, there's nothing she can do. And this road is even narrower than the others, with a low stone wall on one side and the woods on the other, and longer than it first appeared.

But then the road suddenly ends, in front of an unduly imposing gate: on the right is a section of tree trunk with *Les Vieux Oliviers* burned into it, like the lady on the phone said. Visible through the dark-green iron bars are meticulously kept lawns and hedges and trees, for the enjoyment of the rich owners who almost certainly come here very rarely. Around here the use of houses is inversely proportional to their dimensions: the smaller ones are used intensively during the summer and on every holiday, the larger ones remain empty the vast majority of the time. It's not even clear who the owners of the bigger houses are, surrounded as they are by quasi-legendary rumors about tycoons of finance, and soccer, music and movie stars. Some of the names are probably circulated intentionally by restaurateurs and real estate agents, trying to extend to these small towns the mystique of the Côte d'Azur and the more authentic Provence to the west. To avoid them being seen for what they are: completely parceled out, frequented by the Germans and Dutch who like the artificial lake, and by a few wealthy oddballs hoping for some privacy.

Milena Migliari gets out of the van, studies the small brass panel of the intercom on the gate's left-hand column: no name. She hesitates for a moment, then pushes the button, uncertain. No one answers. She looks around, looks up: on top of the column is a blinker and the loudspeaker of an alarm system. She wonders if she should move her face closer to the camera's little glass eye, prove she's not a thief or gossip journalist or whatever else. She presses the button again, looks through the bars again: the house is invisible from here, not a sign of life.

Finally from the grill of the intercom comes a woman's voice, decidedly suspicious. "Who's there?"

Milena Migliari brings her face up to the camera, puts on a smile, which under the circumstances comes out terribly. "I'm here with the gelato."

"What gelato?" The voice on the intercom becomes even more unfriendly; and what's more, it doesn't at all resemble the one that called her at the store, there isn't the slightest trace of an English accent.

"La Merveille Imparfaite, in Fayence? You called me half an hour ago telling me to bring you twenty pounds of it?" Suddenly she feels incredibly stupid for having taken such an unusual order at face value, without even calling back to verify. It's another perfect example of bitter disappointment due to her always hoping for pleasant surprises; it's certainly not the first time she's been played for a fool. When she was a little girl, she fell for it every time her father called promising to come pick her up to spend a wonderful weekend together and then didn't even call back to cancel, infuriating her mother almost more with her than with him. Even Viviane is always telling her that she should try to get her head out of the clouds a little bit, establish a more realistic relationship with life. But if she didn't have her head up in the clouds at least a little she wouldn't be who she is, and she certainly wouldn't have opened a gelateria like hers; she would settle for prepacked mixes and produce standard gelato. Which would probably be much more realistic than what she does, but would certainly give her much less joy. And anyhow she's long since concluded that people are never really able to change, not deep down and permanently.

"Twenty pounds of gelato?" Now the voice on the intercom sounds incredulous. She hears another voice just beneath the first one, then both of them in an incomprehensible exchange; then neither.

Milena Migliari stands there staring at the little glass camera eye on the brass panel on the gate. She wonders if she should press the button again to explain herself, or give up, learn something from this experience, at least enough to avoid falling into traps like this again.

But then there's a click: the gate begins to open, with the buzzing of well-oiled, high-quality machinery.

She hesitates for a moment, then gets back in the van. When the gate is fully open she proceeds carefully along the driveway, which after a while curves to the right. The asphalt is sienna-colored; it would look like actual earth if it weren't so smooth and even. On the left is a laurel hedge, all too perfectly sculpted; on the right a row of cypress and oleander, delimiting a terraced hillside whose grass is all too perfectly trimmed.

Suddenly a large dark animal resembling a llama bursts out from between the trees, comes within inches of running into the front of the van. Milena Migliari slams on the brakes, almost smacks her head on the windshield, the two coolers slide along the flat surface in the back, bump into the backseats. Before she can recover, two more llamas jump out from the opening, race in front of her, and rush off down the driveway after the dark-colored one, in the direction she just came from. She's so shocked by their apparition that she can't move, heart racing and short of breath, she watches them disappear in cushioned bounds around the curve in the driveway. She wonders if there's any chance they can get off the property, if they're domestic animals; but the gate is no longer visible from here and there isn't enough space to turn around and follow them anyway, so she goes forward.

The path continues curving up, still flanked by the high hedges like defensive barriers, then straightens out and the house appears, or at least the back of the house, yellow and wide, with a two-story central body and two single-story wings. In front there's an open space, and a wooden structure with a slanted roof, beneath which several cars are parked.

Milena Migliari looks at the doors of the house, trying to figure out which to park nearest to. She can't decide, so she stops the Kangoo in the middle of the opening, rolls the window up, rolls it down again. She wonders whether she should consider the order genuine since they eventually let her in, or if she ought to talk first with whoever answered on the intercom, figure out what's really going on. Finally she takes the two coolers and goes toward the house's main door, her stomach knotted with embarrassment and the doubts still plaguing her.

The door opens before she has a chance to ring the bell: a huge guy with a shaved head and a hard expression leans out and peers at her through barely open eyelids, looks at the coolers, looks at the van, looks back at the coolers, as if he suspects them of containing who knows what.

SIX

NICK CRUICKSHANK GOES toward the entrance. Aldino is talking to someone just outside the door, turns, and signals for him to stay inside. But he still feels like such a paranoid idiot after the incident in the olive grove; he pushes him to the side, sticks his head out to look.

Outside is a woman with a blue-and-green eight-panel newsboy cap, long hair, a checkered coat, loose-fitting pants, thick-heeled black boots. She has two hard-plastic coolers in her hands and her legs are firmly planted, but she's leaning ever so slightly to one side at the waist: she seems determined to stay where she is, but also ready to leave. A few yards behind her is parked a small orange van, with *La Merveille Imparfaite* written in purple on the side.

"We *jamais* ordered any *glace. Jamais. No glace.* Okay?" Aldino's French is even more limited than his English, which already isn't great; but Nick isn't worried, he's long since realized that the big, threatening, and semi-illiterate Italian is the right man for the job. Once you get to know him he's actually smarter and more sensitive than he looks, at least compared to his average bodyguard colleagues.

"Then who was it that called me and gave me this address?" The woman in the hat responds in Italian, with a strange mix of perplexity and combativeness. She points behind her. "And who opened the gate for me?"

"Not us, that's for sure." Aldino continues barring her way with his enormous body, extending a protective arm backward.

"Hey, relax, Al." Nick Cruickshank knows he needs some protection, but an excess of preemptive defense has always gotten on his nerves, and continues to do so even in times like these. It's true that on the Internet you can still find a video from twenty years ago where, in the middle of a concert in Glasgow, he whips off his Telecaster and smashes it over some guy's head, but that was a case of *actual* defense: the guy had just thrown a bottle of beer at him, was yelling and spitting like a maniac, and trying to climb up onstage to attack him. For two decades he's been trying to explain what really happened, but he's given up; if they want to consider it a demonstration of his extreme rocker savagery, let them.

In any case the woman with the newsboy cap certainly doesn't seem dangerous; judging from the look she gave him when he stuck his head out the door, she doesn't even recognize him. No instant smile, no scurrying around excitedly. In fact, she seems quite annoyed by the situation, though in a pretty bizarre sort of way. She sets the two coolers on the ground. "But someone did open the gate for me, didn't they? Otherwise how could I have gotten in?" She switches to English with ease, but from the way she spoke Italian with Aldino it's clear that she must be Italian as well.

Nick Cruickshank has always had a passion for accents: for inflections, cadences, rhythms, the colors of voices. In England he's almost always able to identify the region, the city, the social origin of his interlocutors within a few sentences; in America he has to settle for less precise coordinates, but he still gets pleasure from recognizing someone as being from Brooklyn or Boston or Houston. A result of his ear for music, sure, but also of his need to decipher the world.

"Yes, how did you manage to get in? You want to explain that?" Aldino peers at the Italian gelato lady, looks around; he's unable to understand.

From the driveway Aileen's red BMW Cabrio pulls up, too quickly, as usual; she slams on the brakes in the parking area. Aileen gets out, elegantly impatient: her bob polished as a horse chestnut, wraparound sunglasses, a piece from her own clothing collection, a red "Anti-leather" jacket, draped around her shoulders, her long legs in jeans torn at the knees by Chinese artisans working in Italy, blue boots—these, too, in Anti-leather, naturally.

Then come Tricia, her thin and bony assistant with the fish face, and Maggie, the makeup artist with the pug nose and the aluminum-colored crew cut: 50 percent appearance, 50 percent substance.

Immediately after comes the station wagon belonging to the photographer Tom Harlan, who gets out and slams the door: thick reddish beard like the fur of some cave animal, extra-short-brimmed hat, black Anti-leather jacket courtesy of Aileen: 60 percent appearance, 40 percent substance. From the other side emerges his assistant what-the-hell's-his-name, thin and shambling. He passes his boss a duffel bag, starts gathering the umbrella lights, accumulators, and tripods from the backseat. The silvery Espace of the *Star Life* team pulls up as well: the editor in chief, writer, photographer, and cameraman get out, in a commotion of voices and gestures: 80 percent appearance, 20 percent substance.

Aileen looks at the Italian gelato lady, points to her little orange van. "*Est-ce que vous nous avez apporté la glace?*" Aileen's French is perfectly natural, like her Italian, her Spanish, and her German:

she has this knack for languages, the result of a childhood spent traveling the world with her diplomat father.

"Yes, but it seems like nobody ordered the gelato." The Italian gelato lady answers her in English as well, more bemused than irritated, now that she's surrounded by this chaos of people.

"What do you mean?" Aileen tilts her head; seeing her next to the gelato lady, it's difficult to imagine two more different women: in features, proportions, ways of moving, dressing, being.

The Italian gelato lady points to Aldino. "They say they didn't even open the gate for me."

"I'm the one who opened the gate! I was right behind you!" Aileen speaks in that extra-expressive, high-energy way of hers. "But I had to stop, because one of the white alpacas and the brown one were biting each other terribly on the neck. They were tearing each other's hair out, so vicious. I tried honking the horn to get them to separate, but they were relentless. I had to let Maggie out to go chase after them with an umbrella!"

"They jumped in front of my van, they really frightened me." The Italian gelato lady gestures to describe the jump: a nice gesture, in fact, very expressive. "I didn't know what they were, I thought maybe llamas."

"The two males need to be castrated, or else it's like keeping two roosters in a henhouse." Tom Harlan, the photographer, is ever intent on confirming his attitude of bristling concreteness; it's always the first thing on his mind.

"Oh, come on, the poor things!" Aileen assumes a horrified expression, though it's not like she's ever shown much sympathy for the alpacas, and certainly not since one of them bit through the sleeve of one of her blouses; but she's well aware that because of the whole Anti-leather thing, people expect her to be pro-animal.

Nick Cruickshank shrugs: the alpacas were a gift from that

idiot Steve McAbee after they'd used them for a video in Scotland; he was convinced they'd do well here.

The Italian gelato lady now seems worried about the alpacas, as if their destiny is connected to a thousand other crucial issues influencing the fate of the world. She has this engrossed expression: firmly planted on her thick-soled boots, surrounded by people generally unaware of her existence. Then she remembers her reason for coming here, points to the coolers. "So do you want the gelato or not?" She hardly seems anxious to sell it; she seems more than ready to take it back with her.

"Of course we want it! We're so sorry for the mix-up! I was sure I'd be able to get back before you arrived!" Aileen rushes over to shake her hand, in that very convincing way of hers.

"No problem." The gelato woman smiles back, timidly.

Aileen turns to Nick Cruickshank. "Liam Bradford wrote on his blog that she's incredibly talented! He says she's able to capture the quintessence of each flavor, with the sensitivity of a true artist. And there are dozens of fantastic reviews on TripAdvisor. How come we didn't know anything about it?"

Then Tom Harlan, his assistant, Tricia, Maggie, the *Star Life* team, even Aldino turn to look at him, waiting to hear him explain how come.

Nick Cruickshank shakes his head, opens his arms. "There are lots of things we don't know anything about." The truth is that they don't know anything about anything that's just on the other side of this gated property. The only places he can claim to know are the airfield; a couple of restaurants (the name of one of which he doesn't even remember); and a few shops where he's made brief incursions, hidden beneath his baseball cap and sunglasses so as not to be recognized by bothersome tourists. Instead of the Canton of Fayence, they could easily be anywhere else in France, Italy,

Spain, or Portugal, as far as their relationship with the territory is concerned.

Aldino gestures toward the two blue-and-white plastic coolers, still unconvinced that they might not be full of explosives. "Is the gelato in there?"

"What do you think?" Now the gelato lady laughs, her eyes sparkle. Her eyes are many different colors, or maybe it's the light of this November sun that's creating the reflections; in any case they're very attentive eyes, and slightly dreamy. She picks up the two coolers, one in each hand. There's confidence in her movements, yet that outlandishness continues to envelop her in a slightly strange aura. She carries the coolers toward the house, shakes her head at Aldino when he tries to take them from her, heads straight for the main entrance.

"The kitchen's over there, on the side." Aldino escorts her, as if to ward off a dangerous violation of the domicile.

Nick Cruickshank looks at Aileen, who seems immobilized by all the interlocking expectations of the people in her entourage. "How did it go with the photos?"

"Ah, really well!" Aileen picks up speed again, as if she's coming out of a freeze-frame: she smiles, leans forward to kiss him on the forehead, mobile on her pretty, nervous legs.

"We were able to create some really spectacular combinations, between the men and the women!" Tricia vibrates with enthusiasm, literally: her structure, composed of skin-nerves-bones, is shaking visibly.

Tom pulls the reflex camera out of the duffel bag, turns it on, brings the display closer to Nick Cruickshank's face. "Look at this one. This one. This one. This one here."

Nick Cruickshank looks, distracted in part by the photographer's excessive closeness and smell: with each click there's a procession of wizened vagabonds, chronic alcoholics, and other assorted wretches wearing jackets in fake tropical-green python, vests in fake shocking-pink ostrich, boots in fake fire-red crocodile, hats in fake electric-blue lizard. Tom Harlan's photographic style aims to accentuate to the utmost the wrinkles and other signs of aging on their faces, creating the maximum contrast with the super-saturated pop colors of Aileen's Anti-leather creations. The idea of using derelicts as models and paying them as such has turned out to be another stroke of genius: it's a way to give concrete help to people in need, get media visibility, reinforce the politically correct image of a material that isn't extracted from either animals or oil.

There are naturally those who accuse her of exploiting these poor souls for commercial ends, but it's now practically impossible to do anything without someone rushing onto the Internet and turning every merit into a cause for shame. They even accuse her of being a leech, for the support he's given to her Anti-leather business, participating in the earliest press conferences, accompanying her to the first fashion shows, letting himself be photographed with her. As if a man can't support his woman because he believes in her, without being the victim of manipulation; the key is not to let all the crap they try to throw at you get under your skin, to ignore it. Just yesterday Linda at the press office in London sent him links to a couple of blogs that say awful things even about the Bebonkers' concert on Sunday, claiming that it's a way of usurping the painful emotions of the Paris massacre, et cetera. A concert *against violence*, whose revenues will go *to the victims' families*? It takes an extremely robust mental shield to block out the hidden spite of anonymous imbeciles, seriously. In any case Aileen was undeniably far-sighted when she secured the exclusive production rights from Andor Kértesz, that crazy Hungarian genius who from agave leaves was able to extract a fiber that seems like leather and is just as resistant; and when she found the right name, in place of the hideous original *Agavleder*. Such a capable and enterprising woman inevitably inspires envy and jealousy, especially when her initiatives meet with success.

"So? What do you think?" Aileen too leans in to take a peek at the reflex's screen: quick, impatient, with new ideas surely racing through her head already.

"Certainly more interesting than the usual models." But Nick Cruickshank has to admit that he *feels* a little unease mixed with the admiration for her resourcefulness. Does it depend on the fact that she simply never stops? That no sooner has she achieved a goal than she immediately has to find another one to strive for? That ultimately there's some truth to the claim that she's using these wretches to promote her goods, even if she does pay them enough to live on for months? She doesn't do it cynically, however; her desire to help people and contribute to the well-being of the planet is genuine. Last year she financed an elementary school in Burkina Faso and even provided it with a well for drinking water; the year before, she donated warehouses, equipment, and even a truck to a cooperative of small-scale coffee growers in Bolivia. Sure, in exchange she gets tax breaks and benefits to her image, but her help is real, tangible.

Aileen nods: she seems happy with the results, happy for his approval. "They were so into their roles, you should've seen them."

"Some of them were showing off a little too much." Tom can't help adding a note of disenchantment.

"Poor things, they were happy!" Tricia intervenes in support of her boss, as always. "We brought them some absolutely delicious croissants, they plowed through them all in a matter of minutes!"

"They'd have been happier with a few bottles of Calvados."

Tom persists in his role, manages to get a snigger out of the editor and cameraman from *Star Life*.

"Then we left the jackets and boots and hats and all the rest with the head of the center." You only have to look at Aileen right now to realize that she is absolutely sincere: her belief that she is doing good is unquestionable, anything but an act. "They'll auction them off at Christmastime, raise a ton of money."

"Well done." Nick Cruickshank wonders if his feeling of less-than-total involvement depends on a sort of growing disinterest for the affairs of the world.

Tom shoves the camera back into the duffel bag, goes toward the house, followed by his assistant, loaded down with equipment. Tricia and Maggie look at Aileen; they go inside as well, followed by the editor, writer, photographer, and cameraman from *Star Life* with all their odds and ends.

Aileen turns to examine his face. "How are things with you?"

"Great, except for the fact that there was a blackout and I almost killed myself with the Ape." Not that Nick Cruickshank wants to be dramatic; it's just that almost every time he sees Aileen return from an expedition he feels like he has been extremely unproductive, and soon feels the need to test how much she still cares about him.

"I've told you a thousand times to be careful with that stupid tricycle!" Aileen scrutinizes him from head to toe to be sure there's no damage, but as soon as it's clear there isn't her gaze shifts to the house.

Nick Cruickshank shrugs: it's tough to find someone more talented than he is at simulating nonchalance. The fact is that the very first thing that struck him about Aileen, when she came to Baz's office in London to apply for the costume designer position on the 2008 world tour, was her attentiveness. Even now he remembers the way she listened to him as he explained what he was looking for: the constant variation of her facial expressions, her audible breathing, the tiny emotional waves in response to each new piece of information. No matter how much fuss and attention and how many acts of zeal and devotion and even adoration he had received until then, Aileen's level of interest seemed of a clearly superior quality: more intelligent, more informed, more capable of making quick connections. That was the reason they began to draw irresistibly closer: because of her readiness to answer every question, her precision in always choosing the right option among the many possible. Because of her looks, too, of course: her eyes, her mouth, her hair, her legs, her way of moving; but what made her seem so special was the miraculous absence of any distraction or mental laziness. There was nothing inexact about her, nothing vague. Aileen's concentration charged their exchanges more than any drug or combination of drugs, and with the advantage of leaving him in a state of total mental lucidity; every conversation became a kind of challenge in which to call on all available resources, including those he didn't know he possessed. A Lennon/McCartney effect (he even said so in an interview in *Rolling Stone*) was forged between them, in which they would both push each other out of their comfort zones and force each other to attain a level they probably would never have reached alone. The Cruickshank/McCullough partnership has produced not so much unforgettable songs (she did inspire two or three of them, sure, but probably not his best) as intuitions and revelations, impulses for renewal and self-betterment. Was it inevitable for such an intense flow of energy, by its very nature, to dry up sooner or later? Or to mutate, at the very least, as they shifted from thrilling infatuation to serious relationship? He's the first to admit that his need for attention is abnormally large, that he feeds off it, can't do without it: it's another reason why he's in this business. Really, how long could a single person's attention stand in for that of tens of thousands of people in a stadium? Realistically? Not even his most passionate fans would be able to maintain the same level of extreme focus they have during a concert, day after day after day, month after month after month, year after year after year.

Aileen continues glancing toward the door to the house; she doesn't want to stay out here anymore, her legs are getting antsy. "Okay, I'm going in."

"Go, go." Nick Cruickshank watches her walk away, a half smile on his lips that doesn't mean much of anything. If he thinks about it, it doesn't feel like Aileen's attention for him has gradually waned, in that almost imperceptible way that any form of attention probably wanes, sooner or later. It seems like he sat down in front of her one night at dinner and began telling her something, then realized that her attention was no longer the same. Or, more precisely, that it was no longer directed solely at him, in the incredibly strenuous mental and emotional ping-pong that made their exchanges so special. At the time he panicked: accused her of not listening to him, pounded his fist on the table, spilled red wine on the tablecloth. Aileen didn't lose her head, but very calmly repeated everything he had said to her up to that moment word for word; which, of course, wasn't the actual issue. He felt stupid, thinking that maybe he had mistaken a momentary distraction for a permanent change. But their mental and emotional ping-pong didn't regain its previous creative tension the day after either, or the day after that. Then he had to begin recording the new Bebonkers album in Los Angeles, and there hasn't been much more time to think about it.

It's not as if they don't get along anymore, don't talk to each other, or don't make love; but there has certainly been a decline;

a part of the electricity that charged every single one of their dialogues has disappeared. Is this what happens when two people have been together long enough? He's certainly no expert on long-term relationships: even if he's always thought of himself as fundamentally monogamous, his relationships have never lasted more than six or seven years. Are both he and Aileen to blame, assuming it even makes sense to talk about blame? Has he too lost interest, curiosity, tension in her regard? How much did it matter that in the beginning he was still married to his second wife, giving their romance an aura of illicitness and adventure, and then he divorced, transforming them into a perfectly legitimate couple? What was the role of the explosive success of Anti-leather in the distraction of a part of Aileen's prodigious attention?

He certainly has encouraged her to raise the bar continually in her work, pushing her to make the switch from costume designer to stylist, stylist to entrepreneur. And it's not like the Bebonkers are always on tour; far from it. What was a skilled, impatient, and energetic woman like her supposed to do? Knit him caps and vests in her free time? Design onstage costumes for a rival band? Work for some stupid TV talent show? It seemed logical to push her to put her skills to work, and even to give her significant financial backing, partly because he believed in her, partly so that he might at least some of the time have an outlet for his extreme restlessness. His accountant was convinced it would be a waste of money, but the Anti-leather business has surpassed even the rosiest expectations. Aileen has revealed a business sense on par with her sense of aesthetics. If as a consequence her prodigious attention is no longer directed 100 percent at him, it's hardly the end of the world: he's certainly not going to start playing the victim. After all, when he really needs her attention, she gives it to him, though maybe not exactly instantaneously, maybe not exactly as intensively or for as long as she used to. But he still gets the right advice, her amazing organizational ability is still there. It's even possible that after Saturday, the situation might improve significantly; it's one of the reasons he let himself be persuaded to take this sort of step. Again, despite the fact that it certainly didn't go too well the past two times.

The Italian gelato lady comes out of the kitchen door with her two empty coolers, followed by Aldino, who keeps an eye on her like he's still expecting some dirty trick.

Nick Cruickshank nods to her with his chin. "Everything all right?"

The Italian gelato lady nods, looks at him with a slightly inquisitive expression. The light has changed, but she's still so full of colors: in her eyes, her clothes, the way she moves. And it's now confirmed that she hasn't recognized him, which, truth be told, is quite unusual.

For an instant Nick Cruickshank feels like he's seeing himself through her eyes, and the picture looks pretty bleak, once he's stripped of his famous name and the echo of the songs he's written, without the legendary aura that envelops the Bebonkers. What is he, to her? A rich and well-aged Anglo-Irish bohemian who comes to the South of France to lounge around with his super-enterprising girlfriend and their hangers-on, drowning in a sea of poses?

The Italian gelato lady puts the coolers back in the van, closes the doors. She looks at him a little uncertainly, then smiles, unexpectedly. Her smile has nothing of the blend of instant admiration and morbid curiosity that he encounters daily; it seems to contain a strange postponement of questions.

Nick Cruickshank is momentarily disconcerted, uncertain whether to make an attempt at conversation, as he sometimes does with the locals; but somehow he thinks it would only end up worsening the already sobering image of himself that he's given her. All he's able to do is raise a hand in a good-bye wave: quite poorly executed, for that matter.

She replies with a rapid gesture, sits down behind the wheel, closes the door, turns on the engine, backs up; in two minutes her little orange van has already disappeared down the access road.

Nick Cruickshank scratches his forehead, thinks about the things he has no desire to do in the next few days, turns to look at Aldino, who seems to be finally relaxing. They both go back inside, with different types of undulating strides.

SEVEN

Milena Migliari opens the smaller side door, pushes the inner gate open with her foot, puts the two coolers down on the ugly tiles of the slant-roofed, glass-enclosed patio. It always reminds her of someplace in Mexico: with these extravagant flowers, the arches, the staircase leading to the second floor, the humid heat that immediately slams into you. She could just as easily use the main door, but for some reason she always comes in here.

Viviane looks out from the second-floor external landing, comes down the steps; one look is enough to see she's really tense. "Damn blackout!" She runs a hand through hair that's longer on top and shorter at the temples and on the sides, pushes back the main tuft. "Today of all days, when I took the morning off to work on the book, for crying out loud!"

Milena Migliari considers telling her how all the equipment in her store suddenly turned off and that if it hadn't been for the Brits' miraculous order she would have had to throw it all away. But it occurs to her that for a while now her conversations with Viviane have turned more and more into an exchange of complaints: about work, the economy, the government, the weather, about almost everything. She still hasn't figured out why, but it happens. Maybe it depends on Viviane's tendency to see things in a pessimistic light, and she ends up conforming almost automatically; maybe it's because finding reasons for being content requires more creativity than complaining. That's why she smiles now, pointing with her chin toward the two empty coolers.

"What?" Viviane looks at her with those blue-gray eyes, intense behind her transparent-frame lenses: faded gray T-shirt, faded jeans, sturdy feet in blue socks with little yellow stars on them. She looks at the coolers, looks back at her.

"Some Brits ordered *twenty pounds* of gelato, just when I was sure I'd have to throw it all away." Milena Migliari makes a sweeping gesture that embraces her shop, the Brits' house, all the space in between.

"Twenty pounds?" Viviane studies her; in her line of work she can glean more information from Milena's posture than from the look on her face.

"They have a large property above Callian, with lots of guests, staff, other people." Milena Migliari touches one of the coolers with the tip of her toe. "But I hope they eat it right away and don't leave it for days in the freezer, when it'll be hard as a rock and all crystallized. Maybe I should only have left them ten pounds, taken the rest back with me."

"Oh *my God*, Milena!" The explosion of Viviane's voice has long-simmering causes. "Artistic integrity or whatever the heck you want to call it is one thing, but for crying out loud! Would it really matter, even if it did get a little crystallized?!"

"It would matter, because it would no longer be *my gelato,* all right? The consistency is one of its most important characteristics!" Milena Migliari gets a combative tone every time she's accused of being too much of a perfectionist, or incapable of dealing with reality. Like back in July, when two rosy-cheeked and corpulent Belgians asked her emphatically for a *non*-dark chocolate and she replied that not only did she not have one, but that for them she didn't have *any* flavors because they obviously didn't know anything about gelato, that they'd be better off getting a couple of cones from the Carpigiani soft-serve machine at the bar under the parking lot. She had said it passionately, though without resentment, but they were mortally offended, and within a few minutes had written horrible things on TripAdvisor. But the worst part was that when she told Viviane about it later that night, partly looking for some sympathy and partly to have a laugh together, Viviane treated her like a crazy fundamentalist, worse than the two Belgians: told her that if she carried on this way they'd never be able to pay back the bank loan, that she needed to stop walking around with her head in the clouds, come to grips with reality. It hurt her even more than she was later able to explain: the sensation that for the first time (maybe the second, or the third) the two of them weren't exactly on the same wavelength.

"Just who were these Brits?" In Viviane's expression there's a flicker of curiosity, but buried under several layers of mistrust.

Milena Migliari forces herself to adopt a lighter tone of voice: she recounts details from her trip to Les Vieux Oliviers, including the alpacas chasing and then viciously biting each other, and the giant Italian bodyguard who couldn't figure out who opened the gate for her, the lady of the house's blue boots and red leather jacket, the master of the house who looked like an old pirate with that earring in his left lobe.

"And what's the proprietor's name?" Viviane rubs one of her stockings on the dog-vomit-colored tiles, the only detail they weren't enamored with when they decided to buy this place, before discovering that the real problem was that the glass roof turns the patio into a furnace and makes it practically uninhabitable from spring through late autumn. Just look at them now: between their agitation, the humidity, and the temperature they're covered in sweat, in the second half of November.

"Cruc something. Cruc . . . Crucshan, I think." Milena Migliari isn't sure she remembers the name correctly, the woman in the kitchen mentioned it while receiving the gelato and listening unwillingly to her instructions on how to serve it.

"*Cruickshank*?" Viviane lunges forward with her face, the way she does when something strikes her.

"Maybe." Milena Migliari nods, noting the sudden change in attitude.

"*Nick* Cruickshank?" Viviane becomes even more pressing, whatever the reason is.

"Might be." Milena Migliari shakes her head. "Who is he?"

"What do you mean, who is he?! Damn, Milena!" Viviane adopts that insistently realistic tone that's now become part and parcel of their division of roles: one absent-minded and the other with her feet firmly on the ground. These are simplifications, because Viviane is also sensitive in addition to being concrete, and because making good gelato requires practicality as well as imagination.

Milena Migliari shrugs. She couldn't say when they began assigning roles to each other. Maybe right from the start, but back then it seemed more like a game than anything, with affectionate and erotic connotations. It made her feel partly reassured, partly turned on; but she thought the roles were flexible, switchable, or even cancelable at any moment. Instead, they've become more and more consolidated, until hers has begun to feel a little too constricting. Sometimes much too constricting.

"Hey, can you see me, from way up there?" Viviane looks up

high, pretends to reel in invisible string around an invisible spool, to pull her down out of the sky. "He's the lead singer of the *Bebonkers*. Ever heard of them? Not even one song? Maybe on the radio, by accident? Does 'Enough Isn't Enough' ring a bell? On top of everything they're doing a benefit concert down at the airfield in Fayence this Sunday. There are posters everywhere!"

"Of course I've heard of them." Now Milena Migliari is getting fed up, seeing herself treated like a naïve simpleton. She *has* listened to the Bebonkers, like practically everyone else living in the Western world during the past thirty years or so. And come to think of it the English guy *did* look familiar to her somehow; but she was nervous because of the blackout and the strangeness of the order, and concerned about the conservation of the gelato, and dazed at being treated like an intruder.

"Well, that's something." Viviane feigns a gesture of relief; she runs two fingers across her forehead, laughs. "Welcome back to earth."

"Sorry, but when you see someone out of context it's easy not to recognize them, right?" Milena Migliari tries to resist the temptation to feel guilty for not recognizing Nick Cruickshank of the Bebonkers: it's something that happens to her when she realizes she's uninformed about world events or has a gap in her general knowledge, and even more so when she makes a mistake in French. And anyway, even if she likes music she's never been one to worship those who create it; she's never had any musical idols. If anything struck her about that Nick Cruickshank it wasn't his rock-star appearance, but rather the deeply perplexed look on his face: deeply perplexed.

"All right, anyway, typical Milena." Viviane is still laughing; she comes closer, gives her a pat on the backside.

Even this "typical Milena" business: sometimes it's amusing, sometimes not at all. Now, for instance, not at all; she immediately tries to reroute the conversation. "And how about you, how's your book going?"

"I'd rather not talk about it, thank you!" Viviane reacts predictably, because she's struggling mightily to put together her manual on the Fournier Method. That's what it's called because Fournier is her last name. It's a method of high-intensity postural massage, which loosens the body's knots and liberates the flow of energy. Viviane practices it in her studio in Draguignan five days a week, and on Monday afternoons in a center for sports medicine in Grasse; by now she's put together a nice following who swear she's made them as good as new. But it's one thing to invent and perfect new massage techniques, another to write a book in which her theory and practices are explained in detail. Viviane has been working on it for months but isn't the least bit satisfied with the results, which naturally influences her mood and their relationship.

Milena Migliari brings her two hands from high to low in a gesture she's learned to use in moments of tension. "Hey, it was just a question, okay?"

"Thanks for asking!" Viviane paces back and forth, the soles of her feet smacking against the tiles; she stops. "You know what, I called Dr. Lapointe, in Grasse."

"Ah." Milena Migliari feels her blood run cold, from one moment to the next. "And what did he say?"

Viviane clears her throat, with that nervous cough she gets when she's going through intense emotions. "That we can start on Monday."

"Monday?" Milena Migliari's stomach contracts, she has trouble breathing. But she's been expecting to hear this for days; for at least a week.

"Aren't you happy?" Viviane scrutinizes her, registers the position of her head, her arms, her legs.

"Yes." Milena Migliari can't get much conviction into her voice, partly because she knows her body language is communicating panic more than contentment.

"I thought you'd be happy." Viviane's eyes narrow.

"But I *am*." Milena Migliari forces herself to find a joyful tone, but it doesn't come. They've been talking about this business for months; *months*. Viviane brought it up on the night of her birthday, when they had drunk a bottle of champagne and were both very tipsy. But she must have begun thinking about it for a long time because she was able to provide very precise details. In the euphoric and unstable heat of the moment Milena thought it was an extraordinarily beautiful declaration of love, a way to further cement their bond and project it into the future; they hugged and kissed, happy. But when they talked about it sober the day after, she was far less enthusiastic about the idea: the clinical and mechanical feeling of the whole story, the need to plan everything out, the responsibility for a hypothetical third person. Her head filled with images of laboratories, doctors in smocks and masks, needles, probes, test tubes, slides, microscopes, tests, injections.

"Well, you don't look like it." Viviane resumes her pacing, unplugs the automatic sprinkler system, plugs it back in.

"What do I look like?" Milena Migliari would really like to know, because she isn't the least bit sure. Out of pure agitation she tears a leaf off one of the geraniums that flourish in the Mexican-like climate of the glass-covered patio; she rubs it between her fingers, feels it fleshy and moist.

"Not very convinced." Viviane's tone is pretty neutral, but it's plain to see how difficult it is for her.

"Come on." Milena Migliari tries to figure out whether hers is a form of egotism, a lack of generosity, a reluctance to make long-term commitments, a lack of love. She wonders why she's unable to throw herself into this venture with enthusiasm, why it feels absurd and even anachronistic to imagine herself with an enormous belly, shambling around like a whale, unable to make her gelato or do anything else in a normal way. She wonders why Viviane's desire for motherhood seems almost like a form of bullying, an attempt to limit her freedom, relegate her to the dimension of primitive female. She wonders whether it's so terrible never to have wanted to bring anyone into the world even before, in her relationships with men; never to have really felt a calling as a breeder and nurturer and educator.

"Yes, you do!" Viviane raises her voice now, doesn't stop pacing back and forth.

"Maybe I'm still a little shaken because of the blackout at the gelateria and everything else, all right?" It's true that she is a little shaken, she even has tears in her eyes; but attributing her state of mind to the blackout seems cowardly, a way of not calling things by their true name.

"Who cares about the gelateria?!" Viviane is furious, red in the face. "What's more, gelato season has been over for weeks! You should already have closed the shop!"

"There isn't *a* season for gelato." Milena Migliari responds with an obstinate tone, but in a voice that's far too meek. "There are *many* of them, each one as different as its raw ingredients, the weather, the mood of the taster."

"But if there are no *buyers*, would you explain to me who you're making the gelato for?" Viviane raises her voice further, gesticulating more and more uncontrollably.

"I make it for whoever *wants* it. The Brits today, for example." It is true that today's order was exceptional, but the point isn't how many buyers there are or are not: it's that making gelato is her work and her passion, and that maybe Viviane is a little jealous of it.

"Right, and the Brits have put you in the black for the next few months!" It's true that in the beginning Viviane gave her a lot of support: encouraged her to give the gelato business a real go, helped her find the space, get the loan from the bank, handle the bureaucracy involved with opening a business, and all the rest. But ever since things started coming together, she's started coming out more and more frequently with sarcastic little jibes and hyperrealistic considerations, as if to say that making gelato is a kind of hobby, more than a real job, and that even if it were, it certainly isn't comparable profitwise with her postural massage center that's now frequented by hundreds of people.

"Well, I'm in the black for today, at least." Milena Migliari tries to hold her ground.

"Yes, how nice it is to live in the moment!" Now Viviane has her hands firmly on her hips, as if to restrain herself from doing anything rash, like smashing a vase of geraniums. "Listen, if you've changed your mind, it would be much more honest of you to say so!"

Milena Migliari bites her lower lip, because she remembers when they both enjoyed living in the moment, and because she can't bear the thought of seeming dishonest about a plan that's so significant for both of them. Ever since childhood she's had notions of loyalty based more on fictional stories than on real life, and has been disappointed so many times by others' behavior that she feels a desperate need to respect agreements, see them through to the end. She takes Viviane's hand, gives it a squeeze. "I haven't changed my mind."

"No?" Viviane looks at her with a sudden glimmer of hope

in her eyes, behind those lenses constantly smudged with fingerprints.

"No." Milena Migliari thinks that it probably is possible to help good intentions win out over momentary second thoughts, if you really want to. "But maybe it's normal to be a little bit worried, don't you think?"

"But of course it's normal!" Viviane hugs her enthusiastically, squeezing her with her strong hands. "It's the most normal thing in the world, *ma poulette*!"

Milena Migliari feels intense relief at having successfully resolved such an apparently irreparable situation with just a few words and gestures: practically a miracle of interpersonal communication.

Viviane kisses her forehead, cheeks, nose, lips, chin, eyes. "This is something that we're doing completely together, *ma poulette*! I'll support you every step of the way, you'll see! It'll be amazing for both of us! It'll be incredible!"

"Good." Milena Migliari dries the tears at the corners of her eyes, dries her nose with the back of her hand. Though she'd rather not, she can't help thinking how time changes the perception of things: for example, she had long considered *ma poulette* a tender and funny nickname, but now it embarrasses her. (And reminds her of the fact that the main reason people keep hens around is for their eggs.)

They both go inside, smiling. Milena Migliari climbs the inside staircase to wash her hands, use the bathroom, and change her shirt; when she comes back down Viviane is starving to death, so she immediately makes her a cheese omelet and a walnut salad.

EIGHT

WHEN HE'S AT Les Vieux Oliviers, Nick Cruickshank spends hours by himself walking or horseback riding through the grassy areas and woods on the property or locked in his studio. Not that Aileen doesn't notice, or bring it to his attention, in a more or less offended tone depending on the circumstances: like she's being deprived of something she has a right to. He usually replies that he needs to feel free to do what he wants; even *not* to do anything at all, without interference from anyone. "*Interference?*" Aileen displays a little grin of feigned astonishment, shakes her head slowly. This is an issue that in his previous relationships as well has brought him endless complaints and accusations, attempted invasions, clashes, escapes. With Aileen the problem arises more here than in London, because in London their lives are largely independent, or at least they have been until now: they each have their own house, their own commitments, their own schedules. They really only see each other in the evenings, if they're both in the city, and almost always to go out; it's not like they've ever had to adapt to what passes for the other's domestic routine. Aileen doesn't come to Sussex willingly, because she says it feels like barging into the life of his first marriage: it bothers her to see the kids' rooms that still have their toys from when they were little, the roses and azaleas that Hoshiko planted. The result is that he too now rarely sets foot there, just occasionally to have a chat with Roman the custodian, make sure that the place isn't falling apart, indulge in a little melancholy. Same goes for St. Barts, where each time they end up tense and unable to relax, slightly worse off than if they'd stayed in a hotel. For Manchester as well, where Aileen claims she feels like an outsider in his small circle of relatives, old friends, and old flames, though for years everyone has been doing their utmost to make her feel at home in every possible way.

So for now Les Vieux Oliviers is the only place where they've attempted to live together for more than a couple of weeks at a time, which makes it a sort of experiment. Aileen has invested all her incredible energy into transforming it: she's had plants added and removed in the garden, hedges moved, the shape of the pool modified, several interior walls torn down, windows changed, the large roof beams painted white. The Provençal furnishings that Nick's second wife, Marie, liked so much have now disappeared, except for two armchairs, a couch, and a carpet that he's been able to salvage in his studio and in the little cottage in the woods. The new style is a mix of high-tech, Arte Povera, 1960s design: interesting, though much less comfortable and comforting than before. And the process of transformation continues, it will probably never end: every so often Aileen calls him from some part of the world in the throes of excitement, to tell him she's found a Philippe Starck glass-and-steel table perfect for the living room, a Tina Paloma sculpture that's made for the entrance, a painting by Hans Herrmann that would look great in the hallway. He lets her, because he trusts her eye, because he appreciates the idea of making creative investments for their life together, and because he's relieved that she focuses her energy more on the *containers* of their relationship than on the relationship itself. The fact is that it's quite rare for him to see her lying in a hammock in repose, or calmly sitting and reading a book for more than ten minutes at a time: she has a constant need to move from one point to another on those nervous legs, be on the phone, organize conference calls, collect information, discuss ideas, solicit answers, explore possibilities, explain, communicate, urge. Yet didn't her mental and physical dynamism strike him almost as much as her extraordinary attentiveness the first time they met? It's true that it was maybe a less-focused dynamism then, almost naïve, before growing more marked as one success led to another until it became unstoppable, inexhaustible, as it is now.

Startled by a knock at the door, Nick Cruickshank jumps up from his old Provençal couch, like he's under attack. "What is it?!"

"*Viens manger, Nick!*" The voice of Madame Jeanne, full of maternal concern, finds its way through the thick wood of the door.

"*Okay, merci!*" Nick Cruickshank puts the acoustic guitar back on the stand, takes one last hit of Wally's weed, puts out the joint in the ashtray; he thinks that he would be happy if only he were able to avoid the others, eat something on his own in the kitchen.

He walks as silently as he can down the hallway, but when he peeks into the vast open space of the living/dining room they're all sitting there, at the long walnut table: Aileen, Tricia, Maggie, Tom, his assistant what's-his-name, the *Star Life* quartet, Wally, Kimberly, Aldino, Damian Baumann, Christie Swoonie, Marguerite and Hugo Bertrand. It's like there's a *committee* around that damn table.

"Oh, look who it is!" Aileen simulates surprise; all the others turn to look at him too. "We thought you'd decided to barricade yourself in there indefinitely."

"I wasn't barricaded." Nick Cruickshank goes to sit to the right of Aldino, who out of embarrassment stuffs into his mouth a piece of buttered bread that's half the size of his hand. Nick thinks that in reality Aileen is right: he *was* barricaded in his studio. But only because he *is* under siege in any other part of the house: one only needs to look at all these eyes and hands and mouths moving, all these poses being endlessly put on display.

Wally and his wife, Kimberly, don't seem too thrilled with the company either, but for the worst possible reasons: Wally, because there aren't too many attractive women on whom to feast his morbid eyes, apart from Aileen and Christie Swoonie (who detests him), and Kimberly, because with the exception of the hosts, Christie and the Bertrands, there aren't enough rich and famous guests to excite her attention. In fact she continues flicking the screen of her giant cell phone, perched on her elbows and forearms: torpid stare, heavy eyeliner, bleached-blond hair forced up against its will, puffed-up cheekbones, lips like inflatable rafts, unbuttoned blouse to show off her tits elevated by a push-up bra, giant-pearl necklace that her darling husband must have given her to apologize for some little slipup. Only Wally Thompson could marry such an empty and vulgar woman, who, at the time of their marriage, fully corresponded to his most squalid adolescent fantasies.

"Wally told me that tomorrow morning you're taking us for a horseback ride?" Kimberly must think that this half-whispered and husky voice is sexy, like the indolence with which she moves her eyelids and head.

"Well, we'll see." Nick Cruickshank has no desire to make any firm commitments with these two, because he's annoyed enough as it is to have them in his home, and because deep down he hopes that, between now and tomorrow, some catastrophe might still intervene to sabotage everything.

Aileen can't stand Wally and Kimberly either, but when it came time to decide on who to let stay here and who to distribute among hotels, villas, and homes in the village, she agreed on the fact that the Thompsons would resent an external lodging more than anyone else. So here they are, like a thorn in their side for four days; what's more, in the grand scheme of things, it's not even the worst of their problems.

The editor in chief of *Star Life* continues scanning the other guests at the table, exchanges quick words and glances with the members of her team; although the agreement is not to film or take photos at the table before Saturday, she's clearly committing every little detail to memory, to be later used from a voyeuristic slant in the long cover piece they're doing.

Madame Jeanne comes in, accompanied by a young and slightly timid server named Didiane, who's pushing a cart bearing a large terra-cotta pot containing the cook's legendary artichoke risotto. They place it on the table unceremoniously, she inserts the ladle. "*Nick.*" Jeanne motions for him to pass her his plate first. It's not that she doesn't know the rules of etiquette; she simply wants to clarify that there's no doubt in her mind as to who the most important person is in here, to hell with formal courtesies.

"*Merci, Jeanne. Vous pouvez le laisser ici.*" Aileen gestures politely but firmly, so as not to give the guests the impression that she has no control over this woman. Early on she tried quite insistently to persuade Nick Cruickshank to fire her, claiming that for the same cost they could find someone much more attuned to their dietary requirements and more familiar with contemporary cuisine, as well as capable of communicating in English with their guests and possibly behaving with a bare minimum of politeness. He had to muster a fierce resistance in her defense, going so far as to say that without Madame Jeanne he wouldn't set foot in this house again. The question lies there dormant, far from being resolved; he has yet to see Aileen give in when it comes to a question of principle.

Madame Jeanne proceeds as if she didn't even hear her: she serves the master of the house, then Aileen, then the others. Kimberly is last of all, but only after being glared at with such intensity that, in a burst of awareness, she decides to put down her cell phone, setting it on the table with her piggish hand and white-varnished fingernails, though without taking her eyes off the screen.

When Madame Jeanne exits with Didiane in tow, Aileen shoots a look at Tom Harlan and the editor of *Star Life*: she rolls her eyes, eliciting chuckles.

"What's so funny?" Nick Cruickshank pretends not to have noticed the silent challenge just thrown down.

"Nothing, nothing." Aileen exchanges more ironic glances with her neighbors, then cautiously nears her fork to the risotto, as if she's sure to find some unpleasant surprise.

Three bottles of Côtes de Provence make the rounds of the table, but no one really drinks, maybe because of the presence of the journalists, maybe in view of the revelry of the coming days, maybe because there's not a very convivial spirit. Wally is the only one who, as soon as he's finished the gin and tonic he brought with him to the table, gulps down a glass in a few swallows and immediately pours himself another; he snickers, gives Christie Swoonie a dirty look, mumbles something to Kimberly, who digs her fingernails into his wrist.

The risotto is extraordinarily good, like everything Madame Jeanne makes. More than once Nick Cruickshank has watched entranced as she prepared it: the outer leaves of the artichoke removed and boiled to obtain a broth that's green and rich in flavor; the inner parts accurately cleansed of their sharp extremities and fluff and then cut into thin strips and slowly sautéed in a pan with garlic and olive oil, before being mixed with the rice in the ceramic pot and bathed in small splashes of white wine and then generous amounts of green broth, and patiently mixed again and again until the final addition of butter and grated Parmesan to thicken. The result is about as close to perfection as you can get with an artichoke risotto: the bittersweet flavor so intense and pure, the deliciously creamy consistency that still leaves each slice and kernel individually identifiable to the tongue. Light-years away from the discolored, overcooked artichoke risottos he's been privileged to eat in the so-called best restaurants in the world. He's sometimes amazed that he has learned to appreciate these nuances; it's been a long road, from his mother's harried and careless survival-style cooking to this. (He has such vivid memories of the three slices of liver dropped into a frying pan with a little salt, no trace of butter or oil or herbs or anything else, then transferred all dried out and blackened to their plates. "Come on, boys, down the hatch.")

The diners are split between those who eat hungrily, such as Aldino, Tom Harlan, his assistant, Maggie, Hugo Bertrand, and the photographer and cameraman from *Star Life*; and those who barely touch their plates, such as Tricia, who's anorexic; Christie, who cares more about her figure than anything else in the world and forces herself not to eat; the writer, who does likewise to suck up to her; Wally, who's already drunk too much and pretty much just keeps on drinking; and Kimberly, who probably stuffed her face with crap earlier and now limits herself to picking at the food.

Aileen scoops up small amounts of risotto with the end of the fork, places them on her tongue, moves her jaws very gingerly, sitting rigidly on her chair. She never has been a big eater; she's capable of going days with only a couple of fresh fruit juices, some pieces of sugar-free candy, and bottle after bottle of water. Not eating much is one of the manifestations of her character, just like not sleeping much: she's able to fall asleep on command (with the help of a pill), but then in the middle of the night she tosses and turns continuously, turning on her light to read, checking her cell phone to see if she's received any important messages, getting up to pee, going back to bed, kicking, pulling the comforter over to her side. Even when she's sleeping it seems like a twitch is always imminent, ready to catch you by surprise as soon as you relax. Sharing a bed with her is a sort of continuous battle, an exercise in forbearance that Nick Cruickshank hasn't by any means gotten used to. Once he even mentioned it to her, as lightheartedly as he could, just to exorcize the matter, and she didn't find it funny at all, rebutting that if he was so annoyed by it maybe they should consider two separate bedrooms. He asked himself whether to jump at the chance and immediately reply that that was fine by him, but he knew she would have interpreted it as the definitive end of the romantic phase of their relationship. He was reminded of when his parents decided to sleep in two separate rooms, and how less than a year later his father had left the house; he decided that a minimum of adaptation might be indispensable if two people want to live together. But the fact remains that with his second wife he slept extremely well, without having to adapt to anything; at least from that point of view the change has not been advantageous.

"*Alors? C'est bon?*" Madame Jeanne sticks her head back in the dining room, to see whether her risotto has been a success.

"*C'est grand!*" Nick Cruickshank smiles at her gratefully but feels genuine displeasure at having to share such a special gift with people incapable of fully appreciating it.

"*Mmmm.*" At least Aldino murmurs with satisfaction; Tom Harlan nods, but without conceding much in the way of words;

his thin and pale assistant snatches another forkful, as if he's afraid they'll take his plate away.

Aileen merely continues to probe the risotto with the tip of her fork, without commenting; she picks up a slice of artichoke, chews it laboriously, resumes telling the Bertrands about this morning's photographic outing, in a clear display of disinterest for Madame Jeanne's masterpiece.

In truth Madame Jeanne is anything but invasive: she's content to reign unchallenged in her kitchen kingdom, coming out only to serve the food and clear off the plates. Her timing is perfect; she arrives neither a minute too early nor too late, there's never any hint of rushing or laziness in her movements. For example, now she has disappeared once again, slipping away without anyone noticing.

Nick Cruickshank tries to focus on the flavor and consistency of the last few forkfuls, but he can't help noticing Aileen's misgivings and Wally's boorishness, the bovine look on Kimberly's face, the meddlesome expression of the *Star Life* editor. He does his best not to look at anyone, but his eyes continue to be pulled left and right as if by magnetic attraction, and with each glance the exasperation seething inside him grows. Finally he's unable to resist. He turns toward Wally. "Don't you like it?"

"The artichokes are chewy," Wally mumbles with his mouth full, a perfectly stolid expression on his face. "And the rice is undercooked."

Aileen turns her head quickly toward the *Star Life* editor, flashes another ironic smile; she couldn't be more pleased with this attack on Madame Jeanne's credibility.

"Yeah." Kimberly goes so far as to twist her frog-like mouth into a disgusted grimace, as if she habitually dines on things infinitely more sublime.

Nick Cruickshank tries to think of a sarcastic and maybe even slightly educational retort, but he's too embittered at the idea of sharing the table with people whom he couldn't care less about or detests, first among them that moronic slob of a bassist who's convinced that seeing as he's been carried in spite of himself to worldwide fame and fortune, he must necessarily be in possession of God knows what profound truths. The realization of having spent decades circling the globe with him and still finding him here now with his revolting wife suddenly seems unsustainable.

"What is it?" Despite his obtuseness Wally must be able to read something in his expression, because his facial muscles contract into one of his most unpleasant expressions. "Eh?"

"Nothing, nothing." A few years ago Nick Cruickshank might have thrown a wineglass at him, or at least a piece of bread; after which the other band members would have taken sides with one or the other, and one of those restaurant- or hotel-smashing brawls would have broken out that have become part of the Bebonkers' most lurid mythology. But since then he's worked hard to rein in his lowest instincts: he simply turns his head the other way, excludes the Thompsons from his field of vision.

Aileen lays down her fork and a piece of bread on the risotto, pushes away her plate of half-eaten food. She turns toward him. "Tomorrow at ten, Lucien Deleuze and Marissa are coming with their teams, with the gazebos and other structures."

Nick Cruickshank suddenly feels like he's up against the ropes, like every other time he's presented with a schedule or a deadline. "Couldn't they come the day *after* tomorrow?"

"No, they cannot." Aileen looks at him with feigned surprise, shakes her head ever so slightly. "You might not realize it, Nick, but time is really tight."

"Ah, right." He sets his fork down on the table, stands up.

Aileen wavers between offended and moderately alarmed. "Where are you going?"

"I'll see you later." Nick Cruickshank succeeds in forcing his lips into a smile, waves to his fellow diners with his napkin before letting it fall on the tablecloth.

"Nick." Aileen tries to hold him with her stare, but certainly doesn't want to make a scene in front of all the guests and the *Star Life* team; she turns toward that giant pain in the ass Hugh Bertrand, pretends to be suddenly very interested in what he's saying.

Nick Cruickshank goes out into the hallway, ducks into the kitchen.

Madame Jeanne is not entirely surprised to see him, just a little apprehensive. "*Ça va?*"

He nods, though he's very tense; almost on the verge of exploding, actually. He goes to the window, turns back, shoves his hands into his pockets, takes his hands out. Over the years he's experimented with a variety of techniques for achieving inner equilibrium, from yoga to shuai jiao to painting, but he's never quite been able to get there: imbalance is always crouching down there inside of him, waiting for the slightest pretext to rear its ugly head. It's true that it is an essential part of his character, the *soul* of his songs, his principal source of inspiration, the engine that drives him. If he did reach a state of permanent calm, so long Nick Cruickshank, and so long Bebonkers. So?

Madame Jeanne points to the great olivewood cutting board where she's setting out the cheeses she's going to bring to the table after the risotto. She doesn't say anything; as usual, they don't need many words to communicate.

Nick Cruickshank reaches out, breaks off a piece of Auvergne bleu with his fingers, eats it as he walks around the kitchen. But he's not hungry anymore, he can't stop feeling that he's under siege, and thinking that the siege is only going to worsen in the coming days, with each passing hour.

Madame Jeanne glances at him two or three times as she repairs the damaged cheese with a knife, sends Didiane out to collect the plates and silverware with the cart. She cleans her hands on her apron, goes to take a white Styrofoam container out of the refrigerator, puts the container on the table and removes the cover, then removes the protective paper beneath the cover. She takes out a spoon and bowl, places them next to the container, gestures to him in invitation.

Nick Cruickshank shakes his head, but nonetheless approaches the table, because he's sorry to refuse her offer. Attached to the white Styrofoam cover is a small piece of straw-yellow paper rolled up tightly and tied with red string. He unties the knot, unrolls the paper: in pen is written *Life is too short to waste it making other people's dreams come true.*

Madame Jeanne observes him inquisitively, seeing him just standing there.

Nick Cruickshank can't move, can't speak: inside him is the strangest jumble of thoughts and sensations, out of which emerges the memory of the time his father quoted this same line to him or to his brother or their mother, probably to the whole family. As if his father, of all people, had ever dedicated even *five minutes* of his own life to making anyone else's dreams come true. And how about *him*? His songs are connected to other people's dreams, it's undeniable: they strike chords, they resonate. But there's a big difference between that and making those dreams come true. And in his *personal* life? In the past? In the present?

Madame Jeanne continues scrutinizing him, starts to look seriously worried.

He rolls up the little piece of paper, sticks it in his pocket. But he's still in a suspended state, struggling to pull himself out of it.

Didiane comes back in with the cart loaded with dirty plates and cutlery; she, too, looks at him with bemusement. Through the closing door come the voices and laughter of the people in the dining room; hard to say if they have dreams, but demands, most certainly. And lots of them.

Nick Cruickshank picks up the spoon from the table, sinks the spoon slowly into the darkest section of one of the four different colors of gelato; he looks at it, brings it to his mouth, savors it slowly.

THURSDAY

NINE

Milena Migliari thinks that she was right about at least one thing in her argument with Viviane yesterday: there is no end to gelato season. You only have to look around this small open-air market in the church square, despite its smaller size in the second half of November, and ideas for the most delicious autumn flavors come spontaneously.

Take these Var chestnuts, which are smaller than the ones from the Ardèche and don't enjoy the same fame or PDO certification: the mahogany color of their lucid skin is simply gorgeous, as Richard pours them into her cloth bag after weighing them on his scale. They have an exquisite flavor, woodsy, hazelnutty, like alpine bread, sweet, comforting, which you could highlight with a little honey from the very same chestnut trees. Or take the pomegranates from Bargemon that she just purchased, two stands back: with a small knifed incision the seller unveiled the brilliant ruby kernels squished one against the other, glossy, alive, overflowing with sourish-sweet juice. Or take the persimmons that Philippe grows near Tourrettes and sells at the stand right over there, in packs of three to protect them, round and orange like little suns, in these days increasingly leaning toward black and white. You don't have to go far to be wonderfully inspired, get ideas for new recipes. As winter gradually approaches, things will get even more interesting: she'll need to think of yet-to-be-developed flavors, and look for new approaches to traditional ones, such as dark chocolate or cream. Revenue will be limited, since there'll be hardly anyone except on weekends, and even then customers will be few and far between; on the other hand, without the constant pressure of people at the counter she'll have much more time to study, to invent. Yes: the end of gelato season is a cliché, and like all clichés serves only to reassure people lacking in imagination.

But if she has to start this hormonal stimulation business at the Centre Plamondon on Monday, with everything that that entails, her mental time and space for thinking about autumn and winter flavors will be notably reduced, that's for sure. And it'll be even worse for the spring and summer ones, to say nothing of those for autumn and winter of next year. She'll be wholly occupied with breastfeeding and diaper-changing and baby-food-making; forget about gelato. She'll be able to dedicate only a fraction of her days to her work, and that's if all goes well; she might be forced to delegate almost everything to Guadalupe, simplify recipes, give up her research and experimentation. Just the thought of it makes her feel dizzy, makes her almost stumble as she passes by Marianne and Richard's stand; every Thursday they come here all the way from Luberon with their goat cheese.

Milena wonders if one of the reasons why Viviane is insisting so much on the baby idea is that she really isn't all that thrilled at seeing her so engrossed in her gelato. Maybe at the beginning Viviane regarded it as simple work, and a good way to keep her occupied; never imagined that she would throw herself into it with such passion. She vividly remembers when she began to achieve her first really good results and find the first customers who appreciated them, and realized she was only at the beginning of her journey. She told Viviane about it, that night, to share her enthusiasm. Viviane stood there listening to her, then smiled as if at an overly excited little girl, and said, "*Ma poulette*, in the end gelato is simply *gelato*. If it turns out good, that's enough." She tried rebutting that a postural massage was just a *massage* and nothing more; that it really wasn't worth all this effort to perfect it, let alone want to write a book about it, with general premises and anatomical explanations and illustrations and quality photos and all the rest. Viviane was offended, as if the two lines of work weren't remotely comparable, divided by the same gap that separates a real job from a hobby. Maybe because Viviane began doing postural massages a long time before she started making gelato, maybe because she views massages as a necessity and gelato as a treat; maybe because her income is much higher, and much more continuous. But there they are again with the roles they've assigned each other, almost without realizing it: the dreamer and the realist, the seeker of the impalpable nuances of flavor and the breadwinner.

The truth is that after a certain point Viviane's moral support has diminished, and it's continued diminishing, to the point of turning into a sort of veiled resistance composed of doubts, criticism, objections, more or less explicit complaints. She began accusing her in an increasingly less playful tone of wasting too much time studying and perfecting recipes, spending too much money on ingredients, producing too little gelato when demand is high and too much when it's low. And complaining about the hours, about seeing her come home late at night, about knowing that when she's not at the shop she's off reading books at the library or doing research on the Internet. Then she came out with the idea of the baby. Tough to imagine that the two things aren't connected;

they are. So where did the idea of having a child really come from? From a sudden burst of love? The need to make long- and even longer-term plans? The desire to create a bond that's difficult to break? The fear of seeing her slip away, caught up in her passion for gelato, or some other passion that's yet to surface?

Another thing that's beyond doubt is that Viviane has become increasingly hostile toward her passion for folk dancing. There too: in the beginning she liked the fact that she wanted to participate in the dance group in Callian on Friday nights, said it seemed like a good way for her to express her sociable nature and physical exuberance. One time Viviane accompanied her and even participated in the Breton dance, telling her as they were returning home that she'd really liked seeing her dance so well, that she was proud of her. But then her attitude changed, revealing itself in jibes and brief provocative phrases almost every Friday morning, at breakfast. "Do you really have to go dancing tonight, too?"; "Don't you get sick of all that spinning around?"; "You do know that no one's going to die just because you don't go this one time." Maybe Viviane is irritated that, for her, dancing is both something fun to do as well as a commitment, annoyed by her loyalty to the other people who meet every week in the room beneath the old town hall. The result is that she complains more and more often about having to eat dinner alone after a hard day's work, while she is out hopping around to the music like a cricket, as if the summer months weren't enough, when she invariably comes home late.

It is true that in June, July, and August she keeps the gelateria open until ten at night and then has to clean up and organize the lab and shop with Guadalupe, such that she rarely pulls down the rolling shutter before eleven. But it's her job, not a pastime or a whim. And even though she bends over backward during those summer months to run home every afternoon and prepare a nice dinner that's all ready to heat up, when she gets home in the evening she invariably finds Viviane in a bad mood, ready to start in with distressing recriminations: the empty house; the sad, solitary meals in front of the television with no one to talk to. Displeasure thus compounds her exhaustion, in addition to the effort required not to overreact when all she'd like to do is cry. But it's even worse with the dancing, because Viviane considers it a useless and infantile game that she could easily do without, if she only wanted to take a little better care of their relationship (which in the evening would essentially consist of lying there half asleep on the couch in front of the television). She has held firm until now, since dancing is too important to her own equilibrium and she truly cares for the people with whom she dances. But every single Friday she ends up feeling terribly guilty, before, during, and after dancing, when she hurries home knowing she'll find Viviane in full-on victim mode. In speaking with other women in the dance group she's realized that her situation is anything but exceptional: almost all the boyfriends or husbands hate the idea that one night a week they want to dedicate themselves to polkas and mazurkas and waltzes and gigues, to Scottish dances and contredanses, to gavottes and bourrées and "Circassian circles."

But this is the point: Why is it that in her relationship with Viviane, which at the beginning was a thousand times freer than any of her previous ones with men, they have ended up not only re-creating roles, but also such *conventional* ones? Why in the world does one of them have to be more playful and the other more serious, one want to open up and one close down, one need her space and one want control? How is it possible that jealousy and possessiveness have gained a foothold almost like they did with Roberto, and the others before him? Is it her fault, Viviane's fault, both their faults, is it the need for security that gnaws at every couple? Is a conflict of aspirations and demands inevitable in every relationship, regardless of the sex of the two people?

Milena Migliari walks back up toward the gelateria with her grocery bags, knocks for Guadalupe, goes to put everything on the lab table. Guadalupe helps her take out the chestnuts and walnuts and persimmons and pomegranates: in no time they're both shelling and cutting and filling the steel basins in the first steps that will lead to some delicious autumn flavors, despite the so-called end of the gelato season.

TEN

Waiting has never been one of Nick Cruickshank's strong suits; in fact, you could safely say that impatience is one of the dominant elements of his character. Not in the sense of an angst to go or do or have; but rather in that of an unwillingness to be at the mercy of schedules, technical procedures, bureaucratic hassles, business decisions, climate changes. Whether it's getting a car from the mechanic or a passport from the consulate or a guitar from the lutist or a final mix from the sound technician or the release date of a new album from the record label, he can sometimes become aggressive if they try to put him on ice. Naturally, this is when the matter is of some interest to him; things that bore him or cause him mental strain he can put off almost indefinitely, relegating them to the status of an elliptical thought that every so often briefly reappears before disappearing again (and then reappearing, obviously).

Anyway, he's just finished a five-mile run around the grounds, three-quarters of an hour in the gym, an energizing shower, a rich breakfast consisting of orange juice, oat flakes, bread and cheese, and one of Madame Jeanne's delicious omelets, neither too dry nor too moist, and it's still too early to go to the airfield. The only thing he can do is sit around in his studio with the door triple-locked, playing a martellato-style boogie-woogie on the piano, his right foot keeping time, hoping no one comes to bother him or ask for anything.

When he's had enough of the boogie and his fingertips start to hurt from all the pounding on the keys, he dedicates himself to variations on a theme in E flat that came to him several days ago. It's a pretty normal succession of chords, without any really mind-blowing harmonic insights, but by now he's sure there's a song in there. Tough to explain precisely how he knows; he just *does*. You might play for weeks (or months) without anything meaningful staying with you, and then at a certain point a sequence presents itself that doesn't dissolve into nothing, like the others, but returns like an idée fixe, with its atmosphere, its shadows, its echoes. It's not something you can plan; it simply happens (or doesn't happen). All you can do is get yourself in sync, be listening for signals, and when they come follow them, like you might follow a trail through the jungle; only this trail is forming as you walk it, step-by-step. There's no need to consult compasses, study maps, or decide on itineraries; the itinerary is there, beneath your feet.

At least, that's what happens to him, since he doesn't know how to read or write music and he's certainly never studied composition. He doesn't have the slightest clue how Bach or Mozart or Beethoven composed their stuff; it's even possible that they saw the paths they wanted to take with perfect panoramic clarity, that they scanned the jungle from a mental airplane. But he's up to his neck in the jungle, with leaves and branches and trunks and every type of climber all around, stretching far above his head; he can't make out a trail until the trail opens up before him. The chords appear to him one after the other, then after a while it's the melody's turn, and even later come the words, at least the key ones, if not all of them. Only then can he try to eliminate the needless deviations, the pauses and backtracking, but always sticking to the trail that's manifested itself to him, without trying to make it change direction. It's a respect far more instinctive than logical and that originates in the awareness that any attempt to alter the route simply wouldn't work, because at this point the trail is *there*. Here's the most difficult part to explain: the fact at first that a song wasn't there and then it is, as if it always has been, as if it's written itself. Which certainly doesn't mean that it hasn't required effort on his part, because before you can stumble onto a trail, you must first *create the jungle*; then there's the infinite care at every step, the painstaking effort to foresee and support, choose the right direction at every crossroads, avoid running into cannibals or stepping in quicksand. This is how it's always happened for him; as far as he knows, it does for others as well. And it's true for every song, not just the great ones: there was a time when even the worst of them didn't exist and then after a certain point it's like they've always been there. Come to think of it, the real problem isn't explaining how songs come about; the problem is explaining *where they come from*. He's long since given up; he doesn't have the slightest idea where his songs were before he sat down at a piano or picked up a guitar and something surprising began coming out of his fingers.

Another really strange thing is that the beauty of a song can be independent of the intellectual or moral qualities of the person who writes it. He knows at least three or four of his colleagues, emotionally arid, intellectually opaque, and artistically compromised, who've happened to write some incredible songs that have touched the hearts and minds of millions of people. It's as if the songs have come into being *despite* them, as if they've simply passed through them. He likes to think he's neither arid nor opaque nor compromised, but even he remembers his bewilderment when "Refound" made its appearance as he was strumming his guitar on a desolate day in East Sussex. The sequence of chords and the melody suddenly revealed themselves to him, as if some luminous force of the universe had whispered them into his ears while he was in a state of perfect receptivity, stripped of intentions, unfocused on an objective. Immediately after came the words, miraculously linked to the music, with the same stupefying naturalness. He didn't have a recorder with him, so he kept playing and singing it for two or three hours straight, to exorcise the fear of it slipping his mind. After that it was like "Refound" had always existed; since forever.

When he played it for the other Bebonkers in the recording studio in London he spied their expressions, expecting to hear them say, "This can't be yours! You've taken it word for word from this or that other one!" But all three of them just stood there staring at him, amazed because it was undeniably a beautiful song, one of those that comes to you once every ten years if you're good or lucky, sometimes never. But he was still unsure whether it was really his; he had to go ask John Wilcox, the man with the most encyclopedic knowledge of music he knew, someone who can write you a piece for English horn in ten minutes or come up with an entire arrangement for symphonic orchestra in an afternoon. He played the tape for him with the terror of having it turned off after a few notes, hearing that there was a traditional Irish or Scottish or even Neapolitan song with the same exact melody. But John listened through to the end and then shook his head and smiled, with an expression marked by the awareness of what had happened. "It's *yours*, Nick."

Some (few) of his colleagues have been graced by one great song, others (very few) have succeeded in being graced by several, in different periods of their lives, like fishermen who make a great catch while their colleagues sit there over the water with poles in hand, waiting for a miracle that never comes. Method and discipline are essential, but alone they're not enough. And there's no amount of theoretical knowledge or studying that's any guarantee; how many great songs have been written by conservatory grads, and how many by people who don't know how to read or write music, like him? The percentages are incredibly unfavorable to the former, bless their hearts. A beautiful song is a *gift*, and a person doesn't take a gift for themselves, it's given to them. But the point is: Who is it that gives you the gift? And then: How do you manage to hold on to it? Or to get it back, if you've lost it? Do you have to rush off in search of a state of deprivation, of unhappiness, of desperation? Because it's beyond a shadow of a doubt that sad songs are more beautiful than happy ones, and that the few beautiful happy songs are nonetheless tinged by a vein of sadness.

The fact is there's simply no way to come up with a beautiful song in the way that Aileen produces her creations in Anti-leather, after learning the cutting and sewing techniques and studying the great stylists and analyzing the costs and doing the market research and putting together a skilled and competent team. If you try to come up with a song like that, all you'll have is a collection of previously heard fragments of sound; radio and the Internet are full of them, and there are people who make a ton of money on them, sure. Yet even the dumbest pop song sung by the most vulgar, exhibitionistic, and ridiculous-heels-wearing ass must contain at least a small part that has *appeared* instead of being constructed, to touch the chords of millions of people. At least *one* element of mysterious origin, one brief sequence that isn't entirely explainable.

Fundamentally it's the same as falling in love: you can't decide it rationally, putting together parameters on the basis of which you'll like someone. It happens, or it doesn't. When it does, is there any way to make it last? And what do you do when it's over? Try repeating the same gestures you made when you fell in love the last time? Go back to the same places? Say the same things you said at the beginning? Dress the same way? Hoping that the magic repeats itself? Even if you know full well that it won't?

Speaking of repetition, has anyone ever studied what goes on in the head of someone who writes a beautiful song and has to continue singing it over and over again for thirty years or more, one concert after another? Trying as well to play it as closely as possible to the way people remember it, since very few of them truly want to hear unrecognizable versions à la Bob Dylan. Not even old Bob's fans like those, apart from those who see him as the Oracle of Delphi, much less fans of the Bebonkers, with their obsession for the so-called original sound. Whatever that means, seeing as their early sound was infinitely freer and more eclectic than the one they now continue replicating with such dependable precision. "Original" probably means the formula the band stumbled on sometime in the nineties, after a long series of experiments in various directions, and which they've since left unaltered. It's quite likely that even Picasso, after passing through his Blue Period and Rose Period and African one and Analytical Cubism and Synthetic Cubism and finally coming to the style that anyone can quickly recognize today, might have wanted to change yet again. But he knew very well that it wouldn't have been in his own best interest; and if he didn't know, then his gallery managers would certainly have explained it to him.

So? Will he be condemned to sing the same songs over and over again forever, trying each time to re-create the spirit with which they came to him the first time? Even if that spirit is long gone?

Shouldn't he try to come up with something that reflects at least a little of what he thinks and feels *today*? Instead of pretending to be a teenager stuck in time (as his mother accurately predicted)? Does he not feel sad and embarrassed for his colleagues who've never stopped playing the part they created for themselves early on, even when it no longer minimally corresponds to their current role in the world? Like Bruce, for example, who keeps on screaming out his animated laments about an outcast alter ego on the run in the New Jersey suburbs, even though people can see him photographed in the tribune of honor at Jumping International in Monte Carlo or the Rolex Grand Prix in Geneva, as he takes in the performance of his twenty-year-old daughter on a horse worth eight million dollars (one of the ten or twelve he possesses)? Or Mick, who at seventy-two prances around the stage gesticulating just as he did when he was twenty-two, hasn't put on a single solitary pound since the sixties, and still ends every concert with "Satisfaction," even if it makes him nauseous? On the other hand, what are they supposed to do, spend their days playing golf? Write songs about their perplexity at having kids who are spoiled and arrogant, completely lacking in any aspirations that don't involve the acquisition of more and more material goods? Have an armchair put onstage and sing sitting down about the annoyance of having their hair dyed every three days, or the difficulty in finding financial consultants who don't run off to Paraguay with their money?

They're pointless questions: inspiration either comes or it doesn't, personal evolution follows paths that are at times unpredictable, and artistic integrity is almost always a pose when it isn't an alibi for failure. The best you can do is cultivate a craftsman's ethic, be honest with yourself, and create forms that allow the light to seep in with miraculous infrequency; the alternative is to give it all up, disappear. If you can't, or don't want to, at least don't sit there complaining. Save the whining and self-pity, thank you very much.

Nick Cruickshank passes in front of a sliding door and sees a small caravan of trucks advancing cautiously on the lawn in front of the house, guided by the gestures of Aileen, flanked by Tricia and Maggie and Tom Harlan and his assistant and the *Star Life* team, while Aldino keeps an eye on them. He only hesitates for a second, then like a thief slips quickly out of the studio and down the hallway and out the back door before anyone can intercept him.

ELEVEN

TO MILENA MIGLIARI persimmons have always seemed like a magical fruit: so intensely orange on the leafless autumn trees, pucker-inducing when they're picked, achingly sweet when ripe, golden and almost liquid just beneath their sheer skin. Many people don't like them, maybe for their viscid nature, the way you have to stick your tongue out to eat them, stretching your lips, sucking, wetting your nose, chin, and hands in their sweet slaver. Persimmons are mysterious. And inside the seeds are concealed tiny white pieces of cutlery: really. She found out only a few years ago, thanks to her childhood friend Alessandra, aka Micior; at first she didn't believe it, not even after Micior emailed her an article with attached photos. She had to see for herself before she was convinced: if you cut the seed horizontally you find a white sprout in the shape of a fork, spoon, or knife, very tiny but precisely shaped. According to certain peasant traditions you can foresee what the winter will be like, based on which miniature piece of silverware you find: a spoon means there will be heaps of snow, a knife that the cold will be piercing, a fork that it won't be too harsh. Too bad seeded persimmons are becoming increasingly rare; if one day plant selectors manage to make them disappear completely, people will think it was just a legend. As far as gelato is concerned the challenge is to keep the final result from being too sugary despite the fruit's natural sweetness, and to maintain its flavor, color, and possibly its consistency. Persimmon gelato is undoubtedly one of the least simple flavors to make, so it's one of the most interesting.

Someone is knocking on the glass door to the shop; the insistent pounding is audible in the lab, over the ugly French pop rock song playing on the radio.

Milena Migliari has no desire to drop everything midbatch; she nods at Guadalupe, who was supposed to pick up a new box of thick Styrofoam containers from Monsieur Deleuze anyway.

Guadalupe goes to see, comes back a few seconds later, in a state of extreme agitation: she's shaking her hands, struggling to find the words.

"What the heck is it?" Milena Migliari goes instinctively on the defensive.

"It's Nick, the lead singer of the Bebonkers!" Guadalupe hops up and down, unable to calm herself. "The ones playing Sunday at the airfield! It's him, I swear!"

"And what does he want?" Milena Migliari is embarrassed at seeing her assistant so excited by a brush with celebrity, and annoyed at the idea of anyone, famous or not, disturbing them when there's a sign on the glass door that reads unmistakably *Fermé*.

"I don't know! He's out there! He pointed at me!" Guadalupe is unable to stand still; she wipes her hands on her apron, adjusts her hair covering, takes another peek into the shop.

"Would you calm down, please? Ask him what he wants." Milena Migliari doesn't stop working with the serrated-edge little spoon to remove the bitter-tasting white filaments from the persimmon pulp, but she too is getting agitated.

"How am I supposed to ask him what he wants?" Guadalupe looks at her, feverish.

"You *ask* him! Open the door and ask him what he wants!" Yes, now she is agitated too; and thanks to someone who she didn't even recognize yesterday when he was standing right in front of her, which is doubly ridiculous. She reaches to turn off the radio, because it's only adding to the confusion.

Guadalupe takes a deep breath, like she's preparing for some daunting endeavor; she goes back into the shop. There's the sound of the key in the lock, a man's voice with a slightly gravelly English accent. "*Bonjour, je suis désolée de vous deranger, mais je voulais . . .*"

"*Pas du tout! Vous ne nous dérangez pas du tout, Monsieur Nick!*" Guadalupe's voice goes shrill with emotion. "Hey, Milena!"

"I can't come out there!" Milena Migliari has no desire to get involved; she forces herself to concentrate on the persimmon pulp.

But Nick Cruickshank is already here, standing in the doorway separating the shop from the lab. He smiles at her, like someone who had a rough childhood but is still a bit of a kid, because he can afford to be or because he's incapable of being otherwise. "Good morning."

"Morning." Milena Migliari realizes she's being anything but polite, but the fact is she feels like her private space is being invaded, in a moment when she's already feeling unstable. She points to the basin with the persimmon pulp. "Sorry, but I'm working."

"I see. I hope I'm not disturbing you." Nick Cruickshank might be a little embarrassed, maybe not. Leather or fake-leather motorcycle jacket, green sweatshirt with an unintelligible design, blood-red foulard, faded black jeans, boots with buckles: it looks like an oft-used stage costume. "I wanted to tell you something."

"What?" Milena Migliari's tone goes curt in self-defense, her expression hard.

With her back to the refrigerator Guadalupe has an air of suffering about her; maybe she was hoping to see the rock star greeted with a festive atmosphere, offers of tastings, compliments on his songs, various kindnesses and attentions.

"Your gelato is incredibly good." Nick Cruickshank's expression is so serious that it's impossible to know whether he's telling the truth or joking.

"Thank you." Milena Migliari smiles faintly, nods faintly; she tries not to commit herself with unnecessary facial expressions or gestures.

"Actually, it's the *best* gelato I've ever tasted *in my entire life*." Nick Cruickshank's slightly hoarse tone has an extremely familiar emphasis, bearing the echo of innumerable songs and associated places, stories, moments.

"Well, I'm glad to hear it." Milena Migliari realizes she's smiling much more openly than she'd like to, but she can't help it; the creases on her face melt away of their own accord. How do you remain indifferent after a comment like that, spoken with such apparent conviction?

Guadalupe, seeing her less hostile, reveals her extremely white teeth, fixes her hair under the hairnet, continues gazing adoringly at Nick Cruickshank.

"I'm not saying it in the intolerably *empty* way it's usually used. It's not a *formula*, I swear." In his eyes is a light of unfiltered, disconcerting sincerity. He smells of patchouli, or marijuana, or both.

"No?" Milena Migliari forces herself back to a more controlled expression, but a current alters her heart rate ever so slightly. But why? What should she care about the opinion of someone whose sense of taste has almost surely been permanently altered by decades of who knows how many drugs? Someone who almost surely smoked a joint before tasting her gelato yesterday, and would have craved anything sweet? Is she too a victim of the impact of celebrity, just like Guadalupe?

Nick Cruickshank gestures: his movements are fluid, but with tiny pauses seemingly dictated by sudden doubts or inspirations, not out-and-out jerks but nearly. "And you're *brave*."

"Why?" Milena Migliari realizes she seems anxious for an answer; she wishes she could rewind a few seconds, limit herself to a shrug.

Nick Cruickshank places his forehead on his hand, like he's pursuing sensations difficult to put into words. "You don't try to make any flavor *simpler* or more *reassuring* than it is."

"Really?" She makes another attempt to hide the emotions coursing through her, but she can't.

Nick Cruickshank nods energetically. "You're able to capture the essence of each flavor and all the marvelous and even imperfect sensations and memories and associations it brings to mind."

Milena Migliari feels herself blush, though it's the last thing in the world she'd want to do; and in the same moment she feels an uncontrollable desire to understand how someone like this could ever have come and said to her what he just said.

Guadalupe's stare shifts from her to him, uncertain. Her English leaves a lot to be desired, but it's not the words she's struggling with: it's the *sense* of their exchange.

Nick Cruickshank motions toward the lab and its equipment. "Any chance I could take a look?"

"Just don't bring those shoes in here." Milena Migliari speaks without thinking, maybe to claim jurisdiction over her territory, make sure she isn't invaded any more than has already occurred.

"Oh, sorry." Nick Cruickshank jumps back with great agility; only his head is still inside.

Milena Migliari feels a sort of tickle, similar to when she knows she's made a better gelato than she was expecting, or she's mastered a particular dance step. She motions to Guadalupe. "Would you give him a pair of overshoes?"

Guadalupe instantly bounds away to get the box from the closet, takes out two sterile transparent plastic overshoes, hands them to Nick Cruickshank.

He takes them, studies them closely as if they're mysterious objects, puts them on with a skill belying his initial puzzlement. He takes two swishing steps into the lab, looks at his feet. "*Wow.*"

"The hairnet, too." Milena Migliari maintains her firm approach.

Guadalupe rushes to get one of the nonwoven bouffant-style caps from the box, passes it to Nick Cruickshank.

He gathers his long partly black and partly gray hair, fits the hairnet over it, and makes a funny face.

"It's because of health rules." Milena Migliari realizes how absurd her requests might seem, but at this moment she feels the need for protective shields of any kind. She's also annoyed at being observed by Guadalupe with her doll-like stare; she gestures for her to pick up the containers from Monsieur Deleuze.

It takes Guadalupe a couple of seconds to react; she stirs. "I'm going, I'm going." Yet it takes her a very long time to leave the lab, and just as long to leave the shop, locking the glass door behind her.

Nick Cruickshank half bows, extends his hand. "Yesterday we didn't even introduce ourselves. Nick."

"Milena." She reaches out from behind the work counter, shakes his hand.

"Nice name. Mi-le-na." Nick Cruickshank walks around the

lab, his clear overshoes and hairnet combining in surreal fashion with his rocker's garb; he studies the glass refrigerators, the pasteurizer, the batch freezer, the maturation vats, the blast chiller. Very respectful, as if in the studio of a great artist.

"And which flavor did you like the most?" Milena Migliari doesn't know why she asks him; soliciting judgments on the part of those tasting her gelato is something she never does, not ever. Early on she asked Viviane for her opinion, but that soon stopped, since her eyes didn't exactly light up; all she said was "good" or "yes."

Nick Cruickshank takes on a pained expression, like he's being forced to make an excruciating choice.

"Just choose one." Milena Migliari wonders why she's being so insistent. Is it the way he's looking at her, his unrestrained curiosity? But didn't she decide four years ago that she had had enough of men's looks, whatever their intentions? Is she simply excited to talk about gelato with someone capable of making meaningful comments and observations?

"The almond one was *stellar.*" Nick Cruickshank makes a wavelike gesture, raising his hand toward the ceiling. His movements have a theatrical quality, but strangely they don't seem rehearsed; it's as if they belong to another dimension, another era.

"And then?" She continues pressing him, doesn't ease the tension; it's absurd, sure, but she can't help it.

"The pomegranate, my God." Nick Cruickshank makes another gesture, semicircular. "The color, the intensity. Inspirational."

"You knew it was pomegranate?" Milena Migliari can no longer conceal anything, not even her surprise.

Nick Cruickshank looks at her; he seems disconcerted. "How could I *not* have known? You were able to preserve so marvelously that sourish-sweet flavor, slightly tannic, *alive.* You didn't trivialize it, didn't soften it, you captured its true soul. You found the exact point of convergence between *truth* and *pleasure*."

"Really?" Milena Migliari realizes she's shaken, but then it is the first time she's heard someone talk this way about her gelato. Sure, she has admirers, such as Katharina and Ditmer Bouwmeester, who produce high-quality artisanal chocolate near Utrecht and come by almost daily in July; or Liam Bradford, whose fantastic review on his blog convinced the English lady to make her huge order; or Marianne O'Neil, who dedicated a poem to her Saint-Paul-en-Forêt wild peach. But no one has ever talked to her with the emotional urgency of this English rock star, equally passionate in gaze and voice, in his gestures, in his gait, in his breathing.

"Yes. Yes. Yes." Nick Cruickshank bends forward at the waist and opens his arms, again like he's on a small stage in the eighteenth century, but during a rehearsal, without a live audience. There are no visible traces of affectation or smugness in his style, only a distinct separation from the behaviors of normal life.

Milena Migliari doesn't know what to say anymore; the words don't come. She pours a certain amount of pulp into the blender, adds the creamy milk she buys unpasteurized from Didier Tornaud in Montauroux, who before making the midlife turn to dairy farming was a computer programmer in Bordeaux.

Nick Cruickshank comes closer to her, his overshoes rustling. "But I wanted to tell you something else."

"What?" Now Milena Migliari feels a small interior wave of alarm: it's rising, from her stomach toward her heart.

Nick Cruickshank makes as if to say something, but switches expressions, as if a different idea has occurred to him. He has this rough grace, which fits with his worn elegance, his ease of movement. "That flavor that tastes like date—"

"You didn't recognize it!" Milena Migliari feels an unexplainable relief at him not having been able to identify the flavor; and a little disappointment, sure. But the relief prevails for some reason.

"Hey, who said I didn't recognize it?" Nick Cruickshank has a sudden angry reaction, as if in response to the most unjust of accusations.

"The date one I make near Christmas." She feels a bizarre urgency to strike down the impassioned definition of truth to which he seems committed; to file him away as superficial and presumptuous, convinced of being able to speak about the complexities of flavor without truly understanding them.

Nick Cruickshank looks at her with flaming eyes. "I *know* what it was. Jujube. *Ziziphus jujube*."

The surprise is so great that it hits her like an electric shock, makes her legs wobble. Immediately after she feels like laughing; she laughs, convulsively.

Nick Cruickshank is puzzled for a moment, then he laughs as well, stomps on the floor with a plastic-wrapped boot heel.

They both laugh, for reasons that are far from clear. And they continue, seemingly unable to stop; it takes them several seconds to recover.

Milena Migliari tries to recover her attitude from when he came in, somewhere between diffidence and mild curiosity, but she can't. "What do you know about jujubes?"

Nick Cruickshank shrugs, smiling. "Already got an idea about what I can or cannot know?"

"Of course not." She shakes her head, though she actually did think she had a pretty good idea, and in that idea there wasn't the slightest chance that he even knew jujubes *existed*.

Nick Cruickshank adjusts his hairnet: he pulls down on the elastic and lets go. "You know in the *Odyssey*, when Odysseus and his men disembark on the island of the Lotus Eaters and give in to the temptation to eat the magic fruit that makes them forget their wives, families, and even their nostalgia for home—"

"They were wild jujubes!" Milena Migliari feels her heart jump, the skin on her face prickle.

"*Ziziphus lotus!*" Nick Cruickshank is excited, too; he does a strange kind of jump.

"Yes!" Their voices overlap; they seem amazed in the identical way.

Milena Migliari moves slightly backward, shakes her head slowly. "*Nobody* knows jujubes. They're a forgotten fruit, practically."

"I have a tree of them in Sussex, really old." Nick Cruickshank gestures, as if to indicate Sussex. "People once thought they brought their house good luck."

"*Yes!*" Milena Migliari is speaking louder than she'd like, but it's her entire perception of herself that's confused.

Nick Cruickshank, for his part, continues to sustain an extremely focused stare. "It's such a simple fruit, and strange. When they're still light-colored and not completely ripe they taste like apples, right? They only take on their true flavor when they become dark and wrinkled."

She nods, far too emphatically. "And they're so sugary, but their leaves contain a substance that cancels out the perception of sweetness. Ziziphin, it's called."

He stares at her without saying anything. He seems bedazzled.

She wants to look away, but still feels that tingle in her face; to avoid looking stupid she tries for a look of impatience, though she's none too sure how it comes off. "What was the other thing you wanted to say to me?"

He puts his hand over his eyes, as if to remember the question; he looks back at her. "Not say, *ask*."

"What did you want to ask me?" Once more she feels the little wave of alarm rise within her.

"Why is the marvel imperfect?" He stares at her, waiting.

She asks herself whether she should look for a precise answer or weasel her way out with humor; in the end she speaks without thinking. "Because it doesn't last."

He continues gazing at her; it's disconcerting how receptive his expression is, how open, how uncompromised by acquired knowledge. "It goes away. Along with the wonder, the curiosity, the meticulous care, the fun, the pleasure, the *joy* it contained."

"Take a *really good* gelato." She realizes her expression is similar to his, that she's speaking in a similar tone, by a strange form of contagion. "One moment it's so deliciously cold, with the most delightful balance of softness and compactness. You're so happy to have it in your hands, to be able to enjoy it. And a moment later it's finished, done. You can't even get another one, because you know perfectly well that it wouldn't be the same."

He's still gazing at her; then he smiles, only just. "You know you're even more surprising than your gelato?"

"You're pretty surprising yourself, when it comes right down to it." Again she replies without thinking, in the uncontrolled spirit that's surrounded them since they started talking. Right away she thinks that she never should have said something like that to him; but now she's said it, it's happened.

His gaze is so totally focused it almost hurts. "And the messages you write on those little pieces of paper tied with red string? I got one that was incredibly *appropriate*."

"Really?" She finds it increasingly difficult to stay calm in this exchange: it's like trying to stand still in the middle of a buffeting wind.

He comes closer to her; his movement seems unstoppable. "You just really have something *special*."

She feels the alarm wave turn into fear that rises up to her lungs, takes her breath away.

He places his hands on her temples, comes forward; he kisses her on the forehead.

She registers the movement of air, the moistness of his lips on her skin, the bodily warmth, the smell of patchouli or marijuana or a combination of both, the rustling of plastic hairnets. She's caught so much by surprise that as soon as he breaks away she feels like laughing again; she laughs, her face burning up, her heart beating erratically.

He laughs, too, only an inch or two away, with an expression that radiates the communicative joy of a child, of a savage.

She wavers between contrasting sensations and thoughts: she can't figure out if this kiss was the most innocent thing in the world, or the most dangerous. Can she continue being natural with him? Should she distance herself as soon as possible?

Nick Cruickshank smiles, but at this point he too seems at least a little uncertain. He makes one of his gestures. "It's just I tend to be *physical* with people I like."

Milena Migliari thinks that she tends to be physical with people she likes, too: she's always grabbing wrists, holding arms, patting shoulders, caressing heads, giving little shoves. More than once she's argued about it with Viviane, who claims that physical contact should be reserved exclusively for intimate relationships, maybe because her own work consists of handling the bodies of strangers every day. But however you want to look at it, this was not about simply being physical: he took her and kissed her, even if on the forehead. Their bodies made contact with a certain degree of pressure, activated tactile sensations, though for no more than two or three seconds. How innocent can a gesture like that be from a man, particularly a man who has almost certainly been a serial seducer for decades?

Nick Cruickshank must perceive these thoughts, because he seems less and less comfortable. From his jeans he takes out a pocket watch attached to a band with a silver chain, looks at the watch as if he suddenly has somewhere to be. "I have to go."

Milena Migliari is trying to understand what happened a moment ago and what is happening now, but she's unable to formulate an answer.

Nick Cruickshank slices the air with his hand. "I'm going flying. With a glider."

"Ah, sounds great." Milena Migliari realizes how generic her reply sounds, but the fact is that her thoughts and sensations keep jumbling together without any semblance of order.

"It is." Nick Cruickshank points to the persimmon pulp in the blender, waiting to be mixed with the creamy milk. "This gelato is going to be amazing, too, I'm sure."

"I hope so." Milena nods, not sure of anything.

There are noises coming from the shop door: it's Guadalupe coming back in and giggling with someone. A moment later she comes into the lab, sets the large box of Styrofoam containers on the floor, directs her dark and bright eyes on Nick Cruickshank, even more excited than when she left. "Sorry, but there's a friend of mine who'll kill me if you don't take a picture with her."

Her friend Delphine, the clerk at the nearby bakery, peeks in: as soon as she sees Nick Cruickshank she starts making faces and squealing. "*Mon Dieu, c'est lui! Je ne peux pas le croire, c'est genial!*"

Nick Cruickshank smiles, his politeness evidently well practiced; he takes off his hairnet, shakes out his hair.

Milena Migliari begins to tell the two girls to leave him be but holds back. Why should she be protective of someone who just disturbed her in the middle of her work and even gave her a surprise kiss, albeit on the forehead?

Nick Cruickshank takes off his overshoes, too, follows Guadalupe and Delphine into the shop, stands with his back to the wall like he's facing a firing squad.

Milena Migliari looks on from behind her work table, half concealed by the doorframe; she thinks that once upon a time the two girls would have been content with an autograph to keep for themselves and maybe show to a few girlfriends; now they demand photographic proof to share instantly with an unlimited number of people.

Guadalupe and Delphine press up against Nick Cruickshank, hip to hip and temple to temple, give toothy smiles in one, two clicks of each of their cell phones. Then, vibrating with excitement, they hug him and kiss him on the cheeks. They certainly don't have any problems with physical contact.

"*Salut, je m'en vais.*" Nick Cruickshank brings proceedings to a close with polite firmness, this, too, well practiced. He leans back into the lab, waves good-bye, still theatrical but significantly less emphatic than when he came in. "Thanks very much for the visit. And my compliments again, really. Bye."

"Thank you." Milena Migliari smiles back in the most restrained way she can; she goes back to her blender, but before turning it on she waits to hear the shop door swing shut. Would he have stayed longer if Guadalupe hadn't brought that friend of hers with the bright idea of taking selfies with him? To talk about what, though, after the conversation was ruined by that kiss on the forehead? Would they at least have clarified the nature of his gesture? Would they have figured out whether it was simply an impulsive act with no particular connotations, or the automatic reflex of a male accustomed to seeking confirmation of his seductive power in every female he meets, even those whom he doesn't like and aren't interested in him? But why should she waste time thinking about it now? And why does she continue to feel so absurdly agitated? Why are her legs shaking slightly, along with her hands on the blender?

Guadalupe says a giggling good-bye to Delphine, locks the shop door, comes back to the lab, still high as a kite. "Did you see how nice Nick was? Can you believe it? And despite his age he's still the coolest around! Just give me a moment to post the photos and I'll come help you."

"Go ahead." Milena Migliari turns on the blender, mixes the persimmon pulp with the creamy milk; Nick Cruickshank's kiss on her forehead and his words and gestures before it whirl around in her head in the very same way, producing the same complete confusion.

TWELVE

THE AIRFIELD OF Fayence-Tourrettes covers an area of more than 110 acres. The runways are in grass; the main one is 2,700 feet long and 150 feet wide. Nick Cruickshank discovered it many years ago, while touring Europe in search of the best places to fly with a glider; and he liked it so much he ended up buying a house a couple of miles from here, and enlarging the original estate with successive acquisitions of bordering properties. It wasn't difficult, since after a certain point everyone began carving up their land into smaller lots and selling them off for the construction of villas and cottages in the so-called Neo-Provençal style. The plain quickly filled with this rubbish, the hills likewise; the towns are quite happy to reduce the minimum requirements for licenses, assuring themselves as much property tax revenue as they can. The nice thing is that he now finds himself with a little breathing room around his home, a few dozen hectares of green where no one can pester him. Which makes it decidedly paradoxical (again) that he's now *actively encouraging* the pests with offers of food and lodging, alcoholic beverages, and various other amenities. But Aileen was so insistent for months and months, with her delicate but constant pressure, never distracted or showing any signs of weakness. And she came up with the idea of combining the private party with the benefit concert, just one day apart, like a package deal to be sold to *Star Life*, the town governments, the local inhabitants, the fans, the other band members, him.

So today the guests will continue to arrive; tomorrow even more of them will swoop in. As there aren't many hotels in the area, Aileen has rented everything she was able to find in terms of villas and local houses. Which, of course, is guaranteed to provoke gratification and resentment in dozens of voracious egos who will measure their own perceived worth according to the quality of their accommodations, split up into opposing factions, those staying at Les Vieux Oliviers against those who aren't. There will be those (such as Noel) who prefer to stay with their Russian oligarch friends in Saint-Tropez as a matter of principle; those (such as Kate) who commute back and forth from Cannes, even though Cannes in this season is pure misery; those (such as Reina) who pretend to adapt effortlessly to a mediocre lodging and then complain about it for the next few months. To say nothing of the perverse mix of true and fair-weather friends, acquaintances and collaborators and business partners, people who'll come to sneak a peek and people who'll come to be seen, photographed, filmed. Then add the sons and daughters, who'll drag themselves here of their own accord or be dragged by female plus-ones ready to record and refer to their mothers every little detail that might someday be useful for blackmail. And, of course, the *Star Life* team, with the arrogance of the one footing the bill, will do everything possible to stir and spice up the various ingredients, to make things as attractive as possible for its voyeuristic and gossip-hungry audience. A lovely prospect, really.

Then, of course, it still has to be figured out how in hell the

Bebonkers are going to find the time and energy for a rehearsal that's any more than a simple sound check before the concert Sunday, considering they haven't played together in at least five months and that half of them will still be wasted after the party on Saturday. Considering as well that Sunday's concert is going to be anything but low-profile: between the charitable cause and the morbid curiosity there are going to be a ton of people on hand for the unforgettable event, as well as local and national television and radio. Plus thousands of cell phones, whose digital zooms will distort Jimmy Rose's carefully planned light effects into god-awful halos, whose three-cent microphones will butcher the efforts of that saint-maniac Jamie Cullingham on the mixer. Within half an hour of the end of the concert, fans around the world will rush onto YouTube to analyze every second of the hour and a half of music under a magnifying glass, make comparisons with last year's concerts and those of ten or twenty or thirty years ago, ready to be inspired, get outraged, confirm their tribal pride, feed aching nostalgia, get riled up with hate. There will surely be those who say that the Bebonkers are amazing because they play each song the same as always, those who say they're pathetic because they insist on doing so; those who say they're living legends, those who say they're dinosaurs. There will also be an army of genuine haters, ex-fans, or people who've never really loved them, anxious merely for confirmation of the fact that the Bebonkers have become a commercial product like Coca-Cola, a group of filthy millionaires who no longer give a damn about the original spirit of their music, despite the rebel image they still try to project. He can already imagine the indiscriminate barrage of accusations, heaped onto the enormous landfill of the Internet: the standardized sound, the lost Zeitgeist, the betrayed ideals, the self-interest behind the good cause, blah, blah, blah. Millions of losers incapable of making anything meaningful or even halfway decent sitting there in front of their screens of various sizes, ready to pounce on nonexistent or barely audible mistakes, to type *Incredible clunker by Nick at 02:24!* or *Wally Thompson's lost his touch and doesn't give a damn* or *Seriously?* or *I'd like to know where all the money from this so-called benefit concert is really going to fucking end up* or *WTF???* And so on and so forth. The more he thinks about it, the more the benefit concert on Sunday turns into a sort of nightmare. And the party on Saturday is even worse.

The only thing he wants to do now is settle in at the controls of his glider, be lifted off the ground and circle up into the sky, gaze down at this valley and the hills and mountains from on high until the houses and streets and existences they contain become so small as to fade into irrelevance.

Jean Leblanc is already there waiting for him beside the Glaser-Dirks DG-303 that he's brought out of the hangar: he shakes his hand with the usual demonstration of strength, blue eyes sparkling in his long face. "*Salut, Nick.*"

"*Salut, Jean.*" They've known each other for roughly a dozen years, and are always happy to see each other, but they tend to be of few words. Now they're taking a walk around the glider for a final inspection: left side of the fuselage, left wing, tail planes, rudder-elevator-trim tabs, right side of the fuselage. They check the tow cable hook, the inflation pressure of the tire, with the blend of casualness and care that results from gestures often repeated but crucially important every time. Lucien, nicknamed "le Petit" for his young age and frail stature, arrives with the parachute. Unlike Jean, who has no interest in music, he's a fan of the Bebonkers: each time he sees Nick he has this eager way of tracking his expressions, his gestures.

Nick Cruickshank puts on the parachute, adjusts the straps on his own, though le Petit does his utmost to offer assistance. Nick opens the Plexiglas canopy, steps into the cockpit and gets settled in the seat, checks the closing lever, verifies the control column and rudder pedals, tests the button for the spoilers and the one for the tow cable. He loves these preparations; they give him the same rapid alternation of anxiety-reassurance he feels when he's looking over the list of technical details with the stage director in his dressing room before a concert, even if he knows full well that he and his team have already taken care of everything with the utmost care.

They're off: Jean pushes the glider, le Petit holds up the right wing to prevent it from touching the grass. They stop about twenty yards behind the Robin DR400, which is already in tow position. The tow pilot waves hello, comes to check the cable, hooks it on, tries the emergency release, checks the glider's safety link. He signals and goes to take his place at the controls, turns on the engine.

Nick Cruickshank closes the canopy, fastens the safety harness, checks the ballast tanks, the control column and rudder pedals again, puts the trim tabs in takeoff position, closes and blocks the spoilers. He verifies the instrument panel, from left to right, first above and then below: anemometer, variometer, two-hand altimeter, turn-and-slip indicator, magnetic compass. He sets the altimeter to zero, turns on the radio, regulates the frequency. The tension grows inside him, like when he's coming out of the dressing room and heading toward the back of the stage with the rest of the band, charged with anticipation for a familiar experience very likely to give him intense satisfaction, but in which the possibility of disaster is always present. Many years ago one of his first instructors told him that a glider pilot is three times more likely to kill himself in a flying accident than in a car accident, and that air sailing is one of the activities least tolerant of distraction, ignorance, and stupidity. He liked the idea then, and still does; it seems like a useful activity, a case in which the risk is most assuredly worth taking. He glances at the windsock hanging limply from the pole, gives the thumbs-up: ready for takeoff.

The Robin DR400 slowly advances, the thirty-yard cable unwinds and goes taut, the glider begins moving across the grass. Le Petit walks faster and faster while holding up the right wing, starts jogging; he lets go. Jean is in the background watching, arms crossed. Nick Cruickshank grips the control column, moves it back; his heart is beating a little faster. Like in the last few steps before coming out in front of the stage lights, when the most primitive part of his brain makes every muscle in his body tense for impact with the crowd of thousands of people electrified with excitement, and the most evolved part forces him to relax his movements and facial expression, in the latest demonstration of "Cruickshank cool."

The tow plane picks up speed, its wings cut through the air and begin to generate lift, the structure of the Glaser-Dirks bounces on the grass with growing frequency. Then the glider rises off the ground, just before the Robin DR400 begins to do so; they both lift off, linked by the increasing tow tension and vibration. Nick Cruickshank keeps an eye on his instruments, moves the control column to keep himself slightly above the wake of the tow plane's propeller, to avoid destabilizing it or himself. It's a game of contrasting forces, a tug-of-war between gravity that wants to pull you down and the density of the air that supports you: an intense oscillation between natural and unnatural. The altimeter reads 60, then 80, then 100 feet; the numbers increase with the distance from the ground and the rustling of the Plexiglas canopy. Slowly and then more quickly the green of the airfield assumes finite contours, the roads crisscrossing the plain become visible and already look tiny, along with the cars driving on them, the houses, the blue swimming pools, the gardens surrounding the houses, the depots, the cement expanses surrounding the depots. One hundred and forty feet, then 180, then 200, then 220. Soon the details of the landscape will gradually start to lose their ordinary meaning, until at release altitude they're practically invisible, no more than marks on the surface of the earth, the fruit of intentions increasingly difficult to decipher as altitude increases, increasingly difficult to take seriously.

Suddenly there's a violent snap: the tow tension is interrupted, there's a sudden drop in speed. The cable has either broken or detached, the tow plane jerks, veers off to the left. Nick Cruickshank feels his heart slow, his blood run cold. He immediately pushes the control column forward in a reflex picked up during emergency simulations, puts the glider into a nosedive to gain speed and avoid stalling, veers to the right. The novelty is that none of the emergency simulations took place at less than three hundred feet from the ground, and he's already fallen to two hundred, and keeps falling. The landscape comes toward him with vindictive rapidity, its elements regaining their ordinary meaning with each passing second. At this altitude the parachute is useless, the alternatives are landing on a knife's edge or crashing. Fifty-five miles an hour; any slower and his room for maneuver is significantly reduced, along with the chances of getting out of this without catastrophic damage.

It's strange, because Nick Cruickshank is extremely focused on the mental calculations and necessary steps to make a 180-degree turn and attempt an opposite-direction landing on the airfield strip, and meanwhile thoughts come into his head that are of absolutely no help in such a maneuver, none whatsoever. The thought, for example, that his feeling of imminent doom yesterday morning in the olive grove was actually a premonition of *this*; that crashing only a couple of hundred yards from where the concert is scheduled to be held on Sunday would be a wonderful conclusion to the legendary biography they've constructed for him; that it would also be a perfect way to cancel Saturday's party; that he wouldn't be able to finish the song he was working on last night; that never again would he see Milena the Italian gelato chef and taste new flavors and maybe give her another kiss on the forehead. Instantaneous hybrids of images and sensations, more than actual thoughts: they flash through a part of his brain separate from the part still trying to control speed, altitude, angle of maneuver, and all the rest. The two parts run parallel to each other and function independently, one hot and one cold, in the super-compressed space of time that's decreasing more and more quickly along with the physical space separating him from impact.

Nick Cruickshank is only fifty feet from the ground, still in his turn, still more or less equally likely to either make it out by the skin of his teeth or sideslip and crash onto the highway down there or into the frighteningly close trees at the airfield's perimeter, and yet a moment later he's above the grassy field, no obstacles in sight; he's able to level off, glide for a few yards, touch down not too brusquely, bounce around on the field, and roll to a stop.

Then he sits motionless in his seat, without unfastening the safety harness or opening the canopy. He breathes slowly, waits for his heart to start beating normally again, watches Jean's old café latte–colored Volkswagen Beetle come slowly toward him across the field. For once he isn't sorry about not being able to sail high up in the sky for as long as possible; for once he's pretty happy to be back on the ground.

THIRTEEN

VIVIANE COMES BY to pick her up at the gelateria to go to the appointment with Dr. Lapointe at the Centre Plamondon, in Grasse. When they're in the car together Viviane always drives; not because they've ever decided on it, it just happens. It might depend on the fact that Viviane is more familiar with the area, and spends more time behind the wheel each day. Anyhow she drives her Peugeot quite aggressively, with sharp turns, accelerations that nearly rear-end the cars in front, last-second braking, sudden downshifting, bursts of speed to overtake and race ahead along the open road. Milena Migliari thinks that at first Viviane's driving made her feel both nervous and safe to the same degree, the way it seemed like an expression of inner tension but also of hurried practicality, a means to an end, without the slightest distraction to contemplate the landscape. Now it's making her more nervous than anything: she digs her feet into the floor, clamps her hands on the sides of the seat, pushes into the backrest.

Viviane checks on her with a quick look. "Everything all right?"

"Yeah, yeah." Milena Migliari thinks that in truth everything is pretty far from all right, but she can't imagine explaining it to her: it would be brutal and disloyal, as well as incredibly overdue. But at this very moment she would prefer to be putting the finishing touches on her chestnut gelato, rather than speeding toward Grasse and ruin. It's true that Guadalupe is now familiar with every step of production and can certainly handle things on her own, but it distresses her to leave a batch unfinished, particularly if it's to go to a darn medical center to discuss the procedures of in vitro fertilization. Which whisks her back to the thought of not being able to work in the middle of summer, when people will line up in front of the counter and even out the door. She might even have to stop by mid-July, because if all goes according to plan she'll be in her eighth month of pregnancy, and Dr. Lapointe has already informed her (with one of his condescending smiles) that the change in temperature from the cold of the lab to the heat outside would certainly not be ideal for an older expectant mother like her. Upon hearing herself thus defined she began to laugh, but Lapointe pointed out that there was no need to be offended, since in the 1970s a woman was considered older if she had a child at twenty-eight, whereas now it's about thirty-five. Which certainly didn't make the term seem less ridiculous to her; on par with the rest of the terminology that she and Viviane have absorbed from meetings with doctors and the Internet and have repeated to each other endless times at home like a couple of parrots, in meticulous summations of the phases of what's supposed to happen in their life in the coming months (and years, and decades).

The fact is that when you dedicate yourself to a joint project with the person you love, especially a project that isn't wholly accepted socially and is even illegal in some countries, you end up adopting the submariner's perspective, to use an expression of her father's that until a short time ago she never quite understood. But now it strikes her as an accurate representation of what can happen between two people who amass a shell of intentions, convictions, and expectations to the point of finding themselves trapped inside it, convinced they can't leave without being crushed by the pressure just outside. So here they are inside the submarine of their maternity plan; the very thought of trying to get out of it makes her feel like a traitor. But what's she supposed to do, go forward out of blind loyalty? Because she's made a commitment? To make Viviane happy? Is it pure chance that yesterday she wrote that quote on one of the messages attached to the Brits' gelato, about how life is too short to spend it making other people's dreams come true? Shouldn't this dream be *hers* as well?

If she's totally honest with herself: no. It isn't. If she's totally honest, she's not at all convinced she wants to jump into having a daughter or a son, let alone in such an unspontaneous and unnatural way. It seems absurd, and even anachronistic, to find herself back in the condition of the egg-bearing hen whose future has been decided. Burdened with all the physical and moral responsibility that comes with it, the pressure of the person she loves, of other people, of society. If she thinks about it, there isn't a single one of her previous relationships in which the guy she was with didn't sooner or later make her feel the full weight of her role as breeder: either because he was terrified of her getting pregnant, or, to the contrary, because he considered it to be the end goal of their relationship. Looking at the question with a minimum of detachment and a sense of humor, it's unacceptable. Maybe it was different in prehistoric times, when the lives of human beings were determined by a struggle between intentions and circumstances in which the latter almost always prevailed. Or in the millenniums to follow, when women didn't have a choice, unless they wanted to become universally pitied old maids, or witches, or lunatics. But today?

There's a blowout: the car jolts, skids, heads for the opposite lane with a terrible rasping noise, just as a truck is coming straight for them.

"Heeey!" She screams and digs her feet in, stares in terror at the radiator grille coming toward her, increasingly large and close.

"Shit!" Viviane yanks the wheel to the right as much as she can, leans on it with all her weight, makes the wheels shriek, succeeds in getting back on the right side of the road, just in time.

The truck blares its horn furiously, rushes past in a clangor of rattling iron; the displacement of air by its enormous broadside makes the Peugeot sway.

Viviane keeps hold of the wheel to avoid losing control, brakes, pulls over, stops.

Milena Migliari's heart is racing, her blood full of adrenaline. "What happened?"

"Flat tire." Viviane adjusts the glasses on her nose, inhales deeply, counts with her fingers: one, two, three. Pretty calm, considering she just avoided a frontal collision in which both of them would have been flattened like pancakes. She puts it in first, slowly scrapes and hiccups along for a few dozen yards, stops in a dirt roadside turnoff. They both get out: there's a gash in the back right tire, it's completely flat.

"What now?" Milena Migliari feels the strangest alternation of terror and relief, for the incredibly close call they just had, and because she knows that visits to the Centre Plamondon follow a tight schedule, and that arriving even a few minutes late means seeing your appointment postponed until who knows when. She wonders whether the blowout is a sign of destiny, to abandon this whole fertilization business. Or is the sign of destiny their not having smashed into the truck? How should what just happened be interpreted? And does it make sense to try to read into these things instead of coming to a rational choice, with no need for external nudging?

"Now we change it, for crying out loud." Viviane goes to open the trunk: she takes out the spare tire, rolls it along the side of the car. She goes back to get the jack and the tool bag, sets it all on the ground.

Milena Migliari certainly doesn't consider herself incapable of dealing with practical difficulties: she regularly takes care of the equipment at the gelateria, she even managed to adjust the batch freezer by herself when one of the blades got stuck. But changing a car tire has always seemed beyond her capabilities: between the heavy lifting, the bulkiness, the resistance, the call for strength, if she had to think of one task that's better left to men, this is it. "Shouldn't we call a tow truck?"

"A tow truck? Come on. It would take half an hour just to get here." Viviane doesn't seem the least bit worried about changing the tire, just very impatient at the possible cancellation of the appointment. She takes the lug wrench or whatever the heck you call it out of the bag, positions it over one of the wheel nuts, presses down on the handle with all her strength, to no avail.

"Don't hurt yourself!" Milena Migliari realizes she's saying this partly out of sincere concern, partly because deep down she hopes that changing the tire turns out to be much more complicated than Viviane thought.

"They screw them on too tight with those damn pneumatic wrenches at the auto shops! Lazy bums!" Viviane leans against the roof of the car, brings her foot down hard on the wrench handle, literally jumps on it, succeeds in loosening the nut. She gives it a couple of turns, then repeats the operation with the next one: positions the wrench, jumps on the handle, loosens, turns.

Milena Migliari stands there watching her, half amazed, half dismayed by how fast she's managed to find the most effective method, by the angry fervor with which she's applying it.

Viviane plows forward, not stopping for a second: she loosens all the lug nuts, then places the jack underneath the car, winds the handle around quickly like a crank; the car begins to lift up.

Milena Migliari is torn between the instinct to offer assistance and the hope that some hitch might still make things take significantly longer. "What can I do?"

"Nothing." Viviane shakes her head; she's already removing the tire, already putting the spare in its place, already tightening the lug nuts, already lowering the jack, already jumping one more time on the wrench handle just to be sure.

Milena Migliari strains to pick up the flat tire, to make at least some contribution. She goes to put it in the trunk, struggling with the weight and the sense of guilt that makes her desire to be stranded at this turnoff waiting for a tow truck that doesn't come, until not only has their scheduled appointment at the Centre Plamondon definitively come and gone, but so too has the very idea of needing one.

Viviane removes the jack from under the car, folds the jack back up, sticks the wrench in its bag, goes to put everything back in the trunk, cleans her hands off with a rag. "Let's go."

"You were lightning fast." Milena Migliari regrets that her dismay is getting the better of her admiration, but that's the way it is, she can't help it.

Viviane stops to look at her with a hand on her hip, like she wants to rebuke her for something; instead she smiles, leans over to give her a kiss.

Milena Migliari is so taken aback, and so full of contrasting emotions, that her eyes fill with tears. She uses the rag to wipe her hands, too, slightly dirty from putting away the tire. "If we don't get a move on, it's good-bye appointment."

In an instant they're back on the road, accelerating as if nothing happened. Ten minutes might have passed since they got the flat, fifteen at the most.

"We'll make it, we'll make it." Viviane drives in that aggressive way of hers, shifting gears decisively; she seems in control of the situation, as always.

"You were *incredible* with that tire." Milena Migliari really thinks so, even if it feels like she's back on the road to catastrophe. But this is the side of Viviane she found so reassuring in the beginning: her ability to take on and solve problems with the same energetic efficiency she employs in her postural massages. No uncertainties, no hesitations, no doubts. That's how she was able to get the loan for the house in Seillans, despite the qualms of the bank; that's how she convinced her to give the gelato venture a shot, despite Milena's fears.

Viviane flashes a couple of looks at her, smiles, adjusts the glasses on her nose.

Milena Migliari smiles too, as she flounders between her affection for such a familiar face and the apprehension that's twisting all her internal organs. She thinks that when they started seeing each other one of the things she liked most about being with a woman rather than a man was the idea of not having to worry anymore about the children question. She was convinced she'd finally gotten free of it for good: finally brought an end to the waltz of expectations, explanations, justifications to give to herself and others, forecasts, hypotheses saturated with implications. And yet after a certain point the question has reemerged and gained ground with more insistence and determination than ever happened in her heterosexual relationships. She doesn't understand how she failed to realize it in time, was unable to explain her position honestly, instead of coming off as undecided but, all things considered, open to any eventuality. As if the priority were avoiding arguments and disappointments, and that the matter could remain suspended indefinitely, or better yet dissolve into nothing. Is this her way of being immature? Her inability to take on any responsibility greater than making delicious gelato from one day to the next? The fact remains that one moment she and Viviane were two free women happy to be together, determined to live the life they wanted without being conditioned by anyone and certainly not by each other, and the next they were trapped inside their submarine of seemingly shared intentions, with this absurd mission-like spirit. How is it possible that tender and loving sentiments have turned into an idée fixe, the idée fixe into a plan, the plan into an increasingly well-defined schedule, and that now the two of them are rushing toward its realization without any more discussion of its reasons or sense? Without being able to talk about it anymore, period?

"What are you thinking about?" Viviane looks at her quickly, shifts down a gear, accelerates with a jerk.

"Nothing." Milena Migliari tries once more to smile, but now it's asking too much of her. She looks at the tattoo on the inside of her left wrist, the two inverted As formed by a little snake that rises and falls in a circle and that stand for *Arte* and *Amore*. She had it done when she was twenty, as a declaration of intent together with her friend Luca, who died three years later in a motorcycle accident in Spain. (They weren't an item, but they were so similar, so close.) Viviane has never liked it, because she says that tattoos are an attempt to show character by those who have none, and it really annoys her to give postural massages to someone who has them. Consequently the tattoo seems like a part of herself that needs defending, just like the others.

"Are you having doubts?" Viviane turns her head again but keeps an eye on the road, continuing to drive fast.

"Why do you ask?" Milena Migliari tries to find the words to answer that yes, she is having doubts; she can't.

"Because it seems clear to me that you are." Viviane's gray eyes flash briefly behind her lenses.

"Of course not." Milena Migliari watches the houses grow ever denser behind the gates and hedges on the side of the road.

"If you want we can go back." Viviane slows down, as if she really is ready to stop the car and turn around. "I'll call and say we've changed our mind, that we don't want to do it anymore."

"No-o." Milena Migliari tries to put more conviction in her voice, shakes her head; she feels terribly not sincere, not honest with herself and with the rest of the world.

FOURTEEN

When Nick Cruickshank returns to Les Vieux Oliviers there are cars and vans of every color and shape parked at the back of the house, on the east side, on the front lawn. Among the cars parked under the shelter there's even the turquoise Bentley Continental belonging to Rodney Ainsworth, slotted in diagonally to occupy two spaces instead of one.

Nick Cruickshank tries to slip inside the house without being noticed, but Tricia intercepts him just past the entrance, flushed as if she's racing in from the front line of some combat zone. "Aileen has been looking for you for hours!"

"I was up in the *air*, all right?" Nick Cruickshank makes a slightly tired gesture; he's permeated by a sense of distance, as if a part of him is still fifty feet off the ground, still suspended between life and death.

"Yes, but Aileen needs you!" Tricia appears to be referring not simply to a specific need but to a more general one, linked to Aileen's emotional stability, perhaps to her very survival.

"And where is Aileen?" From the living room come voices and

laughter, of which stand out Wally's rasping lilt and Rodney's metallic braying.

"On the front lawn!" Tricia clearly views the task she's been assigned of dragging him in for debriefing as a mission of the utmost importance.

"Can I maybe say hello to my friends first, who've come thousands of miles to be here?" Nick Cruickshank points to the living room, but he's hardly sure he really wants to greet them.

Tricia nods, albeit with an extremely vexed expression.

In the living room Rodney, his wife, Sadie; Todd and his wife, Cynthia; and Wally and Kimberly are stationed around the mobile bar, glasses in hand; they turn toward him as if seeing him is both the most wonderful and the most awful surprise in the world, and no real surprise at all.

Nick Cruickshank goes to hug Rodney first, with the false-casual enthusiasm of several thousand of their previous embraces.

Rodney grabs the back of his neck in that classic grip of his, hard enough to cause pain in his cervical vertebrae. He breaks away almost immediately; studies him, in their usual close-up reciprocal evaluation. Rodney's hair is mysteriously thicker than last time in London, before the summer; and unlike Wally, his hairline is more or less unchanged from when the Bebonkers started out. For the hard-core fan watching him from a few dozen yards in front of the stage, or even up on the big screen, he probably looks exactly the same as when they recorded their first album, a lifetime ago.

Sadie too comes to get her hug, pressing up against him with excessive eagerness: face stretched smooth as an apple, dressed in her classic sadomasochistic pantheress style, perfumed beyond belief, as though it might help her control her husband's inclination for infidelity. Rodney's two previous wives were practically identical to her, which if nothing else demonstrates a consistency in his taste, and maybe helps her identify possible rivals before it's too late.

Next up, the hug with Todd: contact between chests and shoulders, two, three decisive slaps in the scapular region.

Todd smiles in his peaceful way, never too involved. "How goes it?"

"How goes it with you?" Nick Cruickshank *is* happy to see him, though he's aware he doesn't have much to say to him. The fact is that for years the relations among the band members have been limited to exchanges of information over the phone about times and places of recording sessions or concerts, or to playing in a studio or on a stage; the rest they leave to their agents and lawyers.

"Pretty well." Todd is fundamentally a mild-mannered guy, he's never let himself get too carried away with the idea of being a rock star. He's the only Bebonker who has nearly always managed to keep his feet on the ground, even when the others were whizzing around the stratosphere, out of their minds with worldwide success.

"Glad to hear it." Nick Cruickshank gives him an additional slap on the back. Yes, he loves Todd: who knows how many Bebonkers concerts would have come unstitched in a chaos of noise without the potent and ever-balanced beat of his drums, how many stupid arguments would have degenerated into savage brawls without his good sense.

Cynthia comes to hug him as well, with the slight rigidity that distinguishes her; she's the lone survivor of the Bebonkers' first wives, and inevitably doesn't enjoy a great relationship with the second or third spouses of the others, a fact that the generation gap only exacerbates.

Of course Wally can't pass up a chance to throw himself into the mix: he goads on the males left and right, slaps the women on the rear end. Then he makes space for himself with his elbows, raises his arms to the ceiling, and launches into his maniacal Celtic warrior cry. "Be-bo-be-bo-be-bonk! Bebonkers forever!" At concerts he invariably succeeds in transforming it into a pulsating choral crescendo that draws in thousands of people, convinced they're part of some glorious tribe, but it's clear that here no one even thinks for a second about joining in.

For a few minutes they continue to exchange displays of surprise and regret for the fact that they haven't seen each other in such a long time, though they know perfectly well they could have seen each other earlier at any moment, if they only wanted to; it's tough to imagine people with more free time and ability to travel. The reality is that for a while now their lives have taken different directions in terms of interests, friends, places of residence: apart from the music they make together, they have very little in common. It's like with any very close relationship that lasts a long time: everyone knows everyone else's flaws so well that a single gesture or word, even a change of expression, can suffice to unleash excessive reactions. They avoid seeing each other as a survival strategy: for the band and for each individual member. They probably wouldn't even play together anymore if they didn't need the continual infusions of money to maintain their expensive lifestyles; if it weren't for the fact that only together are they able to fill stadiums and generate tsunamis of public enthusiasm.

"How was the trip?" Nick Cruickshank tries to stick to current events, avoid opening the door to possible territorial conflicts.

"What?" Rodney has gone partially deaf, after decades of savage guitar work with his Les Paul. On several occasions they've measured the noise level in front of the stage during a concert, and it came out that depending on the song it ranges from 100 to 120 decibels—more or less the intensity of a jackhammer when you're holding it in your hands. A few minutes are enough to do damage, to say nothing of an hour and a half or two hours straight, multiplied by thousands of concerts, and all the other hours of rehearsals and listening on headphones, at nothing less than eardrum-busting volume. It is true that eardrum-busting volume is exhilarating, but Nick Cruickshank began wearing earplugs before anyone else was doing it, as soon as he realized how the postconcert whistling and buzzing in his ears was continuing through the night and into the next morning. Now he uses latest-generation in-ear monitors that let him hear perfectly calibrated sounds directly from the mixer, but he's quite happy he used those construction-site earplugs back then. The ear, nose, and throat doctor who does his regular checkups in London says his hearing isn't perfect, but it's not bad either, all things considered. Rodney and Wally, on the other hand, have always made a point of never taking the slightest precaution in their close encounters with the speakers; they must have felt like some sort of mythological heroes, sacrificing their auditory conduits in the great battle of sound. The result being that they now have to use hearing aids both when they're playing and in everyday life, if they want to avoid playing the wrong notes in songs, or missing one out of every four words around the dinner table; luckily they can afford the most advanced acoustic amplification technology in existence. On the contrary, Todd's ears aren't in too bad shape, maybe because nature endowed him with particularly robust eardrums, or maybe because his drum set is always positioned a little farther back from the speaker columns. Anyway, it's not like a rock musician deteriorates over time solely because of his battle wounds: Wally, for example, has lost part of his ability to invent on the bass not so much because he's half deaf but because of his general carelessness, his lack of discipline, because the only thing that interests him about music now is the money he can still get out of it. For the band it's not a problem, since he more than compensates with his legendary thumping constancy on the strings.

"How was the *trip*?!" Nick Cruickshank mimes for Rodney the gesture of gripping the steering wheel, though he knows quite well he's provoking.

"Great, but would you mind telling us where the fuck you were? We come all the way here like pilgrims, and the man of the house is nowhere to be found!" Sure enough, Rodney immediately gets offended: there's authentic bitterness in his show of indignation. Wally's presence a few steps away certainly doesn't help; during the last American tour the two of them spit on each other in the dressing room on several occasions, and at the party after the Seattle concert things would have ended badly if the security guys hadn't stepped in.

"I was fly-ing!" Instead of dropping it, Nick Cruickshank enunciates, miming two wings with outspread arms. He can't help it: the more he's aware of the risks of a provocation, the more he feels like provoking.

"Cut it out, you son of a bitch!" Rodney used to have a pretty good sense of humor, but it's worsened over time, along with the rest of him.

Nick Cruickshank thinks about how close Rodney and Todd and he were, early on: more than friends, more than brothers. Despite diverse personalities and family origins, music brought them together to the point of making them feel and think and speak and move in the same way. When their instruments were in their hands, or when they were packed inside the van going from one concert to the next, or were seated at the table for a press conference, they didn't need to discuss what to do or say, they just needed to trust in their collective instinct. Before joining forces they had each spent years of self-exclusion from family, school, peers, life in general, locked in their rooms one afternoon after another listening to blues and rock greats and trying to learn their instrument, imitating note by note with single-minded imprecision. Then they met and formed the band, and after a couple of months spent going over the classics they discovered they had a distinctive sound, born of a combination of the qualities and flaws of each of them. It was like digging in your backyard and seeing a jet of oil spurt out: their raw talent dragged them relentlessly toward their first original songs, toward increasingly intense reactions of their audiences, toward concerts in increasingly large venues.

Wally was the last to join, after a series of bassists who either weren't good enough or didn't have enough faith in the band. From their very first meeting no one particularly liked him, but he had a Fender Precision bass and a Fender Bassman Silverface amp with two fifteen-inch cones. He was already playing in clubs and making enough to live on, while they were still semi-amateurs. Despite his unpleasant personality, his technique was superb, and as soon as they began playing with him in the group, the miracle repeated itself. In the space of a couple of weeks of rehearsals he and Todd became the backbone of the Bebonkers, the pulsing and driving rhythmic base upon which the other two could blindly depend. More than a band, they became a little gang of punks, united by a bond of blood (literally: one time all four of them pricked their fingers with a pin, ritually mixed the drops, and swore a loyalty oath until death; thinking back on it now, an incredible display of ingenuousness, and ignorance of the consequences of using a whole other type of needle, for a while longer yet). Nick Cruickshank remembers the first two or three years of the Bebonkers as the only period in his life in which he felt he was experiencing the type of friendship that had thrilled him while reading Alexandre Dumas's *The Three Musketeers* as a boy. "One for all, all for one": it really was like that, the four of them against the rest of the world. Then came real success and real money and real pressure and real managers and real impresarios and real hordes of adoring fans, and the beginning of personality conflicts, power games, the comparisons to see which of them the girls liked most, who was most musically gifted, who had the authority to tell the others what to do. The original spirit declined as their fame grew; the more their fans saw them as a tightly knit group of great friends joined in a thrilling adventure, the less desire they had to stay together. Yet here they still were, in this living room: the band's original formation, an authentic exception in the world of rock, flying in the face of every well-founded prediction. Have they stuck it out on account of self-interest? Mental laziness? Because none of them has ever been able to find a true identity outside the Bebonkers (though each of them has tried, at one time or another)? Because it's simpler to keep up an act in which you don't get along with the others and yet continue to coexist, like in a marriage where the couple decides to stay together despite everything, for the good of the children? Whatever happened to that original spirit? Did it migrate to other bands? Which ones? Did it dissolve into nothing? Must they forever measure themselves against the ghost of what they were in the golden years?

"When are the other people coming?" Kimberly looks around the living room, peeks out through the sliding doors at the bustle of the gardeners and workers on the front lawn.

"Baz should be here shortly, he called from Nice an hour ago."

Nick Cruickshank points, though he isn't 100 percent sure it's in the direction of Nice.

The others nod, half of them content and half not, but Kimberly couldn't care less about Baz Bennett: she keeps staring at him like he's trying to conceal some great secret.

Nick Cruickshank gestures panoramically, to give an idea of the huge range of people on their way between tonight and tomorrow. "There's going to be a full-scale invasion, Kim, fear not."

But Kimberly has three or four specific names in her head, which for her make the occasion and justify the trip here. "When's Kate arriving?" Sure enough: here she is. "Brad and Angelina? George and Amal? The Beckhams?"

"Ask Aileen, she's the one keeping tabs on the arrivals." Nick Cruickshank turns his back to her, heads for the sliding doors. Tricia is on to him like a retriever; she follows him out to the lawn.

Aileen is over by the pool, discussing and gesticulating at the center of a small crowd composed of Tom Harlan, the editor in chief, writer, cameraman, and photographer from *Star Life*, and others whose identity is a complete mystery to him. Meanwhile, the workers and gardeners are dragging wooden structures, digging holes, awaiting instructions. Aldino turns his head this way and that to keep an eye on the various movements, though he seems a little overwhelmed by the task in the midst of this confusion.

"You were looking for me?" Nick Cruickshank comes over to Aileen. It occurs to him how in the beginning he was fascinated by her gestures: it seemed like she was painting in the air with her hands, full of unexpected resources.

"Of course I was looking for you!" Aileen turns around, her face contracted in anger, but it relaxes almost immediately. She smiles; she's only too aware of all the people around her. "We're trying to decide on about a thousand different things! Your contribution would be greatly appreciated!"

"At your service." Nick Cruickshank smiles, too, though he'd rather be off walking in the woods on his own, as far away as possible from here.

FIFTEEN

Milena Migliari sure doesn't like being inspected and probed and measured this way. Even the clinical terms have an ominous ring to them: there's not a single one that's remotely associable with a pleasant image. It would be bad enough if she were actually sick, but it seems decidedly ridiculous to be coming here healthy. And it's even more annoying that to realize this project by and for women there still needs to be some guy poking around inside you down there. She puts her underpants back on, her pants, her shoes: red in the face, extremely irritated. Viviane's participatory gaze from the chair next to the doctor's desk only serves to make her more agitated.

Dr. Lapointe has already taken off his latex gloves, he's already talking about the administration of hormones she'll have to begin on Monday and that will last for a couple of weeks, to stimulate the ovaries and prepare the endometrial tissue. Viviane is perfectly capable of giving the injections, and they shouldn't be painful, because the needles are as thin as those used in insulin shots for diabetics. After the first week they'll need to do an ultrasound every two days, to verify the number of follicles and the thickness of the endometrium; then when the follicles have reached a certain diameter and number, preparation for "pickup" will begin. Does Lapointe use the English term to show how cutting edge his center is? To give the procedure a touch of science fiction?

Viviane has taken lots of detailed notes in the previous meetings, but now she's completing and correcting them meticulously with a blue pen in her beige-covered notebook. She calmly asks all the right questions, doesn't let Lapointe be too vague or hide behind obscure jargon, strong in the knowledge that her job qualifies her as a near colleague; and being French like him gives her a further advantage.

Every time Milena Migliari finds herself in an unpleasant or complicated situation like this, on the other hand, she gets the feeling she still doesn't possess the necessary linguistic tools. Maybe it's only a question of time, but after three and a half years in France she's beginning to think she might never be able to express herself with the same command she has in Italian. Considerations like these come back to mind whenever she has to speak to someone at the bank, or to an inspector at the Health Office, or when she gets into conversations about politics or art or her life with Viviane. As things stand, it almost seems like Viviane and Dr. Lapointe are on the same side: two against one. She knows very well that that's not the case, that Viviane cares for her immensely and is acting for the good of their common dream, et cetera. But the fact remains that *she* is the one being handled and probed, and that *she* will be the one undergoing hormonal stimulation and the ova pickup in Barcelona, thirty-six hours after the administration of chorionic gonadotropin. At Viviane's request, the doctor clarifies that it will be indispensable to keep to the schedule exactly, because being early or late by even a couple of hours could provoke the release of the follicles and the failure of the entire cycle.

"There'll be an ultrasound at the time of the sampling, correct?" Even if Viviane hasn't studied medicine she deals with doctors daily: they're the ones who send her half her clients. She even prescribes ultrasounds when she doesn't want to risk compromising a joint or damaging a cracked vertebra.

"Certainly. My Spanish colleagues will give her a light sedative." Lapointe would willingly do without being pestered by this quasi-colleague, but the clinic he works for is a business, which obliges him to a certain dose of patience.

Milena Migliari wonders just how effective a light sedative can be, because she's read on the Internet that in some cases general anesthesia is used. And what does Lapointe really know about how much pain she might feel? Would he settle for a "light sedative" before having a needle jabbed into his testicles?

"And the sperm selection?" Viviane glances up from her notebook.

"My Spanish colleagues will do it, based on rigorous compatibility criteria." Lapointe seems quite proud to be part of a binational work environment. "Delivery will take place on the same day as ova retrieval."

Milena Migliari has many questions she would like to ask, but each time Viviane beats her to the punch; which seems only logical, given her anatomical knowledge and command of the terminology.

"Then the ova and the spermatozoa will be kept in a liquid culture for twenty-four hours." Viviane reads the notes she's taken, her pen ready for eventual corrections.

"Exactly." Lapointe confirms, though he's starting to look impatient. "After which my Spanish colleagues will evaluate the number and quality of the pre-embryos. The percentage of fertilized ova is on average about 60 percent, if the ova and spermatozoa are of good quality."

"Meaning?" Viviane is determined to clarify everything beyond all doubt.

Lapointe gives a slightly forced smile but continues to play along. "There's a classification by degrees. From the first, meaning excellent, to the fourth, meaning insufficient."

Milena Migliari wonders if her eggs will be of excellent quality, or only good, or insufficient, maybe as a consequence of her previously irregular life or even of some bad habit. During the first visit the doctor explained to her (just to make her feel more comfortable) that it's definitely better not to wait any longer, as her "ovocitary assets" aren't limitless, either in number or in quality, and with each passing year she undergoes an "inexorable impoverishment" (his exact words). She wonders how disappointed Viviane would be by an eventual failure of the enterprise due to the insufficient quality of her eggs; she might even go so far as to reproach her for it, turning it into a permanent shadow, ever present in the background of all their exchanges. She gets angry just thinking about it: at Viviane but above all at herself, for getting into this situation without the necessary conviction, letting herself be carried along by this stupid current of inevitability.

"And if the quality of the ova were insufficient?" Viviane adjusts her glasses, looks at the doctor in that insistent way of hers.

The muscles around Lapointe's mouth contract. "We can use the gametes from an anonymous donor, who has naturally provided written consent for their use."

"And I could be that donor." There's nothing vague about this hypothesis of Viviane's: it's the result of long evening and morning discussions, in which they've explored all the possible scenarios.

"You could be," Lapointe confirms.

Milena Migliari doesn't want to go over this point again, but truthfully, the idea of lending her uterus (and the rest of her body connected to it) to someone else's egg fertilized by an unknown person's sperm doesn't sound good to her at all. She said so clearly to Viviane more than once: the one who provides the egg should provide the uterus. After all, they both have them; and even the law prescribes it. To which Viviane replied (as always) that she is the one who brings more income to the household budget, and that she certainly couldn't do her massages with a belly out to here.

"All clear so far, right?" Viviane would clearly rather move on, not linger anymore on this particular topic.

"Uh-huh." This is the best reply Milena Migliari can come up with. Is she some kind of monster, to feel so trapped? To want to run away from this medical center and never be found? There are so many other things she'd prefer to do in the coming months rather than have a child: research new ingredients, hunt for new flavors, invent new recipes, write the book on gelato she's been thinking about for a while. She has nothing, literally nothing, against children and those who want to have them; all she wants is that they don't ask them of her, that they leave her in peace.

"Good." Lapointe is now anxious to conclude the visit; there are several other aspiring procreators sitting in the waiting room.

"And then?" Viviane has no intention of ending proceedings until she's received assurances on all points.

"Then the pre-embryos are transferred into the uterus with a catheter." Yes, Lapointe has most certainly had enough, by now he's struggling to conceal it. "Two or three days after the pickup."

"And there are three pre-embryos, on average." Viviane scrutinizes him, ready to underline or correct what she's written in the notebook in her round and regular script.

Lapointe nods. "The tendency is not to transfer any more than that, to reduce the risk of twin pregnancies."

"Which still exists?" Milena Migliari has to ask at least this, even though she already knows the answer, they've already talked about it.

"That is correct. But it's possible, as we've said, to minimize it." Lapointe writes something on his prescription pad, to underline that the time available to them has now run out.

Milena Migliari imagines finding herself with two or three alien beings in her belly, sucking the life out of her: more horror movie than science fiction.

"Okay." Viviane considers the topic closed, but still doesn't want to let the doctor go. "Side effects of the 'embryo transfer'?"

"None." Lapointe shakes his head, no longer deigning to make eye contact. "The only precaution is to stay home from work for four or five days, not lift heavy weights or exercise, not go running up and down stairs or anything like that."

"Our house is *all* stairs." Milena's tone is hopeful, as if she expects to hear him reply that in that case they're better off scrapping the whole procedure, that it's no longer even worth talking about. "We only have one room per floor. From the kitchen to the living room to the bedroom to the bathroom to the study to the patio, you need stairs to get *anywhere*."

"Just don't overdo it. It's a question of common sense." Lapointe displays one of his condescending smiles, without looking at her.

"Of course. Then it'll take a couple of weeks to get confirmation of the pregnancy, correct?" Viviane puts away the pen, closes the beige-covered notebook with the elastic.

"Yes." Lapointe signs the prescription. "We'll do the checkups here at the center. Pregnancy test with blood sample, ultrasound two weeks later to examine the amniotic sac."

Milena Migliari thinks that it's terms such as "amniotic sac" that make her cringe. But why give so much importance to a name, however ugly or vulgar it is? For what it describes, for the implications it carries with it? Is her instinctive refusal to be a breeder something to hold up with pride, or be ashamed of?

"Perfect." Viviane is already on her feet. She looks at her watch with a gesture almost identical to Dr. Lapointe's, for almost identical reasons. She too has patients waiting for her, in her studio in Draguignan; this trip to Grasse will end up costing her a good three hours of work, which she'll have to recoup later on.

Lapointe accompanies them to the door, shakes both their hands. "As we've already said, the chances of success on the first attempt are about forty percent. So just cross your fingers, and if necessary be ready to try again."

"Of course." Viviane waves good-bye, her chin raised.

"Sure." Milena Migliari nods as well.

Viviane presses a hand into her back, practically pushing her down the stairs.

And how ought this to be interpreted? Is it a display of protectiveness, or bullying? Will the fact that the gelateria still isn't in the black and that Viviane will have to pay the entire ten thousand euros for the procedure and the trip to Spain have the effect of further accentuating their division of roles? Too many questions, maybe? With the risk of getting lost in a jungle of conjectures and counterconjectures, of never getting out? Wouldn't it be better to abandon her doubts once and for all, and dedicate herself trustingly to their common plan? But aren't things like this supposed to happen spontaneously, on a wave of shared enthusiasm? Is what she's feeling only fear, as Viviane claims, or is it justifiable alarm, which she'd do better to listen to?

SIXTEEN

Nick Cruickshank usually doesn't let anyone into his studio, except for Annette, the cleaning lady, when it's absolutely necessary. An inner door connects the two rooms, the smaller one containing a desk, a chair, and the Provençal couch that survived Aileen's radical furniture makeover. In the more spacious of the two are the tailed Steinway, the acoustic and electric guitars, and other string instruments on their stands, the microphones on theirs, the speakers, the monitor, the mixer. It's the only truly private place he has in the house, where he can shut himself off and think and write and play at any hour of the day or night, when he can't sleep or doesn't want to see someone or gets the inspiration for a song. Here's yet another one of the paradoxes of his life: the bigger the house you buy, the smaller the space in which you're truly protected from intrusions.

But now he is the one who has encouraged the intrusion, because Baz Bennett has been asking him for months to let him hear the stuff he's been working on, and at this point he too is interested in getting some feedback. But they had to come up with an excuse to come here, just the two of them, without Wally or Rodney or Todd trying to latch on.

Baz looks around, in a display of respect for the creative den of the artist, mixed with the anxiety of verifying whether the artist in question is working on something interesting or merely drifting aimlessly. He has been the Bebonkers' manager for twenty years, ever since Stu Abrahams was found drowned in his hot tub in L.A.; he is the one who has sorted out their financial situation, kept them together through a thousand recurring crises, who handles the contracts, recordings, concerts. There's no doubt that he's had a decisive influence in making them all rich, and that thanks to them he in turn has become rich, but it must be recognized that his job is far from easy; very far.

Nick Cruickshank goes to turn on his Mac and the amp, fiddles around with Pro Tools, puts up on the monitor what he thinks is the most promising of the pieces he's been working on. It's a melody that came to him on octave mandolin rather than on the guitar or piano, appearing in the same mysterious way as his best songs. The problem is that it doesn't have much in common with the Bebonkers' repertoire, unless you go all the way back to the first two albums, when they were still experimenting with different sounds and instrumentation and weren't afraid to make incursions into territories distant from their rock-blues base. Before they decided that it was better to simplify matters, concentrate on a few chords played with two electric guitars, bass and drums, and the occasional addition of piano and Hammond organ, seeing as they were so good at it and the vast majority of their fans loved it. Before they convinced themselves and others that this was simply a passion for their roots, when the real reason was that looking in other directions would have required more effort and almost certainly been less appreciated by the masses. Before they passed off this closure of horizons as an admirable choice. But then hasn't everyone else done the same thing? What truly successful group doesn't endlessly repeat the formula that works, that anyone can recognize after just a few notes (until they get sick of it)?

Baz takes a few steps around as he listens, hands in his pants pockets; he seems to be studying the wooden laths of the parquet with great attention.

Nick Cruickshank is perfectly aware that he's always had a playful attitude toward what he does, at least more so than a bank manager or an engineer or a politician, and he's certainly never been one to wallow publicly in his artistic angst. The problem is that people (including fans, including Baz, who should really know better) tend to think that his work is substantially *fun*, the wonderful and gratuitous fruit of inspiration. He sometimes wonders whether it wouldn't be better for him to reveal more of the strenuous effort that goes into each and every song, even without going so far as to construct an image of himself as a martyr to creativity, like some of his colleagues (generally the most mediocre of them, and who in any case have been doing so since the very beginning); but he always concludes that it would be such an uncool thing to do, something so unlike him.

The piece finishes; Baz clears his throat as if he wants to say something, but doesn't.

Nick Cruickshank probes him with his eyes, across the silent space of the studio. "So?"

Baz Bennett raises his head, manages a thin smile. "Uh, interesting. Echoes of Irish folk, Delta blues, baroque influences, an ethnic-tribal backbone. And at the same time absolutely yours, clearly."

"I don't know. It just came to me this way." Nick Cruickshank thinks that it's not true at all that it just "came" to him: there are years of research behind this damn piece, years of listening, of experimentation, of trying things out.

"Very evocative." Baz stares at him with his poker face, like an Egyptian sphinx.

"But?" Nick Cruickshank's tone gets harsher, because it's clear as day that there's a *but* behind Baz's words.

"What do you plan on doing with it?" Baz adopts an extra-calm tone; he's well aware that at any moment he could be standing in front of a very belligerent version of his artist.

"What do I plan to do with it?" Nick Cruickshank senses a dangerous current rising within him but makes an effort to control it. "Finish writing the lyrics and record it in the studio for the next album. I've got four more in roughly the same vein."

"The next Bebonkers album?" Baz is nodding slowly, but it's like he's saying no.

"Why? Does it seem so *inconceivable* to you that we might come up with something different from the usual?" Nick Cruickshank is on the verge of yelling or throwing some nearby object.

Baz opens his arms slightly, his expression still neutral. "Well, you might want to hear what the others think of it."

"I want to know what *you* think of it!" There, he's yelling. At whom, though? At Baz? At the others? At himself? "If the others aren't interested in this type of music, I'll do a solo album!"

Baz shrugs in a way that's barely perceptible. "I told you, it's very evocative. In fact, it's gorgeous."

Nick Cruickshank starts to yell something else, but surprisingly he's overcome by a sense of futility that smothers his anger like a wet blanket. The fact is that he's already tried taking the solo road, as the others have, and it didn't work, for him or for them. Each was convinced that the Bebonkers' popularity would transfer to its individual components. They thought they could free themselves of the band, temporarily or for good, dedicate themselves to the music that really interests them. And instead they discovered that the number of fans willing to follow them on their individual paths is only a small fraction of those that flock to them when they play together. People are interested in the Bebonkers, period; every attempt to stray from the group is regarded as a betrayal, an act of egocentrism at the very least, best-case scenario as a divertissement suitable for occupying the dead periods between the band's albums and tours.

"I'm just trying to figure out what might or might not work for the Bebonkers, Nick." Baz knows that he needn't say more; fundamentally he's a good manager precisely because he's not a great person. Nick Cruickshank and the others took a while to figure out that it didn't behoove them to look for a great friend to handle their ties with record labels and concert organizers. Just think of Tim Hotchinson, who worked so hard to get them their first gigs and drove them halfway around England in his old Ford van: he fell apart as soon as it was time to go head-to-head with the big boys. Or Stu Abrahams, whom they long considered a fifth member of the band: he was well on his way to leading them to rack and ruin in the friendliest possible way when he died. The truth is that they ought to thank Baz every day, even if complaining about him has become one of their leitmotifs. When you give Baz Bennett a percentage of every pound or euro or dollar you make with your music, you certainly can't complain if he pushes you down the most well-traveled path there is. He does so with moderation, because he knows quite well that there are limits, that the Bebonkers have a reputation to uphold, the so-called artistic integrity their fans value so much. He knows quite well that if he wants to sell one of their songs for a commercial he needs to be very careful in pairing it with the product, to avoid having it boomerang disastrously. One brand of cars might work, another not at all; one chain of supermarkets yes, another no. It's all a balancing act, in which the relationship between money and image has to be evaluated with extreme care, and Baz Bennett does it better than anybody else, it's undeniable.

It's also undeniable that the fundamental reason they've kept him around for twenty years is the money, even if it's more pleasant to tell each other that their real priority is reaching the largest possible audience. And what, pray tell, might the goal be of reaching the largest possible audience? Ultimately it all translates into numbers of downloads and tickets sold, which translate into bank accounts, which translate into the number of bottles of vintage champagne Wally can guzzle like beer (after having religiously photographed and posted them on Instagram). Even Rodney has an authentic addiction to money, like he had for decades to sex and cocaine (which of course cost him handsomely); he couldn't do without his Rolls and Bentleys and Ferraris, his boats, his clothes, his guitars with solid gold knobs and black pearl decorations. Even Todd, who is much more restrained than the others, who has probably never set foot in Monte Carlo, likes having spacious and beautiful homes, collecting valuable paintings, playing golf, wearing suits cut on Savile Row.

And him? What is Nick Cruickshank's relationship to material goods? Even if he'd rather not admit it to himself, he has become a serious investor, just like the others. It's true that he often claims to value money only for the freedom it gives him, and to be able to do without 90 percent of what he has, but there are times when he has some doubts. Fortunately in his field what counts is the performance, and he's so good at performing that people believe it, even when it's contradicted by his actual life. People see the image he projects of himself onstage, pick up on the tone of his interviews, so well honed it sometimes risks turning him into a caricature. (Literally: last year Baz got a proposal from Universal to use a character based on him for a cartoon series and negotiated the deal for weeks before scrapping everything because they weren't paying enough.) There seems to be a consensus on the fact that he continues to emanate high doses of so-called rebel spirit, whatever that means at this point; he's yet to slip into the phase of desperately clinging to an unsustainable mask. All horrible false modesty aside, there aren't too many lead singers, including those much younger than he is, capable of generating the same amount of emotion with the same intensity. Even looking at himself in the mirror of his most ruthless critical spirit, he doesn't feel like his charisma has faded. His voice is still full, the tone hasn't deteriorated, the volume hasn't diminished. He still moves with the same degree of elasticity, and his endurance hasn't waned: he can be up onstage for two hours and sing his heart out without fear of his voice cracking or seeming pathetic.

Sure, but the *sense* of continuing to do it? The so-called *reasons*? How convincing can songs like "Hard Hard Hard" or "One Push Too Far" or "On the Brink" still be if the listener isn't preemptively won over to the cause? Don't all those representations of adolescent mind-sets, ranging from sexual frustration to social intolerance to childish laments, sound ridiculous coming from an adult who's been well compensated by a society against which he flung himself with iconoclastic rage in the beginning? How is an eighteen-year-old boy or girl supposed to take seriously his (generic) criticism of the status quo and his (equally generic) invitations to rebel? Yet it happens, incredibly. Is it perhaps a case of the same type of suspension of disbelief that occurs during pro-wrestling matches, where the crowd knows perfectly well that every blow and fall and look of fury or pain is fake, yet they yell and stomp and clap and cry and are thrilled just the same?

But it isn't that simple, because even if they've long since become a commercial machine, each time he and the other Bebonkers go onstage and start playing their songs of twenty or thirty or thirty-five years ago, *they believe.* Really. Maybe not at the first song, but by the second they do; or by the third. It's a question of warming up, and the music drags out their original soul, with almost the same intensity they had back then: the restlessness, the indignation, the raging desire for a different world. Despite everything, despite what they've become, despite the infinitely weaker songs they're writing now. When they play and sing their biggest hits, it isn't just the crowd that believes; so do they. Maybe this is why for years their earlier songs have occupied increasing space on the set list, compared to the more recent stuff. The effect lasts for the duration of the concert, until the final applause; then it's over, it's back to real life.

Every now and then Nick Cruickshank asks himself if the Bebonkers couldn't use the global spotlight they still enjoy to say something meaningful about what's wrong with the world *today*, instead of endlessly rehashing the same generic rebellion from three decades ago. He asks himself if they could write songs with much more specific targets: corrupt and incapable politicians, fundamentalists of various religions, multinational corporations of online shopping, communications giants, oil and tobacco companies, weapons manufacturers, great banks that sequester the people's money, conglomerates that devastate and sack the planet. Would they be able to achieve some concrete effect? To push their listeners to new forms of large-scale boycotting, of generalized dissociation from the accepted rules of the game?

He's become very skilled at answering these types of questions, whether he's asking them to himself or being asked by a longtime fan who has been allowed backstage or by journalists trying to avoid the stereotypes fashioned by hundreds of their colleagues before them. He naturally adopts an ironic tone, underlines how in today's society rebelling against the rules has become impossible, because now the rules are flexible and transgression has become a product for consumption like all the rest, on sale on every damn computer or tablet or cell phone and on every supermarket shelf. In practice what he does is recognize his own irrelevance, even if he's able to give the impression of making a social critique and present himself as a sort of social dissident, a voice in contrast with the mainstream. But for a long time now his voice and that of the Bebonkers have become *a part* of the mainstream, even if their fans refuse to admit it. When they recorded "Enough Isn't Enough" it seemed almost like a hymn to revolution, to the point that the BBC refused to air it; today it's a part of the collective soundtrack of people's lives. A few months ago they even asked him for it for a television commercial for a brand of cookies and breakfast cereals!

It doesn't take much to realize that it's best to set aside any ideas of writing a batch of incendiary songs with more personalized targets than the old ones. Apart from the lawsuits and ostracism they would provoke, and the fact that musically the songs might not be much to write home about, who would they really be of any interest to? A minuscule minority of idealists? Of utopians? Of fanatics? Would they be able to shift something in the general public opinion? It's very unlikely; even if the other Bebonkers were willing to throw themselves in with him in such an enterprise (very unlikely) and were able to overcome Baz's opposition (practically impossible), the commercial results would almost certainly be disastrous. And it's almost equally certain that they wouldn't even be taken seriously: theirs would seem like a marketing gimmick, a cynical attempt to regain a lost virginity, speculating on the wounds of the planet to freshen up their image. It would happen even if they decided to donate the proceeds of albums and concerts to charitable causes: just look at the wild accusations and ridiculous comments raining down on account of this coming Sunday's charity concert.

Most of all: *Why* should they use their music to unleash potentially devastating forces in anything more than a ritual context outside the secure perimeter of a stadium or arena? Because there are so many things going wrong in the world, so many things off-track and unacceptable? Yet they've lived long enough by now to realize that instability isn't *necessarily* better than stability, especially when you're talking about complex social systems. All you have to do is look at the Middle East or North Africa to be reminded that a despotic state is still better than a collapsed state at the mercy of the most atrocious of civil wars; or look around the West to realize that a flawed democracy is still preferable to a democracy held hostage by some freewheeling populist who's foaming at the mouth. Fanatics and aspiring dictators lie in wait behind every mob, with their nooses to swing and their hidden agendas; and it's highly unlikely they'd do any better than the ones they want to replace.

So? So that's it: the Bebonkers will continue playing "Enough Isn't Enough" with angry determination as long as they're able, and tens of thousands of people will continue jumping in the stands or on the grass in the 120-decibel sound wave, pumping their arms and going red in the face and venting all the frustration they've accumulated in their lives, then that night they'll return home exhausted and satisfied, and the next day they'll show up at work and tell their colleagues that they've gone to see the Bebonkers, who even after all these years haven't lost a bit of their original rage, to the contrary.

"You think it would be possible to get some tea with lemon, maybe?" Baz gives him his most lovable smile, which is nonetheless chilling.

"I think so." Nick Cruickshank is relieved to have an excuse to extract himself from these thoughts and this studio; he opens the door, pushes Baz into the hallway.

SEVENTEEN

Milena Migliari walks at a vigorous pace along the high road that leads from Seillans to Fayence, cut into the side of the foothills, despite knowing that the light will soon begin to fade. But she left the van in the parking lot above the shop and has no desire to stay home, as Viviane suggested before running off to her studio in Draguignan, already treating her like she's semi-incapacitated and needs to save her strength. Furthermore, she absolutely wants to check how the chestnut gelato has come out; even if Guadalupe told her on the phone that she'd followed all her instructions scrupulously, she has to see it and taste it to be sure. And even though it's highly unlikely that someone will come by for a gelato on a late Thursday afternoon, it still might happen; in such a destabilizing moment she could really use some validation of why she does what she does.

She likes walking this intensely, the way it works every muscle in her body and helps her think a thousand times more clearly than when she's shut up in a room. It also seems like a way to confirm her knowledge of the territory, step-by-step, one dry-stone wall after another, tree after tree, hedge after hedge, curve after curve. She knows this area well by now; she feels quite at home there, even if not completely. But then she's never felt truly at home anywhere: not Verona, where she was born, not even Padua, where she studied foreign languages in university or the other cities where she spent months or years studying or working or exploring the world. She has often wondered whether she'll ever be free of this stateless condition of hers, whether sooner or later she'll find a place that corresponds to her completely, naturally, effortlessly. Sometimes she's afraid that familiarity with a place is as elusive as that with people and objects, even with herself: an illusion born of repetition that generates predictability, that generates reassurance. A little like walking along this road, which she's gone down so many times that she knows it by heart, but which certainly doesn't feel like hers. All it would take is someone to yell something nasty at her from a passing car, or a dog to come out barking and growling from a yard and bare its teeth, and she would already feel lost, her compass broken.

For as long as she can remember, she's had two recurring dreams, one good and one bad. In the good one she walks slowly into the sea, and when her head is underwater she realizes she's perfectly capable of breathing normally. She feels a sensation of immense calm and euphoria in knowing she can, to dedicate herself to exploring and underwater games and acrobatics, without anyone on land being able to see her. Whereas in the bad dream she finds herself in a city or town she has no knowledge of, and she realizes she no longer has her purse with her wallet and phone and other belongings, she has no idea where to go or where she comes from or why, she doesn't remember the names of any friends or acquaintances to call for information or help; not even her own name. Each time it comes she wakes up in a state of utter anxiety, drenched in sweat and her heart racing, so scared that she's unable to fall back asleep. The two dreams usually alternate, with intervals of a few months, but lately she's been having the bad one more often. She doesn't need a psychologist to see the connections to the doubts and anxieties in her own life, the senses of foreignness and the disorientation that continue manifesting themselves.

Yet when she first came here with Viviane, the summer they met, it *did* seem like home to her: even before finding the real house they have now, when they were in the tiny rental apartment above Madame Voclain's haberdashery. Even though they were crammed into a single room with a kitchenette, and the bathroom was so small you couldn't even fully extend your arm inside the shower, with the plastic flowered curtain that clung to your wet body. Back then it never occurred to her to want more space, or a better view than the one they had, of a small courtyard with a fig tree in the corner. Back then, being at home simply meant being with Viviane; home was *the two of them*. And she continued feeling at home when they moved into the apartment on the floor above, where they now had two rooms and there was an actual kitchen in which to prepare her gelato without having to do any balancing acts.

Come to think of it, she stopped feeling at home precisely when they *bought* a home: the house with the glass-ceilinged patio, so much prettier and more solid and spacious than their previous accommodations, the one they chose as the container for their life together in the long run, rather than for a few weeks or months. What does this mean? That the only house in which she can feel at home isn't physical, but *mental*? An *emotional* house? A place intangible by definition, not permanent, entrusted to the fluctuating fortunes of sensations and emotions?

So her home is her character? Her so-called personality? Her dreams, undefined as they are? Her body, even though so many times she's wished it were different? Her femininity, with all the pleasant and unacceptable consequences that come with it? Her work? Her passion for gelato, the time and research she puts into it, the joy and preoccupation she gets out of it? If she were a man, she would probably say yes: men identify themselves so completely with what they do, like turtles taking their shells with them wherever they go. They might buy their houses, but they certainly don't take care of them; they leave that to women. And women take on the burden, out of a sense of duty or pleasure or a kind of natural vocation, even when they have a million other responsibilities; they end up dedicating to it an incredible amount of their time and energy. To the upkeep of a box, essentially: cleaning it and getting it in order and making it run and comfortable, one room to the next, one piece of furniture after another, object after object. Okay, but before she wasn't talking about homes, she was talking about *feeling* at home, about having a degree of total familiarity with a small piece of the world. Well, she never has. Not even as a little girl, not even when her parents were still together and it seemed like she enjoyed a certain degree of protection, a certain degree of definition with respect to the formless universe. From then on, wherever she's been it's always seemed like her bond with the place was precarious. Which certainly hasn't been entirely negative; knowing that sooner or later she'd be able to leave a place or situation has saved her life countless times, preserved her curiosity and desire to explore.

However, if someone never truly feels at home anywhere, how can they take on the responsibility of bringing another person into the world? Condemning her (or him) as well to never truly feeling at home anywhere? Or might bringing someone else into the world be a way to feel truly at home? Could this be the solution, to create a family? But wouldn't she feel trapped, with no way out for years and years and years? Like with Roberto, and the other guys before him, when it was just the two of them and they talked intermittently about a family on a purely hypothetical basis? The way it's happening now with Viviane, well before the so-called other person begins turning into a reality? The way it began happening when she and Viviane bought the house, and she stopped feeling at home?

It seems to her like the vast majority of people don't even pose themselves the question: apart from those who don't have a home because it's been destroyed by artillery or they have to leave it because they can no longer afford the rent, billions of people feel at home right where they are. They feel at home even in the ugliest and saddest-looking houses, the ritziest or the most conventional or the most squalid, in those that look out on the ceaseless traffic of a city boulevard or a heart-shaped swimming pool or the north side of a valley where the sun never shines. She has never tried it, but she's sure that if she knocked on a random door and asked the person who came to open it if they felt at home, they would say yes. Looking at her like a lunatic, surely, and with a show of defending their territory, proudly, underlining their identification with their home, the visible and tangible proof of their legitimately occupying a small portion of the world.

Maybe the problem is that she is not a normal person, that she's essentially a misfit, her head full of ideas that never gel with the real world. And the real world is well aware of it, and smacks her around every chance it gets, to remind her who's in charge; or tries to build walls around her, to lock her door when her instinct would be to burst out and breathe free air and gaze at the sky.

They're considerations she's made far too often, and nothing useful has ever come of them. Milena Migliari puts all her strength into her leg muscles, pushing herself forward as fast as she can. Fayence has already come into view, its houses perched on the hillside, inhabited by people who have no doubt that they feel at home.

EIGHTEEN

At ten in the evening Nick Cruickshank gets up from the table before dinner is over, with the excuse of having to make a phone call. He ignores Wally, who squawks at him a couple of times, "Who're you calling?" goes to put on a sweatshirt and jacket, sneaks out of the house without even Aldino realizing it. He doesn't have any particular destination in mind; he's only interested in getting away from all those moving eyes and lips and hands, from all those insistent and irrelevant affirmations and claims and observations that have intruded on his living space.

He slips inside the little Mazda, drives slowly with the lights off across the parking area behind the house and down the access road to the gate, presses the remote control; as soon as he's outside his relief is comparable to someone who's just broken out of prison. He turns on the headlights, continues slowly down the narrow road between the short stone walls on one side and the trees on the other, up to the fork between Mons and Callian. He hesitates for a second or two between going up toward the mountains or down toward the plain, between a thicker darkness or a more illuminated one, then turns right, toward Callian. He doesn't shift gears much, pressing on the accelerator with the tips of his toes as little as possible. Nonetheless, in ten minutes he's in town: there's no one around, it seems much later than it actually is. Without really choosing to do so he continues down the road, indolently following the descending curves. He's unable to focus on any particular thought but feels the same sense of generalized nonbelonging he felt as a small child and as an older boy, and then as an adult every time he finds himself ripping out the wires that connect him to a situation, whether out of impatience or intolerance, boredom, stupid or legitimate reasons, a misunderstanding, a question of principle, a mistake.

He reaches the low road, goes right, almost drifting. He passes beneath Tourrettes, beneath Fayence; he makes as if to continue straight in the direction of Draguignan and at the last second veers right, goes up the snaking road with the same sense of inertia he felt coming down. He gets to the town, passes beneath the arch of the town hall, continues on to the outdoor multilevel parking lot that in summer is never big enough for all the tourists' cars and now is almost empty. He asks himself for a moment whether he should continue driving and head back home, and instead turns left and parks randomly in one of the dozens and dozens of free spaces.

He gets out. The air is humid, the temperature down much lower than during the day, a mist hangs in the air. Nick Cruickshank goes down the stairs toward the center of town, passes by the windows of the summer café with its blown-up images of hamburgers and toasted sandwiches and surreally colored ice cream; by the windows of one of the many real estate agencies with photos of pseudo-Provençal villas and houses, their extremely blue swimming pools in the foreground.

Fayence is as deserted as Callian was: not a car on the main road he drove up three minutes ago. The only place open is the bar next to the store selling imitation local specialties, where several silhouettes move behind the illuminated windows; from several buildings the light from televisions filters out through the slats of closed shutters. The semi-lethargy into which the entire zone withdraws in low season is even more evident at night, the silence so dense you can almost feel it. But tomorrow some of the guests of Saturday's party will come here in search of a bare minimum of local color: they'll get a couple of restaurants to open, bring in some money, voices, gestures. There will certainly be some journalists and photographers hunting for interesting subjects, preferably in an altered state or with some illegitimate companion. There will certainly be some fans hoping for a miraculous encounter; some curious locals, some stalkers. Then on Saturday those who want to stake out their place for the concert a day in advance will arrive down at the airfield; they'll set up their tents and sleeping bags as close as possible to the stage. In spite of the decree of the mayor, who claims he doesn't want them there for health and safety reasons, but who, like his colleagues in the surrounding towns, is quite content to be part of such a major event, with the people, the television footage, the attention, the town's name in lights around the world.

The window of the Italian girl Milena's gelateria is dark, closed; the window of the jeweler's just below it, dark, closed; the window of the pizzeria below that, ditto. In the market square that three days a week plays host to stands selling fruit and vegetables and cheeses, ground-level lamps project swaths of warm light onto the sycamores and the church façade. And in the middle of the empty space are roughly a dozen people standing in a circle: they're rocking back and forth on their legs and hitting their arms with their hands, like in an extremely restrained and musicless tribal dance.

Nick Cruickshank pulls up the hood of his sweatshirt, a gesture he makes instinctively the rare times he happens to be out alone among strangers. He wonders why that circle of people is down there: Is it a flash mob of protest, or celebration? For what? Against what? And what could be the point of having a flash mob in a place where there's no one to see it besides him, who is looking on unseen from above, flush against the wall of an old building saturated with moisture? Unless they're Bebonkers fans who have arrived *three* days before the concert, intent on somehow warming themselves and passing the time. It does happen: they adapt to sleeping on the ground, in the cold and even in the rain for nights on end, just to have the privilege of marking their territory before the others, gaining a right of precedence, gearing themselves up with anticipation. But if they were fans of the Bebonkers they'd certainly have a portable stereo to play their songs on, or at least a cell phone with a Bluetooth minispeaker, or a guitar to strum; they'd certainly be launching into the usual mangled choruses, passing back and forth cans and bottles of beer, joints, chillums. But these people are totally silent, and so coordinated, absorbed.

Nick Cruickshank makes his way down toward the square with extreme caution, keeping in the shadows as much as possible. Aldino would be out of his mind if he knew: he'd give him the usual spiel about what was the point of paying him so much to handle his security, just to throw caution to the wind and expose himself to terribly real dangers for no reason. He would reply that he's exaggerating, that the dangers aren't that real, though he knows full well that they *are*: there do exist crazy fans just waiting to transform their veneration into hate. John *was* killed with five gunshots, by a guy who knew all his songs by heart and only a few hours earlier had asked him for his autograph. George *was* attacked in Friar Park, by a fan who punctured his lung with a seven-inch knife and would certainly have killed him if his wife, Olivia, hadn't managed to smash a lamp over the fan's head. Paul's bus *was* surrounded by a dangerous crowd of fans in Mexico City, and who knows how it would have ended if the police hadn't arrived in time. But it's not as if going around with a bodyguard is ever a guarantee of anything: many a Middle Eastern despot has been gunned down while surrounded by entire armed phalanxes. Absolute security doesn't exist; life in general is risky and difficult to predict.

In any case the guys in the circle in the deserted market square certainly don't seem like dangerous maniacs, though they certainly must be a little weird to be doing what they're doing in this place, at this hour. Nick Cruickshank moves a few steps closer, gets a better look at them: they're young, in their twenties, half guys and half girls. If despite everything they did turn out to be Bebonkers fans, the worst they could do would be to crowd around him and ask him for a selfie, or his autograph on a T-shirt; none of them has the physique or demeanor of the potential killer. They've set their bags on the ground in the middle of the circle to be free to move around but kept their scarves and coats and caps on to protect themselves from the humidity and cold of the night. There's a taller and skinnier one who seems to be guiding them, or who at least is the first to do the movements, which the others immediately repeat. The choreography certainly isn't much to look at: they're standing there, rocking back and forth ever so slightly at the knee; now they press their hands over their eyes and then remove the hands, then press them again. This variation too lasts for a couple of minutes, like the previous ones; when it's over they all go back to looking at each other, serious, intent. The taller guy's eyes sweep over the others, then go a little farther and spot Nick Cruickshank. The guy smiles at him, then motions for him to come join them, pointing to a spot in the circle: go over there, go over there.

Only now does Nick Cruickshank realize that he's come too close: he's within a couple of yards of them. But he isn't particularly alarmed, especially since none of the guys and girls seem to recognize him, probably because of the shadows and the mist and the yellow light, the hood he's wearing. Even the tall guy inviting him into the circle does so with an attitude of general benevolence, not specifically aimed at him; or that's how it seems, at least. Anyway, since eye contact has now been established, it would be rude as well as cowardly of him not to accept; and besides, he doesn't have anything else to do just now, if not walk farther down along the narrow and deserted streets, or go back up to the parking lot and get back in his car and drive around aimlessly, or head back home to dozens of people he has no desire to see. So he takes his place in the circle: feet planted, hands in his jacket pockets, hood covering down to his forehead.

The tall guy nods at him approvingly, then turns to everyone, with a low voice that's difficult to hear. "Now let's look at another person in the circle and smile at them." He doesn't have the authority of a leader, nor do the others seem to consider him one. He simply seems to have taken it upon himself to indicate the sequence of actions to be performed, maybe because he knows them better than the others, maybe because he was the one to suggest coming here, maybe simply because his height makes him particularly visible.

The sixteen—no, eighteen—people in the circle look at each other and smile in couples; it isn't clear whether after choosing partners or completely at random. Nick Cruickshank finds himself smiling at a lanky and pale girl, with a blue woolen beret and a gray coat with lots of buttons. The girl smiles back at him in turn:

her face is smooth, clean, her eyes are incredibly clear, devoid of any hidden intentions. He takes a peripheral glance around to see if anyone has recognized him, but they all seem to be absorbed in their smiles, don't pay him any particular attention. The couples continue smiling at each other for a few dozen more seconds: there in the circle, silent in the mist, they rock slowly back and forth, their hands in their pockets and their faces either illuminated or put in shadow by the light of the yellow lamps, and they smile.

The tall guy lowers his head to indicate that this step too is concluded; he seems neither satisfied nor dissatisfied with the results, his attitude is equidistant. He gestures, without any emphasis. "Now everyone will go to someone else in the circle and hug them."

Nick Cruickshank wonders whether the situation will suddenly lose its suspended magic just an instant before the hug. ("You're *Nick Cruickshank*! Hey, guys, it's Nick from the *Bebonkers*!")

The tall guy looks over to encourage him, but once again without insisting. He looks away almost immediately, goes to hug a really short girl, bending over a bit clumsily to put his arms around her.

Nick Cruickshank moves as well, and meanwhile a guy has set out from the other side; they meet in the middle of the circle, look each other in the eye: fortunately there's no sudden change. Again he has the impression he's looking into a face that's extraordinarily uncontaminated: the guy doesn't make the slightest attempt to project an image of himself, doesn't propose any type of exchange. They hug each other and stay that way for several dozen seconds in a manly hug, their torsos touching and their pelvises and legs apart; they give each other a few slaps on the back. Then like the others they go back to their places in the circle; they resume rocking back and forth at the knees, barely moving their arms.

The tall guy nods, in his controlled, mild-mannered way. He's not a persuader, he's not an orator, he's not a firebrand; he simply stands there in the circle, giving instructions. "Now let's hug someone else, but without looking at them first, and let's try to communicate to them the *meaning* of our hug. Only *after* will we look at them and smile at them."

There's a general pause for reflection after his words, then a rustle of movement as the people arranged in the circle feel their way one to another, eyes closed and hands out, searching for an encounter without looking for it.

Nick Cruickshank does likewise: he closes his eyes, steps cautiously until he touches someone who judging by feel and smell is a girl; but he forces himself not to look at her, like the tall guy explained. They hug each other blindly, not too strongly but holding each other tight, with the intimacy of two total strangers who are nonetheless aware of each other's forms. The fact that the hug is so gratuitous, so unmotivated by an attraction or bond of any sort, provokes a strange burst of thoughts and sensations. It's as if an infinite succession of hugs passes through his body, like in a time-lapse video, bringing with it a variety of explicit and implicit requests, which manifest themselves one after another and then dissolve. Is this the *meaning* the tall guy was talking about?

This hug lasts significantly longer than the one with the guy; it's difficult to say whether this is due to the combination of hard and soft surfaces, or because they didn't look at each other first, or because in every ritual there's the expectation of a progression, and this blind hug is more than likely the grand finale. Whatever the case, Nick Cruickshank wasn't expecting the wave of emotion that wells up inside him, the general weakening of his defenses. It's almost like starting to cry in public for no apparent reason, with the most intense feeling of loss, or rediscovery, or both simultaneously. When he tries to break away, he can't. It's unclear whether it's because the girl continues to hold him or because he doesn't really want to break away, because it seems like the moment isn't over yet, because a strange force keeps them locked together. It isn't even clear what the others are doing; there's no sound of rustling or shuffling of stepping back, let alone any final words. So he and the unseen girl continue embracing each other for an undefinable period of time, absorbed by the pressure and the body heat, in the meaning they're trying to communicate, whatever it is.

Finally they separate, with the slowness of someone waking up from an unexpected sleep; they take a step back and finally look at each other in the face, and Nick Cruickshank sees that she is Milena the Italian gelato girl. The surprise has the same unfiltered intensity as the sensations preceding it: it passes through him with the violence of an electric shock, takes his breath away.

She reacts similarly: she jumps back, with a frightened expression.

Nick Cruickshank thinks for a moment about explaining to her that he didn't have the slightest idea who she was, but at the same time he begins to doubt whether he wasn't actually somehow aware of it, imprecisely, as if through an instantaneous glance through half-shut eyelids in bad lighting.

They say nothing to each other, stepping backward until they're once more a few yards apart. But the circle game, or whatever you want to call it, is finished: the tall guy nods, with a slightly sad expression. "Now you can walk around town and hug anyone you want." The guys and girls pick their bags and backpacks up off the ground; they look around, and it doesn't take them long to figure out that around town there's absolutely no one else to hug.

Nick Cruickshank stands there undecided, then approaches the tall guy. "Where are you guys from?"

The tall guy looks at him for a couple of seconds, as though he considers the question contrary to the spirit of the activity. "Digne-les-Bains."

"And you go around doing this thing in different places?" Nick Cruickshank points to the space where, until two minutes ago, there was the circle of people who have now dispersed in various directions.

The tall guy nods, with the faintest of smiles. He collects his backpack, heads toward one of the sloping lanes of the hillside town. Those who haven't already left follow him, in silence.

Nick Cruickshank turns back to the spot where Milena the Italian gelato girl was, but he doesn't see her. The market square is empty, as if no one has ever been there, with the church façade and the sycamores illuminated by the yellow lamps in the mist. He heads back up toward the stepped lane leading to the main road, his breathlessness growing with every step: nothing. He gets to the main road, looks right, then left, and his breathlessness continues to increase, very difficult to explain: nothing, nothing.

FRIDAY

NINETEEN

OF ALL THE moments of the day, the morning is when the differences in personality between Viviane and her seem to emerge the most; Milena Migliari has realized it for a while now, but it only seems to increase with time. The fact is that for her the transition from sleep to wakefulness needs to happen gradually: she needs to sit on the edge of the bed for a moment to reflect, then slowly make her way down to the bathroom on the floor below, look at her face in the mirror, take a few moments to accept that it really is hers. Pee, wash her face, brush her teeth, go back up to the bedroom to get dressed, go down to the ground floor, pull back the orange curtains to gaze out the kitchen window overlooking the street. Calmly fill up the coffeemaker, put it on the burner, fix herself a bowl of oat flakes, add sunflower seeds and little pieces of apple or slices of banana, pour in soy milk and a little maple syrup, still immersed in the sensations of her last few dreams. It might be fifteen minutes in all, but it's important to her; being deprived of it makes her feel out of sorts.

Whereas Viviane throws off the covers as soon as she wakes up and hops out of bed, gathers her clothes off the chair, puts them on and meanwhile starts listing with total lucidity the names of patients, physical problems to be dealt with, her schedule. She goes down and locks herself in the bathroom, and in five minutes she's already on the ground floor, washed and brushed and ready for the day, anxious to drink her café latte and wolf down her rye cookies. Often in a bad mood, on the lookout for existing or even merely hypothetical difficulties, pissed off at the healthcare system or the banking system or the city sanitation system. She gets annoyed at seeing Milena still a bit hazy, not completely free of the arms of Morpheus: asks her curt questions, pushes her for precise answers. Then she jumps up from the table, goes to rinse her cup, plate, and utensils in the sink with nervous gestures, takes the car keys from the Chinese bowl on the table in the entranceway, exits the house, and goes out to the clearing where she left her car to race off to Draguignan.

When they first got together their morning routines weren't nearly so different: if they both had time they would take it easy; if one of them had to rush, the other one would hurry too. It happened entirely instinctively, without asking, without pressure. Sharing the beginning of the day was a joy, a chance to laugh together, tell each other things they wouldn't have said in other moments. Was there an effort to adapt beneath such seemingly effortless harmony? Were they conducting an experiment? Was it the natural contagion that arises between two people who suddenly become intimate?

Viviane was certainly much less pessimistic than she is now, and much less insistent; she'd spend whole minutes enchanted by her expression and her gestures, wondering at them, commenting on them. She already worked a lot back then, but the pleasure of doing things easily prevailed over the need to do them; and no sooner was she free than they would both fully share in the spirit of adventure, of traveling off the beaten path, of taking risks together. After all, they were so mutually attracted, so consumed by curiosity for what they still didn't know about each other, thrilled by even the smallest discovery. Practical problems seemed secondary or became opportunities to put their creative abilities to work; they confronted any difficulty with grace, they got past it. Even the hostile looks and muffled comments of the inhabitants of Seillans amused rather than annoyed them, made them feel like two free women challenging conventions, playing each day at inventing the life they wanted. When is it that that spirit began to change? When did *they* begin to change? Or have they simply stopped being the way they wished to be and gone back to being the way they *are*? At what point did the game of inventing turn into the effort of constructing, commitment after commitment, constraint after constraint? When is it that the lightness turned into weight?

What's certain is that daily repetition amplifies even the most innocent of mannerisms until it becomes impossible to ignore. For example, Viviane's way of clearing her throat with quick little coughs when she's nervous, or of taking off her glasses and wiping the lenses with the hem of her sweater, her napkin, the tablecloth. Or her virtuoso skill in peeling an apple in a single strip, then abandoning it there like an empty vessel on the table, the assertion of who knows what principle. Or her nightly snoring, constant as the hum of a household appliance. Or her way of pulling the covers over to her side, with almost imperceptible little tugs. All things that until a short time ago not only didn't annoy her, but inspired tenderness, a desire to help. And then?

"*Bon*. I have to run; I'll see you tonight." Viviane rattles off three or four little coughs, already at the door, already out of the house. Is she anxious about one of the financial or work issues she's been talking about ever since she jumped out of bed? Does she resent the lack of enthusiasm she senses for the whole fertilization business, for the short-, medium-, and long-term plans they'll have to share starting Monday?

Milena Migliari thinks that even the sex between them has lost the improvised and joyous quality it had in the beginning; it's become a sequence of actions directed at the achievement of a goal in the most efficient (and fastest) way possible. The mechanical side now easily trumps the emotional one; the surprise is gone, there's no longer the slightest hint of chaos. At the start it seemed like such a revolution to have shaken off the demands of a male, his silent needs, his canine insistence, the constant shadow of blackmail, the dormant violence at the heart of every gesture, the voice ever ready to rise up and overwhelm, the offers of protection concealing attempts to control. She had felt such relief at not being scrutinized in every square inch of her appearance, her way of dressing, her attention to detail, her choice of accessories, in a continuous back-and-forth between admiration and disappointment. It seemed too good to be true not to be constantly compared to a catalog of women who were sexier, taller, skinnier, with longer legs, bigger boobs, drawn from a mix of movies, ads, porn sites, workplaces, adolescent fantasies, the gossip of colleagues, the comments of friends. She was so happy not to have to adapt any longer to the predictability and invasiveness of a sexual organ that dominates every choice and behavior of its possessor, and that in certain moments is a weapon, in others an unwieldy tool, in others a distressing proof of weakness. She had so often talked and laughed with Viviane about those stupid anatomical protuberances and the disproportionate importance they hold in men's lives, their thoughts, their language, in their constant comparisons with their fellow men, their pathetic boasting, their latent insecurity, in the exhausting anxiety of maintaining or improving a hierarchical position. She had so willingly done without the declarations of strength alternating with demonstrations of cowardice, the devouring egocentrism that gives way to losses of confidence, the self-importance that gives rise to consternation, the scholastic displays of knowledge followed by admissions of ignorance, the rationality that hides emotional incapacity. With Viviane she had felt free for the first time simply to be herself, with all her virtues and flaws, together with someone who finally really understood her mentally and emotionally and physically (instead of only pretending to understand for a few minutes, in times of crisis), because she too was a woman. It seemed incredible that she'd never thought of it before, never considered the possibility of an alternative to falling time and time again into the same trap.

They lived for months on end without making plans that weren't from one day to the next, sometimes one hour to the next. At night they would talk, make love, laugh, dream of taking trips and doing the most improbable things. Viviane was still perfecting her postural massage technique, working in various medical and sport centers in the area, or at patients' homes. Milena, on the other hand, found a short-term job in a pastry shop in Fayence, and experimented with new gelato recipes in the kitchen of their small rented apartment whenever she had the time. They had very little money, but neither of them worried too much about it; they were sure they would always find a way to get hold of what they needed.

Then what happened? Between them? To them? What the heck happened? And where do they think they're going now, with all this pushing and resisting and dragging? Toward a consolidated family, not much different from the ones they come from? Toward an increasingly defined and enduring division of roles? Must a relationship between two women inevitably re-create the dynamics of one between a woman and a man, purely as a matter of survival? Given that two women in a world of men are in a condition of vulnerability regardless, no matter how evolved and emancipated and independent and intolerant of constraints they might be? Is it possible that, in order not to be overpowered by men, one of the two women is forced to become at least a little bit of a man herself, even against her will? In order to survive the warpaths created by men, so that at least the other woman is free *not* to be a man?

You need only look around to realize that the world is perpetually on the brink of an involution of behavior, language, mental imagery, in which women are guaranteed to get the short end of the stick. There are entire religions that dedicate themselves full-time to denying women's rights or attempting to chip away at or revoke those they've already obtained, to force women back into a condition of domestic servants and procreators. There are entire military organizations, both terrorist and otherwise, whose primary goal is to force human relations to regress toward a system of bullying in which women will invariably find themselves on the lowest rung. There are entire industries that with the support of national governments produce and sell arms to all sides in any conflict, so that males can enjoy killing and destroying with the joyful cruelty of children whose bodies have grown up but not their minds. There are entire obscure networks that provoke and direct the movement of people and profit from it more than from heroin, and push hundreds of thousands of males of a medieval mind-set to look for easier lives in countries whose values they despise, first and foremost the freedom of women. There are entire political parties whose reaction to barbaric threats consists of slogans that regurgitate words no less barbarous. At the slightest occasion, there are displays of primitive manliness: fists pounding against chests, feet stomping the ground, guttural voices rumbling, martial uniforms and parades, beards and turbans, fists and clubs and pistols and rifles raised to provoke fear.

So? Will Viviane always have to be the one who elbows in the ribs someone guilty of pushing in a train station, kicks in the balls some pig who cops a feel in a supermarket, raises her voice with a bully who tries to steal a parking space? And then, once they're home, oppresses her in a way very similar to what a man would do?

Milena Migliari eats another spoonful of muesli, wipes the soymilk from her lips with the back of her hand. She chews slowly, trying to concentrate on the consistency and flavor of the oat flakes and raisins and hazelnuts, but she can't, not one bit.

TWENTY

NICK CRUICKSHANK PRACTICES time and again the first notes of Beethoven's Sonatina in C Major for mandolin and fortepiano that he's considering playing at the party tomorrow, if his mood and the general atmosphere and the sound system were to miraculously (and improbably) come together. It's a fast piece, and the damn arpeggio in C forces you to stretch your hand out to the utmost, makes your fingers skip rapidly over the capos, careful not to produce dirty or muffled notes. It might not present great difficulties for a classically trained mandolinist, unless you wanted to play it twice as fast, like that virtuoso fool on YouTube. But it's a challenge for a rhythmic guitarist and slow learner like he is, and requires a great deal of effort. This might also be why he likes the mandolin, in addition to its being so small and portable: for the way it forces him to get out of his comfort zone, free himself of the automatic reflexes of when he's playing the guitar.

But then he was already fascinated by a variety of instruments during the production of the Bebonkers' first few albums, and often snuck them into the arrangements of their songs, even if every time he had to overcome the others' veiled opposition. They might have been in the studio working on a really fast boogie-woogie, and he would snoop around in the room next door, where a xylophone was stored for some other recording session. He would try banging the mallets on the wooden bars without knowing exactly what he was doing, and intriguing ideas would appear to him as if by magic. So he'd go back to the others, with the attitude of someone completely sure of himself: "I'm going to play over it with a xylophone." The others would snigger and shake their heads, tell him that the xylophone didn't have a damn thing to do with the boogie, and that even if it did he didn't know how to play it. But he would put his foot down and force them to give it a try, and by the second or third attempt it would work: the xylophone would end up producing a sound that was distinct from that of the countless other bands that had their exact instrumentation. In almost all of the Bebonkers' songs from the golden years, there's an unusual instrument adding color to the atmosphere and creating surprising shadows and reflections: a bouzouki, a dulcimer, a sitar, a Celtic harp, a tenor sweet flute, an oboe.

Is his recent passion for the mandolin a pathetically late attempt to get back in touch with his freer and more creative self of the first few albums? A conscious attempt to replicate what he created thirty-five years ago without really thinking, going on pure instinct? To wash away his guilt for acquiescing to Rodney and Wally and Todd and settling for the so-called Bebonker sound? To reduce the clutter of his instruments to a minimum, just when his life in general seems headed in the opposite direction? Isn't it paradoxical (yet again) that he's worked so hard for so many years, writing songs and recording them and churning out one album after another and one tour date after another without a day of respite, to be able to afford an instrument collection that occupies several rooms in several houses in several different places and countries, and he now finds himself playing almost exclusively a Canadian mandolin that weighs so little and takes up so little space? If nothing else, it maintains the calluses on his fingertips and the agility of his finger movements. But for Sunday's concert he'll leave it at home, locked safely in its case; no Bebonkers fan shall suffer the disappointment of seeing him onstage with anything other than a Stratocaster or Telecaster over his shoulder.

But what's the point of learning Beethoven or Bach or O'Carolan by heart after listening to them dozens and dozens of times in different versions since he can't read the sheet music, after figuring out the fingerings and hand positions all by himself, sensing the connections between scales and arpeggios with which he has no familiarity? Might some of these elements someday surface in an original song of incredible beauty? If that occurred, would the other Bebonkers agree to play it, given that it would almost surely have nothing in common with their current repertoire? Baz's reaction yesterday was telling: they certainly would not. And the same would be true for the fans, seemingly determined to demand an infinite repetition of their classics. Is this immersion in music that isn't his, with an instrument that isn't his, merely the umpteenth attempt not to accept who he's definitively become, rather than continuing to imagine who *else* he might have been?

Nick Cruickshank continues to play despite the knock at the door. But they're insistent, so eventually he opens the door, very irritated.

It's Aldino, with the half-angry and half-embarrassed expression he has whenever he'd like to rebuke him for something but doesn't dare. Last night he went berserk after discovering that Nick had left the estate on his own; upon his return he found the Italian waiting at the back of the house with a flashlight in his hand, agitated beyond belief.

"I needed to take a spin on my own, okay?" Nick Cruickshank goes on the attack, the best form of defense.

Aldino shakes his head. "I didn't want to talk about last night, I wanted to talk about tomorrow."

"What part of tomorrow? There are several." It's not that Nick Cruickshank wasn't thinking about tomorrow: for *weeks* his head has been pounding at the idea of tomorrow, with all of its implications. For *months.*

"Well, the security, no?" Aldino has now been working for him for eight years; between the two of them there's always been a sort of role-playing game, the restless protectee and the patient protector.

"What's the problem with the security?" It seems to Nick Cruickshank that of all the aspects of tomorrow, the security is the only one he couldn't care less about.

"Eh, there are lots of them." Aldino has a really hard time being optimistic; maybe that's why he's good at his work. "Allard will be here shortly from Monte Carlo for the inspection, but we already know we'll need men at the gate, behind the hedges, in the house, on the lawn in front of the house, at the edge of the woods. Then there's the question of the local police. Threadbare crew, same goes for their equipment. If, God forbid, we get any nasty surprises, I don't know—"

"What type of nasty surprises could there be?" For a moment the idea that there could be a nasty surprise tomorrow seems almost *desirable*, a glimmer of hope to latch on to.

Aldino raises his chin, opens his arms slightly. "Anything from the lone maniac loser that pops out of the woods, to the commando of three or four well-trained men who smash through the gate, a van with reinforced bumpers, Kalashnikovs, grenades, and the like."

"Christ, Aldino." Nick Cruickshank can't help laughing, because he's reminded of his paranoid reaction toward the workers in the olive grove the other morning; he remembers how stupid he felt.

"It's really not funny at all." Aldino remains perfectly serious, as well he should—that's what he's paid for. "Sunday at the airfield will be even worse, because there we're naturally talking about many, many, many more people, in a completely exposed area. With roads on two sides, anyone can come and go as they please."

Nick Cruickshank forces himself to be serious; he nods, shoves his hands in his jeans pockets. He thinks about when the Bebonkers did their first tours without a shred of private protection, and had to trust in a few local cops, completely unprepared to handle the out-and-out assaults directed at the stage by young men and women viscerally determined to get their hands on the clothes or hair or *chunks* of anyone in the band who came within reach. He thinks about the hysterical yelling, the crazy looks, the gestures in front of the stage by people who seemed possessed, without the slightest barrier in the way; and how all that was set ablaze by his performances, in a tide of primordial energy flowing in both directions. As lead singer he was the main target, but even Rodney had his out-of-control cannibalistic idolizers, even Todd and Wally; more than once their strong legs had been the only things that saved them, carrying them out to their cars and back to the refuge of their hotels just in time. But they wouldn't have complained about it back then: it was a crucial part of the rock mystique that had pushed them inexorably to where they were now. Before the manhunt became an annoyance and then a genuine nightmare, they'd found it exciting, the definitive consecration of their star status.

Today things have changed significantly, among teams of

bodyguards with earpieces, elevated stages, metal barriers, precautionary distances. The price to pay for security has been a loss of contact, not just during concerts but before and after as well: permanently. Nick Cruickshank thinks that between him and his audience there's now a permanent shield; the dangerous thrill of physical contact that can degenerate from one moment to the next is long gone. He's actually glad that for a couple of days there's a little more risk, for once, in spite of what Aldino might think.

TWENTY-ONE

MILENA MIGLIARI IS working once more on her batch of chestnut gelato, since she wasn't too happy with the one from yesterday. Not because Guadalupe didn't follow her instructions properly, but because she did so too well, without taking the liberty to add a personal touch. The fact is that you can teach almost anyone the practical part of a procedure, but you can't teach the *creative* part: that depends on the individual's personality, on their particular combination of qualities and flaws, on how they react to circumstances. Maybe you wake up one day with a dislike for a certain flavor and the atmosphere and stories it carries with it, or you discover you're missing an ingredient and don't have time to find it, so you use another, risking a different combination, changing the entire equilibrium. That's how she has stumbled on some of her best flavors, that's why she always needs to leave herself a margin for improvisation when she's working: to allow herself to be inspired by sight, smell, the weather, the temperature, the mood of the moment, the thoughts passing through her head, even the music coming out of the radio.

Now, for example, the radio is playing "Enough Isn't Enough" by the Bebonkers, with the slightly hoarse but warm voice of that Nick Cruickshank over the urgent rhythm of the bass and drums and the harried chords of the electric guitars, and without thinking she throws a pinch of salt into the mix, and a dash of white pepper as well, to contrast with the sweetness of the cream. As always she doesn't use a scale, measuring amounts on a long-handled spoon, on a small plate onto which she grinds up the fresh ingredients. It's not extreme changes that get you interesting results; it's the tiny deviations from the norm, the almost imperceptible touches that you really feel.

Guadalupe watches her, perplexed as always when she sees her stray from a proven recipe. She still doesn't really understand why yesterday's gelato didn't receive full approval, though it had no evident flaws and tasted good to her. ("What do you mean it's good but not *interesting*?" she asked late yesterday afternoon, after Milena calmly tasted a spoonful and commented on it. "That there's nothing *new* about it," she replied, knowing it might have seemed like a slightly enigmatic observation.)

Milena Migliari reaches over to turn off the radio, because now the rhythm of the song is making her feel anxious. Or maybe it's the words or the voice. Or maybe the song has nothing to do with it, and her anxiety stems from yesterday's visit to the Centre Plamondon, from her thoughts racing forward to Monday, to next summer, to a future that no longer seems her own. She tries to focus exclusively on what she's doing: on gestures and steps, on the slow amalgamation of the ingredients.

But there's someone knocking on the glass door of the shop, like the other day; her heart suddenly accelerates. It occurs to her that she has been expecting it, fearing it; since the other day, since last night. She can see Nick Cruickshank peeking into the lab, smiling at her in that way of his that seems so spontaneous but might be carefully crafted for effect. She can already hear the voice that was singing so angrily on the radio two minutes ago making interesting observations about her gelato and her life, apparently sincere but potentially the product of a bored mind that's accustomed to ignoring personal boundaries.

"Someone's at the door." Guadalupe motions toward the shop.

"I heard. Ignore them." Milena Migliari puts a pinch of dill in the chestnut gelato batter; her heart keeps beating irregularly, though she tries not to think about it.

"What do you mean, ignore them?" Guadalupe raises her head. She doesn't get it.

"This is not a frigging drawing room for chitchat!" Milena Migliari's tone comes out much too harsh, but she's agitated, and furious with herself. What was the meaning of the hug with Nick Cruickshank last night in the market square? Was that innocent, too, like the kiss on her forehead in the morning? Judging by how she feels right now: no. Or how she felt at home, tossing and turning in bed, her head and body full of contradictory impulses. The very dynamic of the hug has uncertain contours, as much as she keeps forcing herself to reconstruct it precisely, which might be partly explained by the fact that they both had their eyes closed. Before they had them open, though. Did they really not recognize each other as they were standing there in the circle, half shivering, among the shadows and lights and mist? There were eighteen people in the circle: What were the odds that the two of them, out of everyone, would come to be locked in an embrace? Did he aim for her intentionally? Did *she* maybe aim for him, without realizing it? Did she let herself get pulled into a stupid magnetic current, already worn out by the two intense hours of folk dancing in the room under the town hall? And what was Nick Cruickshank doing there, among the huggers from Digne-les-Bains? Had he taken up position like a predator? But why should someone like him be interested in preying on someone like her, with all the far more suitable and willing victims he can certainly dispose of? Out of a slightly perverse taste for hitting on a woman who doesn't like men? Even though in truth he had no way of knowing? Even though it seemed like there was absolutely nothing perverse about their hug? Even though it seemed like the *purest* hug she has ever experienced?

The rapping of knuckles on glass keeps coming from the store's door, increasingly insistent: it simply won't stop.

"What do we do?" Guadalupe now looks almost frightened; she clearly perceives Milena Migliari's agitation.

"Go see who it is, tell them we're closed. There is a sign and everything, for goodness' sake." Milena Migliari hates the idea of being so shaken, but she's simply unable to calm down. Maybe the idea of everything that has to happen on Monday has destabilized her even more than she imagined, it's throwing her completely out of whack. Yesterday she had constant mood swings, and now she has this irregular heartbeat, this shallow breathing.

Guadalupe goes into the shop but doesn't follow instructions; she opens the door. A voice says, "Were you planning to leave me outside?"

And it's certainly not the voice of Nick Cruickshank: it's the voice of Viviane. A moment later she appears at the lab door, all smiling and gushing. "Hey, *ma poulette*! How's it going?"

"Good." Milena Migliari is shocked, because she would have placed Viviane at work in her studio in Draguignan at least an hour ago, because they're not in the habit of surprising each other like this, and because she feels a kind of absurd and unjustified disappointment.

"I wanted to show you something!" Viviane waves a hand back

and forth in front of her, continues smiling, excited in a totally atypical way.

"What?" Milena Migliari steps back a couple of inches, defensively, because she's almost positive that the something has to do with their appointment on Monday at the Centre Plamondon, and everything that will follow.

"Look at this! *This!* It's right in front of your face!" Viviane slows the movement of her hand, thrusts her left wrist forward: on the inside of it, in the same place where she has hers, is an identical tattoo, the two inverted As formed by a snake that's slithering wave-like over a transversal line. A real tattoo, not drawn on with a pen as a joke, and freshly done, with the soothing cream on it to protect the skin made hypersensitive by the needle.

Milena Migliari is lost for words: it's the last thing in the world she would have expected from Viviane, after all she's heard her say about the ugliness of tattoos and the stupidity of the reasons for getting them. They've even argued about it several times, when she was defending hers, together with the idea that it can be nice to leave a permanent sign on your body that reveals a side of your character or a glimpse of your dreams.

"*Arte* and *Amore*, no?" Viviane continues showing off her left wrist, doesn't stop smiling. She's trying to pass it off as a caprice, but her eyes are watering behind her lenses; it's not often that she gets this emotional.

Milena Migliari makes as if to say something, but the thought that out of love for her Viviane could have done something so contrary to her own nature pours over her like a bucketful of ice water. It's a small tattoo, and on a part of the body that isn't very visible, but what's overwhelming is the degree of dedication it reveals. Milena Migliari's eyes fill with tears; she bursts out crying, uncontrollably.

"Hey!" Viviane comes over to hug her, holds her tight. "If I'd known it was going to have this effect on you, I'd have thought twice about it!"

Milena Migliari shakes her head, sobs, struggles to catch her breath; she knows full well that Viviane must have thought about it not twice but a *thousand* times before overcoming the resistance of her well-rooted convictions and making up her mind to do it. She leans her head on her shoulder, her facing sinking between coat and sweater, still crying. "You shouldn't have."

"But I was happy to!" Viviane pushes her back to look at her: some tears slide down her face as well; with two fingers she wipes them away from under her glasses. "I thought it was something nice. Right now, no? I went to that patient of mine who has the tattoo parlor in Callian. I showed him the picture of your wrist I had on my phone!"

Milena Migliari would like to stop crying, but she can't; the more she thinks about it the more she cries.

"It's identical to yours, no?" Viviane grabs her left wrist to compare it with her own, puts them side by side.

"Yes." Milena Migliari nods, sniffles. The two tattoos really are almost identical, though hers is slightly discolored with time and Viviane's seems a little smaller, with the As a bit narrower, maybe because her wrist is a little wider.

"So, I have to run, otherwise my clients will kill me!" Viviane lets go of her wrist, gives her a kiss, shakes off the emotion. She nods to Guadalupe, standing by the refrigerator, observing in silence; in a few steps Viviane is out of the lab, out of the shop.

Milena Migliari takes a piece of tissue paper out of a box, dries her eyes, her cheeks, blows her nose.

Guadalupe looks at her, her eyes a bit teary as well. "I would never have imagined Viviane getting a tattoo."

"Me neither." Milena Migliari blows her nose again, looks up at the ceiling to stop the tears. Is her reaction excessive? Has she been overwhelmed more by her own feelings of guilt than by the emotion, because of how she is not equally willing to overcome her own natural resistance in the name of a joint project? Is her resistance really even natural at all, or is it just fear, or excuses dictated by egotism?

"Anyway, it was such a romantic gesture. Really." Guadalupe fans herself with her hand, as if to dissolve the emotion.

"Yes, really." The strangest thing is that as soon as she says it, the possibility dawns on her that Viviane's gesture might not have been a romantic outpouring at all, but an act of *seizure*. These consecutive thoughts are so radically different that they throw her completely, nearly make her drop the ladle.

"Everything all right?" Guadalupe looks at her, apprehensive.

"Can you lock the door to the shop, please? Before anyone else comes in?" Milena Migliari tries to refocus on the batter, but she can't. The surge of emotion comes back to her, she nearly starts crying again, and a moment later the tenderness once again gives way to confusion, the confusion to anger. For a few minutes it seems like she can interpret Viviane's gesture both positively and negatively, like those hologram postcards whose image changes depending on how you hold it. But the more she thinks about it, the more the second interpretation begins to gain ground. She turns over her wrist, looks at it: these two mirror-image As belong to her life before gelato, before France, before meeting Viviane during that torrid summer, vibrant with cicadas. They're traces of a part of her that in Viviane arouses incomprehension, sometimes hostility, maybe because she has never really wanted to share it. The truth is that Viviane has always *hated* this tattoo, claiming she hated tattoos in general; and rightfully so, moreover, because the part of her this tattoo represents is the part Viviane will never be able to possess. She would certainly have preferred to have her get it removed, instead of having to copy it: a couple of times she even suggested it, talking in a falsely casual tone about her client who has a workshop in Nice where they do tattoo erasure with the Q-switched lasers, without leaving any marks.

Milena Migliari grinds more kernels of cardamom, more white pepper into the chestnut gelato mix. The more she thinks about it, the more her ideas become muddled. One moment it seems like Viviane's gesture is emotional blackmail at the very least; the next it seems once more like an act of extraordinary generosity. One moment she feels like the victim of an act of cannibalism; the next like an ungrateful monster. She sways from one interpretation to the other, breathless, unsure.

"Aren't you adding too much pepper?" Guadalupe looks increasingly concerned.

"I don't know." Milena Migliari sticks a teaspoon into the mix, brings it to her mouth, tastes. Yes, of course: there's too much pepper, too much cardamom, too much salt; the chestnut flavor is ruined. Even trying to consider it as an unconventional interpretation, it doesn't work, it's not pleasurable, it's awful. She takes the mixing bowl, dumps the mix into the sink, turns on the faucet, washes it all down the drain.

Guadalupe watches her in dismay, like she's just witnessed an act of pure lunacy.

Milena Migliari turns defiant in her own defense, but she's demoralized to the depths of her soul. "We all make mistakes, okay?! And we'll go on making them!"

Guadalupe nods; she probably thinks her employer is pretty unstable.

TWENTY-TWO

NICK CRUICKSHANK LOOKS out, from behind the slightly pulled-back curtain of one of the windows in his studio: the lawn in front of the house has turned into a frenetic construction site, with workers, gardeners, and electricians setting up gazebos, pavilions, small arches, floral galleries, tables, bars, a small stage, heat lamps, lighting, projectors, speakers. Aileen is going back and forth from one point to another, indicating, explaining, gathering small groups of people, dispersing them, conspiring with her holistic consultant named Fiona, her architect friend just in from Antibes, with the head of catering who has arrived from Nice, with Tom Harlan, with the *Star Life* team, with Nishanath Kapoor, who came out with a thousand requests concerning his role tomorrow before his feet even hit the ground. Farther in the distance Aldino, with his long strides, is sweeping the perimeters of the lawn, the woods, and the olive grove along with his colleague from Monte Carlo; it's understandable that Aldino won't start to relax until all the reinforcements arrive, because already the situation seems difficult to control.

Nick Cruickshank realizes he's torn between his admiration

at the thought of Aileen's ability to handle so many details with so much commitment, and his distress for the exact same reason. How can these two sentiments be practically equal in strength, the former not easily prevail over the latter? And why find suddenly distressing traits of Aileen that he's always valued, like her amazing persistence, her ability never to lose sight of a single goal she sets herself? What did he expect, that she have an on/off button in her head, to switch from the multifunctional frenzy of when she's out and about in the world to an absorbed and even slightly absent-minded tranquillity when she's at home with him? Is it the most isolationist part of him that feels besieged, the one that repeatedly holes up somewhere and cuts ties with the rest of the world, with the excuse of creative needs?

How is Aileen supposed to be in order to satisfy him 100 percent instead of 50? More devoted to him? But she's *extremely* devoted: she's able to solve any practical problem he runs into in the blink of an eye, put to rest any of his artistic doubts with a few words. Calmer? But Aileen being calm is simply an oxymoron: if he saw her lounging poolside on a chaise longue his first reaction would be to call her doctor, or at the very least her holistic consultant. Should she at least now and then be able to set aside her super-organizer vocation? But no one is really capable of changing; he of all people should know. He even wrote one of his best songs about it: "Stop Looking for a Stripeless Zebra (You'll Only Get a Donkey)."

But how come he accepted without argument the idea of the posh party here at Les Vieux Oliviers? With a few initial misgivings, but nothing more? With *lots* of initial misgivings, fine, but all retracted in the face of Aileen's stubbornness? So as not to disappoint her? For the sake of domestic harmony? How come he didn't counter with a proposal of a simple and secret ceremony, perhaps on a tiny Greek island? Because he knew that she would have taken it as an insult, a reduction in status compared to his previous two wives (who certainly didn't go into hiding for their weddings)? Could he have unconsciously gone along with it solely to bring the situation to a head? One thing's for sure: on a small Greek island Aileen would not have been able to give free rein to the inexhaustible enterprising spirit she's currently putting on display, out there on the lawn. And *Star Life* wouldn't be there sponsoring and making public every detail, there wouldn't be the famous guests (at least not the ones he loathes), there wouldn't be all the chatter there's going to be about the two of them, her, Anti-leather. But Aileen is certainly no opportunist, certainly no social climber: her family background is more than solid, she was worldly wise long before getting together with him, she's now a very successful entrepreneur. She certainly doesn't need an occasion like this to garner herself more publicity. Does she?

Nick Cruickshank is suddenly reminded of the circle of huggers from last night: the smooth, disconcerting innocence of their faces, the lack of ulterior motives in their expressions, the total absence of poses or airs. All right, they were all in their twenties, almost certainly still living with their families, still free of the working world, the pressing responsibilities, the wear and tear of all that's tiring and ugly about real life. It would be nice to see those huggers again in five or ten years; many of them probably won't be so picturesque anymore, unless they've become vagabonds or saints. A couple of them might be genuine and not temporary idealists who never develop the craving for material goods or social recognition; but idealists are boring. They show off their moral superiority, always have something to teach you; in the long run they become unbearable. Like Milton Jernigan, who in the 1970s wrote two or three beautiful sad songs and about twenty mediocre sad songs and succeeded in becoming a cult figure because, after a certain point, he refused to collect his royalties and lived like a bum, before hanging himself from that tree in Kinver Forest.

And Milena the Italian gelato girl? She isn't a twentysomething leeching off her family, and neither does she seem like an idealist with a head full of moral, political, and artistic clichés. Yet last night she seemed just as uncontaminated as the others in that circle; she didn't seem to be asking for or proposing any type of barter either. Ditto when he went to visit her at the gelateria to tell her he had never tasted such delicious gelato in his entire life. She smiled, sure, but not smugly; she rushed to change the subject, talk about something else. But what does he really know about her? He's seen her three times: the first they barely said hello, the second they spoke for a couple of minutes, the third they didn't say a word. Is he attributing imaginary characteristics to a total stranger just because she doesn't easily fall into any of the human categories he knows? Just because at the moment he feels like he's drowning?

It wouldn't be the first time he's invested unfounded expectations in a woman with whom he barely exchanged a few words (or none at all), merely on the basis of her features or her way of moving, a look, a gesture, even an unconventional piece of clothing. Maybe without even having seen her up close, letting himself get carried away by what he thought he glimpsed from a distance. How many damn times has he been sure he saw something? How often has he come up empty-handed? It's a childish attitude, no doubt about it, and it's been the cause of numerous embarrassing situations, and others decidedly regrettable. He remembers all too well the dizzying falls upon waking up to reality, the mutual disappointment; the endless confusion, the feeling of being the biggest idiot imaginable.

And anyway, this Milena might very well have a bizarre relationship with her work and maybe with the world, but when he kissed her on the forehead in her gelateria he clearly felt her stiffen. Last night, too, when purely by chance they hugged each other in the market square in Fayence and then opened their eyes and discovered each other's identity, she didn't seem content in the slightest. You only have to encroach on her safe distance, and there's resistance in her looks and gestures; it's there. Maybe in a different moment he would have seen her as a challenge to try to overcome, but not now. He's long since ceased to be the sentimental pirate who seeks out difficult women and uses them and then forgets them the day after without worrying about the consequences, if he ever was. Why has she popped back into his head now? And before? Because of the strange coincidence that he ended up hugging her, of all the people in that circle? But her gelateria is a few steps from the market square; there's nothing that strange about her passing by after closing up. And there were nineteen people in the circle, him included: the chances of hugging her weren't really that small. Does it depend on the fact that the other day when she brought the gelato with her van and he saw her next to Aileen they seemed like women with *opposite* physiques, characters, mannerisms, clothes, everything? That between these two feminine opposites it seemed, if only for a moment, that all his approval went to *her*, instead of to Aileen? That it *ran* to her in a way that wasn't thought out at all, but purely instinctive? What was it, another manifestation of his ridiculous idea that there might be some sort of miraculous encounter awaiting him, somewhere, sooner or later? It's another symptom of that drowning syndrome, no doubt about it.

Nick Cruickshank sneaks out of his studio, goes down the hallway as quietly as he can, careful not to be seen by the guests who are chatting and chuckling and guzzling in the living room, hoping to find refuge in the kitchen, in the protected and comforting kingdom of Madame Jeanne.

But of course the guests see him, just when he thinks he's managed to slip away unscathed: Wally points an annoying finger at him. "Hey, Nick! Where the fuck are you sneaking off to?"

"I have to go check on something," Nick Cruickshank forces himself to respond politely, when he'd really like to tell him to mind his own goddamn business, to keep right on swigging that eighteen-year-old Jameson of his and leave him the hell alone.

Wally sneers; he's always been the most invasive and insistent person he knows. It isn't simply stubbornness mixed with a lack of tact: when Wally wants something he starts hammering away and hammering away and doesn't quit until he gets it, and to hell with any other considerations. It's what's made him the bassist he is, with that unrelenting, incessant, obsessive style that earned him the nickname "The Wall." And that's how he's gone about attaining everything he has today: joining the Bebonkers even though the others didn't like him, forcing his musical ideas into their arrangements even when the others weren't sure about them, investing his money in surprisingly profitable mutual funds even when his financial consultant didn't agree, bedding hundreds or maybe thousands of poor groupies who would have preferred anyone else in the band, marrying nearly identical women three times in a row, all of whom at least at first found him revolting. His uncommon invasiveness and insistence have produced such impressive results, and for so long, that he doesn't have a reason in the world to abandon them: not a one. "That horseback ride you promised us? When the fuck are we doing it?"

"Eh, I don't know." Nick Cruickshank would like to shove him to the ground, like Rodney did on the last tour; it's instinctive with someone like that.

Now his wife, Kimberly, joins them, chomping relentlessly on her chewing gum. "Any new arrivals?"

Nick Cruickshank thinks that this place is rapidly becoming unlivable, inside and out. "Come on, put something decent on, I'll take you on a damn ride."

Wally and Kimberly barely nod; they're probably hurt at being so rudely deprived of the chance to keep insisting.

Nick Cruickshank walks out the back entrance, goes to look for René about the horses, though he's almost certain that Aileen has already put him to work, like everybody else.

TWENTY-THREE

Milena Migliari stands next to the batch freezer, entranced by the sound of the blade that stirs and stirs the mix of the fior di latte to which she's dedicated herself after throwing out the ruined batch of chestnut. Fior di latte is a flavor she comes back to when she needs a fresh start after a failed or disappointing experiment; it's a place to begin again. There's something revitalizing about fior di latte: like a blank canvas, an unwritten page containing a thousand potential stories or none at all. It's such a profoundly familiar flavor, yet so difficult to put into words. Creamy, not quite. Sweet still doesn't define it. Light, soft, essential, candid, snowy? Homogenous, yes, it coats your tongue, creates a patina that's nonetheless quick to dissolve, fleeting. There's nothing predetermined about fior di latte: its apparent simplicity opens onto a universe of soft and velvety nuances that caress the tongue and palate and bring with them memories of naïve thoughts, fresh impressions, innocent experiences of taste and smell. If there's one flavor of gelato that disproves the notion of gelato having a season, it's fior di latte. It goes well in spring, in summer, in fall, in winter, in any weather, on any day, at any time. Like any flavor, its quality depends on the quality of the ingredients, and how you help them express themselves rather than debase them. Most gelato makers use milk and cream from the supermarket; others use junk, such as denatured and devitalized UHT milk, or even worse, rehydrated powdered milk, or condensed milk. Then to conceal the bad taste and make it more pleasant they mix loads of sweetener into the mix, whether saccharine or fructose or dextrose or high-fructose corn syrup; they add vanillin and other artificial aromas, and best-case scenario carob flour to thicken. The result is that commercial fior di latte is often one of the most sickeningly sweet, pointless, and sticky flavors of gelato around. It's empty, bland to the point of being completely without character, a flavor for someone who doesn't know what to choose.

All her milk comes from Didier, who grazes his brown alpine cows on the pastures near Montauroux and lets them feed on fresh grass and sun-dried hay, depending on the season. They go inside only when they feel like it, and even then they're treated with every possible regard, including the music he plays for them every so often on the hurdy-gurdy. They produce much less milk than cows that are shut up in stables between iron bars and stuffed with industrial feed, but it's so naturally creamy that there's no need to add any cream at all, and it has wonderful grassy and floral hints that change from one day to the next, sourish-sweet, honeyed, alive. It's the foundation of all her flavors, and the reason she decided to dedicate herself exclusively to gelato, passing on sorbets. (Sorbets are a whole different world: watery, sugary, grainy, they melt in your mouth before ever appeasing your tongue with the delicious, enveloping, insistent density of gelato.) Given that pasteurization alters any flavor, she employs one that's very brief and at a very low temperature, 140 degrees for thirty seconds tops. To sweeten the mix she uses concentrated grape juice, sometimes acacia honey, sometimes agave syrup, then adds Bourbon vanilla from the island of Réunion; and each one of these ingredients makes a tiny but noticeable contribution to the flavor's final character. Fior di latte is one of the best flavors for verifying the difference between pointless gelato and intriguing gelato, between one that you're tired of after a few spoonfuls and one that grabs you right to the end. It's taken her a long time and lots of trial and error to make a really good one, and she still feels like there's more to discover. Really; it's not just a cliché.

The thickening, at any rate, is probably the part of the preparation that most fascinates her, when the air is engulfed by the liquid mixture and as if by magic transforms the mix little by little into a dense, light, pasty cream. In minutes emerges a gelato that's very close to its final form, but with a temperature of about 17.5°F, its structure is still precarious: all it would take is a blackout like the one Wednesday morning to make it dissolve. She has a five-quart batch freezer with manual extraction; she chose it because she didn't have the money for a larger one, and because she really only needs it to make small quantities for same-day consumption. There are gelato makers who use much larger and more sophisticated machines, others who work with liquid nitrogen, not to make better gelato but to make it more quickly, and more of it. "Optimizing the procedure," as the websites put it, or "maximizing the output." She's always curious to learn about new technical developments, but even if she had the money there'd be no pleasure for her in turning this lab into a sort of space station, with computer-controlled robots doing by themselves in totally predictable fashion what she does by hand with small variations from one batch to the next. She likes the idea of being able to make mistakes, as she just did with the chestnut; she likes the inherent risk.

And these days in particular the whole liquid nitrogen business is even less convincing than usual, reminding her as it does of what Dr. Lapointe said, about women who get their eggs extracted before they turn thirty and have them conserved at very low temperatures with the very same liquid nitrogen, to have them nice and ready for whenever they decide to start a family, five or maybe ten years later. Lapointe calls it "social egg freezing," because the goal is to conserve the coming years for a single's life dedicated to career or partying or exotic travel without the obstacle of children, postponing them for when there's a man who wants them or an optimal financial situation or a couple that's stable (or dying of boredom). The idea fills her with sadness, but she's probably the one who's wrong; in fact, she certainly is. And anyway she has no desire to think about this subject, but the thoughts keep coming back to her of their own accord, with unrelenting insistence.

When the thickening is finished she has Guadalupe help her transfer the fior di latte into the steel container, and the container into the blast chiller, which in a few minutes brings the temperature down from 17.5 to -4°F, reducing the part of unfrozen water that would make it lose creaminess and volume. Then they transfer the fior di latte into the pan behind the counter, next to the persimmon. Taking off their covers and looking at them like this, they make a beautiful pair: white and orange, an excellent autumn combination.

Milena Migliari suddenly feels like she doesn't have much more to do: the shop is empty, the town practically deserted, there are very few cars passing by on the main road up above, a mere four flavors of gelato available at the counter. Two more days and it'll be Monday. She counts them on her fingers, though there's no need: Saturday, Sunday. One, two. Plus today, which is already winding down before her very eyes.

TWENTY-FOUR

NICK CRUICKSHANK GOES to round up three horses in the paddock, seeing as, like he imagined, René has been co-opted by Aileen for the preparations for tomorrow's party. He grabs them one by one by the halter, ties them to the post: Tusk, Muck, and Michelle. With energetic strokes of the scrubbing brush he removes the dry mud from their backs, flanks, stomachs, hoofs, then dusts them off, energized by his irritation at the invasion inside and outside his home. He goes into the saddle room to get bridles, saddles, and saddlecloths, prepares one horse after another in a sequence he knows by heart, even if he's long been accustomed to someone else doing it for him; he tightens the cinch straps, adjusts the stirrups as best he can.

When he goes back inside, the confusion is even worse than twenty minutes ago: there's a steady stream of new guests, a continuous overlapping of gestures and voices. In the living room Aileen's lawyer from Luxembourg is tickling the ivories with "Summertime," unfazed that he is being listened to by actual musicians. Baz is talking about Indian music with Nishanath Kapoor, while Beth Bolton contemplates them like a pair of divinities that have miraculously landed on the same couch. Rodney pretends to listen to a boring couple who must be Aileen's investors, or maybe partners in her charity programs. But there are at least another twenty or so people intent on giving off various poses and attitudes; they turn their heads toward him with varying degrees of interest. Nick Cruickshank excludes them from his visual field, focuses on Wally, who's trying insistently to get Todd to taste his whiskey, even if Todd hasn't had a drink in about ten years. Kimberly is hovering over the writer from *Star Life* as if they're the best of friends; she cackles, gesturing needlessly. He heads straight for her like he's crossing a battlefield, allowing no wandering eyes to distract him. "Are we going? The horses are ready."

"The horses?" The writer from *Star Life* immediately looks around, in search of her photographer and cameraman. "Hold on a moment, I'll call Ed and Simon."

Nick Cruickshank doesn't even reply; he pulls Kimberly away by the arm, waves furiously at Wally, who as always takes whole seconds to react.

Behind the house Kimberly limps pathetically on the high heels of her musketeer boots. Blue shearling jacket with white down on the inside, white hot pants arriving just below the groin, semitransparent black stockings with a darker section at the knees: she hasn't given the slightest thought to putting on something just a little more appropriate.

"You want to go horseback riding like that?" Nick Cruickshank points at her legs; he can't believe he has such close ties with this sort of person.

"You didn't give me any time to change!" Kimberly is absolutely convinced she's in the right, chews her gum in a demonstrative huff.

"Yeah, you practically dragged us outside, fuck!" Wally comes immediately to her aid, two steps behind with his sluggish stride, zipping up the silvered down jacket he grabbed on the fly.

And yet Nick Cruickshank thinks that Kimberly and Wally Thompson aren't even the most obnoxious people he'll have to deal with over the next few days: their flaws are so glaring as to be almost reassuring, and he knows them so well. He's reminded of dozens of other so-called friends and acquaintances who upset him so much more, with their mental mirrors, their stares impervious to light. "Let's get moving, before those *Star Life* jackals find us."

The two Thompsons follow him grudgingly, to the wood construction of the saddle room. Seven or eight pairs of riding boots of different sizes, well oiled and polished by René, who must certainly feel a sense of waste at how little they get used, are lined up on the low shelves. Wally tries on one pair that's too tight, another that's too loose; the third time's lucky. He marches back and forth in the limited space, like a slightly haggard reserve soldier who's still animated by bellicose impulses, stomping emphatically on the wooden planks.

"Don't you want to put a pair on, too?" Nick Cruickshank looks at Kimberly's musketeer boots, with the decorative zippers on the sides; he leans out to look back toward the house, fearing he'll see someone coming.

"No, these'll work fine." Kimberly clicks her heels together a couple of times as well, grimaces in what might be pain but could also simply be one of the expressions she and Wally use to fill up their days of intellectual emptiness.

Nick Cruickshank slips on his boots, takes two red riding helmets more or less of the Thompsons' size off the hook, hands them to them.

Kimberly cautiously presses hers down over her puffy hair,

tightens the chin strap uncertainly. With her jaw constrained she finds it harder to chew her gum, but she chews it just the same.

But Wally sniggers, steps back half bent over, as if to demonstrate that he's wise to the gag. "*Naah.* What the fuck do I need that for? I've been riding a lot longer than you, thank you very much!"

Nick Cruickshank thinks that it's true: when the Bebonkers began earning serious money, starting with the release of their third album, Wally was the first to dedicate himself methodically to the acquisition of status symbols, from a Ferrari to a mansion in Kent to show horses, astride which he could be photographed by magazines and even interviewed on television. The other band members followed close behind, whether it was buying a small building in Chelsea to be more at the center of the action (Nick), delving into luxury sailboats (Rodney), attending auctions at Christie's (Todd); ever since it has simply been a question of continuing to accumulate more and more possessions. Even if they don't really need them, even if they don't really like them. On the other hand, almost all the so-called stars whom he knows spend enormous amounts of money doing things they absolutely *hate*, buying themselves homes on tropical islands where they can't stand the climate or in cities where they live like recluses, buying works of art they don't know the first thing about, filling their homes with furniture and silverware and porcelain they themselves find horrendous, collecting prestigious vintages of French wine they have to struggle to choke down, dedicating themselves to extreme sports that only end up making them look foolish, crossing the world to go to a party for someone who's not even really their friend. They do it out of a sense of social insecurity and accumulative greed, sure, but mainly to present some tangible evidence of their success to parents, neighbors, rivals, and the millions of perfect strangers observing them from a distance. Again, it's a question of not disappointing other people's expectations; the greater the expectations, the greater the effort not to disappoint them. As far as the morbidity of the mass media, the constant attempts at intrusion and the snap judgments based entirely on appearances are concerned: as Rodney once said in an interview, the only thing worse than having all eyes on you is being left alone because nobody cares about you.

"So, where are the horses?" Wally starts up with the insistence again, abandoning the role of foot dragger he's played up to this point.

Nick Cruickshank leads the Thompsons to the paddock, where the three black horses stand tied to the post, saddled and ready, with their long manes and tails.

"Those?" Wally starts laughing, turns to Kimberly, then to him. "These are a bunch of fucking ponies!"

"They're *horses* from Mérens. Also known as *Ariégeois*." Nick Cruickshank knew perfectly well how the ignorant and vulgar imbecile would react, it's not as though he didn't; but it still rankles him.

"They're *ponies*; sorry to break it to you." Wally spends his life comparing what he has to what others have; it's an endless exercise. And since he's totally lacking in intelligence and taste, the only parameters he has to fall back on are cost and size. He weighs up and compares everything, all the time: his electric basses, his dick, his bank accounts, popularity with fans, number of interviews, the poor things he's managed to get into the sack, the ones he's married, houses, cars. When the comparison is unfavorable to him, as it often is, he holds terrible grudges; when he thinks he's got the edge, he prances around like a peacock.

"They're *horses*. Look on the Internet if you need confirmation." Nick doesn't put much emphasis in his voice, because getting sucked into Wally Thompson's comparison games would be too degrading.

"No, my boy, *mine* are horses. Hanoverians imported directly from Saxony, with a pedigree this long, five-nine at the withers." Wally the jackass; he'll never grow up.

"And they make you feel like a better man? More accomplished, more important?" Nick Cruickshank would like nothing more than to give him a nice kick in the shins, or in the balls.

"What the fuck does that mean?" Wally chuckles in that obscene way of his, between throat and nose; he turns back to his wife. "Babe, these look like horses to you? Honestly?"

Kimberly chews her gum, with some difficulty due to the chin strap, shakes her head. "They're really small and kind of ugly." Whereas she looks like an oversized little girl, her face swollen with Botox or whatever she had herself injected with, her big head beneath the red helmet.

"Do you want to go or not?" Nick Cruickshank has to make a titanic effort to control himself. "You've been bitching and moaning about this damn horseback ride for two days."

"Yeah, *horse*." Wally has absolutely no sense of limits; the worst part is that he thinks that at this point he doesn't need one.

"Let's get going, come on." Nick Cruickshank opens the paddock gate, ushers the horses out. He tightens Tusk's cinch, hands Kimberly the reins, helps her up onto the saddle, moves her legs to regulate the stirrup leathers, seeing as she would never think to do it herself.

"Don't get too frisky with my wife over there, eh?!" Wally naturally doesn't let the chance go begging: he winks, chuckles.

"Not to worry." Nick Cruickshank once more fights the urge to say what he'd like to say.

Kimberly lets herself be waited on as if by a stable boy, inert up there on the saddle, no intention of saying thank you. It isn't hard to imagine how these two boors behave with the people who work for them: showy rudeness, demonstrative arrogance. How can he still think of them as the *lesser* evil, compared to the rest of the invasion troops inside and outside the house, and the reinforcements arriving between now and tomorrow morning?

Wally looks at Muck and Michelle with skepticism, like they're completely unworthy of him. "And which of these two asses do you plan on giving me?"

Nick Cruickshank hesitates, because he'd like to tell him that he's not going to give him a goddamn thing, that he can take his arrogant slobbery elsewhere. But they're already here, and entertaining two guests would certainly be more justifiable in Aileen's eyes than going off riding on his own. "Go ahead and take Michelle."

"Michelle? But she's got a beard, she has!" Wally winks, in that horrible way of his.

"Fuck, this one's really jumpy!" Kimberly totters in the saddle on Tusk: she probably never rides her prize-show Hanoverians, or at most takes them out for a few laps, under the supervision of a very well-paid instructor who's always ready to intervene.

"He's not jumpy at all. Just give him some reins." Nick Cruickshank has to call on all the patience he possesses, which has never been very much.

Wally tightens Michelle's cinch by himself, in a show of dismissive expertise; he pulls too much on the strap.

"Not so tight, you'll bother her." One reason Nick Cruickshank chose these horses is that they used to be used by smugglers to cross over the mountains on the most difficult trails, and the idea appealed to him.

Wally pretends not to have even heard him; he closes the buckle, puts his left foot in the stirrup, lifts himself up by the sheer arm strength, plops his heavy rear end down on the saddle. Michelle is naturally annoyed, bucks slightly, raises her head. Wally pulls the reins this way and that like the moron he is, sniggering. "*Whoah!* Seems she's offended by what I was saying about her before!"

"Idiot." Nick Cruickshank tries to keep his voice down as he tightens Muck's cinch, but he's not particularly successful.

"What was that?" Wally's hearing aid must be correctly regulated, nothing's getting past him; he kicks with his heels, turns his mount around.

"Nothing. Let's go." Nick Cruickshank saddles up, clears a path to lead them out of the paddock.

"You called me an idiot, I heard you! Asshole!" Wally trots along behind him, red in the face.

"Hey, Kimberly!" When they're only a few yards from the fence Sadie, Rodney's wife, walks up with her panoramic sunglasses and lynx jacket and thin-heeled little boots that make her even more unstable than Kimberly, an enormous Gucci bag over her shoulder. "We're going to Saint-Tropez, to see Dimitri and Vanessa!"

"To Saint-Tropez?" Kimberly yanks on Tusk's reins as if she's trying to rip his head off, forces him into a panicky retreat.

"Uh-huh. You want to come with us?" Sadie too is chewing gum, with the energy usually dedicated to far more productive pursuits.

"Yeah, yeah. Hold on." Kimberly tries to dismount, in the most incorrect way possible; Tusk starts going around in a circle.

"What the fuck is this, babe?" Wally gives the reins a rough jerk to move back toward her. "You're not coming on this fucking ride?"

"I'd rather go with Sadie; we have to check out a couple of stores." Kimberly tries again to throw her right leg over the saddle.

"What the fuck, babe! You're just leaving me here?" Wally

frowns like an overgrown spoiled brat: he puffs his cheeks out, snorts.

Nick Cruickshank quickly dismounts, ties Muck's reins to the fence with angry gestures, helps Kimberly dismount before she breaks a leg.

"Hey, make sure you keep your hands off my wife's ass!" Here's say-it-again Wally once more. And what's worse, he isn't even completely joking: he watches attentively as Nick is forced to support her until she's painstakingly managed to put her feet back on the ground.

Kimberly immediately rips off the helmet, tries to fix her hair with her hands, snorts, gestures at her husband with a whirling index finger. "See you later, love!"

"Fuck off, babe." Wally, filled with resentment, watches her walk away with Sadie.

Nick Cruickshank really does detest these two, but the strange thing is that he can't help but feel a kind of admiration for how they're united by the same flaws: clearly made for each other. It's disconcerting, making him feel even more alone and encircled than he already did.

"So, are we going?" Wally is already insisting, again.

"Hold on." Nick Cruickshank removes the saddle, saddlecloth, and reins from Tusk, who seems content not to have to carry Kimberly around; he hangs it all on the fence, quickly gets back on Muck, leads the way out of the paddock.

"So, what's the secret to waking this donkey up?" Wally goads Michelle on with his heels, to try to get out in front.

Nick Cruickshank doesn't bother replying; he immediately takes the path through the holm oaks, to avoid the *Star Life* people who are certainly looking for them and not be seen by Aileen and the whole troupe in action on the front lawn.

They make their way through the trees at a good pace, avoiding the trunks, through the moistness of the undergrowth, amid the smell of mushrooms and rotten wood; after a few minutes they come out into the clearing where the secret cottage is located. Nick Cruickshank fell in love with it as soon as he saw it, before discovering that it belonged to a bordering property, which inspired him to make a new acquisition. But he's never wanted to remodel it like he did the main house; he simply had the roof and windows repaired, furnished the inside with the bare essentials. He likes it this way: a simple and innocent place, a refuge when he needs one.

"What the fuck is that?" Wally points to the cottage, continuing to smack Michelle's flanks.

"Nothing." Nick Cruickshank certainly has no intention of explaining it to him.

"What do you mean, nothing? It's your secret fuck pad, admit it!" Wally intensifies his intrusive stare. "Who do you take in there? That young girl who serves at the table?"

"Would you mind not bringing your repulsive filth into my life?" Like so many other times, his disgust for Wally encompasses the thought of having spent decades with him, with all that they have contained.

"Who's repulsive?! Would you listen to him! Asshole!" Wally digs his heels in to catch up. It's incredible that he gets offended at being defined as repulsive, when he puts such ceaseless effort into being that way. "So the little server girl, what's her name? If you're not interested then maybe I'll have a go, while Kim's away!"

"You're disgusting, Wally!" Nick Cruickshank thinks with horror that there was a time when they both shared in this sickness, passing it off as being free-spirited and transgressive, bragging about it like barbarian warriors returning triumphant from their pillaging. The songs he and Rodney wrote about it are still among the most popular with both their male and, incredibly, female fans.

"Oh, sure, and you're so much better!" Wally squawks from behind him, continuing to prod Michelle, who switches into a slow trot and forces him to steady himself in the saddle.

Nick Cruickshank pushes Muck to a trot as well, to avoid being overtaken; they quickly cross through the clearing, slip back into the undergrowth. They continue forward through the holm oaks, both of their two horses now snorting and shaking, competitive.

Instead of calming Michelle, Wally continues goading her on with his heels, though he's already having more and more trouble dodging the branches that risk bashing him in the face.

"Hey, slow down!" To avoid trouble Nick Cruickshank pushes Muck through the trees in the direction of the open fields, lowering his head, bending it to the right or to the left depending on what comes at him. He comes out from between the trees, begins trotting alongside them, toward the olive grove.

But Wally is hot on his heels, with the same fieriness he displayed in the eighties on his interminable bass solos: he slaps with his legs and shakes the reins until Michelle gets fed up carrying such an unpleasant rider and breaks into her much faster and quicker-stepped gallop.

Nick Cruickshank has no choice but to push Muck to a gallop as well, to keep Wally behind him.

Wally naturally refuses to tolerate being restrained: he spurs Michelle on even more frenetically, pants, grunts, leans forward. "Go, go, go! *Go* on, fucking hell!"

"Slow down! Don't be an idiot!" Nick Cruickshank tries to bar his way with his left arm, moving it up and down.

Wally naturally sees it as a challenge and redoubles his efforts: he rides her like a lunatic, yelling in that guttural way of his. In a few seconds the horses are launched in a frenetic gallop, inflamed by their not having been mounted for days and probably by the excessive oats that René feeds them to make a good impression. Nick Cruickshank tries to restrain Muck, and Wally takes advantage to surpass him, crouching low over the horse's neck, head down, ass up in the air—as if, just for a change, he feels the need to prove something to somebody. And at the very same moment there's a rustling in the undergrowth and the brown alpaca shoots out of the woods, the two white ones hot on its heels; Michelle pulls up suddenly at a full gallop, kicks out, bucks furiously. Wally takes flight, human cannon style: he stays aloft for a good couple of seconds, lands badly, rolls like a sack of potatoes, lies motionless on his back.

Nick Cruickshank struggles mightily to rein in Muck, all of whose instincts are telling him to rush off after Michelle as fast as he can.

Wally is lying there still on the grass, in his silvered jacket and designer jeans, his shoes with the ultra-high-tech soles.

Nick Cruickshank jumps down, pulling Muck along behind him, who's still quivering and turning his head and pointing his ears toward Michelle, who only now begins to slow down, a good two or three hundred yards ahead. "Hey? Wall?" He crouches down beside him to get a closer look, tries to evaluate the situation.

Wally emits a sort of wheeze; his stomach rises and falls. He's not dead, but he's certainly damaged.

"Stay calm, Wall, don't move." Nick Cruickshank tries to go back over the accident in his mind, but even though it happened two minutes ago the sequence is confused; he can't be sure whether he saw him hit his head.

"Aaargh." Wally groans anew, moves a leg, meaning that his cervical vertebrae should all be in one piece, but his eyes are closed, his breathing slow, his nose wheezing terribly.

"Wall, can you hear me?" Nick Cruickshank holds the bridle with his left hand and with his right cautiously touches his legs, arms, to see what's broken. He thinks that he doesn't really hate Wally: he hates what Wally *represents*, but they have too much history together, they've been through too much together, all the ups and downs. This jackass is a piece of his life; the thought that from one moment to the next he might become a piece of his past is heartbreaking.

Wally lets out another groan, moves his jaw slightly; he looks to be in really bad shape.

"Hey, Wall?" Nick Cruickshank feels a wave of violent displeasure well up inside him, his trademark "cool" nowhere to be found. "Wall?" He touches his neck, his left shoulder, his right shoulder.

"Fuuuuck!" Suddenly Wally lurches up into a sitting position, with the same expression he had during his worst period of generalized addiction, when he would come to, like Lazarus, after sniffing and ingesting and guzzling any combination of powders and pills and alcohol that came within reach and then crashing to the floor like a deadweight in some hotel suite.

"Wall, good to have you back! You scared the crap out of me!" Nick Cruickshank is overcome by a sense of relief that he wouldn't have imagined, places his hand on his right shoulder again, slowly.

"Aaaaiaaah!" Wally has the raucous and exhausted voice of when he's at his most plastered.

Nick Cruickshank laughs, almost forgetting to hold on to Muck's bridle to keep him from galloping off. And immediately his relief gives way to a disaster film that begins playing out in his head: ambulances with sirens blazing, hospitals where communication is difficult and discretion nonexistent, plaster casts, Kimberly furious, tomorrow's party ruined, Aileen furious, Sunday's concert called off, Baz Bennett furious, the fans furious.

“That fucking pony broke my shoulder!” Wally holds it with one hand: white in the face with the pain, or maybe because he’s gone into one of his famous self-induced states, like the time he took some acid after a concert in Albuquerque and convinced himself that the fingertips of his left hand had become enormous. He continued yelling for hours at the other band members and anyone else he could, “I’ve turned into a fucking *gecko*!” Now he sits there on the grass, all signs of competitive daring vanished, like a professional victim.

“Hey, calm down, Wall. Nothing’s broken.” Nick Cruickshank is not at all sure of it, but he says so to try to calm him down. He thinks that in truth he does hate him *a little*, now that his relief has melted away and he knows he’s neither dying nor paralyzed for life.

“Fuck calming down! Fuck nothing wrong! You put me on that bullshit ponyyyyy!” Wally yells at close to the maximum of his significant vocal capabilities, holds his shoulder, continues grimacing.

“You’re the one who goaded her on like a madman! I must have told you ten times not to do it!” There: Nick Cruickshank once again feels extraordinarily angry at him, and even more at himself, for getting into this situation.

“How the fuck was I supposed to know that you keep fucking llamas in the woods, just waiting to cut you off?!” Wally has always been constitutionally incapable of admitting the truth; no reason for him to start now.

“They’re *alpacas*! And you’re a moron!” Even though Nick Cruickshank keeps telling himself to hold his nerve, the words come out on their own, unstoppable.

“And you’re a fucking asshole, to put me on that dangerous animal, and not tell me that you have a fucking safari park here!”

Wally's expression is a mix of pain and rancor, in which there's no way of distinguishing truth from exaggeration.

"You're the one who's been on my back for *days* to take this stupid horseback ride! And you've never had the slightest sense of limits, as long as I've known you!" Nick Cruickshank knows perfectly well that he's only making things worse, that he shouldn't even listen to him but put his mind instead to getting medical assistance, but he can't help it.

"Son of a bitch! You've always acted so superior, just because you've read a few books and because you're the fucking asshole lead singer!" Wally yells with the liberating power of his most jarring interventions in the Bebonkers' most chaotic encores, when the public's ability to distinguish between good and bad has vanished completely.

Nick Cruickshank makes the herculean effort to focus exclusively on what needs to be done. He takes his cell phone out of his pocket. "Don't move. I'm going to call someone."

Wally too reaches gingerly inside his jacket and takes out his iPhone, with that ridiculous walnut-root cover with the solid gold border; he calls Kimberly, like a stupid and whiny little kid calling out for Mommy as soon as he gets hurt.

TWENTY-FIVE

MILENA MIGLIARI TAKES a small spoonful of fior di latte directly from the pan at the counter, places the fior di latte on her tongue and lets it melt slowly, swallows: yes, it came out well. *Very* well, actually; it's one of the best batches of fior di latte she's ever made, maybe the best. Creamy but not fatty, dense but airy, with an ideal point of sweetness, the languor of the vanilla accompanying poignantly the hints of flowers and grass in the milk. It's a sort of miracle, considering her state of agitation from Viviane's tattoo and all the destabilizing thoughts that continue racing through her head and heart. It could be interpreted as a calming message from the universe or as an alarm bell before everything falls apart. It depends.

Whatever the case, it's very close to the fior di latte she had in mind as she was preparing it, yet it surprises her with tiny unexpected differences. This only happens with her most successful flavors, the ones that bring tears of joy to her eyes: to be able to literally *taste* the distance between what she was aiming for and what she got. It's simple and complicated, like every flavor, like the connections that every flavor moves you to make, the reasons it makes you happy or wistful, leaves you satisfied or restless. This fior di latte contains the essence of things experienced, or even barely grazed, or imagined; a collection of undefinable and elusive elements that to her are the essence of the imperfect marvel.

But now she feels a desperate need for external feedback, and absolutely no one is coming into the shop, nor are they likely to do so in the next few hours. And if there's no one to appreciate the marvel, assuming that she did, what was the point of capturing it? Who can tell her if she captured it, or merely fooled herself into thinking she did? Between tonight and tomorrow some people will probably drop by because it's the weekend, and on Sunday there'll certainly be thousands of people down at the airfield for the Bebonkers concert, but very few of them will be interested in her gelato, fewer still will be capable of giving her the sensitive and intelligent and articulate evaluation she needs. And she needs it *now*, when the fior di latte is literally just finished, incredibly fresh, throbbing, at the height of its expressive capabilities.

Guadalupe is finishing up cleaning the batch freezer and the other equipment in the sink; she turns around as soon as Milena comes back into the lab.

"Would you mind telling me what you think of the fior di latte?" Milena Migliari feels the urgency rush into her voice, her gestures.

"Give me five minutes." Guadalupe looks at her, slightly perplexed; she probably doesn't know what more she wants from her, seeing as she tasted the mix during preparation and told her that it seemed really good.

"No, right now! Please!" Milena Migliari feels the need for a response continuing to grow inside her; she's no longer able to stand still.

Guadalupe turns off the water, dries her hands, follows her into the shop. She tastes a teaspoonful of the fior di latte that Milena hands her, reflects for a few seconds, smiles. "Delicious."

"You're not just saying that to make me happy?" Milena Migliari scrutinizes her, searching for signs of amazement and joy, but doesn't see any.

"Of course not. It's really good. I swear." Guadalupe is undoubtedly sincere. It isn't like her to pay empty compliments, but she doesn't seem particularly grabbed or moved, pervaded by relentless sensations, mental images blossoming one after another.

"Really?" Milena Migliari continues studying her with an expression that she knows is far too anxious.

"Most definitely, Milena." Guadalupe doesn't know how to convince her: she nods showily, moving her whole body, even her hands, to reinforce her words. "It's perfect."

"But perfect doesn't mean anything!" Instead of calming down, Milena Migliari becomes more and more agitated, gesturing convulsively toward the front window. "Haven't you noticed the name of this gelateria?!"

"Sorry, I just meant that it's really good." Guadalupe is starting to worry again. "I meant that it doesn't have any flaws."

"Not having any flaws is hardly a *merit*!" Milena Migliari raises her voice without intending to, but her anxiety is turning into panic. "Not having any flaws is the *worst possible* flaw! It means not having any *character*, nothing that's capable of touching someone's heart!"

Guadalupe takes a step back, looks at her with a light of concern in her eyes.

Milena Migliari neither wants nor has the time to understand why she feels this way; she only knows that her urgent need for answers is transforming into a wave that's threatening to sweep her away. She paces back and forth between the lab and the shop, her breathing labored and her heart racing, her hands sweaty. She feels trapped, with no way out, no escape.

"Hey, what's wrong? Milena?" Guadalupe is now officially worried: in the two years she's worked with her she's seen her in various states of agitation, but always for identifiable reasons, and never like this.

"What's wrong is that I have to get out of here!" Milena Migliari is absolutely incapable of standing still: she takes a one-pound Styrofoam container off the shelf, takes the covers off the fior di latte and persimmon behind the counter, goes to work with the spatula. Despite her extreme agitation, her gestures are quite precise, though more frenetic than usual: she's able to transfer the right amounts without leaving gaps or having to force it down. When the container is full she sticks it in the blast chiller, waits a few minutes, puts a sheet of wax paper and the cover on top, tapes it shut, puts it in a soft-edged cooler. She rummages through the basket with the little pieces of paper with the sayings on them ready to be rolled up and tied with red string, but she can't find any that seem appropriate, so she does without. She puts a small selection of cups, waffle cones, and plastic spoons in three small cardboard boxes, sticks those too in the cooler, along with a spatula; she takes off her plastic hairnet and overshoes, puts on her jacket and cap.

"Where are you going?" Guadalupe doesn't know what to think anymore.

"I'll tell you after." Milena Migliari is already outside the gelateria, walking quickly toward her van.

TWENTY-SIX

Nick Cruickshank thinks that his house certainly doesn't feel much like a home anymore, if it ever has, among people coming and people going, people opening and closing doors, moving furniture, walking through hallways, laughing, flushing toilets, calling to each other, walking, running, talking mindlessly, or making very specific requests.

The Thompsons' room would be calmer, if not for the fact that Dr. Angénieux is now there, having arrived with surprising speed from Draguignan along with his assistant and the mobile X-ray and ultrasound machines, seeing as bringing Wally to the hospital probably wouldn't have been a good idea, with all the jackals already infesting the area in view of tomorrow and Sunday.

Wally is sitting on the edge of the bed in his room, in pain and deeply disappointed at the diagnosis.

The doctor is showing him yet again the X-rays of his right shoulder, clavicle, humerus, and wrist taken by the Fujifilm digital viewer, shaking his head. "*Pas de fractures.*"

"No fractures." Nick Cruickshank translates maybe for the

third time, in an intonation in which impatience has now entirely supplanted the initial relief.

"And why is it then that it hurts so fucking much?!" Wally can see for himself that there are no fractures, but he doesn't accept the idea, because it ruins the self-portrait as victim he'd like to paint for himself at any cost. "I know I've broken something!"

Aileen comes back into the room, followed by Tricia and Fiona, the holistic consultant, and insists on looking at the X-rays and ultrasounds herself. She studies them attentively, observes Wally; asks Dr. Angénieux whether by chance it could be a tear of the *coiffe des rotateurs*.

Dr. Angénieux can't believe she knows the precise anatomical term, and in French, no less; he observes her with a mix of suspicion and admiration.

Aileen explains that her brother had that type of injury while he was playing ice hockey in the Canadian Second Division, in Montreal.

Nick Cruickshank is almost as amazed as the doctor, though by now he ought to be used to the fact that Aileen has an almost inexhaustible stratification of experiences and knowledge, made even more impressive by her ability to make super-fast connections, in different languages, at any moment, in the midst of any activity, without ever stumbling into inaccuracies or slipping into the generic. She was the one who took command of the situation when he and Aldino brought Wally back to the house in the Defender, screaming and moaning like he was on death's doorstep. And she was the one who managed to calm things down a bit despite having a thousand other things to do, identified the mobile radiology center in Draguignan, and convinced Dr. Angénieux that it was an emergency that simply couldn't wait.

"*Non, madame.*" Dr. Angénieux probably continues to find her eccentric, but he knows very well that rich and eccentric foreigners are the best clients to be found in this department, so he treats her with the greatest possible deference. He nods at his assistant sitting at the monitor, points at two or three specific places on the ultrasound images, and presses two fingers on the corresponding points of Wally's shoulder, moving Wally's arm vigorously. "*Vous voyez? Pas de rupture.*"

"Ahia! Get your hands off me! I'm not a fucking lab rat!" Wally doesn't at all enjoy being handled for demonstration's sake, let alone hearing the seriousness of his injuries denied once more.

Aileen is relieved to think that the emergency is in large part resolved; her thoughts are already shifting elsewhere. She smiles affably at Angénieux and his assistant. "*Merci infiniment, Docteur.*" She begins to leave, followed by Tricia and Fiona, but turns to look at Nick Cruickshank. "I really need to talk to you about a few matters."

"Sure, when I'm done here." Nick Cruickshank immediately feels boxed in, points to Wally as the living proof that he certainly can't leave, not now.

Aileen looks quite unconvinced, but nods; she leaves, followed by her assistant and her consultant.

Partly to demonstrate that his presence is actually necessary, Nick Cruickshank asks Dr. Angénieux what can be done for the pain in Wally's shoulder.

The doctor quickly fills out a prescription, not realizing that Wally's intimacy with opiates and their derivatives makes him nearly immune to the normal doses of the great majority of painkillers.

"But is he going to be able to play Sunday?" Nick mimes the

stance of an electric bass player, the fingers of his left hand pressing on the strings, those of the right hand strumming away.

The doctor opens his arms out wide: he seems not to want to express an opinion one way or the other, since he also probably doesn't have the slightest clue what it takes to play the electric bass.

"Of course I won't be fucking able!" Wally bursts into another frenzy of recriminations. "I won't even be able to *move*, for fuck's sake."

"Look, I'm not the one who knocked you off the horse, okay?" Cracks continue to reveal themselves in Nick Cruickshank's façade of self-control. "You're the one who decided to be an arrogant grandstanding idiot!"

"Me, an idiot?!" Wally turns red in the face, almost neglecting his victim's pose to adopt a more threatening one. "Me, an idiot?!"

"Go on playing the invalid, you're better off!" Yes, no doubt about it: Nick Cruickshank has exhausted his already short supply of patience.

"Asshole! I'm going to sue you!" The fact is that Wally has accumulated entire *decades* of rancor: for every bad song futilely proposed to the Bebonkers, for every bad arrangement idea refused, for every rigorous limitation of the stupid remarks he was permitted to make in a group interview, for every photo of the band in which he appears in the background.

"For what? For showing you how stupid you are?" Nick Cruickshank knows he's only making the situation worse, but how the hell is it possible to remain diplomatic with someone like this? "You know, being stupid isn't just a flaw, it's a *fault*! It's the *world* that should sue *you*, for having contributed to making it worse, even if only by very little!"

"Bastard! Son of a bitch!" Wally is livid, spraying saliva. "You were the one who suggested the idea of the horseback ride the other day!"

"I only suggested it because you were so *lazy*!" Now it's Nick Cruickshank's turn to raise his voice to a quasi-concert level, now that the vast majority of his Zen filters have failed. "So totally lacking in *motivation*!"

Dr. Angénieux looks embarrassingly around the room; it's clear at this point that he wants nothing more than to get out of there, return to the calm of his office and more serene and normal patients. He opens his arms. "You could attempt one or two sessions of massage therapy."

"When? Where?" Wally barks like a bulldog, quivering with rage, clasping the side of the bed with his left hand.

"There's a very good therapist whom we recommend in these cases." The doctor takes off the white smock that he slipped on like a stage prop at his arrival, folds it up, takes his cell phone out of his jacket. "If you want I can call her, explain to her that it's urgent."

"I don't want anyone else laying their fucking hands on me!" Wally brays, horribly congested. "I don't want any fucking massage therapist!"

Nick Cruickshank turns his back to exclude him from his visual field, nods at the doctor to call.

TWENTY-SEVEN

Just when Milena Migliari reaches the second-to-last curve in the road, the perplexity comes rushing at her from out of nowhere: with each passing second it dampens the urgency with which she left the gelateria and drove up to this point. An idea that until a moment before seemed good and natural now suddenly seems terribly wrong. She can't understand how she failed to realize that there are simply no grounds for a surprise visit like this; that Nick's turning up at the gelateria yesterday morning and the hug last night in the square not only haven't established any real familiarity between them, but to the contrary have left her feeling bewildered, deeply uncomfortable.

Her not being 100 percent lucid lately only partly justifies the foolishness of throwing herself into such a muddled enterprise, without even reflecting for a second: How could she fail to imagine what it would *really* be like to come back here? After the embarrassment of the other day, when she had at least come to deliver an order? Sure, last night's hug was strangely intense, an unfiltered exchange of emotions that moved her to tears. It even seemed like it was the same for him, judging by his breathing, by the strength with which he held her. But immediately after, the emotion was transformed into pure incomprehension, and both of them went their separate ways without even saying good-bye, without even a wave. And what were they supposed to have said or done, given that the hug didn't stem from their own initiative but was part of the small ceremony of those wacky huggers from Digne-les-Bains? A hug between a woman not interested in men and a man interested in a totally different type of woman? What the heck came over her roughly twenty minutes ago? What mental and emotional state is she in, really? Maybe Viviane is right, she *should* take some sedatives.

Now the large gate is right there, about twenty yards in front of her: Milena Migliari feels her stomach tighten. She slows down, stops the van. It seems very clear that the only thing to do is turn around and go back, forget about ever having had such a stupid idea, let alone coming so close to putting it into effect. And it would be better to turn around right away, before coming into view of the security camera on top of the gate, before the man in jacket and tie with the look of a bodyguard there at the start of the driveway takes down her license plate and notifies the authorities, asks them to run a check on a crazy gelato chef/stalker.

But the road at this point is so narrow, between the little stone wall on the right and the ditch and the trees on the left, that turning around is impossible. Milena Migliari tries to plan out the turn in her head: no, there's no way. She puts it in reverse, turns her head to back up several dozen yards to where the road first widens, but she sees a white van coming up quickly behind her. *Two* vans, in fact, one after the other, and so large that they certainly can't get by with her in the way. She pulls over to the side as far as she can, at the risk of scratching the side of the van against the stone wall, but she can't free up more than five feet of space on her left;

there's no way they can pass. She lowers her window, leans out, gestures desperately to explain that she needs to back up, that they need to do so too, if they'd be so kind. But the white van flashes its headlights, without the slightest trace of comprehension. She feels trapped: she looks in anguish at the gate ahead of her and sees it opening. The bodyguard in the driveway makes hand gestures to say come on forward, come on forward. Seeing as she doesn't move, his gestures grow more energetic, with two hands: let's go, move it.

Again Milena Migliari leans out to look at the two vans behind, but the first one's bumper is now almost touching hers; the guy at the wheel is flashing his headlights again; he even honks at her once. She's startled: she has no choice but to put it in first, go slowly toward the now-open gate, as if toward the jaws of some voracious monster. She can't believe that she's put herself in a situation like this and it's all her fault, that she didn't stop to consider what she was doing for the entire seven and a half miles of road between Fayence and here, that she only began thinking again in the past few feet. She goes forward, urged on by the other two vans, feeling as agitated and embarrassed as she ever has in her life. As soon as she's past the gate she lowers her passenger-side window as well, leaning over to tell the stocky man in jacket and tie that she's come in merely to avoid blocking the vehicles behind her, that she'll leave just as soon as she's able to turn, to leave it open for her.

But the man barely looks at her: slits for eyes, hair shaved at the back of his neck and on the sides, completely in character. He reads the name of the gelateria on the side of the van and nods at her to move forward, switches his attention to the two vans behind her. Milena Migliari waits for him to come back so she can explain, but when he sees her still sitting there he gestures at her furiously. *"Allez! Allez! Dépêchez-vous!"*

So she drives on up the access road, followed closely by the other van, which has also passed through the check. Right away, she feels incredibly stupid. What could she say if she found herself face-to-face again with the enormous Italian bodyguard from two days ago, already so suspicious when she came to make her delivery: that she was forced inside against her will?

The two big vans stay right on her tail, all the way to the parking area behind the house. Compared to the other day there are a lot more cars, several vans, a truck; and a steady stream of men unloading and transporting posts and wooden tables, lamps, chairs, benches, lemon trees, whole boxes of cyclamens in bloom. She doesn't know whether to feel slightly less conspicuous thanks to all the commotion, or that much more recognizable as an intruder; she immediately begins the process of turning around and driving away, leaving as quickly as she can. She forces herself not to look at anyone, fearful they might ask her what the heck she's doing here. But the more she tries not to look, the more she looks; and just when she's finished turning around and is about to pass in front of the main body of the house, the door opens, and a young guy with glasses comes out pushing a machine on wheels that's similar to a mix between a vacuum and a photocopier. Right after him comes an older guy with a gray beard, and after him comes Nick Cruickshank.

Milena Migliari feels her heart jump into her throat; she brakes, even if it's the last thing she would have wanted. For a second she hopes to be able to accelerate smoothly and get back to the access road, not give him time to recognize her; but in that very same instant he recognizes her, or at least the van. He lowers his head, to look in through the open window. "Hey!"

Milena Migliari feels like a thief, caught just when she was about to get away scot-free: paralyzed.

Nick Cruickshank leans in, smiles at her. "What are you doing here?"

Milena Migliari has no idea what to reply, or what expression to adopt. She gives a vague nod, utterly devoid of significance.

"Did Aileen order more gelato?" In this light Nick Cruickshank has decidedly more lines on his face than he did last night; he's more colorful as well, with the bracelets and silver rings, the gold earring, the blue handkerchief around his neck, orange shirt, red jacket with purple stripes. He looks more like an actor from the sixteenth century than one from the eighteenth century, with no troupe and no stage, catapulted into an alien world where he's able to get along pretty well but only up to a certain point.

"No." Milena Migliari tries again to think of another plausible reason for coming here, but she draws a blank.

"*Eh bien, nous allons, monsieur.*" The bearded guy gets Nick Cruickshank's attention, points to the younger guy who's loading the strange piece of equipment into a blue van with the white wording *Diagnostics Mobiles*.

Nick Cruickshank takes a roll of bills out of his pocket, counts several of them off to him, shakes his hand; as soon as the bearded guy has left he leans back in the window. "So?"

Milena Migliari thinks that she'd probably feel more comfortable if she really were a thief come to steal something, but since that's not the case it seems that the only two alternatives are smiling enigmatically and driving away or telling the truth. She takes a deep breath, tries to calm herself down. "I wanted to get your opinion. If you have five minutes."

"Yeah?" Nick Cruickshank seems curious, intrigued.

The younger guy comes back, cell phone in hand. "*Monsieur Crucsànc, un selfie, s'il vous plaît?*"

Nick Cruickshank consents, with only the slightest hint of impatience: he turns to get the right light, moves his head close to the assistant's. He immediately says good-bye, leans back in the window. "An opinion about what? Career choices? Life choices?"

Milena Migliari feels herself blush, though she isn't sure whether he's aware of it. "About two flavors of gelato."

Nick Cruickshank steps back, makes a wide semicircular gesture, as if to offer her the sumptuous gift of the space in which to park her van.

Milena Migliari follows the gesture, even if a part of her would prefer to head straight for the access road while there's still time. She pulls a few feet forward, stops alongside the wall of the house. When she gets out she feels even more exposed than she'd imagined, suddenly deprived of the means of escape. To compensate she immediately walks around the Kangoo, grabs the cooler, holds it up in front of her, like a shield.

The impatient and ill-mannered guy who was tailgating her all the way here has taken a large speaker out of his white van, he's pushing it on a cart; he looks stunned when he recognizes Nick Cruickshank.

"Which flavors?" Nick Cruickshank ignores all the activity around him, staring at her in that extremely focused way of his from yesterday, when he made his surprise entrance at the gelateria.

"Better not to tell you now." Milena Migliari thinks that at this point it's too late to save face; she might as well be herself to the bitter end. "So you'll be objective."

Nick Cruickshank thinks about it, serious; he nods. "Makes sense. But we need someplace quiet to taste it, right? Away from all this chaos?"

Milena nods too, in a way very similar to his; once again it's like their mannerisms are mutually infectious, it's difficult to explain.

Even Nick Cruickshank might realize it, because he stands there staring at her for a moment; then he points in the opposite direction of everyone busy unloading and transporting things and sets off.

Milena Migliari follows him, but she realizes she's running the risk of transforming the gelato tasting into a sort of moment of truth, the opposite of what she had in mind when she followed the absurd impulse to come here and ask for his opinion. She had imagined unceremoniously preparing him a cup or a cone, hearing his impressions; it seems like she's managed to make an already bad idea worse.

Nick Cruickshank guides her to the end of the west side of the house, but instead of opening the door he makes a quick gesture and continues walking, with his strangely elastic and undulated stride. They pass through a patch of lawn, walk alongside a wooden fence inside of which are several small dark horses that approach the fence to observe them. Just beyond is a wood of holm oaks, dense.

Milena Migliari would like to say that it isn't necessary to go so far for the tasting, that any old reasonably quiet room is fine; instead she remains silent and follows him, gripping the handle of her stupid flowery cooler.

Nick Cruickshank turns to glance at her, motions, takes off down a path in the woods without saying anything. He doesn't even have a coat or winter jacket on now, just that red one with the purple stripes.

The farther they go into the woods, the more Milena Migliari wonders whether he hasn't interpreted her request for an opinion on two gelato flavors in the most mistaken way possible: after all, he is a first-class predatory male, probably accustomed to snatching any female who comes within his reach. But she's far from sure about it; and anyway, she continues walking behind him, borne by a current in which puzzlement and curiosity are mixed in almost equal measure.

They walk in silence, at a good pace; Nick Cruickshank turns around a couple of times to check that she's still following him; he gives her just the hint of a smile, in the shadows of the woods. There are leaves that rustle beneath their feet, branches that crunch; the smells of bark, of moss, of mushrooms. Milena Migliari is reminded of an article she read about "forest baths," and the mental and physical benefits of walking among the trees, owing not simply to the purity of the air and the distance from the built-up and inhabited world, but also to several volatile organic compounds that trees release in their immediate vicinity to protect themselves from molds and bacteria. Two Japanese scholars did experiments on urbanites and discovered that after walking for a while in the woods their blood pressure and heart rate diminished, along with their levels of adrenaline. She doesn't know if this is really the case, but it's a fact that she feels less agitated than a few minutes ago, though her confusion hasn't dissipated. But it's a muffled confusion, soft, almost pleasant: more a state of suspension than disorientation. She follows Nick Cruickshank, who walks among the trees with his strange gait and his lively colors against the monochromatic background of the trunks, and in a couple of instances she thinks that this situation could be purely imaginary if it weren't for the very real weight of the cooler she holds in her hand. She also thinks that she'd like to make a woods-flavored gelato; not wild berry, but *woods*, pure and simple. She wonders how she might go about it, without making use of clichés like the pine essences used in air fresheners. It's far from simple: What do the woods taste like?

It seems like they could continue walking along the path indefinitely, but instead they suddenly come out into the light of a clearing, in a circular meadow on the edge of which is a small stone cottage. Nick Cruickshank points to it, with an expression that seems strangely timid.

Milena Migliari would once again like to say something, so as not to worsen any misunderstanding that might have been created; but once again she's silent, gazing at the little house.

Nick Cruickshank heads straight for the door, bends down to fish around in a bush, pulls out a key, opens the door, turns around, and gestures to invite her in.

Milena Migliari walks inside, with cautious steps: it's almost dark, apart from a few swaths of light filtering in. It smells of lemon verbena, damp wood, the smoke of burnt wood and burnt grass. There's a winter jacket and raincoat hanging from a rack, a pair of rubber boots on the rough planks of the floor.

Nick Cruickshank goes to open the shutters of three small windows, lets the light in from outside: the room is spartan, with a stone sink, a camping cooker on a shelf, an old rustic table, three straw-bottomed chairs, a Provençal-style couch, a vertical piano, a wood-burning stove in a corner, chopped wood in a basket.

Milena Migliari sets her cooler down on the table, trying to gather her thoughts. She thinks about telling Nick Cruickshank that this place has too dense an atmosphere, that it risks confounding the gelato tasting rather than making it more transparent. But she doesn't.

"It's the only refuge from the invasion." Nick Cruickshank looks at her, and he doesn't seem at all like the first-class predatory male who just succeeded in attracting a female into his den: on the contrary, he too seems deeply perplexed. He opens one of the windows, looking out in the direction of the main house, but all that's visible are the clearing and the trees. Only noises reach them, muffled by the woods and the distance: electric saws or drills, some yelling.

Milena Migliari starts to ask why he doesn't consider her a part of the invasion as well; then she thinks that she doesn't want to know.

Nick Cruickshank closes the window, goes to open the door to the stove: inside it's already prepared with paper and wood, of various sizes. He strikes a match, lights the paper, blows on the first tiny flames until the fire catches. He crouches there watching, transfixed.

Milena Migliari walks over to the window, turns back; she walks over to the sink, turns back. She tries to keep some distance between them, though she isn't sure it's necessary; the same way she isn't sure it's necessary to light the stove for the gelato tasting. She points to the cooler on the table. "It'll only take five minutes."

Nick Cruickshank nods, but immediately points to a wooden staircase in a corner of the room. "You want to see upstairs?"

Milena Migliari thinks about saying no, but he's already going up, so she follows him, up the little stairs that creak. She looks around extremely cautiously, watches him open the shutters of three more small windows: in the afternoon light emerge the blue of the bedcover, the yellows and reds and greens of some books on two shelves, the black and white of the cases of a guitar and a smaller instrument, the oxidized-copper color of the stovepipe that crackles and pops as the fire below slowly heats it.

Nick Cruickshank gestures as if to say *That's it.* He smiles, again with that strange hint of shyness, so unexpected in someone like him.

"So, are we going to do the tasting?" Milena Migliari tries to refocus on the original reason for their incursion, but she has to make an effort, because she is finding it very difficult to concentrate, every tiny detail distracts her. She goes down the wooden stairs, back to the room below.

Nick Cruickshank follows her down, almost immediately; he stops at the foot of the stairs, waiting.

Milena Migliari opens the cooler on the old walnut table, a bit worm-eaten and fissured but still as solid as the tree it came from. She takes out the one-pound Styrofoam container, the spatula, the paper boxes with cones, cups, and spoons. Arranging everything gives her a sense of purpose, attenuates the confusion inside her. She takes a breath, tears off the tape keeping the cover on.

Nick Cruickshank comes a few steps closer; he stops to look at the container, looks back at her.

"Don't look yet." She thinks that she might as well trust her instincts now, stop trying to complicate matters.

"Okay." He lifts his hands up, covering his eyes.

"Wait." She's surprised at how fluid the communication is between them, as soon as rationality is taken out of the equation. "What do you want, a cone or a cup?"

He lowers his hands, looking at her. "It makes a big difference, right?"

She nods, serious; even if being serious now seems like a kind of game to her, just like everything else.

"Explain it to me." He smiles, but he really is waiting for an explanation; his patience contrasts spectacularly with the urgency he communicated to her the other times she's seen him.

"To begin with, the cone requires only one hand." These are things she's reflected on many times to herself but never said out loud to anyone. "It's perfectly fine if you want to eat your gelato while you're walking and talking and looking around."

"So it's the most *superficial* choice?" He has this way of looking at her, as if he isn't expecting just any old response, but the *truth*, and not only about this.

"Not necessarily." She shakes her head; she feels intense pleasure at the responsibility he just assigned her, and in the attention with which he's observing her, seemingly unlimited in both depth and duration.

"Because, on the other hand, the cone requires no *intermediation*, right?" He continues staring at her; they're on the identical wavelength.

"It lets you establish the most *direct* possible connection between your mouth and the gelato." She realizes she's emphasizing words the same way he does, but it isn't mimicry: she used to do it when she was a little girl, too; she's always done it. They're similar in this.

"Like our ancestors who ate fruit straight off the tree, without even picking it off first with their hands." He moves a hand as if it's a branch approaching his mouth, flaring out his lips with the expression of a ravenous hominid.

She laughs; she thinks that his mimicking abilities shouldn't surprise her, given his line of work, but they do. "Or like a baby sucking milk from a breast."

He laughs too, but quickly turns serious. "So the cup is the most *mediated* choice?"

She thinks that she could have spared herself the comment about the baby and the breast; she shakes her head. "Not necessarily."

He tilts his head to one side: he's clearly examining the question from every possible angle, with a surprising lack of preconceptions. "The type of spoon you use is important as well, right?"

"*Yes*, obviously." She nods energetically, and yet it still doesn't seem enough. "It changes everything; for example, if your tongue slides over plastic, or picks up the cold taste of metal. It makes a big difference."

"*Huge*." The emphasis in his voice might suggest he's mocking her, but one look at his eyes suffices to know that that's not the case. One look at him. "And which one do you prefer?"

"Wood." She gets real pleasure out of replying immediately, without a pause. "Slightly porous, so the tongue has to scratch its surface a little as it seeks out the flavor." It's like a contact sport now: like grabbing each other's arms and pushing each other back and forth, with strength and gentleness.

He pulls on a lock of his hair. He has this extraordinarily flexible physique: forward, backward, to one side, to the other. But he's also very sturdy, standing there with his feet firmly planted. "So what are the advantages of the cup, with respect to the cone?"

She tilts her head as well, practically the same way he did; much as she's thought about it, she's never been able to reach a definitive conclusion. "It certainly forces you to *concentrate* more on the gelato. To *look at it* more as well."

He cups his hands around his eyes as if to look, with a candor that seems impossible but must be real. "You get a better idea of when it's about to *end*, too."

"Yes. *Yes*." She realizes she's had a terrible need to communicate like this to someone, for who knows how long. *Forever*, really. Or at least since elementary school, when she spent entire afternoons talking and laughing and playing with her friend Tania; it's a need both very strange and completely natural. "The little wooden spoon scrapes on the waxed paper bottom, the empty cup makes that sound like the crackle of a small speaker."

"But it *is* a little speaker!" His body trembles, his eyes light up. "When I was a little boy in Manchester my brother and I would take two empty cups of that awful industrial ice cream that every so often we managed to get my parents to buy for us, we'd make a little hole in the bottoms, string a thread through them, knot it and pull it taut, and we had a *telephone*!"

"I did that too, with my friend Tania!" She's shaken by the realization that they both had the same experience, over such a great distance of time and space; and once again it seems like it couldn't be any other way.

"But if you have a cone the end is much more *gradual*, right?" He continues in this unfiltered, exhilarating flow of communication. "Your tongue is able to reach a tiny amount of gelato even when it seems like there's none left."

"And after a certain point the gelato's flavor and consistency blend with those of the cone." She can taste the contrasting flavors and consistencies with perfect clarity, just by talking about them.

"Oh, yes!" He moves in front of her like he's entirely possessed by the sensations they're evoking. "And when the gelato is all finished you can go on munching on what's left of the cone, all the way down to the point. You can make it last a minute longer, or much more. You can even hold that little piece of empty half-eaten cone in your hand for *an hour* if you want."

"Yes, but the gelato is finished." She'd like to say something else, but she's unable to choose among all the different impulses passing through her body.

Both of them are silent, looking at each other and not looking, in the cottage in the middle of the woods, in the damp air slowly warming up from the fire in the stove.

"And how about eating gelato in a *crystal* cup?" He gestures with deliberate theatricality, in a sort of self-reference. "With a *silver* spoon?"

"*Baaah.*" She grimaces in disgust, sincerely. "It doesn't get any more wrong than that, if you want my opinion."

"Of course I want your opinion." He grins widely. "It's an *even* exchange, seeing as how you want mine, right?"

"Uh-huh." But she wonders *what* exactly she really wants his opinion about. About her fior di latte and persimmon gelato? About the *sense* in making it? About what's supposed to happen on Monday? About the future? About right now?

"Anyway, the other night I ate your gelato straight out of the container." He laughs. "Unlike the others, who had it served to them in crystal cups."

She realizes she has forgotten why they're here; she recovers with a twitch, takes the cover off the container.

He backs up, rather than approaching. "But we still haven't decided how I have to taste it."

She shakes her head. "I certainly can't tell you. You have to choose." Yes, there's something delicious about this game, and worrisome, for how innocent it is and is not.

He puts his hand on his forehead: a gesture she saw him make the other day in the gelateria, as well as in a music video a few years ago. He closes his eyes. "Cup. No. Cone."

"Make up your mind." She goads him on; she likes this, too.

"I don't *know.*" He shakes his head. "It seems like each of the two possibilities implies an intolerable sacrifice."

She feels a tickle rise within her, a current of delight that's electrifying. "Who said that there are only *two* possibilities?"

He suddenly looks dismayed; from his expression it's clear that his thoughts are traveling rapidly in various directions. "You mean I could taste it straight out of the tub?"

"No." Yes, yes: she's getting real pleasure from this exchange, she wishes it would never end. "It would be more or less like eating from a cup, only bigger."

"Well?" He looks at her, as if he absolutely must have an answer.

She feels her heart rate quicken, from the electric pleasure of teasing him and being able to surprise him. She takes a paper bag from the table, opens it. "Well, there's the *waffle basket*! The best of both worlds!"

He seems shaken, as if by a revelation: he comes closer to observe the flared and truncated cone she holds between her fingers, he looks at her. "You really are full of surprises, aren't you!"

She smiles; of course she's pleased to hear him say something like that, but it's the tone of his voice that accentuates her thrill. "And then there are also the waffle *cups*, the wafers, and the cannoli."

He watches her hands from very close up, seems bewitched by her gestures.

She takes her coat off, to be freer in her movements, and also because she's starting to feel hot. She thinks for an instant that her green cardigan is a bit discolored after so many washes, and stretched out at the neck; then she thinks that she couldn't care less. She peels off the wax paper protecting the gelato in the container: the white and orange of the fior di latte and persimmon are vivid, gorgeous. She holds the waffle basket delicately in her left hand, sinks the spatula into the fior di latte: even the consistency is exactly the way it should be. She forms a little scoop of fior di latte and on top one of persimmon, adjusts them with two or three touch-ups to give them the final shape she likes the most, roundish but neither puffed up like a mushroom cloud nor flattened. She hands him the little basket, hands him a small bamboo spoon.

He observes it from a distance with his arm outstretched, observes it up close; he half closes his eyes, sticks his tongue out into the persimmon gelato.

Milena Migliari monitors his expressions and realizes that some rational thoughts are beginning to sneak back into her mind, finding their way through the bizarre exhilaration that's been occupying it up to now. Again she wonders whether she hasn't built the whole thing up too much, hasn't made disappointment practically inevitable for both of them.

Nick Cruickshank opens his eyes again, twirling the little basket of gelato around in his fingers; he digs the spoon in, brings it to his mouth. He looks pensive, doesn't say anything, doesn't look at her. He goes over to a window, pulling the spoon out from between his lips, extremely slowly.

Milena Migliari thinks that the first taste has almost certainly disappointed him, and the following ones will continue to do so: that his enthusiastic impressions from the other day have already been deflated by this mediocre result, accompanied, furthermore, by an excess of theorizing and philosophizing. Maybe the fault lies with the tired old grass that Didier's cows are eating, or the overly fresh hay; or with her state of mind, her inability to be a true professional and not let her work be influenced by events in her personal life.

Nick Cruickshank partly licks the gelato and partly eats it with the spoon, without saying anything and without looking at her, his back turned. He's probably searching for the nicest way to tell her that neither the fior di latte nor the persimmon are anything special, and that the waffle basket is just a stupid compromise between a cone and a cup. He'll feel that he was way off when he thought he had tasted the best gelato in the world. Maybe that's what happened, due to his having the munchies after smoking a joint: the smell of marijuana when he came into the lab yesterday was unmistakable, despite being mixed with patchouli. He'll feel stupid for paying her so many groundless compliments; to compensate, he might be just as ferociously sincere now, like in that song of his that was playing on the radio yesterday.

Milena Migliari wonders what the heck got into her to put herself in such a mortifying position. Was it necessary, really? What type of stupid gratification was she after? Did she want to hear him say that they both belong to a world of extraordinary artistic creativity? Maybe Viviane is right about this, too, when she says that gelato is either good or bad, period, and that there's no point in trying to turn it into something it isn't.

It's difficult to know how much time has passed; all perception in this room seems filtered, like the frenetic noises around the house that are barely audible when they reach them through the woods, covered by the crackling and hissing of the stove.

Milena Migliari smooths the wax paper back over the gelato left in the container, puts the cover back on, places the container back in the cooler, along with the spatula and the boxes with cones, cups, and spoons. She thinks that at this point it might be better to say good-bye to him and leave, or leave without even saying good-bye; keep the embarrassment to a minimum, keep the damage to a minimum.

Nick Cruickshank is now crunching on the waffle basket, maybe as a demonstration, underlining the fact that he was at least able to finish it. He turns around, comes toward her, with an expression that she's never seen on him; he sets the bamboo spoon down on the table.

"Listen, you don't have to say anything, okay?" Milena Migliari picks the cooler up off the table, looks toward the door. She should be able to find the path through the woods even by herself, despite the awful turmoil she's feeling inside.

Nick Cruickshank slowly shakes his head; there's still no trace of theatricality in his movements, which only increases the sadness of the moment.

Milena Migliari looks once more at the door. She feels a bit cowardly running away like this, without even asking him to explain why he didn't like the gelato. She feels angry, but not so much at him: at the world in general, at all the faulty reasoning that inflated her expectations, only to deflate them like poorly whipped cream. "It wasn't good?"

Nick Cruickshank shakes his head again.

Milena Migliari now feels the impact of disappointment, though she was convinced she'd already borne the brunt of it and partly gotten past it. Her face is burning, but her blood is cold, her stomach aches. She grips the handle of the cooler, turns around: her legs are already counting the steps to get to the door, to cross back through the holm oak wood, to reach the van, to get off this darn property.

Suddenly Nick Cruickshank grabs her arm, turns her around to face him; in his eyes is a frightening urgency. "You've captured *everything* in that fior di latte and persimmon. The outside and the inside, rediscovery and loss, the miraculous joy of a moment that melts away. Like in a beautiful poem. Like in a beautiful *song*."

She's so caught off guard that she's left breathless; her fingers clamp down even tighter around the handle of the cooler. She tries to create a barrier between the words he just pronounced and the wave of emotions they arouse in her, but the barrier immediately cracks, falls to pieces: her heart slows down, her eyes tear up.

He gazes at her from very close, and a moment later he pulls her toward him with two hands, presses his lips still cold from the gelato against hers.

She shuts her mouth as tightly as she can, but almost immediately reopens it, at the taste of the fior di latte, the growing warmth; their tongues slip over one another with uncontrollable impatience, generating inner waves that spread to every corner of her body. The cooler slips from her grasp, falling to the floor: she registers the sound as if it comes from a dimension beyond the one in which she's currently abandoning herself with increasing speed. Or at least the most familiar version of herself, the years full of tender embraces with Viviane. Familiarity slides off her on all sides and reconstitutes itself as her body and mind absorb the form and consistency and breath of him, so different and at the same time so familiar.

He holds her tight, looks at her with that dark warm light in his eyes, concentrated on her, absorbed. He continues kissing her, his lips so much softer than she imagined, and just as she expected. He passes his hand over her forehead, her eyebrows, her temples, her hair, her forehead again; the continually renewed contact generates torrents of impulses that sweep away all questions or attempts at definition. She makes his identical movements, like in a game in front of a mirror: she traces the contours of his face with her fingertips, slowly. They repeat and repeat each gesture, slowly and precisely as if under a spell, they gaze at each other only an inch apart, too close to bring each other into focus. They read each other's faces with their hands, more than with their eyes; they probe, taste; they press against each other and come apart, they smile: the flow goes on and on, unstoppable.

They continue like this for a space of time that, once again, she'd be unable to measure, even if she wanted to try. He caresses her in ever-broadening circles, like radar whose range gets progressively wider: one pass after another reaches her shoulders, her hips, her waist, her buttocks, her thighs, then narrows its range once more and concentrates back on her face, her ears, her forehead, her eyebrows.

She's completely immersed in these semicircular movements and the sensations they generate, and then just like that her thoughts come back online as quickly as they vanished, dragging her back toward the version of herself from before this embrace began. It suddenly feels like she's standing on the edge of an abyss; the sense of vertigo makes her stagger. "Hey!" She retreats suddenly, her back banging into the wall.

Nick Cruickshank moves back too, in that agile and slightly disconnected way of his. He looks at her: intent, almost scared.

Milena Migliari would like to be able to identify exactly when what was happening between them became wrong. Was it the insistence in his hands, the direction they seemed destined to take, sooner or later? Or has the wrongness been with them from the beginning, ever since they crossed through the woods together and came in here?

Nick Cruickshank makes a gesture that seems to encompass the room and all that has happened inside the room, back to the gelato tasting; back to when he opened the door for her.

Milena Migliari wipes her mouth with her hand, sniffles. She thinks that what happened is unforgivable, but it was both of their faults in equal measure; she certainly can't play the victim, though it would be much more convenient.

Nick Cruickshank has an air of dejection about him; he gestures toward the main house, the preparatory confusion surrounding it. "Tomorrow I'm getting married."

Milena Migliari feels the strangest blend of relief and disappointment well up inside her: it reaches her head with such intensity that she staggers again. She gropes, looking for an answer, and one rises to her lips entirely on its own. "On Monday I'm starting the procedures to have a baby."

"Ah." Nick Cruickshank tries to smile, but it doesn't come

off too well; he looks like someone who just got punched in the stomach.

"Yes, with my female partner." Milena Migliari thinks that she could even enjoy seeing the effect of her words if she herself weren't so incredibly shaken.

TWENTY-EIGHT

NICK CRUICKSHANK STUDIES the expressions of Milena the gelato girl, and it's clear she isn't joking around: she has this direct way of looking at him, with that gleam in her eyes. He searches for something extremely cool to say, but it doesn't come. "Ah, well."

"Well what?" Milena has an attitude of defiance, or it could be strenuous defense; she does not look away.

"I meant, good." Nick Cruickshank realizes he's been caught off guard, and it doesn't happen to him often.

"Good *what*?" Milena is planted firmly in front of him: cheeks red, chin slightly raised.

"Good for *you*, right?" Nick Cruickshank is still slipping into and out of the sensations of two minutes ago. What was that kiss? An attempted escape? An attempted invasion? An act of desperation? There was something so unexpected, though: it was like he recognized her from an unknown point in space and time, and that he recognized *himself*, or a part of himself that he'd lost, or given up looking for. Which probably speaks volumes about the state he's in at present.

Milena continues staring at him, a stare that's less defiant or defensive than it is extremely attentive, scanning him and not liking what it sees. "Which means?"

"If I were a woman I'd prefer to be with a woman too." Nick Cruickshank thinks he could have articulated the idea better, but that's how it comes out.

"Ah, sure." Milena moves her head, snorts. "The typical man, playing the game of imagining himself as a woman for two seconds. A nice little erotic trip, eh?"

"Not at all, no, *no*." Nick Cruickshank can't believe he's incapable of putting together even the shortest sequence of words to accurately convey his thoughts.

"Then tell me why." Milena continues scrutinizing him: inflamed, almost furious now.

"Because men are so *awful*." Nick Cruickshank tries to channel as much truth as he can into his tone, seeing as his verbal tools are disabled. It's as if a hapless sound technician has turned off his microphone in the middle of a song, and he still has to try desperately to make himself heard, over the protests of the crowd.

"Why?" Milena keeps the pressure on, doesn't let him wriggle free.

"Because of how *limited* they are." Now Nick Cruickshank is answering without even reflecting anymore. "How *predictable* they are. Because of how *mean* they are, too."

Milena makes a visible effort to remain serious, but she can't; she starts laughing.

Nick Cruickshank feels an unexpected relief; he laughs too. "Being in a rock band for a few decades is a good way to get to know the worst sides of men."

"So is being a *woman* for a few decades, I can assure you." Milena has this nice way of laughing, of looking at him; there's something independent about her, restless.

"I can imagine." Nick Cruickshank thinks that yes, the situation *is* absurd if he thinks about it with a minimum of perspective; but if, on the other hand, he stays inside it, it's so natural that it doesn't even seem like a situation.

Milena shakes her head. "So you hate even yourself, given that you're a man?"

"Yes, it happens to me quite often." Nick Cruickshank focuses on her features, watching to see if she finds the idea amusing or tragic.

Milena has turned serious again as well, but there's still a sparkle of amusement in her eyes. "All right, then we have something in common."

"That's not all." Nick Cruickshank realizes that his sensations are turning into words without first becoming thoughts: they're skipping that step completely.

"No?" Milena tilts her head to the side, studying him.

He feels a tickle in the vicinity of his heart. The space dividing them vibrates with a magnetic tension that he doesn't think he's ever felt before, except maybe when he was thirteen; although he was able to describe it pretty well in a couple of songs.

"What else do you think we have in common?" She looks away, glances at the cooler sitting on the wooden planks of the floor.

"We're just all wrong, the both of us." Once again he doesn't think before speaking: the thoughts arrive after the words, chasing after them like tired old dogs, with no hope of reaching them in time.

She turns back to look at him, and there's an almost frightened look in her eyes now, her pupils are dilated. "All wrong how?"

"That we don't *belong* anywhere." He makes a semicircular gesture: unconsciously, this too. "That we've never quite *fit in*, despite everything."

She clamps her eyelids down tight, as if to be sure what he really means.

He feels his heartbeat quicken. It's ridiculous; he thought he was immune to these feelings, permanently. "Wherever we are, whomever we're with, whatever we do, even if things work out. Even if they work out really well."

"Define wrong." In her expression and in her words is a mix of curiosity and diffidence, a need for raw, unadulterated answers.

"Our roots are never long enough, in any place or situation. Even if from the outside the opposite might seem true." It's another sensation he's described in a couple of songs; but his songs limit themselves to alluding; they certainly don't explain anything. They might come very close to a precise meaning, then wander off in other directions.

She nods, nearly the same way he does. "I see myself almost as a sort of *intruder*."

He's excited by how well attuned they are, and frightened at how she continues to catch him by surprise. "*Me too*."

"Come on, you even invented your own *style*." She doesn't trust words, and she's right not to. "I even read on the Internet that they call it 'Cruickshank cool.'"

"Ah, right." He shakes his head; it seems like such a stupid definition, and he certainly wasn't the one who invented it. He takes off his jacket, as if he could also shrug off the definition, and the attitudes that go with the definition. "You know what Cruickshank means, in medieval Scottish?"

"No." She shakes her head.

"Crooked leg." He laughs; points to his legs, which luckily are pretty straight. In truth he discovered that his name probably derives from the River Cruick, in the old county of Kincardine; but the first interpretation has always seemed more appropriate, metaphorically speaking.

She smiles; she has this total honesty in her features, in her eyes. Like last night, when they were in the circle of huggers; like when, after the hug, they looked at each other without saying anything. "It almost seems like I'm playing the part of *someone else*. And I'm afraid of being found out, sooner or later."

He realizes he's hanging on her every word, on the snapshot images they create; the idea inebriates and terrorizes him to the same degree. "But not when you're making your *gelato*?"

She wipes her forehead with her hand: she has these strong and delicate fingers, these fingernails cut short, not painted, like a woman who works with her hands. "Not *while* I'm making it, no. But all I have to do is move from the lab to the shop counter, and I already feel like an impostor."

"But you shouldn't!" His voice comes out with almost desperate emphasis, because it's as if they're talking about the songs he'd still like to write, the reasons for his frustration and unhappiness and inspiration and passion.

She laughs again: solid yet graceful, standing firmly yet flexible. She comes forward, lowers her forehead.

He comes forward as well and lowers his forehead, and a moment later they're locked once more in an embrace, even more passionately than before: like they're sinking into each other, like the meaning of the distressing information they've exchanged has dissolved their contours, along with the space that separates them.

They stroke each other's faces, their fingers trace the curves of their foreheads, the lines of their noses, of their ears: they pass over them again and again, as if moved by a need to register the data flowing through their fingers toward a more internal, more ancient memory. They separate briefly and come back together again, kiss again; they sway back and forth in their warm and liquid natures, move back a few inches to look at each other, then resume painting each other's faces with their fingers, annihilate the distance once more, kiss each other once more.

Then his hands are under her sweater, and hers under his shirt; but with a need to touch everywhere, so different from the more targeted search for sensitive points that occurs with Aileen. So different, too, from every other embrace before Aileen, though he's not really able to think about it now. Here, it's as if each touch is felt by the one touching and the one touched in the same way; as if there's no separation, as if their two parts are rejoined in a whole, containing polar opposites. There's an incredible degree of innocence in every single one of their gestures: of noncalculation, nonintention. And despite what they now know about each other, they throw caution to the wind: they continue activating cascades of sensations, letting themselves be carried beyond. They breathe into each other's mouths, ears, bite each other's earlobes, kiss the tips of each other's noses; they gaze at each other from a few inches away and then from no distance at all, their features losing their contours and regaining them, then losing them anew.

It's strange, because he's aware that even one false move could ruin everything, yet he gives in completely to the wave that's passing back and forth between them. He makes no effort whatsoever to imagine where this embrace might lead; it seems to him that the embrace *in itself* contains all its reasons. It's not a point of departure, but a point of arrival; and it contains the shadow of latent pain that could become acute at any moment, just as easily as their features go from unfocused to crystal clear at the slightest step back. Try as he might to remain light, he feels a heaviness grow with each exchange, a danger that continues to increase, that frightens and thrills him, counseling him to lie still and pushing him to act.

Then they're on the wooden steps of the staircase, and it isn't clear how they've come to be there, or how their intentions and movements can be so perfectly coordinated. The only thing for sure is the undeniable need for contact running through them, the convulsive grasping, the continuous transfusion, the feeling and gazing at and breathing into each other without interruption.

They're halfway up the stairs; they're upstairs, where it's colder, even though the metal pipe of the stove burns the hand he places on it; they're in the middle of the room and they continue to kiss and hold each other; they're on the bed and still they kiss, rubbing against each other with the strangest blend of urgency and calm, precision and vagueness.

Shards of thought flash through his mind intermittently: What does she like? What doesn't she like? Are there limits? What are they? Luckily, he doesn't have a goal to reach: he's more than happy to continue kissing and caressing her like he's doing now, moving back slightly every now and then to distinguish her features, tracing the lines of her eyebrows with his fingers again, moving closer again. But now she slides a hand under his shirt, passing it over his stomach and descending still farther, with lightness and determination. And there's a language in her breathing, in the movements of her tongue. Despite their closeness, it's now nearly impossible to tell who is responsible for a specific movement, which movements are the cause of which sensations; the relationship between cause and effect seems to fluctuate continuously.

And yet at a certain point, they've thrown off the final pieces of shaped and sewn fabric they each had on, both naked under the comforter, warm between the still-cold sheets, clasped tightly to each other, chest to chest, stomach to stomach, legs to legs. Suddenly he too has slid his fingers over her belly, and farther down, down, down over her smooth skin and slipping inside the warmest place, hidden like a secret they both know well, pausing there and lingering in the damp that becomes wet as she presses against him in rhythmic vibration. And then at a certain point he rolls on top of her and kisses her and kisses her again and slips inside her, with infinite caution, in the surprising and moaning and gasping and rubbing closeness that doesn't die out but instead continues to feed itself on the beats of their hearts. Suddenly it seems to him like everything that matters and makes sense is *here, now*: in this moment that continues to expand, in this fusion of contours, in this convulsive exchange of breaths, exchange of skins.

He's able to think about it only fleetingly, but for all the combinations of bodies and desires he's experienced in the past, he doesn't ever remember feeling this sense of completion, this naturalness, this harmony, this trading of proportions, forms, images. And he doesn't ever remember being involved with a female being he knows so much about, question for question, answer for answer, in every shade of color, in every curve, in every fold. Not one element of this stupefying proximity raises obstacles or creates difficulties, there's no discordance, no dissonance: it's like a game for ecstatic and unruly children, or adults extremely aware of the miraculous rarity of what's occurring, absurdly mindless of the seriousness of the consequences.

TWENTY-NINE

A PART OF HER continues to register difference of shape and consistency compared to Viviane: of weight, proportions, anatomical parts, to be sure. But it's a part that shrinks with every movement and every breath, until it virtually dissolves into the combination of filled and empty space that makes possible a physical invasion that strangely doesn't feel like a seizure but is surely a form of possession, even if encouraged, even if compensated by an envelopment that in turn is a form of possession.

They continue on and on, in the fusion of gestures and looks, in the vibration and friction, in the quick beating of hearts and the flowing of blood, with mental images that crop up and vanish constantly, questions that take shape only to lose it immediately. At a certain point she gets scared that she's misunderstood completely, that despite everything the game of possession might at a moment's notice turn into a game of domination; she stops. And in the same precise moment he withdraws, as if he has read her mind, picked up on her fears. He smiles at her, and in his smile there's an unthinkable power of reassurance; again he caresses the line of her eyebrows, the curve of her forehead. He doesn't seem dominated by the animal obstinacy she remembers in the males she's been with, doesn't seem fixated on the reaching of a goal; he seems lost in her, around her, in their closeness, in what they have in common, in what differentiates them. It seems like he could easily stop right here, without getting carried away by an enslavement to instinct, without wanting to rush off toward a mechanical conclusion. She smiles back, caresses a surprisingly smooth temple, a surprisingly full shoulder, a surprisingly muscular arm; slowly but surely she abandons herself again to the current surging through her, and feels a kind of unknown yet familiar bliss expand within her.

He kisses her lips with lips that burn now, kisses her on the forehead, eyes, nose, chin, neck, breasts. He sucks on her nipple, with the biting and aspiring insistence of a hungry newborn baby, sending waves of almost painful pleasure through her body. Between them there's a communication based on breathing that rises and falls in intensity, like a totally accurate nonverbal alphabet, like a precision scale on which to measure the reactions at every step, the repercussions, the echoes. His lips descend toward her navel, he presses on her waist, on her hips. There's something so profoundly familiar at the heart of this need to know each other. Where does it come from? From an unidentifiable and yet so perceptible, so extraordinarily tangible *before*?

He slides farther down, down over her mons Venus, down between her thighs, his tongue receiving and transmitting shivers, like a sort of ecstatic veneration of a female divinity, in which the pleasure of giving is equal to that of receiving, and in fact there seems to be almost no more distinction between giver and receiver. It's an alternating current, in which each tremor of the provoked rises up through the tongue of the provoker and saturates him with an intoxicating pleasure that leaves and then returns. He continues to lick her, with method and patience, as if he could go on like this forever; his tongue accelerates, slows, interprets her expectations with incredible accuracy. He passes over and over again with the sweetest insistence, and she wouldn't want to make comparisons, but the comparisons make themselves: it's better than with Viviane, even though she had seemed infinitely better than the men before her. How is it possible that something like this is happening with a man? After deciding years ago that she didn't like men, that she was finished with them? After being so profoundly convinced that she'd found her center with a woman? Is there something about this difference of polarities, this magnetic attraction between positive and negative? In the fact that he's a rock star, a being that transcends the sexes because he attracts them both, consciously? In his evident, profound knowledge of women, maybe in his genuine love for the female gender? But how authentic can love really be coming from a male, a potential enemy even when, in this case, at least for the moment, he lacks aggressive intentions? Without the disruption of the unpredictable, without the surprise, without the novelty (that's nevertheless so familiar)? Does even the latent dangerousness have a role to play in this encounter? In the way he grips her thighs, his approach at once playful and determined? In the finger he slips inside her, very delicately but without hesitation? Curving it and pressing upward as he presses down with his other hand on her stomach in just the right place, while his tongue continues gathering and provoking sensations to the rhythm of the sighs and moans she produces, without worrying at all anymore about the impressions or judgments they might arouse, without worrying about moaning or raising her voice or moving around with less and less control. How can this ancestral dance be so easy, so spontaneous? Where does the idea come from that it's so *right*, unlike all the things that are so wrong in their lives, and in general?

He continues without tiring, without stopping, as she begins to feel the tension building in her feet and in her calves and rising upward like a series of small waves that gain more and more strength and seem to weaken and vanish and grow stronger and fade again and return with more determination until they become one single and continuous wave that rises and rises, maybe unstoppable now, maybe not, but yes, yes, yes, unstoppable, a wave that crashes into her and knocks her over and throws her and makes her yell from deep in her belly, deep in her throat, makes her thighs squeeze so tightly she might be hurting him, but she can't really think about it because she's too flung backward and dragged back forward in an undertow so slow and sweet, it makes her smile uncontrollably, immeasurably.

Here he is coming back up, in a long, sliding movement, skin on skin, heat on heat, sweat on sweat, eyes on eyes. He looks at her from very close up, smiling at her exactly like she is smiling at him. It comes naturally: she relaxes her lips, he relaxes his, she breathes, he breathes. No longer like looking into a mirror: like being *inside* the mirror. He pulls up the blue comforter, to cover her and cover himself; he holds her tight, caresses her face, her hair. They look at each other, lying on their sides; they keep smiling, time keeps expanding. Thoughts have fled the field, sensations taken over all the space there is. He doesn't seem to expect anything in return for what he's done: he doesn't make requests, apply pressure. He seems happy that it has happened; to be close to her, to caress her slowly and smile.

She stays immersed at length in the deep reverberation, in the light contact of his hands, then follows a sudden impulse, takes him by a shoulder and pushes him onto his back, with a determination that surprises her as much as him. He thinks about resisting, then lets out a sigh, closes his eyes, and lets go. She has a fervor she thought could only come with Viviane: she blocks his wrists, her lips descending over his body, doing more or less what he did to her. She sucks him as if she's going to swallow him whole, make him a part of her, definitively annihilates any distinction. This too is quite strange: and exciting, something so simple but that activates within her a pleasure unfelt, a search for the very origins of what he feels and what he makes her feel, in the increasingly panting exchange of breaths and murmurs and moans, until he arches backward and yells like she yelled, shakes like she shook as their fluids mix and their contours melt into each other again.

Then he looks at her, across the mountains and valleys of the displaced and battered comforter. "Heeey." He reaches out a hand, takes hers, lifting it toward the ceiling.

"Hey." She holds his fingers tightly.

"There's the imperfect marvel." He's still smiling. "The highest degree of perfection that imperfection could ever reach."

"Yes." She smiles again as well, because she can't help doing so; and meanwhile her thoughts return, and the imperfection of the marvel begins to manifest itself, like a hairline crack that gradually widens across the surface of a beautiful porcelain cup, thin and fragile as an eggshell.

Nick Cruickshank turns to look at her, and though he continues to smile, his expression is changing too. "We've really done it now."

Milena Migliari nods; she knows.

THIRTY

HE REALIZES HIS words were childish, completely inappropriate given the situation; but the more inappropriate they seem, the less he's able to find any better ones. He lies next to her, caressing her hair with the same repetitive gesture. He feels like he could continue doing so indefinitely, or else be forced to stop at any moment, because there's simply no measure to what's happened.

It isn't the single acts or their sequences; he's experienced similar moments many times with varying degrees of conviction, to the point of concluding that they're substantially senseless. On more than one occasion he's felt dishonest, for contributing with his songs to the oft-perpetrated mystification, the scam erected by the dealers of consumption and their willing servants, with their advertisements and their romantic advice columns and their pornography and their films and their books full of prefabricated fantasies. As if the close encounter between two people attracted to one another is the *guarantee* of a marvel to which everyone is entitled, the equivalent of any other commodity on the market that's endlessly available to be bought and sold. As if the marvel can be reproduced as many times as there are billions of people in the world, and isn't actually an extraordinarily rare occurrence, extremely difficult to predict and almost impossible to preserve, a miraculous blink of an eye in an infinite succession of unpleasant or neutral moments.

So what's just happened here? What was this exhilarating fusion, this loss of boundaries, this inexplicable impression of familiarity and reunion, this instantaneous combination of equal and opposite elements, this complete and utter naturalness? And why now, when the choices he's made with great difficulty and after long consideration, forcing himself to overcome complex forms of resistance and obstacles, are about to come to fruition?

He gets up, collects his boxers and pants off the floor with vague gestures, puts them on. He turns to look at her, her body still immersed in the long wake of sensations that show no sign of dissipating.

She looks at him; she sits up on the edge of the bed, pulling the blanket over to cover herself. The temperature in the room seems to diminish noticeably with each passing second, along with the light coming in through the windows.

He'd like to say something, but he knows that nothing he could say would seem right, so he remains silent, picks up his shirt.

She gets up too: light-skinned, supple and strong, exactly as he saw and felt her earlier, a girl-woman, a warrior-philosopher, a female of both sun and moon, contemporary and ancient. She too picks her clothes up off the floor, looking at them as if surprised by their shapes, their colors, their consistency.

He motions that he'll leave her to get dressed; he goes down the stairs with an uncertain step, his legs trembling. He puts more wood into the stove, blowing to help rekindle the fire. Then he lights the oil lamp on the table, staring fixedly at the yellow light, as dilated thoughts pass slowly and uncertainly through his head.

From his jacket pocket he retrieves the corncob pipe and the bag of Wally's weed, fills the bowl, lights up, inhales.

She comes down the staircase with cautious steps, and he only has to look at her to know that she feels exactly the same way: crash-landed on earth, unable to find the true names of things.

He hands her the pipe; it feels like he has to stretch his arm out over an incredibly vast space to reach her.

She turns it over in her hand, puts the mouthpiece to her lips, takes a hit.

They're both quiet, their movements extremely slow. Words are suspended between them, the anticipation of gestures that continue to remain unmade; the only sounds are the breaths and crackles of the stove. Every so often they pass each other the pipe, take a hit, hold in the smoke, then softly blow it out.

"So you're getting married tomorrow?" She looks at him, her head tilted ever so slightly.

"Looks that way." He realizes he's talking about it like something that doesn't regard him, but there's an entire sea of uncertainty between him and the event. He hands her back the pipe with another exceedingly slow gesture.

She nods, but with an air of not finding his answer completely comprehensible. She takes a hit, holds in the smoke.

"And you're doing this child thing, with your friend?" The words he finds are as imprecise as his thoughts; if he had to write a song right now, it would end up frighteningly muddled and meaningless.

She blows out the smoke. "With my partner." There might be something almost interrogative in her tone, or maybe not.

"I meant with your *partner*." His mental image of her partner is purely hypothetical: inexplicably, she's dressed in gray, with short hair and glasses, a serious expression on her face, as if in wait.

She passes him back the pipe. "It's complicated." She looks at him, from the old chair where she sits in graceful balance. "And you two?"

"We two who?" He feels a chill pass through him. Or maybe it's the room that's cold, maybe the stove is no longer able to heat it. Yet, just before, it was so warm: they were both covered in sweat, their skin burning.

"You and your future wife." She also seems to be having trouble finding the words and pronouncing them properly; but then she isn't speaking in her native tongue, unlike him. "You don't want children?"

He blows out the smoke, shaking his head. "I've already got five of them, and they give me enough problems."

"But you don't have any with her, do you?" Her curiosity is so transparent, so free of implied judgments, so disarming.

"No. I don't." Again a chill passes through him, as if he's still naked.

She looks at the stove; maybe she's as cold as he is.

"How do these things get created?" He feels the need to ask, though he doesn't really expect an answer.

"What things?" She continues to seem so incredibly familiar, even now: so simple and so complicated, so calm and yet so full of worries.

"The permanent bonds between two people." He's hearing his voice with the same detachment as when he hears it back over the mixer after a recording session: imprecise, the intonation in constant flux. "When the best reasons that kept them together have dissolved, and all that remain are the *worst*. When what's keeping them together is habit, fear, and regret."

She sucks on the mouthpiece of the pipe, though it's no longer lit. "Do you believe in the idea of twin flames?"

"What's that?" He shakes his head; he's suddenly afraid of being in the dark about some fundamental notion of the universe.

"Two parts of the same soul?" Yes, her tone is interrogative here, like she isn't completely sure he'll be able to understand. "They separate and then pass through a long series of reincarnations to gather experiences, and at a certain point are reunited."

"Ah, like soul mates? The two halves of the apple?" He smiles: he wrote a song about that five years ago, "Twin Soul Reunion." Wasn't bad, the maximum soppiness you could hope to get out of the Bebonkers without provoking a mutiny among their fans.

"And each of the two halves is a complete soul, but with a different polarity." Now she's speaking with a sort of charmingly didactic intent, at once wise and naïve, mysterious. "Two complementary opposites that meet and recognize each other again, and are irresistibly attracted. The fusing of the sun and the moon; total and perfect understanding, with no need for explanations."

"Doesn't everyone think it's like that when they meet someone new?" Her honesty pushes him to be honest, too, but the sound of his own words causes an inner pain that stabs at his heart and stomach.

"Maybe, but they're almost always wrong." She speaks like she's intent on offering the most accurate reconstruction possible. "Because a *true* reunion between twin flames is extremely rare."

"And because their illusions are quickly contradicted by direct experience, and by time." Nick Cruickshank certainly doesn't want to be cynical, but he feels like the search for truth comes at a price.

It's unclear whether Milena's expression is one of disappointment, or profound thoughtfulness. "Not if it's a *true* reunion."

Nick Cruickshank looks off to the side; he's suddenly afraid that his insensitivity and impatience have just ruined something incredibly precious.

They're both silent, listening to the sounds of the stove.

"What now?" Nick Cruickshank feels a sort of desperation rise within him and doesn't know how to stop it.

"Now?" Miraculously, Milena is still there with him; she truly seems to want to understand.

"I mean, what do we do *now*?" Nick Cruickshank couldn't say exactly what that now was referring to: To the now of the next few minutes? The next few weeks? The next few months? The next ten years? To the two of them? To him and Aileen? To her and her partner? To a universal, neutral now?

Milena moves her foot, pointing at the cooler on the floor. "You want some more gelato?"

"Yes!" His relief is so intense that he reacts with a totally not-mature, not-appropriate enthusiasm, which she seems to share completely, inside their safety zone on this side of the *now* where it might still be possible to find refuge.

She grabs the yellow-, red-, and pink-flowered cooler, pulls out the white container, then sets it on the table, takes out one of the two little cardboard boxes, and from it two little wooden spoons. She drags her chair up to the table, sits down, then sticks one of the spoons into the white of the fior di latte, brings it to her mouth.

He does the same with the persimmon: the same movements, the same timing. The gelato seems even more surprising than before, sweet and acidulous, only slightly viscous: a cold, delicious distillation of all that's wonderful to discover and taste in the world.

She slowly draws the spoon out from between her lips. "It's strange, don't you think?" She gestures to indicate the floor above, the room where they are now, the two of them.

"It certainly is." He thinks that "strange" doesn't even begin to define what's happened, and what, while it lasts, is still happening.

"Yes." With her spoon she reaches back toward the gelato, sticks it decisively into the orange of the persimmon, and brings it to her mouth. There's an aching gluttony to her movements: the woman of sun and moon who continues to be delighted by what she finds here on earth.

He takes a spoonful of white fior di latte: calming and satisfying, with all the connections to shapes and thoughts that it stimulates. He looks at her, and in him grows the desperate desire that this moment not end. "Can we try to stop time?"

Her eyes in the lamplight are full of colors, like the first time he saw her two days ago; a lifetime ago. "Yes."

They eat the fior di latte and persimmon directly from the container with insatiable pleasure, as if each spoonful is their last, and the next one their first. On and on they continue, in the uncontrollable need to replicate the wonder and joy that have surged through them time and time again, as if this moment that contained them could go on forever. One spoonful after another, they finish off the entire tub: suddenly they're there, scraping the bottom like a couple of famished children. They look at each other and laugh.

Then she turns to look out the window, and he does the same, and they realize that time hasn't stopped: darkness has fallen.

THIRTY-ONE

When they come out of the cottage in the woods it seems like night more than evening. She thinks about getting her phone out to check what time it is but changes her mind. He tries to lock up but has trouble doing so, fumbling around with the key in search of the lock. Time has flown by, with all it contained, and now they're like two survivors of a natural disaster who don't have the slightest clue how long their luck is going to hold out. She's bewildered at the idea that it's become so late without them realizing it, but incredibly it doesn't seem to make her anxious: the waves that have crashed into them and tossed them around have left her permeated with well-being, under her skin, in her heart, in the pit of her stomach, in the back of her thoughts. She doesn't even seem to feel guilty: try as she might to rewind, she can't think of a single squalid or petty thing they've done, not a single word or gesture that wasn't beautiful. Is this her way of absolving herself? Of pretending not to be jointly responsible for an episode that could have disastrous consequences?

They pause in the clearing, then he turns toward the heavier darkness of the woods. "Shall we go?" It seems like an actual question, as if they could decide to stay here instead, go back inside, to the shelter of the cottage, hide out in there indefinitely. But he's moving, and she follows him, with the strangest alternation of fluidity and clumsiness, her right hand gripping the cooler that contains the empty container that contained the gelato, the reason or pretext of her coming here. He holds her left hand, in a protective way she's not at all accustomed to, stroking it as they walk. Protective for how much longer? Ten minutes? Five? What then? They don't say a word to each other, maybe because they don't know what to say, maybe because they've already said far too much.

The dense darkness of the woods wraps around them, with the smells of damp wood, rotted leaves, moss; they feel the path beneath their feet, more than see it, but he goes forward with such confidence, he knows the way. Every so often they stop and breathe each other in, shoulder to shoulder, temple to temple. They start walking again, but slow down as they gradually move forward, as if trying to prolong the time they have left: and of course they can't, time slips away from them one step after another, one pause after another.

They come out of the trees, and all the lights of the big house are there: more numerous and closer than she expected. He grips her hand even tighter, but still they say nothing to each other. They walk alongside the paddock, where by now the little dark horses are almost invisible but their snorting can be heard when they approach the fence.

When they're about fifty yards away from the house he lets go of her hand; his fingers slip away, the warmth of contact disappears.

An emptiness passes through her, makes her waver momentarily.

He must realize it, because he stops again, leans over to kiss her on the side of the head.

She feels the warmth return and it calms her, though she knows it's absurd; she smiles, in between the darkness and the light. And no sooner does she marvel at being able to calm down than the dormant alarm inside her awakens and takes possession of her: it makes her heart race, fills her head with anxious anticipation and incessant questions. If his future wife were to see them, would she know what's happened between them? Just by looking at them, without any need for conjectures, let alone questions? And even if she doesn't see them, what are they going to do now? Will they say good-bye and that's it, go their separate ways? With what *internal* consequences? What doubts that will never go away? Or will they both be able to forget about what happened, once the swirl of sensations still enveloping them has dissolved? Will they be relieved when this afternoon becomes just another piece of their past? Will they be sad? Will they perhaps feel a small pang of guilt every now and then? Of perplexity? Of nostalgia?

By now they've almost reached the house; with each step their physical closeness to each other seems less sustainable, yet between the darkness behind them and the lights ahead she isn't even sure how close they really are, because it seems like she's almost touching him and instead when she turns there's far too much space separating them. But it's certainly not a question of physical closeness: it's the traces of what's transpired, on their faces and in their ways of moving, as much as they might try to pretend otherwise. Not that they're trying very hard, though. Their states of mind change every second, without one being able to prevail over the others long enough to control the situation. She now feels much worse than when she arrived here with her van, and at that point she already felt like a thief. One moment she feels like what's happened was so magical that it was worth any risk; the next that it was the stupidest thing in the world; the next that it was the most ridiculous. One moment it seems like she did absolutely nothing wrong; the next she feels like a criminal. She turns toward him, to tell him something or grab his hand or even just to look at him before leaving, but a violent beam of white light accosts them.

"It's him!" An enormous black silhouette is in front of them, a high-powered flashlight in his hand.

"Of course it's me. Lower the light, you're blinding me." Nick Cruickshank uses a hand to shield his eyes.

The enormous silhouette complies, and it's the Italian bodyguard who stopped her the other day at her arrival; now that his face is visible, he looks embarrassed.

Just beyond is Nick Cruickshank's future wife, illuminated by the lights from the windows and sliding doors and the lower garden lights and the ones higher up; behind her are several men and women, all in a state of obvious tension.

Nick Cruickshank gives her a little wave. "Hey, Aileen." Incredibly light, incredibly out of place. Is this the provocation of a rock star who ignores conventions and the rules of cohabitation and even other people's feelings, or an absurd show of loyalty? To *her*?

Milena Migliari would like to sprint around the corner of the house, get to her van, jump inside and turn on the engine, drive away as fast as she can; but she already knows that it would be a very undignified way to go, as well as being useless, since they'd certainly stop her at the gate. It would actually be so undignified and pointless that just thinking about it makes her want to laugh. She tries to restrain herself, because she knows that laughing would be even more unacceptable than Nick Cruickshank's attitude, but she can't; she laughs.

Nick Cruickshank turns to look at her, with an expression that's so comic it makes her laugh even harder; and he laughs with her. He tries to look serious, tries straightening up but can't. He walks chuckling and slightly bent over toward Aileen and the others.

Milena Migliari follows him, since she can't come up with any acceptable alternatives. Even though she keeps on laughing it feels like her feet are glued to the ground, each step forward requiring a conscious effort.

They meet in the middle of the lawn: Nick Cruickshank, she, and the bodyguard on one side, Aileen and her little group on the other. Just beyond a small army of men are planting, hammering, assembling, setting up arches, lengthening walkways, widening cupolas in the shafts of light.

"What is so amusing?" Aileen makes a visible effort to restrain herself, maybe because of her two friends or assistants standing at her sides, the other people standing just behind her. But she's so tense it looks like she's about to snap: you only have to look at her dilated nostrils, her hands, her nervous legs.

The enormous bodyguard points the flashlight toward the darkness behind them, possibly to make sure there are no other intruders ready to pop out of the woods. Then he makes a gesture of disengagement, awkward like his other gestures, and goes toward the men working in the distance.

"Well?" Nick Cruickshank looks at his future wife, as if he isn't that sure who she really is.

"Would you mind telling me where you've disappeared to all this time?" Aileen's very white teeth sparkle in the lamplight, but certainly not in a smile.

"Ah." Nick Cruickshank turns, gestures toward Milena Migliari standing two steps behind him. "She brought me some gelato to taste."

Milena Migliari feels a bit thrown in at the deep end, but she lifts up the empty cooler, confirming that at least this detail is authentic, demonstrable.

"Some gelato?" Aileen looks at her like she's just now becoming aware of her presence, which clearly isn't possible. Or maybe it is. Who knows?

Milena Migliari thinks that if this woman attacked her now she wouldn't know how to defend herself. Should she play dumb? Take responsibility, salvage a little dignity? Very little, after being caught like this, the thieving Italian seductress/gelato maker who slinks into the life of the woman who only two days ago came to her rescue with the largest order she's ever received.

"Yes. Fior di latte and persimmon. They were extraordinarily *good.*" Nick Cruickshank gives his voice that theatrical emphasis, as if convincing Aileen that the extraordinary goodness of the gelato could cancel out all the guilt and suspicion, dissolve all the tension.

Aileen tightens her lips in another nonsmile, which must require an enormous dose of self-control. "I bet they were, if you spent *hours* tasting them."

"*Hours*?" Nick Cruickshank seems genuinely surprised, turns to look at Milena Migliari, as if to ask her how much time has actually passed.

Milena Migliari shrugs; if she had to guess based on how she feels, she'd say that an entire day and evening and night have passed, or just a few minutes, bursting with incredibly unmanageable gestures and sensations.

Aileen shifts her gaze from her to him, scans their expressions in the lamplight. "Are you high?"

"*Naaah.*" Nick Cruickshank tries to look serious, but once again starts laughing. He snorts, hunching slightly forward like before.

Milena Migliari is immediately infected, though she tries desperately to restrain herself. She bites her lip, but it takes her whole seconds to stop.

Aileen excludes her from her visual field, goes back to focusing on her future husband. "And where did you do this pothead's tasting? We've been looking for you everywhere, inside and out."

Nick Cruickshank gestures toward the woods behind him, maybe because he knows how unrealistic it would be to claim to be coming from anywhere else.

"The damn cottage in the woods?" Aileen makes one of those incredulous faces so common in Hollywood comedies: her eyes and mouth go slightly sideways.

"Well, there's an *invasion force* here." Nick Cruickshank points to the men still intent on every sort of preparatory activity on the illuminated lawn behind her.

Aileen glances over her shoulder, as if to verify that there truly is no way of saying a word or making a gesture without being observed by dozens of people. She tries giving another of her non-smiles, but she's so incredulous and indignant that it cracks immediately. "Here we're preparing the *party for our wedding*, Nick!"

"I *know*." Nick Cruickshank smiles, but not arrogantly, not thoughtlessly; despite everything he seems aware of the fact that there are different points of view in the matter.

Aileen turns back to Milena Migliari, comes up to within a couple inches of her. "Could I speak to you for a minute? Inside?" She makes a small, nervous gesture: eyes nervous, arms nervous, legs nervous.

Milena Migliari feels terribly uncomfortable but doesn't know how to refuse; she moves with her toward one of the sliding doors.

"Hey, hold on a moment." Nick Cruickshank touches his future wife on the shoulder. "If you have something to say, say it to me, too."

Aileen turns around, barely in control. "I'd like to speak with *her* for a minute alone, all right?"

"No, it's not all right at all." Nick Cruickshank shakes his head.

"The same goes for you." Aileen gestures at her two friends or assistants, who get the message right away and freeze where they are, though unwillingly. She motions at Milena Migliari to come on, almost pushes her toward the sliding door.

Nick Cruickshank starts to follow them, but an Indian man with a beard and gray hair in a very elegant dark-blue kurta-pajama takes him by the arm. "Nick! I've been looking for you for such a long time! We absolutely must talk about tomorrow!"

"We'll talk about it later, Nishanath. Okay?" Nick Cruickshank tries to free himself, but the Indian man has no intention of letting him go, grabs both of his wrists, holds him there as if he has something of vital importance to communicate to him.

Milena Migliari goes in, Aileen one step behind her: it's a large living room with a high ceiling with great white beams, full of couches and armchairs and carpets and drapes and paintings and sculptures and lamps, a space a hundred times larger and more open than the cottage in the woods where she was with him until a few minutes ago. The cooler she has in her hand seems to accentuate the unsustainability of her position; she sets it on the floor.

Aileen looks over at a couch, as if she wants to invite her to sit down, but fortunately doesn't: she studies her from head to toe, rocking slightly at the ankles. "Milena, right?"

"Yes." Milena Migliari is a little unsure even of her own name at this point. She studies Aileen as well: the straight line of her nose, her slightly sunken blue eyes beneath a protruding forehead, her almost colorless lips, her slender neck, her thin arms, her long legs. She has this elegant and nervous figure, spring-loaded.

Aileen turns toward the sliding doors, through which the activity on the lawn is intermittently visible, amid the lights; she looks back at her. "Listen, whatever happened between you and Nick out in the cottage in the woods—"

"*Whatever*?" Milena Migliari isn't trying to deny anything: she would like to know exactly what happened, out in the cottage in the woods, if there's a specific name for it.

Aileen shifts her weight on her legs, tilts her head. "Listen, it's not like I don't know what type of man I'm marrying."

"And what type of man is he?" Milena Migliari thinks that it would be interesting to hear it from her; it might help in her own useless attempts to figure it out. She wonders if the wake of sensations and states of mind that still envelop her is clearly noticeable from the outside, if there's something in her eyes, her features, her way of breathing.

Aileen stops trying to maintain that nonsmile of hers, looks her right in the eye. "What matters is that you know it too. And that you don't get any ideas."

Milena Migliari shakes her head slightly. "What ideas?" Again, it's not an empty question: What ideas *does* she have about him? About herself? About their disturbing, inexplicable encounter?

"I think you understand perfectly what I mean." There's an underlying ferocity beneath Aileen's ultracivilized surface, though it's veined with fragility.

"No, I actually don't." Milena Migliari realizes how stupid she might seem, or how devious, but she truly doesn't understand. She doesn't understand what happened, doesn't understand what she's doing in this living room, doesn't understand what keeps racing through her heart and head.

"All right, then I'll explain it to you!" Aileen's voice goes up, in a sudden burst of volume. "If you think you've achieved any sort of position with Nick because you screwed him out there in the cottage, you've got it all wrong!"

"Any sort of *position*?" In the general incomprehensibility of the situation, it seems to Milena Migliari that even individual words have become incomprehensible, completely disconnected from what she's feeling.

"Sorry to interrupt, but would you mind telling me who screwed *who*?" Another woman's voice reaches the living room, from the hallway side.

Aileen whips around, Milena Migliari does likewise. A couple of yards from them, wearing the white shirt and pants she dons to do postural massages, her sleeves rolled up, a hand on her hip, face twisted with tension, is Viviane.

To Milena Migliari it seems like such an absurd apparition that she thinks she's just imagining it, a side effect of the extreme sensorial uncertainty she finds herself in; but her heart stops just the same, her blood freezes.

"And who is she?" Aileen's tone becomes haughty, the lady of the manor surprised to find some crazy vagrant wandering around her home.

"Who are *you*?" Viviane certainly isn't one to be intimidated by anyone's tone of voice.

"I'm Aileen McCullough, and this is *my* house," Aileen shoots back even more harshly. "How did you get in here?"

"You called me here urgently, on account of that pig who fell off his horse!" Now Viviane is losing her temper; she bangs into a couch in the form of a water slide.

"Viviane, calm down." Milena Migliari says it only because she doesn't like seeing her so agitated, certainly not because she cares about keeping up appearances.

"I will certainly not calm down!" Viviane is getting more and more furious. "And what the hell are you doing here, you want to tell me?! What was she talking about?!"

Milena is so disconcerted that she has absolutely no idea what to respond; the only reaction that comes to her is to shrug.

Viviane turns to Aileen with a very aggressive tone. "Well? What were you talking about, you want to tell me? Who fucked who in the woods?!"

Hearing herself berated like this, Aileen attempts to regain some control, to recover from her utter lapse in style just now.

"Whatever I was saying, it was between me and this young lady. I don't understand what business it is of yours!"

"It's my business because she is my *woman*, all right?!" Viviane shakes a furious finger at her; out of anger and excitement a little white foam appears at one corner of her mouth.

"What the devil is she saying?" Aileen turns to Milena Migliari as if for an explanation, a bewildered look on her face.

"I am nobody's woman." Milena Migliari doesn't like Viviane's tone one bit, let alone her proprietorial attitude.

"Ah, no?!" Viviane immediately interprets her words as a distancing, becomes even more furious. "It's good to know, really!"

"I am *me*, all right?" Milena Migliari tries for a tone of conviction but realizes she's not even sure who she really is anymore; realizes how perplexed her voice sounds.

Aileen gives that stereotypical look of incredulity again, accompanying it with that sideways movement of her head. She seems on the point of saying something but turns around again, because just entering the living room is a stocky guy with long grizzled-blond hair, grayish fuzz on his chest, a beer belly, and naked, except for a small white towel around his waist.

"Hey, you!" the guy barks in Viviane's direction, with a guttural voice of notable strength. "Who're you calling a pig who fell off his horse?!"

"You're the pig, you fat tub of lard!" Already infuriated, Viviane's venomous reply is instantaneous.

"Giant fucking dyke!" the guy yells at her even louder; the

veins in his neck pop out, he turns red in the face. "Instead of fixing my shoulder, you've half destroyed it with those hard fucking hands of yours!"

"You never should have dared to touch my ass, cockroach!" Viviane heads straight for him, shoves him in the chest, hard. He staggers, flails, possibly tries to punch her but misses, loses his balance, trips on the carpet, grabs on to her, drags her down; they fall on top of each other in a tangle of arms and legs.

"Ahiaaa! Cunt!" the grizzled-blond guy screams in pain, but this doesn't prevent him from punching Viviane in the back with his left hand.

"Keep still, idiot!" More than anything Viviane tries to immobilize him, maybe for fear that he might do even more damage to his shoulder.

Milena Migliari goes toward the scrum but doesn't know where to begin to try to separate them, especially since they continue grasping at each other like in a game of rugby.

"Stop this *immediately*!" Aileen yells with a shrill register, at a volume that can almost compete with the grizzled-blond guy's. "I will not allow you to behave this way in my house!"

"And here's the bitch!" From the ground, the grizzled-blond guy screams at her as well. "Fucking manipulator!"

"There is no end to your squalor, Wally!" Aileen tries to raise her voice even more, but it's clear from how worn out she sounds that unlike him she's not used to these volume levels.

"Gold digger! Fake!" the grizzled-blond guy named Wally screams hideously, like a barbarian warrior in agony.

"You're an embarrassing failure of a human being!" Aileen is almost as red in the face as he is. "Nick should have kicked you out of the band at least twenty years ago!"

"The band is *mine* as much as his, bitch! I'm one of the founding members, got that?!" Wally pulls himself up to a sitting position, even if Viviane tries to restrain him. "You dyke cunt, get off me!"

"Lousy prick, hold still!" Viviane grabs him by his healthy arm, twists it to block him.

"*Aaargh*!" Wally yells inarticulately and kicks wildly, fortunately without connecting.

"What is this circus?" Nick Cruickshank has entered the living room, followed by the very elegant Indian man still trying to get his attention, and by Aileen's two friends or assistants. He shifts his gaze from his future wife to Milena Migliari to Viviane and Wally on the floor, with the curiosity of an anthropologist.

Milena Migliari feels that sense of absurd relief again at seeing him, even less justified than before; once more she feels like laughing.

THIRTY-TWO

Nick Cruickshank again wriggles free, and not tenderly, of Nishanath Kapoor, who continues trying to talk to him with mystical urgency about his role as celebrant in tomorrow's ceremony. "I said we'll discuss it *later*, all right?!" The situation in the living room is distracting, with Wally half naked on the floor, where the massage therapist is holding him down, Aileen assailing Milena, Tricia and Fiona the holistic consultant shoving each other to be the first to offer practical assistance and moral support to their boss.

"Ahiaaa, you ugly fucking whore, get off me!" Wally is part complaining and part insulting, part trying to land some kicks.

The massage therapist manages to pin him down without much difficulty: she has his left arm in a hold and meanwhile jabs two fingers into his right shoulder, it isn't clear whether as the continuation of her professional treatment or as a way to inflict pain.

"Ahia! Cunt!" Wally writhes, alternates more whining with renewed attempts to land a surprise punch.

"Would you quit it, prick?! You want to hold still or not?!" The massage therapist strengthens her grip on his left arm, like a skilled wrestler.

"Ahiaiaah! That huuuurts, fuuuuck!" Wally immediately reverts to victim mode, moaning and kicking, the big pathetic crybaby.

"Nick, tell these two to stop it immediately!" Aileen comes so close to him that her forehead is almost touching his; she's literally trembling with anger and indignation. "It's completely unacceptable. Do you realize that?!"

Nick Cruickshank starts to answer, but again he can't help but laugh. It might depend on the general regression taking place in the living room, but truthfully it seems like ever since he set foot in the cottage in the woods he has undone any progress he might have made toward so-called maturity.

"Cut it ouuut! Noooow!" Aileen yells with a register he didn't know she was capable of, stomps her heels like a psychotic flamenco dancer.

Milena looks like the only reflective person in this living room: she watches Aileen and Wally and the massage therapist in that unfamiliarity of hers, as if she's from another dimension, making her overwhelmingly attractive in his eyes.

"What the fuck is going on here?" Kimberly comes into the living room, panting; Sadie and Rodney are right behind her.

"This bitch threw me on the ground!" Wally really does seem like a child now, even if hideously ugly and bearded, half naked and flushed pink there on the floor.

"He called me a giant fucking dyke!" The massage therapist continues holding him down, for whatever reason.

"Well, are you or aren't you?" Kimberly peers at her, her features contracted in suspicion.

"That's my business!" the massage therapist shoots back just as aggressively. "And this pig tried to make a move on me!"

"That's not true, babe! Ahiaaa!" Wally shrieks as if he's being tortured.

Kimberly immediately turns on him. "What fucking move did you try to make?! Tell me!"

"None, I swear!" Wally is so shaken he could even seem sincere if you didn't know him.

"Answer the fucking question! What move?!" Alas, Kimberly knows him all too well.

"That other manipulative bitch called me a failure of a human being!" In an attempted diversion Wally points a trembling finger at Aileen; all that's missing now is for him to start whimpering.

"*You* were the one who said some absolutely atrocious things to me!" Aileen is completely outside her habitual register, which is visibly worrying to Tricia and Fiona. "And you continue *to do it*! A guest should have at least a shred of decency!"

Kimberly looks at Aileen, looks at her husband on the floor, as if unable to decide who to tear into. She goes for Wally, probably in light of any number of episodes of marital infidelity and general sexual squalor. "You want to tell me why the fuck you're naked?!"

"She was giving me a massage!" Wally is yelling, completely red in the face. "I swear! I mean, look at her, babe!"

"Look at yourself, you disgusting little worm!" The massage therapist is disgusted; she lets go of Wally's arm, leaps to her feet.

Kimberly throws herself on her husband: with that mass of bleached-blond hair, the short-sleeve blouse with the puffed sleeves, the white hot pants above black two-tone stockings and knee-high boots, she's a triumph of outraged vulgarity. "If you wanted a fucking massage, you should've told me, and I'd have given you a fucking massage!"

"But I fell off that fucking pony, I told you on the phone!" Wally latches on to her to pull himself up, stumbles: the towel falls down, he pulls it up, but he's too agitated and the towel too small, his knob and his rear end take turns playing peekaboo.

Kimberly turns her attention to Nick Cruickshank, her face now twisted by her protective instinct for her vile husband. "You told us those fucking donkeys were calm! You even convinced me to get on, for fuck's sake!"

"Yes, it was a tragic error in judgment." Once again Nick Cruickshank starts laughing—he can't help it.

"What the fuck are you laughing about, asshole?!" Wally yells, like a man possessed. "I nearly wrecked my shoulder!"

"Exactly, *you* nearly wrecked it." Nick Cruickshank says it with the tone of a statement of fact; the fact is that the overwhelming majority of his thoughts and sensations couldn't be further away from Wally and his tumble.

"What the fuck does that mean?!" Wally shouts, looking to Kimberly for support. "He's the fucking head of the house, is he not?! He's the one responsible, is he not?!" He turns toward Rodney and Sadie, hoping for their solidarity as well.

"Of course he's responsible!" Kimberly joins in her husband's shouting, though she continues to glare extremely suspiciously at the massage therapist and look hatefully at Aileen. "We've come all the way here just for your fucking wedding, and look how you're treating us, you and that bitch!"

"We invited you out of pure *obligation*, my dear little whore!" Aileen fires back equally virulently, though at a lower volume. "We would have happily done without you and your abominable slobbery!"

"You're the whore!" Kimberly screams and gesticulates like she's at the fish market, swaying back and forth on her high heels. "You think you're hot stuff because you're the daughter of the fucking ambassador, but if you hadn't reeled in that asshole Nick, like fuck you would've been able to set up that whole fake-leather business."

"You are aware that being the daughter of an alcoholic thief doesn't give you any type of moral prerogative, right?!" Aileen raises her sound level so it's almost on par with Kimberly's, but not quite.

"My father is not a thief, you biiitch!" Kimberly shrieks even louder, to drown her out. "It certainly wasn't his fault he ended up in prison!"

"But of course!" Aileen tries to smile, but in these conditions the only result is a grimace. "He was the victim of a political conspiracy, I'm sure!"

"Biiitch! Biiitch! Biiitch!" Kimberly launches into a loop of undoubted vocal effectiveness: not by chance did she meet Wally when she was a backup singer.

"For your information, I had a very successful business long before meeting Nick!" Aileen tries to reestablish some semblance of stylistic distance, though she must be aware of how difficult it is. "But when you got your hooks into this incredibly vulgar imbecile you were nothing but a two-bit groupie! And you have the courage to call me an opportunist!"

"Because you are, you are, you are!" Kimberly comes out with another loop, seeing as she has such a talent for them. "And then you gave those god-awful so-called creations of yours to the dregs of society, but to me not even a motherfucking purse!"

"I simply didn't want to be associated in any way with a poor embarrassing cow like you!" Trembling, Aileen is white in the face with rage.

Aldino bursts into the living room ready to clobber someone, attracted by all the yelling; his expression turns to dismay as soon as he realizes that the enemy is internal.

"Biiitch! I'll tell you what I'd do with your fucking purses!" Kimberly's voice is literally able to shake the glass of the sliding doors. "Besides, if I want something in leather I buy it *in leather*, certainly not in that horrible cheap plastic of yours!"

"Anti-leather is made entirely from *plants*!" Aileen is almost able to match her in terms of decibels, but a lack of training strains her vocal cords. "But clearly someone like you isn't capable of understanding such things!"

"She understands them much better than you, bitch!" Now Wally intervenes in defense of his wife, though he's unable to gesticulate freely due to the pain in his shoulder, and the fear his towel will fall down again.

"You're a half-wit, you're a troglodyte!" Aileen is so upset she doesn't realize that the photographer and cameraman from *Star Life* have come into the living room with their equipment, accompanied and guided by the editor in chief and the writer.

Nick Cruickshank wonders whether he should alert her, or intervene himself, but he turns the other way, because the massage therapist is trying to drag Milena away by the arm.

"Do you mind telling me what you did out there in the woods with him?!" It's not clear how much she knows, but she's very aggressive, trying to push her into a corner of the living room.

Milena backs up, twists free: agile, flexible, even in this free-for-all she's able to maintain an enchanting natural grace.

Nick Cruickshank would love to take her hand and whisk her away from here, jump into the first car they find, just keep driving; but he's barely able to catch her eye from a distance.

"Excuse me, no photos or filming!" Aileen has finally realized that the photographer and cameraman from *Star Life* are recording everything. She tries to stop them with gestures that are super-determined, though slightly imprecise.

The photographer and the cameraman continue unabated, as if they haven't even heard her.

Aileen goes toward the writer and editor, with uneven steps. "You tell them to stop it immediately!"

"I'm sorry, but they're only doing their jobs!" The editor, who until a short time ago was gushing with feigned courtesy, now reacts in a decidedly discourteous fashion.

"This is not their job!" For that matter Aileen too has almost completely abandoned her usual elegance. "This is a *private* situation!"

"I'm sorry, but I'll be the one to decide that, thank you!" The editor becomes increasingly aggressive.

"No, my dear! *I* decide, because this is *my* fucking house!" Aileen seems on the verge of a total loss of control, something Nick Cruickshank never thought possible.

Aldino moves toward the photographer and cameraman, clearly intent on blocking them physically, but the writer steps in. "If this guy lays a finger on them, we'll cancel the contract and sue you!"

"The contract specifies that private situations are excluded from photos and filming!" Aileen worked for weeks to define every aspect of the agreement; she seemed so sure she hadn't left any room for misunderstandings or ambiguities.

"Private situations are those in the *bedroom* and in the *bathroom*!" Seeing herself challenged, the editor's tone turns nasty. "The terms are absolutely clear, and even your lawyers approved them! You've all signed!"

"It's not a question of *rooms*, but of *what happens* in them!" Aileen refuses to accept the idea that the contract might have an interpretative hole precisely at its most crucial point. "Oh, don't worry, I'm calling our lawyer immediately, but there isn't the slightest doubt that this is a *private* situation!"

"This situation is all too terribly *public*!" The *Star Life* editor switches to an authentically cannibalistic register. "You could hear the yelling all the way out there, for God's sake!"

"So you're implying that a conversation's *volume* determines whether it's public or private, not its *content*? Do you realize the extent of your legal ignorance?!" Aileen's tone is decidedly ferocious as well, but she's frantic; she turns to look at Nick Cruickshank, as if to plead with him to intervene.

Nick Cruickshank shrugs; ever since she came out with the *Star Life* idea he's tried to explain in every way possible that there was no reason in the world they needed to have their party paid for by a magazine, let alone a magazine that caters to despicable voyeurs. He ended up caving out of pure exhaustion, after she repeated time and again with unshakable conviction that supervised coverage would be infinitely preferable to the inevitably uncontrolled infiltrations of paparazzi, in addition to helping out the cause of Anti-leather and reviving the Bebonkers' image. In other words, they willingly put their personal life up for sale to the highest bidder, and it's absolutely pointless to complain about it now.

"Sorry, Nick, can you explain to me when the hell we're going to find time to rehearse for the concert Sunday?" Rodney couldn't choose a worse moment to present his demands, nor a more petulant tone.

Nick Cruickshank opens his arms out wide; to him Sunday seems so infinitely far away. "I don't know. Ask Baz."

"I'm asking you!" Rodney immediately gets upset, showing how irritated he already was. "Because after the party tomorrow half the band is going to be in far from ideal shape, and without a decent rehearsal it'll be even worse!"

Nick Cruickshank looks at him thoughtfully and can't understand how he managed to write dozens of songs (on the first three albums, after which everyone wrote their own, even if they've continued taking joint credit for them) and play thousands of concerts for decades with someone he now dislikes so strongly. "We did decide on the concert Sunday together, did we not?"

"Yeah, but until last week no one thought to tell me that your wedding party was the day before!" Rodney too has countless reasons for feeling bitter, starting with the fact that the fans consider him a phenomenal guitarist but not exactly *the soul* of the group. No one's ever dreamed, for instance, of talking about "Ainsworth cool." His fault, naturally, a result of his pedantry, his obsession with technique, the way he's become more and more wrapped up in the virtuoso spirals of his solos, but just try telling him that.

"We didn't tell you before in order to maintain a minimum of *privacy*, okay?" Aileen retorts, her voice hoarse. As always, she's able to divide her attention over various channels simultaneously, even in her current state of agitation.

"Some privacy, with *Star Life* running around!" Sadie points to the cameraman and photographer, who continue recording every exchange, the writer and editor right behind them.

"This from someone who would never dream of putting her life on public display, nor that of her dear ones!" Aileen can't bear another attack on this front.

"Meaning what?!" Unlike Aileen, Sadie still has untapped stores of vocal power at her disposal, and she certainly doesn't intend to let them go to waste. "No, you're going to explain this to me now! What do you mean?!"

"Even Todd says that we can't play if there isn't any time to rehearse!" Rodney continues down the same blind alley, obsessively unperturbed, pointing to the center of the room with his chin.

Todd is there, it's unclear since when; he looks at Wally, who is half naked and slightly curled up on his side, hands gripping his exceedingly small towel. "How're you doing?"

"I'm doing great. Isn't it obvious, shithead?" Wally rips into him, despite the fact that Todd is the only Bebonker with whom he's maintained quasi-amicable relations. (It really is difficult to argue with Todd.)

In confirmation of his amiable nature Todd doesn't reply, he turns toward Rodney. "Then who's playing bass on Sunday?"

Rodney turns immediately toward Nick Cruickshank, as if to get an answer from him.

"Are you going to tell me what you meant?! Eh, are you?!" Meanwhile, Sadie continues shouting at Aileen.

"I don't need to tell you anything at all!" Aileen puts all the disdain she has left into her voice. "All you have to do is go on any gossip website to find a few dozen photos of you with your tits and ass on display beside some pool, husband and children a few steps away!"

"At least I can!" Sadie hits back savagely but smoothly. "You maybe not, seeing as you're practically anorexic!"

"You're embarrassing! You're embarrassing! You're embarrassing!" Aileen throws herself into a loop as well, not knowing she doesn't have the slightest chance of competing with an ex-pro on her own ground.

Nick Cruickshank is amazed how little he cares about the people getting upset and yelling in the living room of what's supposed to be his home. The only person that matters to him is Milena: each time he looks at her it's like he sees a halo of thoughts, gestures, and words suspended all around her and waiting to be set free. But each time he tries to get closer she moves to avoid the grasp of the massage therapist, or someone else gets between them. If he were more lucid he'd certainly be able to reach her; but he isn't, not at all.

"What do you mean, who's playing bass?!" The mere idea of

being excluded makes Wally start shouting even louder than before.

"And you, do you mind telling me what you think you were doing?" Aileen abandons Sadie and goes back to interrogating Milena, at a lower volume, as if she could manage not to be heard by the others, *Star Life* team included.

Milena looks at her: it's clear she doesn't understand the question, or the reasons behind the question.

Aileen turns toward Nick Cruickshank, her face upset; her hair, incredibly, disheveled. "Well, can you explain it to me, Nick? What did you think you were doing?"

"We weren't doing anything." Nick Cruickshank shakes his head, and at least in this he feels like he's being perfectly sincere. "It *happened*."

"Ah, sure." Aileen kind of hops in place, employing more nerves than muscle. "You've followed your instincts, naturally! Isn't that just marvelous?!"

"We can call anyone on bass! That's the least of our problems!" Rodney has never loved Wally, but in the past ten years it's quite possible he's developed an authentic desire to kill him.

Todd nods, his head of curls looking slightly frizzy. "We can ask Jack, or Tim."

"Or Ronan." Nick Cruickshank throws out a name, purely as a reflex.

"Excuse me, but we were talking about something completely different, it seems to me!" Aileen takes him by the arm, her voice so beleaguered it's painful to the ear. "Could you forget about your stupid band nonsense for a moment?"

"It's actually not nonsense, Aileen," Todd intervenes, in that impartial way of his. "Without the bass we can't do the concert on Sunday."

"The bass is the least of our problems, compared to not being able to have a decent rehearsal!" Rodney is right, because time really is short, and after the party they'll be in the worst possible condition for playing; but that doesn't make his attitude any less annoying. But then he's always been this way, ever since he was still a maniacal, aspiring solo guitarist spending his days locked in a room playing scales after scales until his fingers hurt. He had a brief period of creative glory during the Bebonkers' first two years, then his obsessiveness swallowed it whole.

Nick Cruickshank is totally incapable of taking any real interest in the matter; in truth he doesn't even try, keeping his eyes trained on Milena.

"Either I'm on bass, or there are no Bebonkers! That clear?!" Wally shouts himself hoarse, gesticulates with his good arm, lets his towel fall again, struggles to pick it up, pushes Kimberly away gruffly when she tries to cover him up.

"It's certainly not our fault you're in this state, you slob!" Rodney dumps on him a portion of the anger accumulated during decades of exasperating arguments over questions of principle, countless hours waiting for the night owl to wake up, continuous competition for visibility.

"Son of a bitch!" Wally takes a Walter Kottke ceramic duck off the coffee table and throws it at him with his left hand. Naturally, he misses—the duck crashes into the awful Stephan Muchensky bronze cone that Aileen bought at Christie's for a price that's best forgotten, shatters into a thousand pieces. Wally turns immediately toward the *Star Life* cameraman who has filmed this episode as well, tries to take the camera away from him. The cameraman retreats, still filming; his photographer colleague takes advantage to get a sequence of rapid-fire shots of the clumsy attempted assault. Wally yells, grunts, kicks out, flails with his good arm: he's not aware of it, but this is a sort of pathetic replay of when all four of them used to devastate hotel suites just for the fun of it, because they had nothing better to do, because ultimately it was what was expected of them.

Todd shakes his head, with that unnerving calmness that over time has become just as much of a role to play as the poses of the others. "Anyway I've said right from the start that I didn't like the idea of the party before the concert."

"I didn't like it either, if you really want to know." Nick Cruickshank looks at the spot where Milena was two minutes ago but doesn't see her anymore. A vein of misery wells inside him, unstoppable.

"Is that so?!!" Aileen's tone and manner, which she's honed for so long, with such care and intelligence, have deteriorated in impressive fashion. "You might have told me! I certainly didn't force you! You're being totally unfair!"

"Come on." Nick Cruickshank thinks that he certainly has the vocal capabilities to yell much louder, but he's too despondent, his sense of foreignness too intense. "The pressure of your *expectations* happens to be worse than any obligation."

"Then find yourself a woman completely *devoid* of expectations, and devoid of the qualities allowing her to have expectations, and then tell me if you're happy!" Aileen no longer seems to care that she's being targeted by both the cameraman and the photographer from *Star Life*; in fact, she seems to be turning her face to give them a better angle. "Unless you'd rather flee again in that damn glider of yours!"

"It's not for fleeing, it's for *flying*." But Nick Cruickshank wonders if there's really a difference, since in reality glider flying is hardly as graceful and poetic as people say, or as it might seem from the outside: it's mechanically complex and anything but natural, as yesterday demonstrated. And even if not every flight ends in a crash, it does inevitably bring you back down to earth; even the greatest combination of updrafts can't keep you in the air forever.

"Sorry, but these are your issues, resolve them between the two of you!" Rodney yells, in that donkey-like register of his that half the Bebonkers' fans incredibly seem to like, maybe for the simple fact that it's been buzzing in their ears for so long. "I want an answer right now about the bass and the rehearsals, or else I'm not doing the concert!"

"How exceptionally loyal of you." Nick Cruickshank can't resist giving him a little bow complete with mimed hat removal, though he knows he's exacerbating the situation.

"You're the one who's mixed your personal affairs with those of the band, as usual!" Rodney brays with asinine vehemence; all he needs to do now is start flapping his ears.

"Yeah, you're the one who created this situation!" Sadie immediately supports him, with a perfect blend of malice and stupidity.

"I think the situation created itself *by itself.* Like every situation, right?" Nick Cruickshank wonders if that's really true: in the present case, as well as in the other situation he's thinking about.

"You created the situation, asshole!" Wally spits up some more wild fury: he sprays saliva, turns toward Rodney and Todd, as if he wants to attack them. "And you two as well, you little shits, saying that the bass is the least of your problems!"

"Only as far as replacing you is concerned!" Rodney raises his voice, so out of character for him; his beef with Wally is longstanding as well, though it's never come to the surface. "In the sense that *anyone* would be better than you, both personally and musically!"

"You're a little shit, Mr. fucking Quick Hands! Your solos are about as exciting as a fucking Japanese porno, but you don't even realize it because you're so convinced you're a god of the guitar!" Wally is screaming like a beast, foaming at the mouth, gesticulating; the towel comes and goes. "If you even think of getting up on that fucking stage without me on Sunday, you're dead! I mean it, I'll go and get a shotgun and you're *dead*!"

"Which would be appropriate at a benefit concert for the victims of an act of terrorism." Nick Cruickshank can't help himself, again.

"We can cancel Sunday as far as I'm concerned!" Rodney doesn't budge from his line, braying like never before. "Without some decent rehearsals and a guarantee on the bass, I'm going back to the coast!"

"On Sunday you will do me the huge favor of respecting the commitments I've made with the sponsors, TV, radio, as well as the mayors of four towns!" Baz Bennett has arrived in the living room as well, immediately adopting the attitude halfway between grammar school teacher and big-money drug dealer that's allowed him to keep them together until now. "I'm talking about money already paid, having nothing to do with the proceeds going to charity! And if you don't give a damn about the money, at least think of your responsibility toward your fans! And to those who work for you!"

"Yeah, and so disinterestedly!" Rodney immediately turns on him, with the pent-up rage of thousands of travel hours toward destinations whose names you don't even remember, press conferences where there's nothing to say, extenuating meetings with record label functionaries that don't know the slightest thing about rock, arrangements made and unmade to please the market, arguments in front of the mixer until dawn. "At least try not to be a pain in the ass until the day you retire, Baz!"

"I really wish I could afford to, Rod!" Baz is speaking only a little louder than normal, but in his voice there's a current of several thousand volts. "But I'm afraid that in the space of a few months I'd have to come and put flowers on the tomb of the Bebonkers!"

"*Hah, hah, hah,* very funny, really!" Rodney spins around, raising his hands in the air, as if to incite a nonexistent audience.

"I don't think you'd be very amused, dear Rod." Baz's habitual sarcasm now has a more sinister tone than usual. "Having to sell your pretty sailboat to pay for your house in Santa Monica, and then having to sell the house in Santa Monica to pay for the one in the Highlands, and so on and so forth, until you find yourself out on the street!"

"You do know that without us you wouldn't be in too good shape either, Baz!" Rodney attacks him with even more rage, seeing his material possessions suddenly called into question.

"Without us today you'd be managing a few groups of dance hall losers!" Wally attacks him abruptly, even though Kimberly is holding him back. "You'd be going around collecting coins in a hat without us!"

"You should be calling me on the phone every goddamn day to say thank you, Wally dear!" Baz raises his volume a little more, though he keeps himself far below the level of the others.

"Is that right, and why the fuck should I?!" Wally tries to free himself from Kimberly's hold, but she doesn't let go.

"I don't know, for managing to keep you out of jail, among other things?" Yes: the voltage in Baz's voice is lethal.

"What the fuck are you saying?! What the fuck are you talking about?!" Wally barks, roars, spits.

"Let it go, all right?!" Baz's tone is decidedly blackmail-like, which falls fully within his habitual methods.

"I'm certainly not going to fucking let it go!" By now Wally seems in the throes of a convulsive fit. "What the fuck are you referring to? Say it!"

"I prefer not to in front of your lady, all right?!" Baz positions his index finger in front of his nose and mouth, pure Mafia style.

"The story about the underage girl in Rio?" As incredible as it might seem, in the general mayhem even Todd abandons his proverbial discretion, along with his proverbial calm.

"What underage girl in Rio?!" Kimberly looks at Wally like she wants to rip him to shreds with her nails and teeth. She looks at Todd. "What underage girl in Riooo?!"

"You're not actually going to listen to him, babe?! That asshole just wants to ruin me!" Wally doesn't even try to keep his towel on anymore. He grabs a Lucien Lunot ballerina off a stand, throws it at Todd.

Todd sidesteps, but the ballerina still hits him on the side of the neck. It must really hurt, because he gives an awful cry.

"That is a one-of-a-kind Lunot! It's worth three hundred thousand pounds!" Aileen emits a scream that's almost as terrible: she rushes to collect the ballerina, turning it over in her hands to verify any damage.

"I'm suing you!" Todd is bent over, one hand pressed against his neck. "Lunatic, psychopath!"

"And I'm going to kill you, you goddamn Judas!" Wally makes as if to charge at him, newly naked, pink and hairy.

"No, I'm going to kill you first, you gigantic fucking pig!" Kimberly grabs his hair, scratches his face, jumps on his back in a sort of crazy rodeo. Terrible sounds are unleashed by the two of them; they spin around, end up crashing into the Le Corbusier couch.

"*Assez!*" Madame Jeanne arrives in the middle of the melee, more enraged than Nick has ever seen her. "*Vous agissez comme des enfants! Comme des barbares! Celle-ci est la maison d'un poète! Ayez un peu de respect! Si vous ne savez pas vous tenir, je vous mets tous à la porte!*"

Everyone shuts up instantaneously, like a group of children or savages hushed by someone with moral superiority. In the sudden silence the only sounds are the panting of Wally and Kimberly and the clicking of the camera; then that stops too.

Nick Cruickshank goes toward Madame Jeanne, a bit uneasily since he too feels like part of the gang. He puts his hand on her arm. "*Merci, Madame Jeanne.*"

She looks at him: severe, protective, ironic. "*Tu devrais mieux choisir tes amis, Nick. Et tes femmes.*"

"*C'est vrai.*" Nick Cruickshank nods; he exits the living room, slips down the hallway, goes to the door, opens it. At the back of the house the air is cold and damp, a mist is rising just like last night. Milena's orange van is nowhere to be seen. Ten whole minutes must have passed since she left this circus, together with her partner and future co-mother.

SATURDAY

THIRTY-THREE

MILENA MIGLIARI TOSSES and turns again and again under the covers, after hours of talking and crying with Viviane, in the ground-floor kitchen and in the tiny first-floor living room and in the little study at the top of the stairs and then in the bedroom on the floor below and then back in the kitchen, back in the bedroom. It's now six in the morning, Viviane has fallen asleep from exhaustion and after taking a Xanax, snoring in that regular way of hers, head under the covers. She, on the other hand, continues to toss and turn, without peace: first on her side, then on her back, on her stomach, on her side again. She pulls up her knees, extends an arm, bends a hand uncomfortably, kicks out, presses her face against the pillow—useless, sleep simply won't come. Her eyes burn from all the tears, her throat hurts from the sobbing, her vocal cords are worn out from all the useless attempts to reconstruct and explain, all the going back and jumping forward. She's exhausted from the sound of her own words, the intentions they contained, the sensations they tried to translate, the reactions they provoked.

What's most absurd is that she feels like she absolutely *agrees* with Viviane: with her amazement and indignation and anger at a betrayal that's worse than the normal types of betrayal, because their relationship is not a normal relationship, because of how they've had to fight for it and defend it at every step, one day at a time. She agrees to the extent that she did not even for a moment try to deny what happened, nor try in any way to play down its seriousness or the scope of its consequences. She was not able either to explain it or justify it; she was not able to say that it was a mistake due to a moment of confusion, a slipup in a stupid game, a temporary loss of clarity. Nor was she able to say that if she could go back in time that she wouldn't do it all over again, that from this moment on she would do everything possible not to think about what happened ever again. Ultimately, Viviane wasn't asking for anything more, despite all that yelling and despairing. Even now she'd be satisfied with a confirmation of their present, a declaration of intents for their future. Beneath her hard shell, she's never been a spiteful woman, and over the years she's provided more than enough proof of her generosity and comprehension, in addition to her solidity of character and practical reliability; she'd certainly do anything in her power to close this chapter and look ahead, if only she were able to reassure her. What's making her despair is that she was completely unable to do so, capable only of repeating that Viviane was absolutely right, that she's terribly sorry for making her suffer.

Viviane replied that she doesn't give a damn about being right, that her sorrow is of no consolation, nor is it of any use at all to their relationship. She told her that at the very least she should help her understand why she was so overwhelmed by an encounter with someone she hadn't even recognized when she saw him for the first time; why she decided to throw away their pact of solidarity, their struggle to affirm their right to be together, despite the prejudices of their families and the inhabitants of Seillans and the rest of the world.

But she wasn't able to help her understand anything at all; all she could say was "I don't know, I don't know, I don't *know*" a thousand times between tears and sobs, feeling like the most awful and disloyal personal on earth.

In the absence of her own explanations, Viviane even suggested some: the stress of being about to embark on the endeavor of having a child, the worsening of their sex life due to exhaustion and everyday worries, the fascination of celebrity, the skill of the professional skirt-chaser, the desire to verify one last time what it's like to make love to a man.

She was unable to confirm a single one of these hypotheses proposed with such effort and displeasure, continuing to flounder helplessly in the painful frustration of the not-explainable and the not-explained.

"You do know that I'm not your master," Viviane said to her at a certain point, when by now they'd reached an extreme point of attrition. "I'm not your limiter of dreams. I'm not your imposer of roles. You do realize that I'm not a fucking *man*."

Milena Migliari repeated to her four or five times, through more tears and sobs, that she'd never thought she was. And yet on this point she wasn't completely sincere, because it simply seemed too unfair to say it at this point in time, after having years to do so: in truth Viviane *has* become something of a prevaricator. She *has* to a certain extent limited her, *has* to an extent forced her into a role. Perhaps to protect her, perhaps to help her, perhaps to reassure her, perhaps out of a need for control deriving from insecurity. But on her part she has let her do it; she didn't protest, didn't draw any personal line in the sand and defend it. Out of laziness, out of cowardice, because she didn't want to deal with the issue, because she hoped things would get better by themselves. What would Viviane be like after this betrayal if they managed to stay together? Lighter, freer, more trusting, more respectful of her autonomy? Of course not: trust is long gone now, suspicion has spread to every corner of her thoughts, and it's there to stay. They will go on as damaged couples do, every smile tinged with pain, a shadow of resentment ready to reemerge at the slightest occasion.

And how the heck will she be able to justify it to herself? Will she tell herself it was a blip caused by her worrying about the short-, medium-, and long-term commitment she's about to take on with Viviane? Will she be able to write it off as an accident, the moral equivalent of slipping in the bathtub and breaking a couple of ribs? Will it be possible for her not to feel permanently guilty after this kind of episode? Not to see it as the sabotage of an entire life's journey? Will she ever be able to file it away like a secret event, perhaps to be revisited every now and then, with a mix of wonder and nostalgia? Is this how traitors live with their betrayal?

On the other hand, purely hypothetically: What follow-up could there ever be to what happened with Nick Cruickshank? She's embarrassed even to think about it; she feels ridiculous, pathetic. Yes, in that cottage in the woods the attraction between them was so deep and unstoppable that it slammed into her without giving her time to think. Its echoes continue to course through her: the extreme amplification of signals, the exaltation of impulses, the overpowering activation of currents. Nothing like that ever happened to her with a man even when she still thought she liked men. Who could've imagined it happening now? It's never even happened to her with Viviane, not even during their passionate beginnings. She never would have thought she'd be able to communicate with such disarming ease with someone who's supposed to belong in the enemy camp; to feel so gratified in her unconfessed desires, so motivated in undeclared requests, so satisfied in unrecognized needs. And she certainly isn't referring only to the physical dimension of their encounter, no matter how intense and surprising it was: the mental dimension shook her just as much, maybe more. The *spiritual* dimension, even? The sense of reciprocal recognition, of recovery, of long-forgotten familiarity that suddenly reemerges and cancels out all separation; the instantaneous complicity, the automatic intuition, the laughing with exactly the same spirit. But how real were these feelings? To what extent were they the result of a blend of confusion and suggestion, as Viviane tried at least ten times to suggest?

And anyway for someone like Nick Cruickshank yesterday was almost certainly just one of many similar trysts, at most a little unusual given the circumstances. Maybe he's already forgotten about it this morning, caught up in the last preparations for his wedding celebration; or he'll file it away along with a thousand other similar episodes, sources of curiosity or amusement. Or perhaps he'll remember it because of its unpleasant consequences, for that whole mess that occurred after they were discovered coming back from the woods. But it's hard to imagine him turning his life upside down for her even for an instant, despite the marvelous and surprising things he said to her when they were in the cottage in the woods; despite the incredible transfusion of energy from the universe that took place between them. Does he not *make his living* coming up with marvelous and surprising things, to sing to an unlimited number of female listeners? Is he not a professional *enchanter*, and one of the best around? Yes, he clearly has an uncommon ability to resonate with the mind (and body) of a woman, to pick up on and translate her sensations and sentiments; but this is likely independent of the specific woman he's involved with. Or maybe the specific woman has a specific value, but only while he's making love to her, or while she's inspiring a song; then it's over, he's off to search for new sources to tap into. What sort of continuity could be expected from someone like that? How reliable could he ever be?

But now she gets truly furious with herself: When has she ever been one to sit on her little throne calmly evaluating gifts and the promise of gifts before deciding whether it's worth it to offer her body, heart, and soul in exchange? And if we're talking about reliability, Viviane is the most reliable person she's ever met. And not *only* reliable: she's someone you can talk to about anything, about plans and even about dreams. All right, lately not with the same intensity as when they were just starting out together; but if they succeeded then, they could do so again. If reliability is what she's after, why desire it if only briefly from someone who's clearly incapable of it? She should stop thinking about it, give up trying to defend herself with Viviane, admit that what happened was an incredibly stupid error in judgment. No different than if she'd had an accident in her little van with one of the many reckless maniacs who rush full throttle along these hairpin curves between the mountains and the valley, oblivious to the fact that there might be a woman coming in the other direction who's deep in thought, absorbed in the music that's playing in her head.

Enough, it's completely useless to stay in bed tossing and turning like this any longer: Milena Migliari slips out from under the covers, gathers her clothes up off the chair, puts them on in the bathroom, goes down to the kitchen. She makes herself a hibiscus-and-ginger-flavored tea, adds a tablespoon of thistle honey, mixes, mixes, mixes. She tries to calm herself but it doesn't work: her heart beats faster and more erratically than it should, her thoughts keep jumbling together, her sensations keep expanding and shrinking and expanding.

There's an English author she now detests after reading three or four of his books, for the way he manages to be culturally alternative and commercial at the same time, moderately radical, politically correct, lovable. In every novel he presents flawed but captivating characters and guides them through plots in which at the end, after a series of vicissitudes that seem to lead toward ruin, everything miraculously works out: each character somehow compensated, no irreparable wrong done, no permanent damage. What annoys her most is the strategy of not arousing displeasure in the readers, not leaving them with any sad thoughts. And yet in real life it doesn't work like that, not at all: wrongs *are* irreparable, damage permanent, sad thoughts might vanish for a while but they return. What's happening to her now is a perfect demonstration; in fact, an *awful* demonstration. However she tries to examine the situation, she can't see a way out that doesn't include a definitive betrayal or a definitive renunciation. What should she do, then? Resign herself to persevering with Viviane, despite knowing that she'll be unhappy? Throw herself body and soul into a romance that for Nick Cruickshank has almost certainly not even begun?

However, every time that even for a second she imagines herself not going forward with the in vitro fertilization idea and being totally free to do what she wants, her mind is flooded with all the marvelous gelato flavors she has yet to try. *Flower* gelato, for example. Sure, she made a rose-flavored one last spring and it came out well, but there are dozens of others to experiment with: jasmine, forget-me-not, violet, lavender, wisteria, chamomile, bluebottle . . . truthfully, she could make as many flavors as there are flowers: hundreds, thousands. All she has to do is close her eyes and she can already see their colors, smell their fragrances, taste their flavors.

And what if this was a bit like the false alternative between cone and cup, in which no one usually contemplates the existence of a third possibility? What if the solution was to choose *her own* life before choosing *with whom* to share it?

THIRTY-FOUR

NICK CRUICKSHANK HAS a problem with his cervical vertebrae, a result of his famous fall from the stage of the Hollywood Bowl in 2006: if he doesn't put his pillow in the proper position under the back of his neck, his fingers start to tingle, guaranteed. But the tingle is just an added annoyance, on this night of ceaseless agitation, in which there seems to be no way of getting to sleep. Images from the afternoon and evening continue returning to him, mixed with the feelings in his body, and the dozens of questions overlapping sloppily one on top of another: about what happened, what's about to happen, about Aileen, about Milena the Italian gelato girl, about himself. His heart is double-timing it, his ears are buzzing, he's drenched in sweat. He really doesn't want to lay there anymore thrashing around like a fool on this five-layer mattress that should be the most comfortable in the world and instead is terrible; he might as well get up.

He rolls to the edge of the bed, jumps to his feet, stumbles on the carpet, bangs into the chest of drawers he never wanted in there, feels his way to his bathrobe hanging on the coat rack, puts the bathrobe on. Aileen turns over under the comforter, grunts, snorts, resumes her regular breathing. Despite her insomniac tendencies, she has the impressive ability to create mental compartments between one activity and another, one phase and another of the day or night: it's how she's able to maintain her lucidity and stay operative even in the most difficult moments. Agreed, last night she was infected by the climate of general lunacy, eventually turning into an extremely deteriorated version of herself; but then at about one in the morning she called time on her extenuating attempts to reconstruct events and attribute responsibility and brought the proceedings to a close. "I need to sleep, tomorrow's going to be a long day." She went into the bathroom to remove her makeup and take a sleeping pill. Ten minutes later she was in bed with a mask over her eyes, five minutes later she was asleep.

He on the other hand has never truly been able to absorb the techniques of mental detachment, and not for lack of trying, with yoga, tai chi chuan, shuai jiao, Transcendental Meditation, and all the rest. Not that he doesn't zone out, from situations, relationships, practical problems: he does so far too often, even in situations that to others seem tremendously important. He does it out of boredom or disinterest, laziness or impatience, often with the result of inviting accusations of arrogance or indifference. But it's precisely when he's emotionally involved that he's unable to: all it takes is a gesture, a word, a look that pursues him through his thoughts and eventually pierces his heart, arousing in him an unending sense of loss and guilt, catapulting him into the deepest sadness. It's a good thing deep sadness is his primary creative fuel, because he has an almost inexhaustible supply of it, whether from stability disrupted, dreams shattered, separations, abandonments, distances, voids. He'd have enough to write *dozens* of great tearjerkers, if only he had the guts to go down that path more often.

He leaves the bedroom, closes the door with extreme caution, walks down the hallway as silently as he can, so that Aldino or one of his bodyguard colleagues that arrived yesterday doesn't think there's an intruder and spring into action. From the north-facing windows at the back of the house only darkness is visible, though it's already less dense than an hour ago. He passes the rooms assigned to Wally and Kimberly, Rodney and Sadie, Todd and Cynthia. He isn't overly astonished that they've all stayed, despite yelling such horrible things at each other: theirs is a bond that by now is difficult to break, held together by a tangle of consolidated roles, rooted habits, thirst for revenge, fear of the unknown, economic interests, even a worn-down and extenuated form of affection. He thinks of the relationships in which the others too have gotten bogged down over the years: the conquests put hurriedly on display, the getaways, the secrets slapped on the pages of newspapers, the public declarations of love, the lies inspired by press offices, the families ruined only to form new and very similar ones, the harm done by having too much and not having enough, the constant disproportion between merit and compensation.

He opens the door to the kitchen, goes in. It has a strange effect on him so empty and calm, without Madame Jeanne intent on dicing and kneading and cutting and mixing and frying and boiling and opening and closing oven doors and refrigerators. The first light of day begins entering through the eastern windows, bathing this motionless heart of the house, this core that once activated produces warmth, comfort, and sustenance for those present, when they're present. It occurs to him that if for any reason he ended up giving in to Aileen's badgering and fired Madame Jeanne, this house would become a lifeless place, frighteningly cold. It occurs to him that ultimately this has never really been *his* house: it's just a property that he purchased, too big, with too much land around it, in a place where he has no roots, whose language he doesn't even speak very well. Not that he feels more rooted in London, or in Sussex, or in the other places where he invested in real estate, each time as if he were investing in the idea of a stable life, to come back to at the end of his tours or leisure travel. Those ideas of stable life had the false vividness of dreams, or television commercials: breakfasts in the kitchen, lunches outdoors in the gorgeous light, gallivanting on the lawn with children and dogs, evenings in front of the fireplace, music in the living room, amid the warmth of family and friends. Not realistic; at least not for him, not for how he's made, not for his highly flawed mental and emotional profile. The lives his houses contained have invariably broken apart after a few years, shifted elsewhere, dispersed, and always because of him; the containers have remained, within them the tenuous reverberations of hypotheses no longer verifiable. Better, then, to continue flitting here and there around the world? On the road at least there's the advantage of not having too much time to think about insufficiencies or nostalgia or doubts, of filling up your days with activities, even if they're mainly tedious. But now he's had enough of the string of air and ground transfers, hotel suites, sound checks, set lists modified to avoid going insane from the repetition, crowds in varying states of enthusiasm, each tour stop already projected into the next.

The only property of his that makes him feel a sense of belonging right now is the little 450-square-foot cottage in the clearing in the middle of the woods, where yesterday he was with Milena the Italian gelato girl; it hurts to think that that too is empty now, after being filled with such burning intensity for a few hours.

It's there that his thoughts continue to return, back through the sleepless night spent trading accusations: to the caution of their initial circling, the growing curiosity of their approach, the exhilarating joy of their contact, the overpowering surprise of their fusion. There was a rightness never previously felt in the combination of their expressions, their shapes, their desires, their spirits, their breathing. He's amazed he doesn't feel the slightest shred of guilt, but it's true; even all these hours later it's as if what happened was too pure, too untainted by intentions to be wrong. He has all these images in his head: Milena filling up the waffle basket with her fior di latte and persimmon, Milena handing it to him, Milena observing him seriously as he tastes it, Milena worried, Milena smiling, Milena laughing. And the many colors of her eyes, the white and orange of her gelato, the yellow light of the oil lamp, the red of the fire in the stove, the black of the evening beyond the windowpanes when they awoke from their enchantment and looked outside. His mental state is far from limpid but his fingers contain a precise memory of the lines of her forehead and the curves of her thighs, in his nostrils the smell of the skin between her neck and ear, in his ears the sound of her sighs, on his tongue the taste of her tongue, so similar to the taste of her gelato: and each one of these memories so recent and yet already so far away brings with it a sense of lack that knocks the wind out of his lungs, makes his stomach muscles contract.

Nick Cruickshank thinks that he knows almost nothing about her, and that nevertheless it seems like he knows everything. And he's convinced that it's the same for her: he felt it. It seems absurd to have met her just the other day, to have greeted her like a stranger, before their mutual unfamiliarity melted away. He's reminded of when she talked to him about the twin flames: about the instantaneous, complete harmony of their rejoining. He didn't even let her explain the idea very well, feeling the need to interrupt her at all costs with his stupid disillusionment, his stupid "Cruickshank cool." But doesn't this notion of twin souls seem like something out of a book of illustrated fairy tales? Could he have played along anyway? Pretended to believe? Perhaps even tried to believe *for real*?

After all, how many other times has he felt such a deep familiarity in such a short time? How many times has he *recognized* someone who in theory (and practice) he didn't know? Limiting himself to *real* life, thus excluding the lyrics of "Twin Soul Reunion," and his adult years, thus excluding his thirteen-year-old pining for Mia Lees (who never even looked at him because she considered him a little boy): never. From this perspective, as a purely mental exercise, could Aileen be his twin flame? No. But it's a stupid question, the wrong question. Theirs has been a mature relationship from the beginning, conscious, realistic, keeping in mind previous experiences and giving priority to each other's practical and professional needs, not teenage dreams. Isn't this precisely what he needs now?

Then what is behind what happened yesterday with Milena? An infantile tendency to give in to instinct, despite the damaging precedents? An irresistible predisposition for choosing imagination over reality? A desire to flee responsibility? An intolerance for what Aileen has become these past few years? For what she probably always was? An inability to accept the fact that every person is the result of a combination of qualities and flaws, and that it makes no sense to want to keep the former and get rid of the latter? If there's anyone who ought to be able to appreciate people's flaws as much as, if not more than, their good qualities, it's him. Of course, it depends on *which* flaws, because ideally two people's flaws should combine just as well as their qualities. Which opens the door onto some dangerous terrain, because there are so many couples who get on so well together thanks to the combination of the *worst* things about them. Without having to look too far, you only have to look at Wally and Kimberly: from this standpoint they're a rousing success (at least they were until last night, before the matter of the underage girl in Rio surfaced). Too bad the result is only twice as unpleasant for everyone else.

And him, what the hell does he want? What is he searching for? Is he still chasing after fantasies inspired by the novels he devoured as a boy to get away from a life he wanted nothing to do with, and that then gave life to his songs, which in turn nurtured the fantasies of millions of people? Is he actually responsible for deceiving them, a ruse that's now coming back to bite him?

But the sensations he felt yesterday with Milena seemed so damn *real*, not products of his imagination. In that cottage in the woods he sensed he'd found the soft and sweet yet strong and intelligent woman he's always desired, ever since Aunt Maeve. That he *rediscovered* her and rediscovered himself. And it had seemed by contrast that Aileen had the characteristics of his mother that so upset him as a child: the sentimental coldness, the hardness of character, the tendency to deal with too many things at the same time, eyes and thoughts in constant motion. But how reliable are these sensations? In the (growing) light of the day after? The sensations of a few hidden, illicit hours, between two people shaken and confused by the crucial choices they're about to make? And what's *truly* special about Milena? Her sincere passion for what she does? But Aileen is passionate about the Anti-leather thing too; and she used to be about her job as a costume designer, when he met her. Her artistic spirit? But Aileen is certainly much more than an entrepreneur: she's also someone who designs her own creations, who works with shapes and colors. Is it her devotion to the search for nuances that are difficult to capture? But it's not like Aileen is insensitive to nuance; in fact, she's extraordinarily quick to pick up on it. Her disinterestedness? But is the fact that Milena's not interested in catering to the widest possible audience a merit? Does it give her a degree of moral purity and integrity that Aileen doesn't have? And that *he* hasn't had either, for a long time now? Is this the focal point of their encounter, right here? Or is it in the fact that they both feel like two lunar creatures fallen to earth, and yet still have such sunny warmth, such radiance in them, as yesterday made clear? Are they *terrestrial*, too?

The problem is that by now he's all too familiar with the stupidity of falling in love: the indiscriminate enthusiasm for novelty, the excessive amplification of minuscule differences, the attribution of incompletely verified qualities, the exaggeratedly generous interpretation of mundane gestures, the mental photoshopping thanks to which you end up seeing only what you want to see. And the linguistic regression, the ridiculous simplification of thoughts, the systematic repression of doubts, the inability to step back. If he tries thinking back to the times he's fallen in love in the past, they appear like a collection of superficial impressions, illusions produced by a yearning for surprises, judgment errors dictated by impulsiveness, steps taken without really reflecting on the consequences. Today not a single one of them seems based on solid, genuine reasons; not one of them would last for even half a day in light of what he now knows. In the end, his two relationships *not* based on falling in love are the ones that have lasted the longest, and left the most durable memories, composed of small daily harmonies, the sharing of simple gestures, understandings on the essentials without unreasonable expectations, without fireworks or drumrolls. And what's left of the relationships that seemed so extraordinarily intense, each one a thousand times better than the last, so unspeakably important that they justified the criminal devastation he committed in their name? Only the vaguest *idea* of physical and emotional sensations, tiring to recall, exasperatingly vanished, impossible to grasp.

So? What substance could there ever be with Milena the Italian gelato girl, who's about to have a child with another woman? How long could the conviction last that with her everything is so much more natural and free and right than in any of his past relationships, with no need to adapt or to attempt to transform, no self-deception or sensory distortions? Didn't the distortion of the senses begin the moment they first kissed? Even earlier, the moment he went to visit her in her lab? Even earlier, the moment he tasted her gelato in the kitchen, under the vaguely perplexed gaze of Madame Jeanne? And is her gelato really that extraordinary? So essentially different from the still-delicious gelatos he's eaten at other places and times? How long would they be able to replicate the sensations he felt with her in the cottage in the woods, and that continue to play havoc with his heart and leave him short of breath? For months, for years? For an entire *life* together, like he wrote in a couple of songs so absurdly sentimental that common sense and shame dictated he discard them immediately, without even letting the rest of the band hear them?

And yet *there was* a previously unfelt naturalness in what happened between them: a total lack of poses, including the pose of not having any poses. They both seemed to be simply what they *are*, in all their incredible resemblance and diversity. Try as he might, he can't remember ever before having felt a similar blend of the physical and the spiritual; bodies and souls communicating as one (another good line never to even think about putting in a song). *There was* a mutual recognition: it emerged from every look and every gesture, every breath, every word they said or didn't say. There was the continuous *surprise* in a continuous flow, and the *joy* at the surprise. There was the *marvel*. Imperfect, yes, and it did end, and badly, for that matter; but it was there.

But would he really be willing, on the basis of sensations impossible to verify, to ruin his consolidated relationship with Aileen, a woman whose qualities and flaws he knows beyond any possible doubt? To destroy the plans for a life together that she has been working on for months, aligning them with so much care, intelligence, and know-how? To make her look terrible in front of dozens and dozens of friends and acquaintances who've come here from around the world? In front of the *Star Life* team, who certainly wouldn't miss the chance to transform the report of a fairy-tale ceremony into the chronicle of a catastrophe, for the perverse enjoyment of its audience? Knowing furthermore how he would get off practically scot-free in the matter, as it would gel perfectly with the persona he's constructed for himself since the beginning? Not only would the majority of his fans not disapprove of such a gesture, they would applaud him enthusiastically for it; you only have to consider how they've continued keeping tabs on him all these years, always looking out for signs of possible bourgeois backsliding, ready to accuse him of betrayal. They would almost certainly interpret such an unforgivable slight as confirmation that the author of "I Won't Have It (Any Other Way)" is still very much alive and kicking, with the same proud aversion to social etiquette he had thirty-five years ago.

Nick Cruickshank looks in the freezer, with a sudden desperate desire to find one of the containers of Milena's gelato. He'd even settle for one that's only half full, even one with only a little corner left; just enough to see the colors, pass his tongue over it. His hands search frantically among the containers of baby carrots and peas and zucchini that come from the estate's garden, but of Milena's gelato there isn't a trace: gone.

THIRTY-FIVE

MILENA MIGLIARI SLIPS out of the house, closes the door behind her, trying not to make noise, though the last time she checked, Viviane hardly seemed on the verge of waking up. The sun is still low, the sky a very pale blue, but the air is clear, the light painful to the eyes. She walks with a slightly uncertain step, down the cobblestone lane between the close-in walls of the houses; she bypasses the ramp of the small castle, the front window of the tourist office, the boulder beside what's left of one of the old gates. She continues down to the parking lot, gets into her van. For a while she just sits there, the cold making its way through her jeans: the compartment smells a little moldy, but it seems like the only space where she can feel safe. Then she begins not to feel safe here anymore either; she turns on the engine, pulls out, goes up the road that follows the ridgeline and then curves downward toward the valley. She doesn't have any actual thoughts in her head: only the perceptions of shapes, colors, sounds, movements. There isn't even a precise direction she's going in; she turns the wheel and shifts gears automatically, with an emptiness that grows with each curve, as if she's driving along the edge of an abyss that might suck her in from one moment to the next, make her vanish into thin air.

When she reaches the valley, the emptiness increases further: she'd like to go back up to the top of the hills so she could come down again and lose herself in the curves, and once down go back up again and then come back down, never having to decide on a direction, never having to decide on anything. But she can't make up her mind to go back up; she goes around and around the traffic circle: six, eight, ten times, like on a merry-go-round or a slow spin cycle, until her head begins to spin and she's forced to take an exit. She drives along the straight road out of pure inertia, so slowly that a car behind her blasts its horn, surpasses her with a surge of acceleration. She continues driving for several dozen yards, pulls off into the turnout in front of several ugly new buildings housing a real estate agency and a florist and a bakery, a medical supply store. She turns off the engine, sits there still, in the displaced air of every car and truck that passes. She wonders whether Viviane has gotten up yet, what state she must be in. Will she already be searching for her, up and down the stairs of their vertical house, in the glass-ceilinged patio? Already outside, on the streets of the town? Will she go back inside to explore the kitchen, to see if she's at least left her a note somewhere? (She didn't; she would have needed a few dozen pages at least, and she still wouldn't have been able to explain anything.) Will she jump in the car and drive along the high road to Fayence, thinking she'll find her at the gelateria? To tell her what? That she's shameful, that she'll never be able to forgive her? That she's already forgiven her, despite the fact that she really hurt her? That what happened can be forgotten if they both really want to? That their plan is still intact, and that on Monday they can begin the procedures at the center in Grasse? That she wishes her the best, whatever she decides to do now?

Milena Migliari sits still in the van for maybe half an hour, maybe an hour; other cars park beside her, people get out, go into the stores, come back out, the cars back out and leave, more cars arrive. Her ideas are no clearer than before, her questions find no answers, not even attempts at answers; her heartbeat does not return to normal. She's reminded of what Nick Cruickshank said yesterday afternoon or evening, about how they resemble each other in that they're both wrong with respect to the world. She doesn't know about him, but she certainly has no doubt about being wrong, as wrong as you can be: 1,000 percent wrong, without even the smallest portion of right. As a little girl she would sometimes look at herself in the vertical mirror near the front door of her parents' house and think (every now and then she would say it, too), "I'm all ugly," because nothing about her appearance seemed right, much less her thoughts, her dreams, her interpretation of things.

When she can't bear sitting there in the van any longer she turns the engine back on, turns around, gets back on the straight road through the valley, barely touches the accelerator with the tip of her toe. She turns to look at the nursery, the pseudo-Provençal houses built on new lots of turned-up earth, the sign for the supermarket, the sign for the retail outlet for construction materials. She registers each element of the landscape as if she might be able to get something useful out of it, but all she receives is a growing sense of foreignness. It's like she's inside her worst recurring dream, the one where she finds herself in a place she doesn't know and no longer has her purse or phone or wallet and she wants desperately to get back home but doesn't have the slightest idea where her house is or even if she has one, and no matter how hard she tries she can't remember any names of streets or cities or countries, any numbers, anything. Viviane told her that the dream certainly has to do with having changed her life and residence so many times without ever putting down roots, and that the only possible remedy is to stay put in a place and build something, establish a system of solid and durable points of reference. It worked for a while, here, even though she was skeptical at the beginning; but now she's in that terrible recurring dream of hers *for real*, in an unrecognizable territory, lost, her heart in her throat and her breathing labored.

On the right is a sign that says *Aérodrome*, which for some reason seems vaguely familiar, though she doesn't know why, though she doesn't even want to know. She drives so slowly she doesn't even have to brake: all she needs to do is turn the wheel, follow the road between the fields and built-up lots.

Up ahead the houses end and the meadows extend out into the valley as far as the eye can see, with mountain chains on two sides, like great protective walls. She stops the van among the parked cars behind the airfield building, gets out. It's windy, the sun is getting a little stronger, but the air is still cold. She half closes her eyes, walks on the gravel and then on the grass, hands in her coat pockets, looking down, chin against her chest. Whatever it was that happened yesterday, it's left her feeling dazed, like she had a serious accident and has yet to receive a reliable picture of the consequences.

Over on the grassy field are some gliders, resting on one wing: white, slender, soft-lined, smoothed over as if by a process of natural evolution.

Closer to her are trucks and vans, several workers putting up the structure of the stage for the concert tomorrow: the platform where the Bebonkers are going to play, the towers of metal poles for the lights and speakers. On the field in front of the stage, boys and girls as well as older-looking people have spread out blankets and sleeping bags, to ensure themselves a place beforehand. There's even a police car: two cops are talking with a small group of fans, probably to try to get them to pack up, but they're unable to persuade them, and they too look uncertain. It seems like they're *all* uncertain this morning: the cops, the fans, the workmen putting together the stage, the airfield technicians, the glider pilots. They're all moving around as if they have to overcome some inner resistance, a fundamental lack of motivation.

Milena Migliari observes the gestures and expressions of the people on the field and wonders if they know that Nick Cruickshank is getting married today. She wonders how the fans really feel about him, coming all the way here from who knows where to wait for him at least a day and a half ahead of time. Do they have the slightest idea who he really is, beyond the part he plays in public? At least the most devoted and longtime fans, the ones who've followed him for decades, listened to all his songs, read everything that's been written about him, seen all his photos and all his videos? Do they know about his curiosity, his attentiveness, his sense of humor, the surprising sensitivity of his observations? Do they know that he knows the scientific names of plants and the stories behind them? Do they know that he's read the *Odyssey*? Have they ever seen him listen to someone with that intent expression? Or are they content with the image of the artist-outlaw who's all instinct, the shaman of the stage, the anarchic iconoclast? Do they prefer not even to think about there being anything else, prefer to believe that the character coincides perfectly with the person? And do they have the slightest clue about the bad feelings between the members of the band, or do they continue to consider them a glowing example of brotherly friendship that has survived the test of time and the waves of success and adversity?

Milena Migliari looks at the sky, thinks that she'd like to see at least one glider twirling around up there. But there isn't even one, though she turns in every direction, her nose up in the air. How much of her life before yesterday is recoverable? Will she and Viviane ever be able to reassemble the pieces of what they had? Or should they go on living together, a black hole exercising its destructive force of attraction every time they come anywhere near Chemin de la Forêt? And the two of them aside, what about *her*? In the folds of her sensations, at the back of her thoughts, would she be forever left with the idea of having briefly gazed upon the imperfect marvel, and then lost it immediately? Should she propose to Viviane a change of scenery, a different country, anywhere else? Portugal? Ireland? Costa Rica? But would it ever be enough, or would they be haunted everywhere by what happened here? And how would they get by? She might be able to open another gelateria elsewhere, but Viviane's work is rooted in this area, it's taken her so much effort to build up a reputation and a good clientele. Then there's the loan on their house, and the one for the gelato equipment. How would they manage to pack up and start over again somewhere else when their baggage is so weighty, tied together by so many cables, anchored by so many stakes? In any case, wouldn't it be a much better idea to confront her problems openly and *resolve them*, instead of running away? Hasn't she already run away far too many times before meeting Viviane? As a child, as a teenager, as an adult? Isn't it thanks to Viviane that for the first time in her life she's been able to build something, day by day, with visible results? Is it possible that instead of being destroyed by what happened yesterday their relationship could come out of this even *stronger*? Maybe not tomorrow, not even the day after, but in a few months? In a few years? Is it possible that coming so close to the edge of the precipice might make her more aware of the importance of having her feet firmly planted on the solid ground of reality? Or is it already too late, her life condemned to be forever full of regrets? Regrets for what? Sensations grazed ever so slightly or simply imagined, and not reproducible in any case?

She's standing still on the airfield, her head full of questions, her heart heavy, when she feels someone touch her shoulder. She whirls around.

Nick Cruickshank is hidden behind a pair of very dark sunglasses and the hood of a sweatshirt underneath his jacket, but it's him. He motions toward the stage under construction, smiles. "Did you come to make sure you get a good spot?"

Milena Migliari shakes her head, smiles, but she isn't amused; not at all. She struggles to steady herself on her legs, struggles to gesture toward the gliders on the field. "Did you come to fly?"

Nick Cruickshank shakes his head, more or less like she did. "It's early, for the updrafts."

They're both silent. A cold wind has blown in from the mountains to the north and swept away any trace of mist; now the air is far too clear, the light too intense. It's an absurdly rarefied morning, when even breathing seems difficult.

Nick Cruickshank looks around cautiously, not wanting to be recognized by the fans. He smiles again, but he doesn't feel comfortable either. "What were the odds of us meeting here, now?"

"I don't know. Low? High?" Milena Migliari thinks that when she turned off the main road she imagined him still in bed with his now almost-wife, or already focused on the preparations for the wedding party; or here.

"So?" He takes off his dark glasses, looks at her with that strange unfiltered intensity of his.

"So what?" She feels a potential inner bursting, the anticipation of a breakdown of defenses with incalculable consequences.

"Shall we walk?" Nick Cruickshank gestures: not one of his

theatrical gestures, just a movement of the hand, with no emphasis, but as determined as his gaze.

Milena Migliari tries to decide what to do, and it feels like she can't; but she looks down at her feet and sees that they're moving of their own accord, right next to his.